D1524428

Still Life with Strings
By
L.H. Cosway

Books by L.H. Cosway

Contemporary Romance
Painted Faces
The Nature of Cruelty
Six of Hearts
Hearts of Fire

Urban Fantasy
Tegan's Blood **(The Ultimate Power Series #1)**
Tegan's Return **(The Ultimate Power Series #2)**
Tegan's Magic **(The Ultimate Power Series #3)**
Tegan's Power **(The Ultimate Power Series #4)**
Crimson **(An Ultimate Power Series Novella)**

For my readers.
You are a drop in a gigantic ocean but you mean
the world to me.

A Note from the Author

Dear reader,

The story you are about to read is set in my home city of Dublin. It may not seem this way to strangers, but it is in fact a very small place. Lives can be interconnected in little ways that may seem unbelievable, but are actually very possible given how tiny the city, and indeed the country, really is. My heroine, Jade, works in a concert hall that is loosely based on but not a one hundred percent accurate portrayal of the National Concert Hall on Earlsfort Terrace. Similarly, my hero Shane is the concertmaster of an orchestra that is loosely based on but not a one hundred percent accurate portrayal of the RTÉ National Concert Orchestra. Just a short walk from the concert hall is Grafton Street, where Jade busks as a street performer, and just around the corner from Grafton Street is St. Steven's Green, where Jade's mother used to sell her paintings. If all this information seems random, I promise it will make better sense once you've read the story. However, if like Jade you are a dreamer at heart, you can simply choose to put it all down to destiny.

I sincerely hope you enjoy *Still Life with Strings*.

Yours,

L.H. Cosway.

At eighteen years of age, he never knew true grief
until he saw her crying on the six o'clock news.
It was so palpable he could almost mould it with his
hands.
His fingers itched to create a melody that would be
the musical embodiment of her mourning.
So he picked up his violin and began to play.

One

They call me the Blue Lady.

The more poetic would say a dark angel, or an unexpected, fantastical surprise standing upon the mundane street. I wear a long midnight blue dress, a matching wig, white paint on my hands and face, and glorious, feathery blue wings affixed to my back.

I feel like a gap in reality, a moment where people can pause mid-stride and say in a breathy, wonder-filled voice, *wow, look at that.* For the more cynical, *wow, look at that nutjob.*

Perhaps for a moment someone will think that they've stepped into a world where normal is not the rule anymore, that the extraordinary is. That my wings aren't false but real, that my skin is really this white, my hair really this blue.

Unfortunately, none of it is real.

But it's nice, isn't it, for a brief moment to imagine that it is?

In reality I'm a twenty-six-year-old woman with a stack of bills I'm struggling to pay and two younger siblings who are reliant on me to keep a roof over their heads, clothes on their backs, and food in their bellies.

I do this living statue act whenever I have the free time. It gives me an artistic outlet, while also making me some much-needed cash on the side. Admittedly, I don't normally do it at one o'clock in the morning in the middle of Grafton Street, but it's a Saturday. That means there'll be lots of tourists. More to the point, lots of drunk tourists with loose pockets and even looser inhibitions about who they hand over their cash to – such as women who stand very still while dressed like a Manga fairy.

I stare directly ahead, unblinking, controlling my breathing using a *qigong* method, just as I hear the recognisable loutish shouting and laughter of a stag party up ahead. When they come into my line of sight, I see that they're all wearing black T-shirts with their nicknames written across the back and *Jack's Stag Weekend* across the front.

No shit.

I am an island, an inanimate object among the to and fro of humanity. I brace myself for the possibility that the stag party is going to be trouble. Moments later, one guy stands in front of me, waving his hand in my face and trying to get me to blink. How original.

Sometimes I feel like those guards who stand outside Buckingham Palace. And like those long-suffering buggers, I have also perfected the art of remaining still and giving no reaction at all.

"Are you blue all over?" he slurs with a drunken sideways grin.

As a street performer, you have to take the rough with the smooth. When you put yourself out there, you're going to encounter every facet of society: the good, the bad, and the drunk off their arses. Kids are the best. They haven't yet lost the sense of wonder that makes them stare up at you and truly believe you're some sort of blue-fairy-bird-woman-thing.

"That's a real nice rack," says another of the stag partiers.

Yeah, you try carrying it around all day and dealing with the back problems, and then tell me how nice it is, I think. Soon they lose interest and continue on their way. A half an hour passes, and several more pedestrians throw some coins into my hat.

The moon is full tonight, a round white orb perched amid the stars. I want to go up there and see what everything looks like from on high. I flutter my wings and prepare for flight, flapping them through the air and then leaping into the sky. My ascent is an easy one. I pluck a star out of the blackness and stick it in my blue hair as an adornment. When I reach the moon, I find a comfortable spot and sit. Leaning my chin on my hand, I gaze back down at the street. The people look like tiny black ants, the buildings like less brightly coloured blocks of Lego.

I blink, and I'm back on my box, back on the street. I was never really on the moon. My wings are a pretty accessory, but they're useless for flying. Sometimes I can imagine things so hard that I feel like they're really happening.

My eyes catch on a group of people I recognise. They all play in the symphony orchestra at the concert hall where I work as a ticket attendant and bartender. I don't talk to most of them, but I'm friends with a couple of the ladies. I know that one of the violinists is leaving to move to Australia with his family, so tonight must be his big send-off.

Often on my breaks I'll sit at the back of the hall and watch their rehearsals, allowing myself to be swept away with the music. My favourite sound is at the very beginning of their performances, when all the instruments clamour together to get in tune. It builds up this addictive sense of anticipation.

I envy their lives as musicians, travelling the world and playing for amazing audiences in historic venues. It's so much more beautiful than the life I live. I think a lot about the fact that I'm constantly near these people, and yet my reality is so far removed from theirs.

None of them even know that the woman with the painted skin dressed all in blue is the same inner-city girl who sells tickets for their concerts and serves them drinks at the bar after their practices.

In a way it's quite a wonderful feeling. For a moment I am unchained from my own humdrum identity.

By the time I withdraw from these thoughts, the orchestra musicians are gone. Slowly, I turn my head slightly to the left and find a new position. I stand in the same pose for fifteen minutes at a time, and then I'll make an almost imperceptible move to ease some of the strain. It takes willpower and the patience of a saint to do this. Fortunately, I've had years of practice being responsible for my younger siblings.

I'm all about the willpower, especially since I'm a recovering alcoholic who works in a bar. Most people say that to properly get over an addiction, you have to purge all presence of the drug from your life. I take a different approach. The fact that I can be around alcohol and not drink it, well, I like to think that makes me stronger. It's been five years, and I haven't touched a drop.

Anyway, what with jobs being so thin on the ground these days, I can't exactly afford to be picky. You'll be amazed by what you can achieve when necessity sets in.

Once I settle in my new position, I notice a man standing by the shuttered window of a shop on the other side of the street. He's got brown hair in what my mother would have called a "gentleman's haircut" when she was alive. It's all neatly combed and swept to the side. His facial features are exotic yet not, giving the impression that he was born of a white father and an Asian mother — or vice versa.

He's just standing there staring at me, looking fascinated and a small bit lost. I sometimes encounter people like this. Adults who see me and are touched by whatever emotion my appearance has managed to evoke in them.

These are the things I live for. Aside from the money, it's the main reason why I do this.

Up until this moment, though, I've never had someone I'm attracted to show a similar sort of wonder. His eyes crinkle in a smile. I think he knows that I've noticed him. A couple who have also been watching me for several minutes finally drop some money in my hat, and I give them a small bow for their generosity.

My legs are starting to get a little too stiff, so I decide it's time to call it a night. Stretching my arms up over my head and stepping down off my box, I pick up my money hat, fold it in half, and shove it into the box.

The beautiful man across the street stands up straight when he sees me move. I pull off my wig and stick that in the box, too, loosening my real hair out of the tight bun I'd had it in under the wig. Making sure not to damage the feathers, I shrug out of the wings and place them inside as well.

When I glance up, the man is standing before me, too close almost. His eyes are a deep golden brown, like a glass of fine brandy, and his features have a delicate masculinity. Strong yet vulnerable.

"Hello there," I say with a hint of amusement, pulling my long cardigan from the box and shuffling out of my blue dress. I always wear a light slip underneath.

"Hey," the man replies, watching as I fold the dress neatly and place it in the box before ducking into my cardigan. "You're blonde," he says then, eyes on my hair.

I'd expected him to be foreign, given his semi-exotic appearance, but his accent is middle-class Dublin through and through.

"That I am," I answer, giving him a look as if to say, *are we done here?*

It's almost two in the morning, but the street still has quite a few people on it, so I don't really feel on edge about this stranger standing near enough that we're practically touching.

His gaze travels down to my feet, a wry smile shaping his lips when he takes in my black biker-style boots. As he scans my bare legs, I feel a shiver run down my back, lingering erotically at the base of my spine.

Hmm, it has been a while, and this man is utterly gorgeous. He's wearing a dark suit with a white shirt, no tie. He hovers over me, standing only a couple of inches taller. His breath whispers across my skin, smelling faintly of gin.

"Would you like to have a drink with me?" he asks, reaching out to run a hand through the waves at the end of my long hair.

Despite his forwardness, it feels good to be touched. Sometimes it seems like no one ever touches me like this — just for the sake of it. I had a really stressful day with my younger brother Pete acting the brat; a little relief would be nice. A bit of physical interaction. Some skin on skin.

Something thickens in the air between us as we make eye contact. The man sucks in a quick breath, his gaze flickering back and forth over my features.

Once I have everything put away, I close my box, pulling it along on its wheels.

"How about a quick shag instead?" I ask back, uncharacteristically brazen. It's the middle of the night, and I'm never going to see this man again. He's just what I need. A pretty stranger to lose myself in, to make me feel new again for a short while.

He laughs out loud, thinking I'm joking. Then his eyes widen and his nostrils flare when he realises I'm being serious. A touch of red colours his cheeks, possibly displaying his embarrassment. His hand moves from my hair to my neck and strokes downward to my collarbone. He might be embarrassed by my proposition, but he wants exactly what I want. I can tell.

"Okay, Bluebird, that sounds much better," he says, breathing harshly now.

Taking his hand, I lead him away from the main street and down a dark, secluded alleyway. I rest my box against the wall, and seconds later he's on me. Hands in my hair, lips on my lips, tongue in my mouth caressing my tongue. He tastes nice, like toothpaste and an expensive dinner. I undo three buttons on his shirt, slipping my hand inside and feeling his taut nipples and hard, muscular pecs beneath.

His hands move along my bare thighs to the backs of my knees, where he applies pressure and pulls my legs up around his waist. He holds me there, my back pressed hard against the concrete wall. His erection hits me right between the thighs now, nudging exquisitely in and out. All of his embarrassment has disappeared, his lust overriding it.

"You smell great," he rasps, sucking on my neck. "You want me up inside you, Bluebird?"

"Yes, hurry," I moan, allowing my face to fall to the hollow between his shoulder and neck. His hand slips inside my knickers, and he groans when he encounters my wetness. He shoves a finger in experimentally, and when I cry out he allows another to join it.

I reach down and fumble with his belt, undoing his trousers and pulling them down just enough to free his cock. The next thing I know, he's tugging my knickers all the way down my legs and shoving them into his pocket. He rummages in his other pocket and whips out a condom, which I suppose isn't too unusual a thing for a man out late on a Saturday night to carry around with him.

Rolling it on, he lifts his head to meet my gaze. He tilts his neck to the side, those gorgeous golden eyes hooded with desire. I don't make a habit of propositioning random men on the street, and yet I have to admit that none of my previous one-night stands have ever progressed this quickly — or this smoothly. Usually there's a bit of awkward fumbling before a rhythm is found, if at all, but with this guy it feels so natural. I guess the late hour has brought out my uninhibited, adventurous side.

He positions his cock at my entrance, still holding my gaze, and pushes slowly into me, letting out a guttural, "Fuck."

I lock my legs tight around his waist, and he grips me firmly before he starts pumping into me fast. In this moment we're base and animalistic. No reservations, no pretences, just two people seeking relief and some small piece of a human connection.

"You feel…really good," he groans, flicking his tongue along my earlobe.

"Yeah, go harder," I whisper, needing to be fucked so hard that I fall into the pleasure and forget.

"You're a dirty, beautiful little thing, aren't you?" he says, a glorious smile on his face. He lets go of one of my legs and pulls down the strap of my slip, my cardigan hanging loosely at my elbows. Then he pulls free one of my breasts and moulds it with his palm, pinching the nipple. I sigh and undulate, biting my lower lip.

"I'll be whatever you want me to be — just fuck me harder," I tell him, throwing my head back when he thrusts up into me deep.

His eyes grow dark as he zeroes in on my mouth, then captures it with his lips. He slides his tongue in and out, as though mimicking the motion of his cock inside me. When he withdraws for air, I notice he's got some of my shimmery white face paint on his cheeks and stains of it on the shoulders of his suit. For some reason, it makes me smile.

"You like that?" he growls and I nod, unable to find my voice.

His thrusts become even faster, harder, as he reaches down between my legs and rubs at my clit, coaxing me to orgasm. I can tell he's going to come soon, so I let go, allowing myself to climax along with him.

He's got a delirious look on his face as he spurts into me, letting out a long, deep, stomach-clenching groan. The noise is the essence of male sexuality. My orgasm hits me quick and intense, shattering through my system.

He holds me there long after he's come, stroking my hair away from my face and cupping my cheeks. "I think I might have dreamt you," he breathes, kissing one side of my mouth and then the other.

That makes me grin wide. What a romantic thing to say to a woman who let you shag her minutes after you just met.

"You're a sweetheart," I reply, giving him a soft kiss goodbye and then dropping my legs to the ground. I take a moment to right myself, fixing my cardigan back in place. Then I walk over to my box and grab the handle.

"So, I'll see you," I say, dipping my head to him in farewell.

He's still leaning against the wall, trying to catch his breath. For a split second he seems taken aback by my abrupt departure, and then his cheeks redden like before.

"Yeah, see you, Bluebird," he replies with a sombre smile.

Feeling him follow me out onto the street, I turn right at St. Steven's Green in the direction of home. For a while it feels like he's still behind me, but a minute or two later when I summon up the courage to look, he's gone.

Perhaps it wasn't that he dreamt me. Perhaps I was the one who dreamt him.

Two

I live in an area of inner-city Dublin known as "the Liberties." There's a historical reason for the name, but essentially it's similar to what they call "the Projects" in America. The name is ironic, because there's little that's liberating about living here. In fact, it often feels like the opposite way around.

My house is on a street close to St. Patrick's Cathedral, a short walk from where I had the encounter with my nameless stranger. I smell his cologne on me, something citrus and fresh. His spit and his sweat linger, too. It dawns on me that I never even asked him his name. When a soft breeze floats up my dress, I remember that he still has my knickers stuck in his suit pocket.

The street is empty, apart from a group of teenage boys hanging out at the end of the row of houses. I eye them as I pull the front door key from my pocket and notice a familiar red baseball cap. Oh, it better fucking not be. Taking a closer look, I see that it *is* him, my fifteen-year-old brother Pete. For the last year or so he's been hanging out with a bad crowd. It's been an absolute nightmare trying to keep him on the straight and narrow.

Opening the house door, I drop my box down in the hallway and then march my way toward the group. They all begin nudging each other as they see me approach, and then Pete turns around, a gigantic scowl on his face.

"Get home now," I tell him firmly, allowing my gaze to touch on each individual present.

You can't be eye-shy with these little shits. You have to show them that you mean business. It's scary, because they're all taller than I am and most likely carrying weapons, but when you strip that away, all you have left are scared little boys living in a world with no privileges. Some of them are a good deal older than Pete, too, maybe even eighteen or nineteen. And when eighteen- and nineteen-year-olds are befriending boys Pete's age, you know there's some variety of grooming going on.

"Piss off, Jade. I'll go home when I'm ready," Pete hisses.

Not bothering to retort, because I'm tired and want to go to bed, I simply step forward, twist his arm behind his back in a simple lock, and drag him away.

"Hey, let go, you fucking strong bitch," he yells, clawing at my hand.

It's true — I may not look it, but I am pretty strong, mainly because I practice Tai Chi twice a week at my local community centre. A lot of people don't know that it isn't all about waving your arms through the air and meditating. It's actually a martial art as well. My teacher is a really cool hippy lady from France who only charges a small fee for the classes.

A lanky, well-built boy steps up and spits just short of my feet, a snakelike grin shaping one end of his mouth. He gives me a squint-eyed look that only the truly inbred can do justice, and calls, "Your sister's a fucking freak, Pete. Why don't you give her a slap and teach her a lesson?"

"I'll give you a bloody slap," I shout back. "And don't be getting mouthy — I know your mother!"

I have no clue who his mother is, but it's a tried and tested threat that always works to put wayward teenagers in their places.

He spits on the ground one more time for good measure just as I shove Pete into the house and slam shut the door.

When we're inside he pulls away from me, cheeks red, clearly fuming. "Why'd you have to do that? You made a complete show of me, Jade!"

"Good! If it keeps you away from scum like that, I'll be happy to make a show of you every day for the rest of your life." I pause, hand on my hip, taking in his appearance. He's got grey bags under his eyes and looks paler than usual. I've been suspicious that he's started smoking and selling marijuana, but I don't yet have any proof. "Is this what you want for yourself? Do you know how long most teenagers who deal drugs last before they get caught and sent to prison, Pete? Not very long, let me tell you, especially considering how idiotically dumb most of them are."

"You're the dumb one. You haven't got a clue about anything. I hate you."

"If I'm the dumb one, then what does that make your aesthetically challenged friend out there?"

Pete mouths the words "aesthetically" and "challenged" to himself like a question, shaking his head.

"Whatever, Jade. Damo knows his stuff. He's headed for big things. He's also going to set me up with some work. I'll make a tonne of money."

"The only big thing Damo's headed for is slopping out in Mountjoy Prison. And if I see you anywhere near that tool again, you'll regret it. Now get to bed."

"Fuck you."

I roll my eyes. "Ah, so sweet. Get to bed. *Now*."

With that, he turns on his heel and stomps loudly up the stairs. I drop down onto the last step and breathe an exhausted sigh.

My mother died four years ago from lung cancer. She lived a hard life and smoked like a chimney, so it was only to be expected that the big "C" would take her. I miss her every day. Her death meant that at the ripe young age of twenty-two I had to step up and become the guardian of my three younger siblings. Alec is twenty-one now, so I don't need to worry about him anymore, but I still have fifteen-year-old Pete and April, who's seventeen, to look out for.

I know, lucky me.

I love them like crazy, but they aren't little babies any longer, and sometimes it's a lot to deal with. The two of them are going to send me into an early grave one of these days.

The situation with Pete is pretty much self-explanatory, given the fight we just had; he's a confused, angry young man who lost his mother too soon. But April I worry about for another reason entirely. There's been a couple of men way too old for her sniffing around. I feel like a guard dog half the time, barking at them to keep away.

Speaking of dogs, our family Jack Russell terrier, Specky, is trotting her way down the hall to me. We all named her Specky because she's got two little patches of brown around her eyes that look like a pair of glasses. She nuzzles my hand and I pet her soft head, picking her up and carrying her with me to my room. I don't normally sleep with her, but after what just transpired with Pete, I feel like I need her company.

"I was with a man tonight, Specky," I confide, and she lets out a little yip upon hearing her name. "He just might be the most beautiful man I've ever seen."

Inside my room, I plop Specky down on the bed and strip off my clothes. I use a makeup wipe to remove the rest of the paint from my face and hands, but it seems I've sweated most of it off already anyway.

Climbing under the cool sheets, I rest my head on the pillow, and Specky snuggles into me. Seconds after I close my eyes, I'm dead to the world.

At ten o'clock the next morning, my alarm clock chimes and I reach out, grumpily shutting it off. My shift at the concert hall doesn't start until twelve, so I allow myself an extra half an hour's sleep. When the scent of male cologne hits my nose, memories from last night come flooding back to me in vivid detail. His hand on my breast, his mouth on my neck, his eyes on my eyes. Smouldering.

It was unlike any casual sexual encounter I've ever had. I mean, the sex was actually good — *really* good. And considering it happened in a dirty alleyway, *standing up*, that's saying something.

Once I'm thinking of these things, I can't get back to sleep, so I get up, throw on a robe, and shuffle my way into the bathroom to take a shower. As usual at this time on a Sunday morning, the house is blessedly silent.

I work through my morning routine: shower, dress, breakfast, and by eleven-thirty I'm out the door. The walk to work takes fifteen minutes, so I go slowly, perusing the news headlines in a corner shop and buying a packet of mints.

I'm on duty in the first-floor bar today. There's a lunchtime concert on, attracting elderly and middle-aged couples mostly. Young people don't really go in for classical music, which is a shame, because getting to listen to it on a weekly basis has become something of a love affair for me. Just the sound of it gives me hope for a better life for me and my siblings. A life where I don't have to worry about my kid brother going to prison or my teenage sister falling pregnant.

It's funny that I've become the parent figure in our house, because I'm actually the only member of my family with a different father from the others. That's why there's a slight gap in our ages. My dad was a plumber from Galway whom my mother met at the wedding of a mutual friend. Two months after I was born, he got knocked over by a car and killed while walking home from the shop.

My siblings' father's name is Patrick. Unfortunately, *he's* still alive. I don't mean to sound callous, but it would probably be better for all of us if he weren't.

He's a drinker and a gambler who lives with his girlfriend, Greta, on the other side of the city in East Wall. Every once in a while he'll show up looking for money, or a place to stay if he and Greta have had a fight. I can't stand the man.

Making my way inside the building, I slip in the back and put my bag away. Then I head out to the bar. The place is already filling up, and I serve the patrons their drinks. A whole lot of white wine (for the middle-aged couples) and orange/cranberry juices/tea (for the elderly.) Once the concert begins and everybody's in the main hall, I go to take a break and have a chat with my friend Lara, who works in the box office out front most days.

We sit down in the staff room with a cup of tea and some sandwiches, Lara telling me about her three-year-old daughter's latest attempt to escape her crèche. When Lara works during the day, she has to use child-minding services, and little Mia is constantly trying to run away from them.

"I don't blame her," I tell Lara, laughing. "I wouldn't trust some of the women they employ in those places to mind my dog, let alone my child. I remember Mum tried putting April in a crèche when she was little, and she took her out of it after only a week, said the workers were way too pushy and shouty."

"God, that's the perfect way to describe them. But I haven't got another choice at this point," she says, rubbing at her temples. "It's a nightmare."

"Hey, maybe I could get April to babysit for you. You know she finished school a couple of months ago and still hasn't managed to find a job. That way Mia could be kept at home where she's comfortable. I bet it's the strange environment and all the other kids that upset her."

"That's actually not a bad idea. Run it by April and see what she says."

I smile and sip on my tea, feeling like I've just killed two birds with one stone. This babysitting thing will help out Lara, and will also keep April busy and away from all those older men.

"So, did you go out busking last night?" Lara asks, breaking my thoughts.

"Yep. Made eighty quid. Not too shabby. It was a godsend, actually. I'm screwed money-wise for at least the next month. The bills just keep piling up."

"Ugh, I know the feeling."

Soon it's time for the intermission, so I make my way back out to the bar. A man in his fifties wearing a wedding band orders two glasses of pinot grigio and eyes the top of my shirt, where there's a small hint of cleavage showing. He tells me I have nice hair and very pretty green eyes. I take all his compliments with a polite but reserved smile, wishing older men wouldn't

~ 27 ~

always pigeonhole me as the young blonde they can have a wild, midlife crisis–style affair with. I seem to put out certain vibes without being aware of it, because I get hit on by these types all the time.

Once the concert ends, the building slowly empties out, and I go about cleaning up and restocking the bar for the evening event. Lara and I take the same break again, and chat some more about this and that.

Hours later my shift is almost done when the floor manager, Ciaran, comes and asks if I'll make up refreshments for the musicians, who will be spending some time at the bar once the building has finally been emptied of patrons. I give him a quick nod and begin preparing some water and juices, alongside a couple bottles of wine. I also set out some peanuts and crisps in case they're feeling peckish.

Slowly, the men and women from the symphony start filling the seats by the bar. Noeleen, one of the trumpeters, slides into the stool in front of me and asks for a shot of vodka. She's a talkative middle-aged woman with red hair, and one of the few musicians who I'm on first-name terms with. She's one of those people who will chat with anyone; there could be a three-year-old sitting beside her, and she'd start telling the kid about her recent colonic. I like that about her.

I chat with her for a minute before I get swept up serving drinks. I've just handed two men their glasses of orange juice when I feel someone's eyes on me. Glancing quickly up, I get the most unexpected surprise.

For a short while time seems to move in slow motion, because standing before me is my next customer, who also happens to be my handsome stranger from last night. I pray that he doesn't recognise me without the face paint, but the look in his eyes tells me he knows exactly who I am. How long has he been watching me? More to the point, what on earth is he doing here?

Three

My voice comes out scratchy when I say, "Uh, hi, what can I get you?"

He tilts his head, eyes hot, perusing me from top to bottom before he allows his gaze to rest on my face. Suddenly, I feel flushed in my work blouse and skirt.

"Hey, Bluebird," he says, voice low. "Isn't this a surprise? I'll have a gin and tonic, if you don't mind."

I nod and go about making up his drink. A surprise is right. One of the violinists takes a stool beside him. I recognise her because she sits in the lobby a lot, drinking fancy coffees and reading bridal magazines. I once asked Noeleen when her wedding is, but my trumpeter friend simply gave me a wry look and shook her head, telling me the woman's name is Avery and that she's not getting married, she's just obsessed with weddings. It made me feel really sorry for her when I heard that.

She's got straight brown hair and nice eyes, but a slightly long nose that makes her face less conventionally attractive than it would be otherwise.

"Hi, Shane," she greets my stranger politely. "How did you find things? If you need any help getting settled, just say the word."

Shane. Now I know his name and why he's here. He's in the orchestra. He must have taken the place of the violinist who left. It dawns on me that I had sex with a man who can create the beautiful music that bewitches me. Suddenly, I feel this urgent need to witness him play, to see him hold his instrument with those skilled hands of his. I shake myself out of the thought.

Shane turns to her with a pleasant smile. "I had a great first night, thanks, Avery," he says, his eyes landing on me for a moment as he continues in a low voice, "And it just got better."

Avery misinterprets his statement as being directed at her, blushing and letting out a delighted titter. Now I feel bad. Oh, well, I'll let her enjoy it. I set Shane's gin and tonic down on the bar and then look to her to see what she wants.

"Oh, could I have a sparkling water, please?"

"Sure, hon," I reply, turning to the fridge to grab a bottle. I slide a slice of lemon onto the rim of a glass, pour in some ice, snap open the lid of the bottle, and put them down in front of her. All the while I can feel Shane's attention on me like a warm caress.

Everybody seems to be set for the time being, so I wipe down the counter and turn to talk with Noeleen again. I think I see Shane perk his ears up to listen in to our conversation.

"What was the symphony you played tonight?" I ask her while drying glasses. "I know I know it, but my brain is on a go-slow."

"It was Beethoven's Ninth," she answers. "What did you think of the choir?"

"What I could hear from the bar sounded wonderful."

"I agree," she says, sipping on her wine. "My hand didn't act up, either, so it was an enjoyable performance all 'round."

I give her a sympathetic look. Noeleen has some wear and tear damage in her fingers from years playing the trumpet. Her doctor says that it's most likely only going to get worse as time goes on; however, it doesn't stop her from playing. She's been in various orchestras for more than two decades now.

"Isn't there anything the specialists can do about it?"

"There are some therapies, but mostly they just throw painkillers at me and hope for the best."

Shaking my head, I turn to serve a man who's asking for a red wine. Shane's voice fills my ears then, requesting, "Oh, barkeep, could I get another gin and tonic?"

I give him a polite smile, wondering if he's trying to be funny with the "barkeep" bit. "Sure."

Avery chats away to him about brands of strings for the violin. As I'm about to slide the glass across the bar, he instead reaches forward and takes it from my hand, allowing his fingers to touch mine briefly. My face gets hot and flushed. It's like we've switched places. Last night I was in the driving seat, and now he is. It's just really thrown me for a loop to see him here.

I never thought I'd see him again, to be perfectly honest. I mean, it's one thing to proposition a guy on the street in the middle of the night, but it's another entirely to have him show up at your place of work. Not only that, but he works here as well.

A memory hits me of how I saw the orchestra musicians out last night, and it was right before I'd noticed Shane watching me. Now it all makes sense; he'd been with them.

He's looking at me now like he wants to go for round two, and no matter how nice that would be, it can't happen. I swore myself off relationships when I stopped drinking. It's kind of like that saying, *once burned, twice shy.* Only in my case I was burned over and over again, making me a million times shy.

The whole point of last night with Shane was that he was a random stranger. Someone I could have a heated encounter with and then let drift into the recesses of my memory. Yet here he is, flesh and bone and sexy, pretty manliness.

"What's your name?" he asks.

Avery's chatter dies down as she realises he's not paying attention to her any longer.

"What's yours?" I counter.

"Shane."

I give him a smirk. "Funny how we managed to forego first names, isn't it? I'm Jade. Pleased to meet you, Shane."

I reach out to shake his hand, and he takes my fingers into his warm palm before releasing them.

I think he's blushing a little because of my comment, that adorable shyness creeping back in that's so at odds with his polished confidence.

"So I guess I can stop calling you Bluebird, then," he whispers.

I smile and joke, "I have you pegged. Women are all birds and bitches to you, right?"

He gives me a startled look, and I hold back a grin.

"I'm pulling your leg, hon," I tell him, and the startled look fades.

Several moments of silence ensue before he regains his confidence. "So what's with the living statue thing? They don't pay you enough here or something?" He's trying to be flirtatious now.

"That's a hobby. And no, to answer your second question, they don't pay me enough here. Not when I've got two mouths to feed at home."

His brow furrows before he asks, "Are you a mother, Jade?"

I let out a small laugh and shake my head. "The look on your face! No, I was referring to my younger brother and sister." I lean against the bar so that our faces are inches apart, then whisper, "I'm a poor little orphan, Shane. You want to come rescue me?"

He swallows, his Adam's apple bobbing in his throat. My eyes flick to Avery when I hear her make a small noise of surprise. Damn, I'd almost forgotten she was listening to us.

"In what way do you need rescuing?" Shane asks back, his voice gravelly.

I stand up straight then and return to drying glasses.

"Contrary to popular belief, not all orphans need to be rescued," I tell him with a wink, and walk to the other end of the bar. Soon the musicians begin to head home, and I finish closing up for the night. When I look back to where Shane had been sitting, I find he's gone. Avery has left, too. Hmm, I wonder if he went home with her.

I call goodbye to a couple of other workers, hitching my bag up on my shoulder and making my way out through the employee exit. I give a surprised yelp when somebody emerges from the side of the building. Clutching my chest, I see it's only Shane carrying a violin case and a small backpack.

"Shit, you scared me," I exclaim, my breathing fast.

He gives me a sheepish grin. "Oops, sorry." He pauses, biting at his full bottom lip. "I've been waiting for you."

Smiling now, I reply, "Oh, yeah?"

"Yeah. I was, uh, wondering if I could take you out some time?"

"Aren't we past all that?" I ask.

He looks to the ground and then back up at me, scratching at his jaw. "I don't think so."

I take a step closer to him, putting my hand on his arm and letting it drift lightly downward. He closes his eyes at my touch. Wow, this guy really likes me. Like, *really* likes me. All those posh women in his line of work must be prudes. Perhaps that's why my overly forward ways have him so affected.

"You don't think so, Shane? So it wasn't you who fucked my brains out in the back of an alley last night?" I whisper.

"Bloody hell, Jade," he exclaims, looking around to make sure there's no one within hearing distance. Breathing heavily, he continues, "That wasn't my initial intention. I did actually mean it when I said I wanted to have a drink with you. You're amazingly beautiful — in your costume and out of it."

I smile softly now. "You like my wings, honey?"

He nods. "Very much so. Your appearance as a living statue is striking, to say the least. I couldn't look away when I saw you. You had this expression on your face like you were imagining heaven."

I give him a full-on grin for that one. I don't think I was imagining heaven last night, but it's a nice idea. Now I'm trying to remember what I had actually been imagining, but it's not coming to me. I think I was just noticing him and thinking he was incredibly attractive — him fucking me was pretty heavenly, though.

I smile up at him. "Are you a bit of a poet, Shane?"

He smiles back, and I see a dimple deepen in one of his cheeks.

"Nope. Just a lowly violinist."

I start walking now and he moves, too, keeping pace with me. "Ah, I like a bit of modesty in a man. So, you must be thrilled to have snagged a place in the symphony. Where did you play before?"

His eyes light up at the fact that I'm asking questions about him. "Yeah, I was over the moon, actually. I had to do a number of auditions and interviews. Up until about a year ago, I was in a string quartet. We had a fairly large European following, so I got to do lots of travelling."

"Wow. That sounds exciting. What was your group's name?"

"The Bohemia Quartet. Ever heard of us?"

"Sorry, can't say that I have. Do you have any recordings?"

"Yeah, three albums. You can buy our stuff on iTunes." He gives me this cute little self-deprecating grin.

"Cool. I'm going to look you up sometime. So why did you leave?"

His shoulders slump as he shoves his hands in his pockets. "That's a depressing story."

"I can deal with depressing," I tell him.

He shakes his head. "Nah, not tonight. Perhaps some other time."

"Okay. So are you planning on walking me all the way home?" I ask, noticing we're almost at the end of Harcourt Street now.

Shane glances up and down the road. "How much farther is your place?"

"Five minutes from here. You can head off if you like. I might see you around at work." I begin walking away, but he rushes to catch up with me.

"Hey, what's your hurry? I can go another five minutes."

I stop and turn to face him, giving him a sad look. He's like an enthusiastic puppy — a darkly exotic enthusiastic puppy.

"We're not having sex again," I state, getting straight to the point.

He blinks and sputters. "Is that what you think I'm after? Jade, I just want to talk with you some more. I like you."

Putting my hand comfortingly on his chest, I tell him softly, "That's really sweet, and I've no problem talking. In fact, I'd love to be friends, but I just need to know you understand that what went on between us last night won't be happening again. 'Kay?"

He stares at me, and his eyes tilt downward. Great, now I've kicked the puppy. For a moment I think he's going to argue with me, but then he simply replies, "I'd love to be friends, too."

He gives me a small smile, one which I return. "Friends it is, then. Come on, buddy. Walk me home."

A few minutes later we're approaching my house. I take a glance at the group of boys who seem to be continually camped out at the end of the street. Then I breathe a relieved sigh when I confirm that Pete isn't with them.

Pulling my keys from my bag, I turn to Shane. "Well, this is me. Thanks for the chat. It was good talking to you. Hopefully we can do it again soon."

He stands at the end of my front step, hands dug into his pockets. He doesn't say anything, but he's staring at me, real intense.

"What are you looking at me like that for?" I ask, letting out a small nervous laugh.

"I've never met a girl like you before," he says.

What am I, a mermaid or something?

"Well, I wouldn't imagine many of the girls from around here hang out with men who play the violin, nor do they attend any string quartet concerts," I reply jokingly, gesturing over to a couple of girls standing by a house across the street, puffing on cigarettes in their pyjama bottoms, massive gold hoop earrings in their ears.

Shane looks to them and then back at me. "No, I don't suppose they do. You know, I've never actually been in this part of the city before."

"No, I don't suppose you have," I say, teasing him.

He narrows his eyes, giving me a tight-lipped smirk. "I, uh, don't think I remember the way back."

I laugh. "Well, that was silly, now, wasn't it? Where do you live?"

"Ranelagh. I was going to catch a cab."

"In that case, come on inside and I'll call one for you. My neighbour Barry drives a taxi. He'll do you a discount if he knows you're a friend of mine."

I turn my key in the door and step into the hallway, my ears immediately getting blasted with loud rap music. Great. I forgot my brother Alec usually has his friends around for a few beers on a Sunday night.

"Sorry about the noise. It's just my brother and his mates. Come on into the kitchen."

I gesture for him to take a seat at the table. "Do you want some tea while you're waiting?"

"I'd love some."

I put on the kettle and then pick up my phone to call Barry. It rings out twice before he answers.

"Jade, what can I do for you, love?"

"A friend of mine needs a lift out to Ranelagh. Are you free?"

"I will be in about fifteen minutes. You at your house or somewhere else?"

"My house."

"Right, give me half an hour, tops. I'll beep when I'm outside."

"Great. Thanks, Barry."

The music coming from the living room gets louder, and I find it hilarious when Shane furrows his brow as though offended. I can't blame him. If I spent my life playing classical music, I'd be offended by rap, too.

I bang my fist on the wall, shouting, "Keep it down, Alec."

The volume lowers, and I go about making the tea. A minute later Alec walks into the kitchen, opening the fridge to take out more beers. My eldest brother is a sight to behold these days. He's been working for a construction company, so all the hard labour has bulked him up, and he's taken to tattoos in a big way. He's already got a full sleeve on his right arm and is building another on the left. His light brown hair, the same shade as that of all my siblings, is cut in a Mohawk down the centre of his head.

"Sorry about the music, Jade. Some of the boys got carried away." He notices Shane then and gives him the once-over. The two couldn't be any more opposite: Shane in his black shirt and slacks, and Alec in his jeans and ratty T-shirt.

"You a friend of Jade's?" he asks, taking the cigarette that had been resting behind his ear and lighting it up.

"Yeah, he is. This is Shane. Shane, this is my brother, Alec."

"Nice to meet you, bud," says Alec, reaching across the table to give Shane's hand a sturdy shake. What with his appearance and his deep inner-city accent, Alec can come across like a bit of a scary bastard, but he's actually a really amiable guy. He's the funniest fucker I know, brilliant sense of humour. You'll never get one over on him in a battle of wits.

"Nice to meet you, too," says Shane, smiling urbanely.

Alec grins when he hears Shane speak and gives me a look that says, *haven't you done well for yourself, snagging the posh fella.*

I give him a look in return that says, *we're just friends!*

"Right. Well, I'll leave you both to it," says Alec finally, picking up the beers and strolling back into the living room.

"And keep the music down," I call after him.

"So, you've got two brothers and a sister?" Shane asks as I set a cup of tea down in front of him.

"That's right, though Alec's big and ugly enough to take care of himself now."

Shane laughs. "Right, yeah, I can see that. What happened to your parents?"

"Whoa, bit of a personal question there," I say, pulling out a chair and sitting down across from him.

He looks embarrassed. "Sorry, I shouldn't have asked."

"No, you're all right. Mum died four years ago from lung cancer. My dad died a few months after I was born, got knocked over by a car. The others have a different father, though — that's why I'm the only one with this mad albino hair. Their dad's name is Patrick, absolute waste of space. He shows up every once in a while, but mostly I try to keep him out of the picture."

"Sounds complicated."

"It is. So, do I get to ask about your family, or does this interview business only go one way?"

Shane sits back in his chair. "You can ask. My situation is fairly simple, though. I'm an only child. My parents live in Dalkey."

I grin. "Well, I'd never have guessed. Is that where you grew up?"

He eyes me speculatively. "Uh-huh. And what do you mean, 'you'd never have guessed'?"

"I was just teasing. I knew you must have been raised somewhere around that area, given your accent."

"Ah."

"Yeah. Are both of your parents white? Correct me if I'm wrong, but you look like you've got some Asian blood in you."

"Bit of a personal question," he says with a smirk, throwing my own words back at me.

"I like asking personal questions." I lean in closer to him, my elbows on the table, and bite flirtatiously on my lower lip. I do it jokingly, but Shane's expression heats up nonetheless, his eyes zeroing in on my mouth.

"I bet you do. And yeah, both of my parents are white. They lived in Beijing for several years in the eighties where my dad was working for the Irish embassy. While they were over there they tried for a baby, but something wasn't working. In the end they found out that Mum was infertile, so they hired a surrogate."

"Say what?" I exclaim humorously. Shane shoots me a narrow-eyed look. "No, seriously," I go on. "I thought only crazy celebrities and millionaires hired surrogates."

"It's actually more common than you'd think. So anyway, they paid this nice Chinese woman to have a child for them. Basically, they used my dad's sperm, and the surrogate got pregnant through artificial insemination. So I'm my dad's biological son, but not my mum's."

"Wow. And have you ever met your birth mother?"

"No. Mum thought it would be best to sever all the ties. When I was five we moved back to Ireland."

"What age are you now?"

"Twenty-nine. I'll be thirty next month. You?"

"Twenty-six going on fifty."

He laughs. "You don't look fifty."

"I feel it sometimes," I sigh.

He gives me a sympathetic expression and reaches out to softly squeeze my hand. He doesn't keep doing it for long, but it's nice while it lasts.

We stay locked in a moment as he drags his tongue over his bottom lip, wetting it. I stare at his mouth, half mesmerised.

The moment is broken when a car horn beeps loudly from outside, signalling Barry's arrival. "Ah, there's your ride home, and the conversation had just gotten interesting," I announce with amusement.

Shane stands and gulps down the last of his tea. "Well, we can continue it tomorrow if you'd like. Are you working?"

"Yep. Eleven o'clock until seven."

"I have a rehearsal until four. Can I stop by the bar and see you?"

"Sure. You'll be bored out of your tits watching me work, but I'll try my best to fit in some talking time." I smile and stand up, ushering him out to the front door.

"It's a good thing I don't have tits, then, isn't it? See you, Jade," he calls, blowing me a cheeky kiss and making his way over to Barry's taxi.

I make a show of catching it with my hand, like a big fat nerd. Standing on the step, I watch him go until the car disappears out of sight. A second later, my sister April and her best friend Chloe saunter up to me, wearing outfits that almost match. They've both got some variation of a white cotton top on with similar denim miniskirts and fake UGG boots.

"Hey, Jado," Chloe calls to me as they approach. She's got this annoying habit of making up nicknames for everyone, normally ending with an "O." She calls April "Apro." You get the picture.

"Eh, *who* was that?" April asks, her voice booming halfway around the street.

"A friend."

"Your friend is a fucking *ride*," Chloe puts in, fanning her face theatrically. For those not in the know, "a ride" is Dublin slang for "hot."

"Yep. That he is," I reply to her, deadpan. "Where have you two been?"

"Nowhere," says April, tight-lipped, which might as well be slang for "up to no good."

"Okay. Have you seen Pete around?"

"Nope."

"You're a fountain of knowledge tonight, April, really you are. Here, I've got a proposition for you," I say.

Chloe snickers at my use of the word "proposition." I'm dealing with a future Nobel Prize winner in this girl. April looks at me appraisingly.

"What is it?"

"Lara's looking for a babysitter for little Mia. What do you think? It'll earn you some money until you can find a full-time job."

"Yes, I'll do it! How much is she paying?" April asks enthusiastically, while Chloe's eyes simultaneously light up as she mouths the words *free house* at April.

"I saw that, Chloe, and there'll be no free house." I wag my finger at her. "If April's going to do this, she's going to do it properly. You can't have boys over if you're going to be responsible for a three-year-old. Do you hear me?"

"Yeah, I know. Don't snap at me — it was Chloe who said it. I know I have to take it seriously. I'm not stupid."

"Good to know. Now, are you coming in or what?"

She rolls her eyes at me and walks into the house, she and Chloe heading straight for the living room so that they can flirt with Alec's friends. I spend the next half an hour trying to get a hold of Pete, but he's not answering his phone. Eventually he arrives home, giving me the silent treatment after our argument last night. He shuffles up the stairs to his room, shutting himself inside with a slam of the door.

I really don't know what to do about him anymore. In my room I fall onto my mattress, exhausted. This is what I mean about teenagers being a handful. To be honest, I'd much prefer two wailing babies.

Reaching for my handbag, I pull out my phone and check my messages, of which there aren't many. The rap music is still thumping from downstairs, so I grab my headphones and stick them into the phone, scrolling through my music. Nothing tickles my fancy, so on a whim I go onto iTunes and search for the Bohemia Quartet. Their albums immediately pop up, and I download the most popular, titled *Songs for Her*.

I know I shouldn't, but I immediately wonder who "Her" is. There's a picture of the group on the cover, and all of them are equally good-looking guys, so it could be any one of their girlfriends or even a relative. Anyway, seeing the picture makes me understand why they were so popular. I'm sure they had a *huge* female following.

I hit "play" on the first song, and the opening notes hit me right in my soul like a soothing balm. All remnants of the rap music below float away as I get lost in the beauty of the strings.

Four

When I wake up the next morning, I realise I fell asleep with my earphones on, Shane's music having lulled me into a slumber. Later that day at work, he shows up at the bar at a quarter past four, looking invigorated.

"Whatever you've been taking, can I have some?" I ask him jokingly.

"I sometimes get like this after playing," he explains. "Could I have an ice water?"

"You can indeed," I say, pouring him a glass. He knocks it back in three long gulps and then asks for another.

There's a writers' talk going on in the main auditorium at the moment. It just started, so the bar is empty. I decide to take a break, grabbing myself an orange juice and a gin for Shane before walking around to take the seat beside him.

He eyes my orange juice. "No drinking alcohol on the job, eh?"

"No drinking at all, actually," I reply, pulling up my sleeve to show him the five small blue sparrows tattooed onto my inner forearm. "One for each year I've been sober," I explain.

"You were an alcoholic?" he asks softly in surprise, eyes tracing up and down my tattoos. One of the best artists in the city did them, and the blue has the effect of looking like watercolour paints.

I give him a grave nod.

"But you work in a bar. Isn't that kind of tempting fate?"

"For some, maybe, but not for me. I find being around alcohol is like working a muscle, so the more I do it, the stronger I become. The sparrows represent freedom from my addiction and my commitment to staying free of it. There's nothing more committed than ink permanently under your skin."

Shane reaches out and traces his fingers over the birds, his head tilted as he studies them. "They're very pretty. Are you going to keep getting a new one each year?"

"Probably not. I mean, I only have so much real estate," I joke. "They start at my wrist, so I guess once they reach the top of my arm I'll stop. If I get ten years under my belt, I don't think there'll be anything that could ever drive me back to drinking."

Shane looks at his gin now, like he feels guilty for having it in front of me.

"Oh, don't be silly. Drink up. I know that most people can enjoy alcohol responsibly. I'm just not one of them."

"When did you start drinking?" he asks, giving in and taking a sip.

"You probably don't want to know the answer to that."

He arches an eyebrow but doesn't say anything.

I let out a sigh. "Eleven when I had my first taste, fifteen when I began drinking properly."

"Fifteen, shit."

I pick up a cardboard coaster and begin picking at it. "I had a few…issues when I was younger. I guess drowning them in a bottle of vodka was the only thing that worked for me back then. I got my stomach pumped several times, almost died from kidney failure once."

Shane moves his stool closer to mine. "Is that what made you quit?"

I'm lost in my own thoughts for a second, and I don't hear his question. "Sorry, what was that?"

"The kidney failure. Is that why you quit?"

"Oh. No, actually. My head could have been falling off and I wouldn't have given up drinking. Didn't care enough about myself, I suppose. It was my mum getting sick that gave me the final push. I suddenly realised that she was never getting better and that my family needed me. Pete and April were still just kids at the time, and there would be no one to look after them, not their waster of a dad, anyway. I couldn't stand the idea of them being put into foster care, so I had no other choice but to step up."

I look down at my hand, at my healthy skin tone, remembering a time when I was so ill it had almost turned yellow. I shake myself out of the memory. "God, I'm being really depressing now, aren't I?"

"I think you're fascinating," he breathes, and then winces. "Did I just say that out loud?" he asks, shaking his head at himself.

I laugh. "Yep. Don't regret it. It's a good feeling to be fascinating to another person."

He knocks back a gulp of his drink and turns to me properly, his eyes searing. "I really like making you feel good, Jade."

His expression grows heated as he prolongs our stare. "Well, mission accomplished," I tell him, a touch uncomfortable under his attention. "So, how about we trade one depressing story for another? You still have to tell me about why you left your string quartet."

"Ah, can we not? It's an awful story."

"Surely not as awful as mine."

"Want to bet?"

"Okay, no big deal. You don't have to tell me."

He looks sadly into his almost empty glass. "How about I tell you something else, something equally depressing?"

"Go ahead. I'm all ears."

"I have no friends," he states, deadly serious.

Resting my elbow on the bar, I stare at him quizzically. Our faces are inches apart now as we conduct our intimate little conversation. "What you do mean?"

"I mean I have no friends. I have acquaintances, yes, but not friends. The only proper friends I did have were the three guys from my string quartet group: Leo, Justin, and Bryn. I don't talk to any of them anymore, so now I have no friends."

"Surely you have some. What about your childhood pals? You could reconnect with them now that you aren't travelling all over the place any longer."

He gives me an embarrassed look and then glances away shyly.

"What? You don't have any childhood friends, either?" I ask in a surprised voice.

"Maybe when I was under five. At six my mum decided to bring me to have piano lessons. You know, at the music school on Westland Row?"

"Yeah, I know it. You can always hear the sound of instruments drifting up onto the street from down in the basement."

He smiles fondly. "That's the one. So, anyway, Mum had an old friend called Jill who worked there as a music teacher and brought me for my first lesson. She tried teaching me 'Mary Had a Little Lamb' on the piano, but I had no interest. Then when Mum came to collect me, she and Jill were having tea and left me to my own devices in the music room. I picked up a violin, began messing around with it, and within a half an hour I had 'Mary Had a Little Lamb' down pat. I don't remember all the details, but I do have a very distinct memory of it being like I'd found an extension of myself in that one small instrument. All of the strings made sense, and I knew exactly how to create the melody I wanted."

"Wow," I breathe, enthralled by his story.

Shane smiles and continues, "I was proclaimed a child prodigy after that. Mum began having me homeschooled by a private tutor so that I could spend more time focusing on the violin. So basically, I was isolated and rarely met other kids my age, hence the 'no childhood friends' bit."

I briefly reach out and give his wrist a squeeze. "That sounds very lonely."

"It was and it wasn't. Mostly I was so focused on my music that I didn't have time to realise I was lonely. Then when I got older, though, I'd see other kids my age out having fun, and I'd envy them. But I always had my violin. Often I'd wonder if I could be a normal teenager but had to give up music, which would I choose? Music always won. When you want to be accomplished at something, especially playing an instrument, you have to sacrifice other things in life. Natural talent only goes so far. You have to spend so much of your time trying to get better and better."

There's a small note of strain in his words, giving me the impression that he struggles over this on a regular basis. Being a virtuoso versus having a social life.

"Well, you do realise you can have both now, right? Music and friends, I mean."

"I can?" he asks, looking at me in hope.

I laugh tenderly. "Of course you can. You already have a friend in me, so you telling me you have no friends isn't true."

He gives me a tiny smile. "I didn't know if you really wanted to be my friend or if you just felt sorry for me."

I shake my head at him in awe. "Are you serious? Of course I want to be your friend! In fact, I envy your life. If anyone should be felt sorry for, it's me." I pause to hold up a finger as I list off my reasons. "Recovering alcoholic, orphan, responsible for two wayward teenagers, lives in a shitbox area. Need I say more?"

Shane laughs at my humorous tone. "I guess you're right."

"I am *so* right. And you, Shane, are far too young, handsome, and talented to be so troubled," I proclaim.

"Not handsome enough for you to want to sleep with me again, though," he says, putting on a mournful face.

I give his shoulder a friendly slap and wink. "I don't remember any sleeping being involved. But anyway, if I was the relationship kind of girl, I'd be sleeping with you all over the place, my friend. You're a hot piece of arse. You should be getting out there and finding some willing females."

"Why aren't you the relationship kind of girl?" he asks with interest, ignoring everything else I said.

"We're back onto me again, I see. Well, when I was a drunk I found myself in a very messy, co-dependent relationship with another drunk. When we were happy, I drank. When he hurt me, I drank. For me, boyfriends are closely tied to my alcoholism. So when I decided to start over fresh, no boyfriends was my number-one rule. You see, when my heart gets broken I turn straight back to alcohol, and I have too many people relying on me now for that to happen."

"Who says I'd hurt you?" Shane asks seriously.

I shrug at him. "I can't predict the future. Who knows what we'd be like together?"

"I think we could be good together," he says in a low, flirty voice.

I suck in a breath at how his eyes rest on my breasts. "Feel free to elaborate on that," I flirt back, picking up my orange juice and gulping some down. All of a sudden I'm really thirsty.

He grabs either side of my stool and pulls it into his so that our thighs collide. Next, he brings his mouth to my ear, his breath touching my skin and giving me tingles. "Well, for a start I'd lay you down on my bed and take my time worshipping your full, beautiful breasts. Then I'd spread your legs and use my tongue to…"

"Okay, I get the picture." I laugh nervously, not having anticipated such a detailed erotic description, especially considering how shy he can come across. Perhaps that gin and tonic has already gone to his head. I quickly stand up from the stool and hurry back behind the bar, saying, "I think my break time is up."

I can feel how fast his words got me wet, which I find startling for some reason.

Shane stares at me in confusion. "You did tell me to elaborate, Jade."

"Yeah, well, sometimes I'm my own worst enemy," I mutter, picking up our empty glasses.

"What was that?"

"Nothing. Never mind."

"We're still friends, aren't we?" he asks, worried that he's ruined things.

"Of course we are, silly. The intermission is coming up, so I need to get back to work."

"All right. I should probably be getting home anyway," he says, unsure, grabbing his violin case from where it had been resting on the floor. He's about to leave but then turns back to me. He remains silent for a moment before stating, "I really like talking to you, Jade."

Giving him a warm expression, I answer, "I really like talking to you, too, Shane."

Five

The next day there's a free lunchtime concert on at work. I haven't bumped into Shane since our conversation at the bar yesterday, and I'm really curious to see him play, so I quickly eat a sandwich and then make my way to the hall.

I take a seat close to the back of the room, not wanting to be noticed. There's a decent-sized audience assembled, mostly nearby office workers who've decided to do something classy on their lunch break. I realise I'm in for a treat when the conductor announces that they'll be playing Mendelssohn's Violin Concerto in E Minor.

I don't see Shane anywhere; however, there is an empty seat in first violins belonging to the concertmaster, which in my limited knowledge I know is the second most important position after the conductor. The fact that this seat could be Shane's must mean that he's pretty good.

What am I saying? I've heard his album; I know he's good. In fact, I fell asleep listening to it again last night. I probably shouldn't make a habit of that.

The conductor turns to address the audience, saying, "We usually have a guest violinist join us to play this piece. However, we recently welcomed a new and very talented member to our orchestra, Mr. Shane Arthur, who I have invited to play the solo today."

Those in attendance clap, and the conductor turns to take his place in front of the musicians. Shane appears and walks to the centre of the stage before the music starts up. Just seeing him standing there holding his instrument has me a touch hot and bothered. Immediately he begins playing, with the rest of the orchestra accompanying him, and my ears soak up the familiar melody.

It fills me with emotion, as classical music always does. Shane's entire body is a work of art as he moves with his violin, and I realise that he was right, it really is like an extension of him.

My head wanders as I become enraptured by the music. I hardly see or hear any of the other musicians, my attention solely on this intriguing man. Musical notes float out of his strings in a cacophony of colours and textures. They fly up into the air. A treble clef drifts to me, catching onto the edge of my shirt. I pick it up and smooth it beneath my fingers, fold it in half, and stick it in my pocket for safekeeping.

There's a lull in the music at one point, with Shane playing a low and sad melody. When he plays this, I see grief and misery in his entire form. I see loss. He's so emotionally involved in the piece that I can't help falling in love. Maybe I'm not in love with *him*, per se, but I'm definitely in love with something about him.

How fortunate I was that our paths crossed. I've a feeling that having this sad, lonely, lovely man in my life is going to change it irrevocably. Even if from now on I only ever get to observe him from afar, he will mark me somehow.

All of a sudden, his eyes seek me out. I go rigid in my seat as he plays to me for a long few moments before focusing on something else. For the remainder of the symphony I close my eyes and just…imagine.

In turns joyful, mournful and triumphant, I see streams of paint in my head, swirling and dancing to the music. All of the pain I've experienced in my life feels like it's being expelled simply through Shane's manipulation of the strings.

I remain seated even when the concerto is over, my eyes still closed. Minutes later I feel someone sit down beside me and take my hand in theirs. I can tell it's Shane even before I open my eyes to look.

"You never told me you were coming to hear me play," he says just as I lift my head to look at him. He's closer than I expected him to be, his face hovering inches from mine.

"I'd hoped to remain incognito," I reply, giving him a soft smile. "You're amazing. The way you play is just — wow. I still have tingles."

I lift my arm to show him how my hairs are standing on end.

He lets go of my hand and sits back in his chair with a satisfied look.

"I'd love to play for you alone sometime," he says after several moments of quiet.

I breathe harshly just imagining it. I don't think it would be humanly possible to sit in a room alone with

Shane and have him play for me, and *not* want to fuck his brains out afterward. Even the way he holds the bow turns me on. For a brief moment I imagine him standing above me, reaching down and running it lightly down my naked abdomen.

"I'd give anything to know what you're thinking right now," Shane murmurs, breaking me from my dirty thoughts.

"Oh, nothing much."

"It didn't look like nothing. It looked like a whole lot of *I'm thinking about sex*."

I smirk and try to deflect from the stone-cold truth of his words. "You *wish* I was thinking about sex."

"Yeah, you're right about that. So when are we next spending some time together, friend?" he asks, giving my arm a little nudge with his elbow.

I take several moments to think about it before giving him a considering look. "That depends. How do you feel about haircuts and Indian food?"

He shrugs and runs his hand over his head. "I'm in favour of both?" he replies like a question.

"Good. Come to my house tonight at six, and we'll hang out."

"Okay. You aren't going to explain?" he asks with interest.

I stand up. "Nope. I have to get back to the bar now. See you tonight."

"See you tonight, Bluebird," he breathes, shaking his head and smiling as he watches me walk away.

Once a month my friends and I get together at my house for a catch-up night. The group consists of me, Lara, Lara's cousin Ben, and Ben's boyfriend, Clark. Ben is a hairdresser and Clark is a counsellor, so we combine haircuts with talking about our feelings. I like to think of it as grooming for the inside as well as out. We also love Indian food, so we always order some in.

I'm beginning to wonder if Shane's going to show at all when a quarter past six hits and he still hasn't arrived. Ben is moving furniture about the kitchen to create a makeshift styling station, asking Lara what kind of a cut she wants this month. She tells him she'd like seventies-style retro layers, like one of the *Charlie's Angels*. She's far more adventurous than me in this respect. I always keep my hair long and just have a basic trim to keep the split ends at bay.

"So what's he like, this new friend of yours?" asks Clark, sitting down beside me at the table. He and Ben are both in their late thirties, and I love having them around because they kind of feel like my two gay big brothers, giving me guidance and advice. Ben also had a drinking problem when he was younger, so we've bonded over that shared experience for years.

"Well, at first I just thought he was this good-looking, slightly shy violinist, but then I spoke to him some more and got to see him play, and now I kind of feel unworthy of his friendship. He's like one of those, what do you call them? Virtuosos. He was a prodigy at the age of six."

When informing my friends about Shane, I left out the part about us meeting on the street in the middle of the night and instead simply pretended we met at the concert hall after a show.

"All those classical musicians are mad in the head, though," Ben puts in as he runs his hands through Lara's auburn hair. "You know, like Beethoven. Oh, and the guy out of that movie, *Shine*."

"Beethoven went mad because he had all this beautiful music to create but couldn't hear it because he was deaf," says Lara.

I look at her in surprise.

"What? Haven't you ever seen *Immortal Beloved*? I cry at that film every time. The unrequited love that wasn't unrequited after all."

"I have, actually. I couldn't watch it more than once, though. I was literally in tears for days afterward. Anyway," I say, looking back to Clark, "I'd forego sanity any day of the week to be able to play like Shane."

"Are you having a little cerebral crush?" Clark asks with a knowing grin. "You don't want him for his body, you want him for the music he's got inside kind of thing?"

I love how Clark uses words fancy words like "cerebral." He's one of the only people I know with a college education, so I'm always stealing his phrases.

"Oh, his body is something to be coveted just as much as his talent, let me tell you. But anyway, stop reading into this. I think I'm just fan-girling."

There's a knock at the front door, and my heart leaps. I give each of my friends a look urging them to be on their best behaviour and then rise to go answer it.

I stare at my reflection in the hall mirror for a moment. Little zinging gold sparks radiate from my chest, and butterflies flit around my head. I think I even see a love heart or two. I swipe them all away, not reading too much into their presence. When I finally open the door, Shane is standing on the step, holding a bottle of sparkling grape juice.

"Hey," I breathe.

"Hey, Bluebird."

We both smile and take each other in for a moment.

"You look great," he says.

I'm wearing an old sundress, no shoes.

"Thanks, so do you. I see you brought refreshments."

"Yeah, I almost grabbed a bottle of wine, but then I realised that would be counter-productive."

"Counter-productive, indeed," I say with a smirk, taking the bottle from him and helping him out of his jacket. I catch a whiff of his cologne and get assaulted by memories of our one night together…if you could even call it a night. Swallowing hard, I hang the jacket by the end of the staircase and lead him into the kitchen to meet the others.

Jacinta Lennon loved to paint pictures of her daughter.

It was one of her favourite things to do.

She took one final look at the painting she was about to sell to a passer-by, admiring the brush strokes and the quality of the canvas.

Her daughter stood within the frame, a blue beacon on the grey street, standing so still on her box.

Closing her eyes briefly, she made a wish that it would bring its new owner as much pleasure as it brought her.

Then she handed it away. She would never see it again.

Six

Shane pauses halfway down the hall as he turns to study a painting hanging in a dark wooden frame. It's one of my mother's. She never really held down a steady job when she was alive; however, she managed to keep the household afloat with welfare payments and the money she made selling her paintings on St. Steven's Green. She loved to paint scenery and sometimes portraits. Often she'd make me sit for her. There are dozens of paintings of me up in the attic. I hate looking at them because I find it weird seeing myself through the eyes of another person.

"Where did you get this?" Shane asks, his gaze roaming over the country scene depicted.

"My mother painted it. She did lots of pictures like this one. Do you like it?"

"Ah," he says with a sharp breath, as though something has just made sense to him. "It's very good. Your mother was a talented woman."

"She was. Come on, everyone's dying to meet you," I say, linking my arm through his and leading him into the kitchen.

Clark is the first to greet Shane, thrusting his hand out for a shake and introducing himself. I catch sight of Ben shooting Lara an *omg, he's fucking hot* look. Lara gives him an *omg, I fucking know* look back. I smile to myself a little in satisfaction.

Though to me Shane's not just hot, he's beautiful. Man-beautiful.

Dangerous, slippery-slope thoughts I'm having these days.

I put the grape juice in the fridge as Shane says hello to Ben and Lara, taking the seat at the table where I had previously been sitting.

"Oh, Jade, Shane took your chair. Now you'll have to sit on his lap," Ben chirps with a saucy wink.

Shane shifts to look at me apologetically. "I'm sorry, I didn't…"

"Oh, would you stop? I'll grab a chair from under the stairs," I say, shaking my head at Ben. If I know my friend, he's going to go out of his way to try to embarrass me tonight. Ben just has that way about him.

When I return with the chair, I set it down beside Shane, and we watch as Lara has her hair cut. Ben already washed it before Shane arrived. It's hard to talk once he whips out the hairdryer, but we just about manage to make casual chitchat.

Ben takes me upstairs to wash my hair in the bathroom when he's done with Lara. We return a few minutes later, and I find with relief that Shane and Clark are deep in conversation, about politics of all things. Lara looks like she's ready to nod off from boredom.

I can't help myself when I brush my hand along Shane's shoulder as I pass him by. He stiffens and then relaxes, turning his head to stare up at me hotly. I shouldn't be teasing him like this, but every time I see him I feel this overwhelming urge to touch him.

"Clark, will you call for the Indian now? That way it'll be here once Ben's finished with my hair."

"Will do," says Clark, standing to retrieve his phone.

Shane watches as Ben starts to trim the ends of my hair. I stare right back at him, unable to pay attention to Lara and Ben, who are talking about the latest episode of their favourite soap opera. My body gets all warm as we continue to fuck each other with our eyes. Jesus, I want him so badly.

The eye-fuck Olympics are interrupted only when Clark starts asking everyone what they want to eat. Shane's voice is gravelly when he speaks. I feel a silly little satisfaction deep in my belly to know I've affected him. Immediately afterward I reprimand myself for being so careless. I know I can't have a relationship with Shane, and yet here I am, leading him on.

The moment he breaks my heart, I'll be straight back on the vodka, and that just can't happen. There are too many people who need me sober and functioning.

The food arrives just as Ben has finished blow-drying my newly trimmed hair. Shane bends forward and reaches out to run his hand down it. I watch him curiously. A second later he pulls away and clears his throat, getting up to assist Clark in dishing out the Indian.

"So, tonight's theme is anger," Clark announces once everybody's seated with their food.

Hmm, we've never done anger as a theme before.

"Someone care to explain?" says Shane with a bewildered expression.

"Clark's a counsellor," I tell him. "Every month he gives us a new theme, and we have to talk about it. The theme is always an emotion. You have to discuss the time in your life you felt the given emotion most intensely."

"Ah," he furrows his brow. "Do I have to take part?"

"Of course you do!" exclaims Ben, reaching out to pinch Shane playfully on the arm. "Otherwise it's just voyeurism, and that's no fun unless there's sex involved."

Shane laughs good-naturedly, and I'm surprisingly relieved at how well he's getting along with my friends. *You are not grooming him to be your boyfriend, Jade, so stop it.* I have to scold myself into submission; otherwise, my girl-brain will lose the run of herself.

I like to think that I have two brains. One is my girl brain and the other is my boy brain. They both have their good sides and their bad sides. For instance, my girl brain is great for organising, while my boy brain is good for fixing shit, and when you live in a house like mine, stuff gets broken all the time. My boy brain is crap at counselling night. He doesn't want to talk about his feelings. My girl brain is ace at counselling night. She loves to talk about her feelings. In fact, sometimes she likes it a little too much.

"There's no need to be anxious," Clark reassures him. "What gets said on counselling night stays in counselling night. Or something like that." He grins and dips some naan bread into his korma.

"Well," says Lara. "I think I'd like to go first because anger is something I know *all* about."

"Here we go," says Ben, rolling his eyes teasingly. We all know the story Lara's going to tell. In fact, she's told it for a number of different themes already: sadness, despair, heartbreak. She eyes Shane, seeming eager to recount it again for new ears.

"Hey! Don't take the piss. I've had a lot to be angry about in my life. The thing that made me most angry, though, was when I came home and found 'he who shall not be named' shagging my slut neighbour Leonie McEvoy. Leonie McEvoy lived in the apartment next to mine for two years, and she'd always be hanging around making 'fuck me' eyes whenever my boyfriend came to visit, wearing the tightest pair of jeans and the most revealing top she could find. She knew when he was there because she'd recognise his navy Ford Fiesta parked outside.

"'You're crazy, Lara,' he'd say whenever I'd warn him not to go near her. 'I only have eyes for you,' he'd declare, the lying toe rag. I swear to God I felt like I was turning into the Hulk when I sauntered in tired after a long day at work, and there he was going to town on that wrote-off walking advertisement for chlamydia."

We all burst out laughing while she pauses for breath before addressing Shane. She's been addressing him the whole time because she's well aware we've already heard this story before. "He'd moved in with me at this point, you see, and I was three months pregnant with my little girl, Mia. I didn't care that I'd have to raise my baby by myself — I wasn't going to stay with someone who cheated on me. I was so angry I smashed almost every plate I owned before kicking him out and telling him not to show his face ever again."

"Well, that sounds pretty hardcore," says Shane with a low whistle when Lara's finished with her story.

She folds her arms, looking satisfied with his reaction. Ben goes next, detailing how there'd been a boy who'd bullied him brutally at school for being gay. Years later Ben had been standing on the street watching the pride parade go by, and who did he see sitting atop one of the floats wearing a crystal tiara on his head and a pointy Madonna bra? The very same bully who'd made his life a misery. Ben was so angry that he marched straight into the parade, climbed atop the float, and pulled the guy off it by the hair before punching his lights out.

I can see Clark eyeing Shane as Ben's story comes to a close, and Shane looks sort of uncomfortable at the prospect of having to share a story, so I volunteer to go next.

"Hmmm, do we only get to tell one story?" I ask Clark. "I've been equally angry in the extreme about a few things over the years."

"Just one story, Jade. Pick the one when you were most angry."

I make a show of scratching at my chin as Ben gives me a sympathetic look. He knows exactly when I was most angry. It's not something I'm ever going to share, and he knows it. So I select a substitute and lie.

"Well, there's not much of a story to tell about when I was most angry. It was the day my mother was diagnosed with lung cancer. She had a lot of years still left, but that bastard of a disease took her. It's hard to deal with anger when there isn't an actual person to focus it on." I give Ben a sad smile. "You can't pull cancer down off a gay pride float and beat the shit out of it, no matter how much you might want to."

They all chuckle, and relief washes over me as I push my true story back down into the recesses of my mind. I can't think about that. It was one of the main reasons why I began drinking at such a young age. I might have been angry when Mum got her diagnosis, but mostly I was just sad. Sad and determined not to keep living my life in a drunken stupor so that I could block out the guilt and loss I felt for so many years.

Shane leans forward and squeezes my hand comfortingly, his eyes full of empathy. We stare at each other for a long time, and then he excuses himself to go use the bathroom.

My friends get quiet when he leaves. Ben breaks the silence by declaring, "Jade, that man seriously wants to Channing all over your Tatum."

I let out a burst of laughter. "You watch far too many YouTube videos, Ben."

"Oh, Channing Tatum," says Lara with a dreamy sigh. "Now there's one hot slice of shepherd's pie."

"Number one," says Clark, pointing at Lara. "If you're going to use the 'hot slice of pie' analogy, the pie in question needs to be dessert-based. Apple is always a popular choice. Savoury pies just sound wrong. And number two," he goes on, giving me a cheeky wink. "I think Jade would much prefer if he Colined all over her Farrell."

"Oh, my God, would you all shut up! He might hear you," I exclaim.

"What? I know for a fact you keep a DVD of *Alexander the Great* hidden under your bed. And let's face it, you're not watching that movie for the history."

I narrow my gaze at him. "You're evil."

"I do try."

At that moment Shane returns to the room, and they all start smiling at him.

"So, Shane, I think it's your turn to share," says Ben, clasping his hands together.

"Ah, right," says Shane, sitting down beside me and grimacing. "Anger. Well, I guess my story is quite similar to Lara's. I came back to my hotel room in Vienna after returning from a party to find my fiancée of two years *in flagrante delicto* with my best friend Justin. He was the cellist in my string quartet, and we'd been doing a set of shows there."

"*In flagrante* what?" Lara asks, confused.

"He caught them having sex," Clark explains to her.

"Oh, shit," she blurts out, and then reaches over to put a comforting hand on Shane's arm before pulling away again. "That's awful. Your fiancée and your best friend!"

Shane winces a little when she reiterates the fact, and I can't stop staring at him. Now I know where the almost tangible sadness comes from when he plays his violin. And now I also know the reason why he left his string quartet.

"Were you in love with her?" Ben asks in a low voice.

Shane gives him a mournful smile. "I should hope so. I'm not in the habit of asking women I'm not in love with to marry me."

I can't hold back from reaching to him under the table and taking his hand in mine for a moment. Our fingers intertwine effortlessly, and tingles shoot from his skin into mine when we touch. I don't keep holding on for long, and when I let go I feel like I've lost something vital.

"Well," Lara chimes in, "once a cheater, always a cheater, that's what I say. You're well shot of her, just the same way my Mia and I are better off without her lying man-whore of a father."

The edges of Shane's mouth curve up in a grin, and we continue eating our food. We chat for another hour or so, and then everyone begins to say their goodbyes and leave. Shane is still there when my friends have gone. Once I've waved off Ben and Clark, I return to the kitchen to find him standing by the sink, rinsing dishes.

"Hey, you don't need to do that. I'm the hostess," I say placing a hand on his shoulder.

He turns his head to look at me, and there's an intensity in his gaze when his eyes wander to my hand on him.

"My grandmother always told me it's good manners to help with the clean-up when you've eaten at somebody's house. Let me do it — I'll feel weird if I don't."

"Okay, but that means I get to dry," I reply, grabbing a towel. "Sorry we don't have a dishwasher."

I don't go into the fact that a dishwasher is a luxury I can't afford right now. Shane only shrugs, and continues rinsing plates and cups. As we quietly clean up together, I'm aware of him watching me, but I'm too self-conscious to make eye contact. I don't know what it is about being alone in the room with him that makes me get shy.

We're almost done when the front door opens and shuts, and my sister April struts in. She's wearing leopard-print leggings and a pink diamante Paul's Boutique hoodie that's probably a fake from the markets. God bless the teenagers these days, but they haven't got a clue about fashion. Although to be honest, neither did I at that age. All I ever wore was baggy jeans and even baggier band T-shirts. My only nod to style was the fact that I used to dye my hair purple and colour my eyes in with copious amounts of black eyeliner, because, you know, I considered myself to be "different."

April opens the fridge and pulls out a carton of orange juice, taking a long swig before she even notices anyone else is in the room. When her eager eyes land on Shane, a grin shapes her mouth.

"Hey, I'm April, Jade's sister," she says, thrusting her hand out for him to shake.

I watch the entire exchange with amusement as Shane turns and takes the dishtowel from me to dry his hands off on it.

"It's a pleasure to meet you, April," he says.

"Oh, nice accent. Posh," says April, nodding her head as she sizes him up. "I bet you're loaded, too. You look like you're loaded."

Shane bursts out laughing as April eyes his designer shoes. She might not seem like it, but my sister can spot expensive brands from a mile away. She's like a baby gold digger in the making, and I can't really blame her for wanting to improve her circumstances, given her less than lavish upbringing. Still, she can keep her eager little eyes off Shane.

"I'm sorry," I apologise to Shane while giving April a light slap on the arm. "My sister was too busy donning her leopard print this morning to remember to put on her manners as well."

"And I'm sorry that *my* sister talks like a nerd. Seriously, Jade, who uses the word 'donning'?" she asks, grinning and sticking out her tongue.

"I do," I reply, guiding Shane from the kitchen and into the empty living room. Alec must be staying with whatever girl he's shagging this month, because he hasn't been around this evening, and Pete's upstairs in his room, playing computer games.

"She's a character," says Shane, sitting down on the couch as I turn on the television.

"Mm-hmm, that's one way to put it," I scoff.

It's just gone half past ten, and I'm kind of wondering what he's still doing here. It's not that I don't enjoy his company (to be honest, I enjoy it slightly too much), but it feels like he's waiting. Like maybe if he sticks around long enough, something will happen between us.

"Do you want me to call you a cab?" I ask casually, standing and flicking through the stations, afraid that if I sit down beside him I'll want to do something crazy...like grab him and stick my tongue down his throat.

"I don't need a cab. I drove here tonight," he replies, and I turn to look at him with wide eyes. I didn't know he had a car, since he didn't drive to the concert hall the other night.

"You drove here? Where did you park?" I ask with just the tiniest hint of urgency.

"Just around the corner. There were no spaces any closer to your house."

"Right, and what kind of car do you drive?"

"A Range Rover," he says, and his brow furrows at my panic. "What's wrong, Jade?"

Great, a flipping Range Rover in this neck of the woods. He'll be lucky if it hasn't been stolen and sold on the black market already — and I'm not exaggerating.

Without thinking further, I hurry into the hall, grabbing my boots, coat, and keys on the way. "I should have warned you. You can't just leave a car like that around here," I tell him as he follows me out the door.

Seven

We walk around the corner, and the anxiety that had been building in my chest dissolves when I see his car is still there. That only lasts a moment before I clock two shifty-looking characters hanging around nearby. One of them is leaning up against a wall, looking from side to side — keeping sketch, in other words. The other is craning his neck to look in the window of Shane's car. I guess he's thinking the whole rigmarole of selling a stolen vehicle is too much hassle when he could just do a smash and grab, steal something valuable from the glove compartment, and run off.

"Hey, Babyface Nelson, keep walking," I call sarcastically, and the guy startles, his attention shifting quickly to me.

The other guy narrows his eyes as he chews on a wad of gum. "We're happy where we are, thanks," he replies in a hard tone.

Babyface Nelson walks to his friend and folds his arms. "Yeah, that's right."

Shane puts his hand to the small of my back in a protective gesture as he guides me to the car. "We don't want any trouble here," he says, pulling his keys from his pocket. Both their attentions light up when they see the keys, the plan for a quick clean steal formulating in their heads. I wish I'd thought to warn Shane not to take his keys from his pocket. Now they know he's the owner.

Quick as a flash, one of the thugs pulls out a short flick knife, making sure Shane gets a good look at it and understands the threat.

"Throw those keys over here," says the thug, and Shane eyeballs him.

"Fuck off," he answers, his hand on my back pressing in harder.

The thug's expression turns angry as he moves towards us.

"I said give me the keys, or I'll fuck up your pretty little girlfriend."

"And I said fuck off." Shane stands firm.

I don't like where this is going, not one tiny bit. I'm about to tell Shane to just give him the keys, because he obviously has insurance for a car this expensive, and it's not worth getting stabbed over. But I don't get the chance to do that, because the thug with the knife moves fast, running directly toward me with the blade. Before I can move, Shane twists his body around mine, and the thug ends up sticking him in the side instead.

I see red just as Shane clutches himself from the shock of being stabbed and the thug dives for the keys that have dropped to the ground. Leaping into action, I kick him hard right between the legs. The thug grunts in pain and I grab his wrist, twisting it so the knife falls from his hand. I pick it up quickly and hold it out.

"Get out of here now, both of you, before I call the police."

Once they've scarpered, I turn quickly to Shane, pulling his shirt up so that I can check the damage. He didn't get cut too deep, just enough to make him bleed, but it might need stitches.

"You okay?" I ask, slightly out of breath.

His lips turn up in an almost smile. "Yeah, I've been worse," he says, giving a pained wince as I lead him to the passenger door. "I have to say, I'm feeling slightly emasculated."

I grin. "What?! You got stabbed for me. That's about as heroic as it comes. Come on, I'm driving you to A&E in St. James' to get you looked at."

He doesn't complain about me driving his car, and since I'm used to my old Mini that I had to sell last year, it takes a bit of getting used to driving a Range Rover. Shane grins at my mistakes but doesn't comment on them. I think he's in a little too much pain to speak but is trying his best to hide it. I park close to the hospital entrance and hold Shane's hand as we walk inside. We explain to one of the nurses on duty what happened, and she gives us a form to fill in before instructing us to take a seat. It's eleven o'clock at night, so suffice it to say there are more drunks and junkies hanging around than actual sick people.

It's an environment I recognise well. I've been hospitalised a few times over the years, all self-inflicted of course. With my life being so clean now, it's hard to be reminded of when it wasn't.

A woman drinking a bottle of strawberry Ensure is sitting in the row in front of us, having an argument with herself. I imagine all the nutrients and vitamins sinking into her damaged system, trying to repair a body fucked up by drugs. Vitamin A, vitamin B, vitamins C, D, E, and K. All in liquid form, because she can't handle solid foods, or maybe she just doesn't care enough to go through the hassle of chewing.

I know I didn't.

Often I'd shun a bowl of cereal for breakfast in favour of a cigarette and a bottle of something strong.

"We could be waiting a while," I say to Shane with an apologetic expression. I feel to blame for all this; the reason he's injured is because he was protecting me (which makes me feel all mushy inside) and also because my neighbourhood is so crappy that he couldn't even park his car there for a couple of hours without someone trying to steal it.

"I have good health insurance," he replies. "Does that make a difference?"

His eyes light up for a moment, like he's actually enjoying this or something.

"Oh, I'm not sure. Maybe."

Our question is answered no longer than twenty minutes later, when a nurse calls his name. Yep, the insurance definitely makes a difference. I've spent my whole life on free healthcare and sometimes have had to wait several hours to be seen. I try to go with Shane, but in a clipped voice the nurse informs me that's not allowed. Huh. I wonder why she's being so snotty. Maybe I gave her a hassle years ago and she remembers my face.

I sit back down in the seat and pull out my phone, dialling the number of the police station nearest my home. A male voice I recognise answers, a cop I've had to deal with a few times over the last couple months when Pete's gotten himself into trouble. He's a bit of an old prick, but aren't they all? Sergeant Finnegan, I think I remember his name being.

I quickly tell him the details of what happened, and he says he'll look into it. I get the feeling he doesn't exactly play things by the book, because I'm sure he should have told me to come down to the station.

When Shane returns, he has that pleased look in his eye that shows he's been given some good painkillers. He lifts the side of his shirt to show me his hip is all bandaged up.

"Are you going to be okay to play your instrument?" I ask with concern, trying not to ogle his momentarily bared abdomen.

He waves me off. "Oh, yeah, it was only a little cut."

I grin and make a funny swooning noise. "Such a man."

"The manliest." He smiles and dangles his keys in my face. "Now take me home, woman. I strangely enjoy watching you drive my car."

I swipe the keys and stand up. "What, like a comedy of errors?"

"Nah, more like foreplay."

Snorting, I reply, "Oh, God. Did you really mean to say that?"

He continues, smiling happily, "Yes, Jade. Yes, I did."

"I think they might have given you too much meds. You know sometimes that stuff works like truth serum."

Pretending like he needs to lean on me for strength, despite just claiming his injury was only a little cut, he puts his arm around my shoulder. "This was a great night," he declares. "I love being around you. You really know how to live."

We've just reached his car when I slip out from under his arm and open the passenger door for him.

"Yeah, I know how to get my new friend stabbed and his car almost stolen. Such a great life I live," I reply mockingly as I start the engine.

We're driving out of the hospital when Shane says, "It's better than being sheltered. You live in the real world, Jade, and you don't know how desperate I am to join you."

Turning from the road for a moment, I give him a funny look. "You live in the real world, too, Shane."

"I live in a world of privilege."

"Just because it's privileged doesn't mean it's not real. It means you're fortunate."

He shakes his head and reaches out to put his hand on my arm. "It's stifling and fake. And so fucking lonely. I want you to teach me to be like you, to live like you."

For a while I remain quiet. Then I reply, "My life is one long series of fuck-ups, bad luck, and mistakes. I have nothing good to teach you. By the way, we're almost in Ranelagh. Where's your house?"

"Turn left here," he says. "And I'm not letting you change the subject. Teach me, Jade."

"You're very strange sometimes."

"Teach me."

"I'm not sure…"

"Jade, please, just say yes." He squeezes my arm. "I need this. You don't know how much."

The sincerity in his eyes startles me; he seems almost desperate. And so, despite the fact that I have no clue what I'm signing myself up for, I reply, "Okay, Shane, I'll teach you."

He grins big. "Thank you. My house is just at the end of this street."

I let out a breath and park outside the red brick Victorian house. It has a really nice garden and white plantation shutters on the windows. Getting out, I throw him his keys.

"I need to call for a cab to bring me back to mine, but my battery's dead," I say as he catches them easily.

"Come inside. You can use the house phone."

I eye his place warily, wondering if it's a good idea that I go inside. He opens the door and turns to look at me when I haven't moved.

"You coming in or what?"

"Yeah," I answer finally, and walk into the foyer. The place has obviously been lovingly restored; it even has those old coloured tiles on the floor. Shane leads me to the living room and shows me to the phone, where I quickly dial Barry's number. It rings out with no answer, so he must not be working tonight. Putting the phone back down on the receiver, I try to remember the number for my local taxi rank.

Shane's sitting on his vintage brown leather sofa, watching me. We lock eyes for a long minute, a dozen emotions passing between us.

"Barry, the guy who drove you home the other night, he's not picking up. I need to Google the number of another rank."

Shane reaches into the pocket of his trousers and pulls out his sleek black iPhone. "Here, use this."

I walk to him and reach out for the phone, but when I grab it, he doesn't let it go.

"Stay," he breathes, gaze intense.

"What?"

"Stay the night."

"Shane, I can't."

Gripping my wrist with his other hand, he pulls me down onto his lap before I can resist, and then his hands are in my hair, trailing down my spine.

"We can't do this," I tell him, breathing heavily. My thighs are straddling his waist, and I can feel him hardening against me.

"Jade, please, just let me…." He trails off and pulls my face to his. Then he does the sweetest thing by running his nose along my nose before nuzzling my neck. It's so simple, yet feels incredibly intimate. I close my eyes, wanting so much to give in and let him slip inside me. All he needs to do is hitch my dress up and undo his pants. So very fucking easy, and yet I know I have to be strong. Temptation is around me all the time, and Shane is just another form of it.

Shakily I open my eyes and get off his lap. He watches me, a sad expression on his face. He knows I'm not going to stay. Without another word, I quickly search for a number on his phone and then call a cab. The lady on the other end tells me a car will be there in ten minutes, but that could be ten minutes too long if I have to stare at Shane and think of all the things I can't allow myself to have.

I look around the room for a distraction and see his violin perched on a stand. Walking to it, I run my fingers over its surface.

"It's an original Stradivarius," Shane says in a quiet voice, almost like he's telling me a secret.

I turn to him, open-mouthed. "You're joking."

There are only a couple hundred of these violins left in the world, and Shane just leaves this one sitting in his living room for anyone to steal. Is he crazy? It's at least worth several hundred thousand euros, if not millions.

"Not joking," he replies, smiling.

"Uh, shouldn't this be locked up in a safe or something?"

"Now, where would be the point in that? The beauty of an instrument is to play it, not to leave it to get dusty in a safe. Besides, it's insured up the wazoo."

I can't stop staring at the violin, a piece of wood that was created perhaps two hundred years ago. What historical figures have held it in their hands? What great musicians have made it sing for them? Hundreds of multi-coloured fingerprints rise up on the shiny wood, dancing along its length, telling a thousand tales of music. I blink, and they're gone.

"But how can you even afford this? I know your string quartet was popular but...."

"My grandfather left me a sum of money when he died. The rest I took from my own savings. I dreamed of having this instrument since I was a boy, and then a few years ago I finally had the means to pay for it."

"Wow."

"You sound impressed."

"I am impressed, very much so. But you need to keep it locked up when you're not at home."

Shane shrugs. "I usually do. This time I forgot. Anyway, very few people would think it was anything other than a plain old violin if they saw it."

"Hmm, that's true." I hesitate before continuing impulsively, "Play something for me."

Shane tilts his head, studying me, then nods and goes to pick up the instrument. I watch him; he hasn't even started playing yet, and I'm already enraptured simply by the way he moves. Bringing the bow to the strings, he plays a slow, sad tune. I recognise it from his album, the one I've been listening to far too much. He only gets a couple of notes in when there's a harsh knock at the door, breaking my too short reverie.

"Damn, that's the taxi."

Shane nods, placing the violin back on its stand. "We're forever being interrupted by those blasted things," he says, referring to the other night in my kitchen.

"Yes, strange that," I say with a smile.

"Are you working tomorrow?"

"I am." God, why is my voice coming out so breathy?

"I have two concerts to play, so I might see you around."

Walking to him, I give his wrist a light squeeze. "See you tomorrow, then."

And I go, walking straight out the front door and leaving behind what could very well have been an incredible night I'd never forget.

Eight

The next day I walk into work tired as hell. I had a rough time of it trying to get Pete up and ready for school this morning. Then I had to talk down an anxious April, whose first day as Lara's child-minder is today. She might act like the cock of the walk most of the time, but April is prone to panic attacks, especially when she has to try something new.

In the end I got them both out the door with just enough time to shower, have breakfast, and take Specky for a quick walk before my shift. I'm manning the first-floor bar again today, and when I walk in I spy two men seated off to the side, deep in chat. I immediately recognise one of them as Shane, and the other I've never met before.

I take over from my co-worker and start restocking the fridges with bottles. Shane and the man he's talking to are close enough for me to hear most of their conversation; I quickly catch on that he's a journalist and Shane's being interviewed for some magazine or newspaper. I guess it makes sense, since he is sort of a celebrity in the classical music world.

"So, you're enjoying being back on home soil?" asks the journalist.

"Oh, sure. It's great to play around the world, but there's something that little bit special about being home. My parents used to take me to see concerts in this hall when I was just a boy. I idolised the violinists in the symphony, and now I'm one of them. Plus, there's a great sense of community in an orchestra that you don't get in smaller groups."

The journalist chuckles. "It must be very fulfilling, but let me ask you, your departure from The Bohemia Quartet was somewhat abrupt. You say you left for health reasons, but now you're playing again, so what I want to know is if that was really the reason why you left?"

Whoa, diving straight for the juicy tidbits there. Shane's jaw flexes ever so slightly, but he quickly covers his anger at being asked such a personal question by laughing good-naturedly. "Yes, that was the real reason. I know everybody likes a good scandal, but in this case there wasn't one."

"So why haven't you rejoined the group? You're obviously back to health now."

"As you probably already know," says Shane patiently, "our manager, Jack Campbell, replaced me with a new violinist, Andrew Hollows. He's a very talented musician, and I couldn't have asked for a better replacement to bring the group into a new era. Besides, it was time for a change."

"But didn't you just say you left for health reasons?"

"Yes, but I also wanted to move on with my career, do something different."

"You just mentioned your manager, Jack Campbell. Might I ask you about your relationship with his daughter, Mona Campbell, the concert pianist?"

Mona was his fiancée? Perhaps that's who the album *Songs for Her* was named after. He must have really loved her to have done that. Shane drums his fingers on the table for a moment, and I wonder if it's a sign that he's getting ticked off with this line of questioning. He swallows visibly. "What would you like to know?"

"Word is that you two were engaged to be married, but she broke it off. Now she's in a very public relationship with the Bohemia Quartet's cellist, Justin Burke. Do you still keep in contact with either of them?"

"I wish them both every happiness, but no, we're not still in touch."

"Sounds like there's a story there," the journalist replies brazenly.

Shane doesn't say anything, but simply eyes the man like he can't believe what a prick he's being. Neither of them have noticed my presence in the empty bar, so I decide to interrupt and give Shane a little break from the interview.

"Can I get you guys anything to drink?" I ask, approaching their table.

Shane's eyes widen when he sees me, confirming my suspicions that he didn't realise I'd come in. Damn, now I feel bad for eavesdropping. He might not have wanted me to know some of the stuff that was just said.

"Oh, an orange juice for me," says the journalist, and I turn my attention to Shane.

"I'm good," he says abruptly, and I frown.

Perhaps I shouldn't have interrupted, but I was only trying to help. I walk back behind the bar and pour an orange juice into a glass of ice. I don't really want to return to their table, given Shane's somewhat frosty reception, but I don't have another choice now.

Silently, I place the glass down on the table and quickly return to my station. Shane doesn't meet my eyes the entire time, and I can't tell if he's pissed off or just embarrassed. They've moved on to a lighter, less personal topic now. I lose myself in my work, focusing intently on stacking glasses and stocking the bar for this afternoon's event; a famous opera singer has flown in from Italy to do a handful of shows, and she'll be accompanied by the house orchestra.

I like opera. Even though I can't understand the words, somehow my brain translates the emotions, in the same way an instrumental piece can tell me a story with no words at all.

I'm in the small storage room at the back of the bar when I get a text from Alec telling me he'll take care of dinner tonight for April and Pete since I'm going to be working until eight. As I type out a quick thank-you in response, I hear somebody enter the room from the soft click of a shoe. Turning around, I find Shane standing mere inches away from me.

"Uh, you're not supposed to be in here," I say while his eyes roam my face. Tingles seize my chest at his closeness. I can feel the air of his breath hit my cheeks.

"I know. I just wanted to apologise for being cold with you earlier. It wasn't you — I was just pissed with the guy interviewing me."

Sucking in a quick breath, I nod. "Yeah, he seemed to be going right for the jugular. How are your stitches?"

"They're fine, a little stingy and a lot itchy. You look good in that shirt," he says, the words tumbling out like he hadn't meant to vocalise the thought.

I give him a small grin. "This is my work uniform. You've seen me in it before."

"And you've always looked good in it." His hand moves to my shoulder, his thumb brushing slowly back and forth.

I swallow.

"So, um, what was the interview for?"

He rolls his eyes and smiles. "They're doing a feature on me in *Hot Press*, though you'd think it was for a gossip mag by the way that guy was carrying on."

"Yeah, stupid nosy bastard," I reply jokingly. "Asking lots of questions like it's his job or something."

Shane squeezes my shoulder and narrows his eyes, but he's still smiling. "Think you're clever, huh?"

I raise my chin and continue to taunt him. "Yes, I think I'm very clever, Shane Arthur."

He moves an inch closer. "Oh, really?"

"Mm-hmm." His chest rubs off mine, and now I'm pushed up against the wall.

He dips his nose to my neck and inhales deeply. "You smell good," he whispers, and I momentarily lose the ability to speak. The next thing I know his mouth is on my neck, sucking, and I let out an involuntary moan. Jesus. My willpower is really being tested as I force myself to pull away from him. His body is hard and strong, so it's difficult to pry him off me, especially since he seems so determined to keep his mouth on my neck. If I don't stop him soon, he's going to leave a mark.

Perhaps that's his intention.

Finally, I twist my body, duck, and swing under his arm. My chest is rising and falling quickly, and his gorgeous brandy-coloured eyes have grown dark with need. I move to the door, wrapping my fingers around the handle.

"You're taking liberties here, Shane. I already told you where we stand."

His eyes dip at the ends sadly as he continues to stare at me. "Yeah, that's right, you did. I'm sorry, couldn't help myself."

"Well, you should've tried harder. I can't be in a relationship. You know this." My words come out sounding weak and desperate. I really need him to stop pushing, because if he doesn't, sooner or later I'm going to give in.

He walks to me and takes my hand into his. "I'm sorry, Bluebird. I promise not to do anything like that again."

God. How could I ever stay mad at a face as beautiful as his?

I look at him seriously. "You promise?"

"Cross my heart."

"Okay, then."

He smiles big. "So, um, now that we're friends again, could I ask a favour?"

"You can ask," I allow.

"Well, I've got to do this ridiculous photo shoot for the *Hot Press* interview, and I was wondering if you'd come with me? You know, for moral support. I hate doing these sorts of things, but it's good publicity for the orchestra."

My lips curve in a grin. "You're doing a photo shoot! Of course I'll come. When and where?"

The idea of watching Shane getting dressed up by some stylist like a living Ken doll is oddly appealing to me. Perhaps I'll get to watch him try on outfits, catch glimpses of his perfect body. You know, like the best and worst kind of torture all rolled into one.

"Tomorrow at lunchtime in the Clarendon Hotel. You don't have a shift then, do you?"

I shake my head. "No, tomorrow's my day off. I had planned on doing some busking, but I'll put it off to go with you."

"Great. They've booked a suite. I'm not sure how long it's going to run, but there'll be food, so you won't get hungry."

I hold up a hand, laughing. "Hey, you had me at photo shoot, there's no need to sweeten the deal with free food, although it's always a plus."

Shane lets out a breath as though in relief. "Thank you so much, Jade. It would have been torture going alone."

When he says this, I realise that what he's told me is true; he really doesn't have any friends. I feel quite honoured that he's allowing me into his life, but I also plan on remedying his friendlessness, so I say, "If I come with you to the photo shoot, will you come somewhere with me this Sunday?"

"Sure, I'm not working. Where do you want to go?"

"It's a surprise, but I promise you'll like it."

"Has it got to do with you teaching me how to live?" he asks slyly.

Hmm, I'd forgotten about that one. "Yeah, in a way I guess it does."

"Then I'm all in."

For the rest of the day I'm rushed off my feet with work. It's almost a full house for the afternoon and evening concerts, so I don't get the chance to see Shane again. We exchanged numbers before leaving the storage room, and when I get home I'm tempted to send him a text. I don't even have anything important to say, but for some reason I feel this need to touch base. I hate to admit it, but I love interacting with him, love talking to him about anything and everything.

I resist the urge and instead give in to a different temptation, one that I'm sure to regret. I Google his ex-fiancée, Mona Campbell, and discover that she's a semi-famous musician just like Shane, and a concert pianist at that. She even has a Wiki page. My gut sinks when I see how drop-dead gorgeous she is. The facts I glean are that she's twenty-nine years old, the daughter of manager mogul Jack Campbell, is world-renowned in her field, and has the silkiest chestnut brown hair I've ever seen.

There are one or two old pictures online of her and Shane when they were together, taken at some sort of awards ceremony. They look perfect. There are also a couple of newer ones of her with the cellist, Justin, and I don't get it, because he's not half as good-looking as Shane. Deciding to cut myself off — otherwise, I'll be browsing through pictures for the rest of the night — I go and check my emails.

A notification tells me that Shane Arthur has just added me on Facebook.

Interesting.

I laugh out loud when I check out his profile and see he's got a grand total of 1,213 friends. Well, now, I'm definitely going to have fun with this. Immediately clicking to accept the friendship, I go straight to the private message function and type:

Jade Lennon, 21.43 p.m.: Only in this day and age can a man have 1,213 virtual friends while still having no friends at all. Here's to number 1,214 being a real one ;-) P.S. How did you find me on this?

At first I put a few kisses at the end but then decide that might give him the wrong impression, so I change them to a winky face. Scrolling down his wall, all I see are messages from women proclaiming their love of his music. One girl called Suzy Carmine has posted almost every day for the last month. That's kind of alarming, taking into account the fact that Shane hasn't responded, but only "liked" the first few. A couple of minutes later he writes back:

Shane Arthur, 21.50 p.m.: It's pathetic, right? They're all fans and work contacts. I'm thinking 1,214 is going to be the magic number. Found you through your phone.

Jade Lennon, 21.53 p.m.: I am magic, aren't I? And no, it's not pathetic. I'm going to transform that low self-esteem into high self-esteem if it's the last thing I do, mister! Btw, what's the deal with Suzy Carmine? She seems...enthusiastic.

Shane Arthur, 21.54 p.m.: You've been busy, or should I say nosy! Sometimes the fans can be a little intense. She'll get bored and move on eventually. P.S. Yes, you are fucking magic. Xxx

Jade Lennon, 21.54 p.m.: You're too sweet.

Shane Arthur, 21.55 p.m.: You should let me show you how sweet I can be.

Jade Lennon, 21.55 p.m.: Shane...

Shane Arthur, 21.56 p.m.: I know. Sorry.

Jade Lennon, 21.56 p.m.: Okay, you're forgiven. You nervous for tomorrow?

Shane Arthur, 21.57 p.m.: Dreading it :-/

Jade Lennon, 21.57 p.m.: Don't be. You're going to be fantastic. Are you bringing your violin?

Shane Arthur, 21.57 p.m.: Yeah, they want to get to some pics of me with the Strad.

Jade Lennon, 21.58 p.m.: Oh, this is going to be so much fun. For me, I mean. :-D I get to be a spectator.

Shane Arthur, 21.58 p.m.: You're cruel.

Jade Lennon, 21.59 p.m.: Mwah ha ha.

Shane Arthur, 21.59 p.m.: I just realised your name is three letters off John Lennon.

I laugh when I read this.

Jade Lennon, 21.59 p.m.: That's because I'm John Lennon reincarnated as a female. I was born seven years after he died, so it's entirely possible.

Shane Arthur, 22.00 p.m.: Well, in that case I'd like to take this opportunity to thank you for writing some of the best songs of the 20th century.

Jade Lennon, 22.01 p.m.: You're most welcome.

Shane Arthur, 22.01 p.m.: Lol.

A couple of minutes pass and I'm tired, so I decide to say my goodbyes for the night.

Jade Lennon, 22.05 p.m.: Right, I'm gonna get some sleep. Talk to you tomorrow, friend!

Shane Arthur, 22.05 p.m.: Cool. Dream of me, Bluebird. Xxx.

His last message makes my belly flutter. He doesn't know it, but I've dreamt of him practically every night since I met him. His kisses make my cheeks grow warm even though they aren't real ones.

The next day I dress casually in jeans and a cream blouse. I'm on my way to meet Shane at the Clarendon when a little kid slides in front of me. He can't be any more than eleven or twelve, and he has the gall to ask, "Hey, missus, gotta smoke?"

"No, I don't. And you're too young to be smoking," I say before walking by him.

"Yeah, well, your arse is too big to be wearing those jeans, but that didn't stop ya, did it?" he shouts after me, brazen as you like.

Ah, lovely. If I ever feel I'm getting too full of myself, all I'll need to do is walk down this street, and I'm sure some little fucker will take me down a peg or two. Continuing my walk, I surreptitiously check out my bottom in a shop window. It's certainly well-endowed, but...oh, fuck it. I'm not thinking about this.

My phone buzzes in my pocket, and I find a text from Shane telling me he's already at the hotel and that he left my name at the reception desk. When I get there a couple of minutes later, I'm ushered on through to the elevators by a helpful receptionist.

Oh, yeah, one of life's mysteries, why do elevators always have to be lined with mirrors? After my run-in with "little mister gotta smoke," I'm feeling decidedly paranoid about my appearance, so I could really do without the three-dimensional view right now. I run my fingers through my wind-tossed hair and wipe a fleck of mascara away from under my eye.

When I reach the suite, I knock on the door and get greeted by a pretty redhead, the photographer's assistant. Stepping inside, I find quite the professional setup. They must be planning on putting him on the cover or something.

Shane's sitting in a chair while a stylist does his hair, which in my opinion doesn't really need doing anyway. He looks so out of his comfort zone that I have to stifle the urge to laugh. There's a free-standing clothes rack lining one wall and it's full of classy men's outfits — designer suits and the like.

His eyes are constantly scanning the room while his hair is fussed over, and when he sees me he gives me a full-on smile; it's one part happy to see me and two parts relieved his friend is here to make him feel less awkward at being primped up like a show pony.

"Jade," he says, standing to greet me while the stylist scowls that he's moved out of her reach. He takes my hand when I get to him and gives it a soft kiss, which makes a little swoosh rush through my chest.

"Hey, look at you," I reply, gesturing to the sharp grey suit he's wearing.

"Do I scrub up well?" he asks modestly.

"Hell, yeah."

"Mr. Arthur, I need to finish your hair," the stylist, a twenty-something honey blonde, interrupts impatiently.

I give him the nod to sit back down and he does, while I peruse a table of sandwiches and drinks set up nearby. I pick up one that looks like smoked salmon and cream cheese, and pop it discreetly into my mouth, all *la di da I'm just taking a look around.*

"Jade, could you bring me some of those? I'm starving," Shane calls, and I turn in surprise to find he'd been watching me. Caught red-handed. It causes me to gulp the whole thing down in one go like a bird of prey swallowing a live robin.

I purse my lips at him and suppress a smirk of my own, while putting a couple of the tiny sandwiches on a paper plate and carrying them over to him. The stylist lets out a sigh as I approach; I'm obviously making her job harder here, but Shane did ask for something to eat.

Feeling playful, I lift a sandwich to his mouth for him to take a bite. His eyes stay on mine the entire time as his mouth closes over it. Okay, perhaps that was a questionable move.

I didn't anticipate how hard it would be to stay platonic with a man I'm this strongly attracted to. There's an underlying note of sex in everything we do. I can barely look at him without remembering what it felt like to have him fill me up, for him to effortlessly hold me and fuck me against a brick wall.

I hand him the plate then, deciding that feeding him was a little too...sensual for my liking. A couple of minutes later, the photographer, a dark-haired man in his mid-thirties, strolls into the room and starts giving Shane directions as to where he wants him. I sit back and watch as he removes his violin from its case and goes to sit on a chair by the window.

The photographer tells Shane to look out the window and try to affect a thoughtful expression. He flattens out his mouth and narrows his eyes, giving a faraway look. I can't help smiling, because he's clearly not enjoying this at all. His posture is all ramrod straight.

The photographer tries to give him more directions, but he's sort of useless at taking them. I butt in, saying, "Hey, why don't you try squinching?"

The photographer turns to me, shakes his head, and laughs.

"Do I even want to know what that is?" Shane asks, hesitant but amused.

"It's all the rage right now," I explain. "You just sort of squint your eyelids and it's supposed to make you look better in pictures, you know, like, all moody and smouldering. Ben and Clark both swear by it."

I internally chuckle, remembering Ben showing me his holiday pictures from Spain last summer, and in every one it's pretty obvious that he and Clark were trying to out-squinch each other, which just ends up looking ridiculous. So yeah, a rule of thumb, if you're going to squinch, make sure there isn't anybody else in the photo doing it as well.

"If I squint I'm going to look constipated, Jade," Shane replies, deadpan, and I let out a bark of laughter.

The photographer puts his hand on his hip, looking back and forth between the two of us. "Is she your girlfriend?" he asks while snapping a couple of shots. Shane is still looking at me and smiling.

"Nah, just a friend," he answers as he regards me warmly.

"Mm-hmm," the photographer responds in a very *sure she's just a friend* sort of way.

"Ugh, I'm so bad at this," says Shane dejectedly, rubbing at his forehead for a second.

"Honey, nobody with a face and body like yours is bad at getting pictured," the redheaded assistant butts in, all sass and flirtation. I automatically give her an evil look without realising I'm doing it. Shane is the only one who catches me, and he seems pleased as punch about it. Great, now he thinks I'm jealous.

"Hey, I know. You should play something and not think about trying to pose," I say. "Forget anybody else is in the room, and just pretend you're practicing. I bet you'll look really natural in the shots if you do that."

The photographer clicks his fingers at me. "That's a fabulous idea." Turning his attention to Shane, he says, "I like your friend — she's good."

"All right, I'll give it a try," says Shane, lifting his bow and setting the violin under his chin. He starts to play a really lovely, almost dreamy song, and the photographer is like a bat out of hell snapping pictures. I smile, satisfied that my idea is working. Sitting back on my stool, I watch the images float out of the camera and sail through the window like bubbles floating on air, capturing a moment of musical brilliance. The melody sparks off the images and makes them shine, makes them that much more vital.

A picture is just a picture, but add music and there's emotion. There's a story.

Shane plays for about five minutes, and I'm sure at least a hundred or more shots have been taken within that short space of time. In a voice that is unexpectedly quiet and entranced, I ask him the name of the song he just played.

"*Méditation de Thaïs*," he answers, setting his violin down on his lap, gaze on me.

"It's beautiful," I reply, mentally repeating the name over and over in my head so that I'll remember to download it onto my iTunes later on. I'm too embarrassed to try to write it down, because then he'll know how affected I am.

A moment later the stylist abruptly calls for a wardrobe change, and my special moment is broken. This time she puts Shane in an all-black ensemble. Her phone starts ringing just as she's about to put on his tie, so she hands it to me instead while she goes to answer the call.

Walking up to him tie in hand, I feel my throat go decidedly dry. Since he's a bit taller than I am, I have to reach up to wrap the fabric around his neck. My fingers slide over his smooth skin, and I notice his Adam's apple bob as he swallows.

"You always dress well, but I have to admit right now you're looking pretty dapper, Mr Arthur," I say softly, and his head dips down a little while he watches the movement of my hands intently. He's not speaking, and for some reason that makes me extra nervous. Our breaths mingle. We're so close, and my stupid girl brain makes me go slowly with the tie, wrapping it once in a loop, pulling it up and over, and then slotting it through the loop. I tighten it a little, and several seconds tick by before I cough and step back.

"There you go. Perfect," I whisper.

We lock gazes for a long moment, and then the door to the suite opens and shuts. When the sound of heels clicking on wood rings out, a posh female voice declares, "Oh, don't you just look marvellous!"

I turn to see a tall, slim brunette lady wearing a tailored business suit standing a couple of feet away from us. Looking back to Shane, I'm not sure if I'm mistaken when I see him grimace.

"Hi, Mum," he says. "I didn't know you were coming."

Nine

A moment later Shane's mother notices me standing there, and her brow furrows for a split second.

"Hello. I'm Mirin Arthur. I don't believe we've met," she says, holding out her hand to me.

"Hi, Mirin. I'm Jade, a friend of Shane's."

She moves her lips in a weird way when she hears my accent and then says, "How nice, and where did you two meet?"

"Jade works at the concert hall, Mum," Shane interrupts. Is it just me, or does he seem annoyed?

Her gaze darts to him and then back to me. "Oh, really, are you in management there?"

"Uh, no, I'm just floor staff."

Usually I like to think I'm a decently confident person, but there's something about this woman that makes me feel inferior. I've always been pretty proud of my job; I get to work in a wonderful place, but Mirin Arthur stares at me like I just told her I clean rat-infested sewers for a living.

"Right, well, it's lovely to meet you," she says with a fake smile, and then she turns her attention to the photographer. Striding toward him, she requests to have a look at the pictures taken so far, before proceeding to *ooh* and *aah* at how well they turned out.

Shane and I remain silent. I never considered the fact that his parents might not approve of our friendship, and let's face it, I'm sure I'm aeons away from the women he usually sees. Not that we're seeing each other. I'm definitely nothing like Mona Campbell, anyway. I bet she and Mirin got along like a house on fire.

While his mother talks on and on in the background, Shane takes a few steps towards me and discreetly laces his fingers through mine. He gives my hand a tight squeeze and whispers in my ear, "Don't let her get to you."

I pretend not to know what he's talking about. "What do you mean?"

"I know how she is. My mother has this knack for sucking the life out of people. I have first-hand experience."

My eyes are drawn to the woman as he tells me this. Now she's arranging a vase of flowers on top of a chest of drawers. They're bright and purple, but they wither away when she touches them, until they're all black detritus.

"She does have a certain…way about her," I finally agree.

Shane huffs a breath, like I'm putting it way too mildly, and let's face it, I am.

"My mother is a fucking snob, Jade. I promised myself I'd stop caring about her opinion a long time ago, and I have. Do you know when I discovered Mona had cheated on me, I was more anxious about what my mother would think than anything else? How fucked up is that?"

I stare at him, my mouth open. "Jesus."

"Yeah. I knew that she'd blame me for it, and of course she did. She thought the sun shone out of Mona's too shiny and perfect-to-be-true arse. In fact, she still does. She thinks it was somehow my fault our engagement didn't pan out."

God, this poor man. He says he's stopped caring, but the way he's talking right now tells me he's far from over the hold his mother seems to have on him. Perhaps that's what his whole "teach me how to live" thing is about. He wants me to teach him how to get free from the emotional bondage.

Our hushed conversation is interrupted when Mirin calls, "Oh, Shane, come over here and stand by the door. I think it will make for a good background."

I smirk when I notice the photographer giving the stylist an eye roll. Yeah, I'm pretty sure he's not thrilled about Mommy Dearest coming in and taking over. Shane kisses me lightly on the cheek, sighs heavily, and goes to his mother. When I see Mirin looking at me in a puzzled way, I realise she saw the kiss and is none too happy about it.

My phone rings in my pocket, a welcome distraction. I pull it out to find Pete's number flashing on the screen. I can only imagine what this is going to be about. I always make sure to call both April and Pete at least once or twice a day if I'm not in the house to make sure they're okay. When Pete's the one calling me it's usually because he's in trouble or needs money. He hasn't called for money in a while, though, which is worrying, since he's a fifteen-year-old boy with no form of income. It begs the question, where is he getting his cash from?

"Hey, Petey, what's up?" I answer, walking into the next room of the suite to take the call.

There's an audible sigh, then, "You need to go to my parent teacher evening."

Jeez, is it that time of year again already? "Oh, yeah. When is it?"

"Uh, tonight."

"Okay, you could have given me a few days warning."

"This is me giving you warning, Jade. It's two-thirty — the whole thing starts at seven."

"Yes, but I would have liked some time to organise a decent outfit and all."

"Fuck, are you going or not?" he grits out.

"Don't swear at me. I'm not one of your pals on the street. And yes, of course I'm going. I'm your guardian, after all."

"Good. Hanging up now."

"I'll be home to make dinner. I love you."

All I get is an embarrassed, "Jesus Christ," before he makes good on his promise and hangs up. I don't care how much it annoys him — I'm going to keep telling him I love him until it finally sinks in.

A word to the wise, fifteen-year-old boys are perhaps the most emotionally stunted individuals on God's green earth. And, I'll add, they do not do well with compliments, affection, or any form of kindness, especially when given by older sisters.

Walking back into the room where Shane is being pictured, I mentally calculate how much time I'll need to go to the shop for groceries, get home, cook dinner, find something to wear, and be at Pete's school by seven. Yeah, I should probably get going soon. I hate to leave Shane since I said I'd stay with him for this, but his mum's here now, so he won't be entirely alone.

Though from our brief conversation earlier, I'm guessing he'd probably prefer to be alone than to have his mother here.

The photographer is sorting through shots, so I walk up to Shane to tell him I've got to go.

"That was my brother Pete. He decided to spring it on me that his parent teacher evening is tonight. I hope you don't mind if I leave early?"

Standing from his seat, Shane replies, "No, of course not." He pauses and then randomly volunteers, "I could go with you if you like?"

Giving him a funny look, I respond, "To the parent teacher evening?"

"Yeah, why not?" He lowers his voice. "That way I can pay you back for the moral support."

I rub my forehead. "These things can be pretty stressful, especially when you're dealing with a kid like my brother." I go quiet for a moment, considering it and thinking about how the snobbish teachers sometimes look down on me because of my age and the fact that I'm only Pete's sister. Having someone like Shane by my side could definitely make me look more respectable…they might even think he's my husband or something. Okay, *so* not going there.

"You can come, but are you even done here?"

He quirks an eyebrow. "They've taken enough photos of me to last a lifetime, Jade. Besides, I don't think I can stand much more of this," he says, casting his eyes in his mother's direction as she continues to pester the photographer.

A small chuckle escapes me. "She likes to take the lead, I see."

"A long career as the CEO of an international charity will do that," Shane mutters under his breath.

"She runs a charity? That's impressive," I tell him, letting out a low whistle. Mirin Arthur might not have been particularly nice to me, but I can respect a woman with that kind of drive.

"Think of it more as a business than a charity, but yeah, 'impressive' is one way of putting it."

The tone of Shane's voice tells me he doesn't exactly agree. Loosening his tie, he says he's going to go change. As I wait, I shove another tiny sandwich down my gullet to see me through until dinnertime (and a few in my handbag for Specky), and then I play with my phone for a bit.

Somebody clears their throat, and I glance up to see Mirin standing in front of me.

"My son likes you," she states, all matter of fact, and I don't know how to reply or if she even expects me to. Instead I stay quiet and wait to see what she'll say next. Her eyes trail over me intently. Jeez, what's she doing, taking my measurements or something?

Unable to stand the silence, I blurt, "Yeah, me and Shane are tight."

Oh, God, did I just say that to this woman? That was probably one of the most ridiculous sentences to have ever come out of my mouth. Mirin gives me an almost imperceptible smile.

"Have you known each other long?"

"Not long."

"I see." She presses her lips together before continuing in a voice that's not quite threatening, but it's not *not* threatening, either. "My son is a vulnerable man, Miss…"

"Lennon."

"Miss Lennon. He's been through a very rough year, and I wouldn't like to see him being taken advantage of."

Vulnerable. What exactly does she mean by that? I nod along to what she says before I realise what she's getting at. She thinks *I'm* trying to take advantage of him? Fuck, if this is the way she talks to all the people who've ever been in his life, then I get why he doesn't have any friends.

"I assure you, Mirin, that when it comes to your son, I have only the purest of intentions. You have nothing to worry about." Okay, so maybe I didn't mean for that to come out sounding so sarcastic, but I can't help getting riled up by her. You'd think her son was the King of England and I'm some hussy trying to sleep her way to the throne.

"Listen to me, if you think you can wheedle your way into his affections with your obvious...attractions" —her gaze flicks briefly to my chest and then back up to my eyes before she continues— "you are sadly mistaken. I will not see you hurt him. He has already been hurt enough."

"Maybe you should look in the mirror and you'll see who's really hurting him," I whisper, unable to help myself.

"What did you just say?" she whisper-hisses back at me.

"Is everything all right?" Shane asks, just entering the room, his expression suspicious as he takes in his mother's fuming face.

"Fine and dandy," I reply. "Are we off?"

"Yes. I'll talk to you later, Mum," he says, stepping forward and giving Mirin what seems to be a very strained kiss on the cheek.

"You're leaving? But I was hoping we could do dinner at Marco Pierre's?" she replies, affecting a disappointed demeanour.

"Another time, Mum," is all he says before he's putting his hand to the small of my back and ushering me out the door.

All the way to the elevator I feel like I'm holding my breath. Once we step inside the car, I let it all out, slumping back against those aforementioned pesky mirrors.

"Your mother is a character," I say as Shane eyes me with some sort of intensity. His hand is still on my back, right at the base of my spine, and he's rubbing small circles into the fabric of my shirt.

"My mother is never happy, not with anything. She's always striving for something better, and then when she gets it there's something else she wants."

Even though he's right beside me, his eyes are faraway.

I turn to face him, feeling far too close in the small space, yet I don't move to put any distance between us. "Don't let her make you feel like you're anything other than perfect, Shane," I say, my voice barely a whisper.

His faraway eyes come back to me. "What is perfect, anyway?"

"Whatever you want it to be. Think of it more as a feeling. I think perfect is just feeling content with your lot."

The elevator doors open just then, signalling we've arrived on the ground floor. Shane doesn't respond to what I've said, but from the look on his face I can tell he's really thinking about it. I ask him if he drove in, but he tells me no, that he left his car at home. Parking in the city is shit and all that jazz.

"I have to go grocery shopping first. Are you sure you still want to tag along?"

"Of course," he replies enthusiastically, like I just told him I'm going on a roller-coaster ride instead of picking up a few things for dinner.

When we reach the supermarket, I surreptitiously stand aside and pretend to be searching for something in my bag, when really I'm toting up how much money I have to spend. I think Shane notices what I'm doing but he doesn't say anything.

I decide I'm in the mood for something creamy, so I grab the ingredients for a spaghetti carbonara. April always complains when I cook Italian, too many carbs apparently (cue heavy sigh), but she'll just have to put up with it for one evening. Shane follows alongside me as I stroll the aisles, like a really well-behaved dog. He watches me pick stuff up and mull over prices as though it's the most fascinating thing he's ever witnessed.

To be honest, it's starting to weird me out. I'm beginning to learn that this man can be pretty full-on.

"What do you normally like to eat?" I ask to break his rapt attention.

He grins sheepishly. "I usually order my food from this gourmet delivery service. I never really have time to cook. They do a chicken and avocado salad that I'm seriously addicted to."

"Gourmet delivery, you say," I tease him while twirling my invisible moustache. "What, is Dominos not good enough for you?"

"Dominos is fine, but if I don't want to put on ten stone, then I try to avoid fast food."

"Hmm, what do you do to keep in shape?" I ask, placing a bag of dried pasta in my basket.

"I run. I've never bothered with gyms because I haven't really been in one place for long enough to justify a membership. Running is something you can do anywhere."

He must run a lot, because let's just say his violin is not the only thing that's finely tuned, if you get me.

Thirty euros' worth of groceries and one cab ride (courtesy of Shane) later, we reach my place, and Shane offers to put the food away while I feed Specky. She starts yipping like a maniac at the back door when I come in, so I let her into the kitchen.

"Okay, okay, come inside out of the cold, you mad little bitch," I tell her — because I'm one of those ridiculous (often lonely) people who have whole conversations with their pets.

When she sees there's a stranger in the house she goes quiet, though, eyeing him with suspicion. I pick her up in my arms and give her a kiss on the top of the head.

"Shane, I'd like you to meet Specky. Specky, this is Shane," I say, bringing her close so that he can pet her. He puts the new carton of milk in the fridge and then turns his attention to my dog. Because she's only a miniature Jack Russell, she's particularly tiny.

"She's fucking adorable. Is she still a puppy?" he asks.

"Nope, just the runt of the litter," I reply, smiling.

"Why Specky?"

"See the spots around her eyes? I think they look like spectacles."

His lips curve up when he glances at me. "That's the cutest thing I've ever heard."

"Oh, shush," I say, sticking out my tongue at him.

I let Specky down so that she can eat the food I just put in her bowl. She's been clawing at me to get to it, suffering through the introduction to the new human. Shane sits down on a chair, suppressing a smirk at my embarrassment over him calling me cute. I turn on the radio and start to throw together the dinner. The great thing about carbonara is that it's cheap and you can make it in only a couple of minutes.

Over the next half an hour my siblings all arrive home, eager for something to eat. They sit at the table with Shane, shoving food into their mouths and asking him a million nosy questions. I wish they'd stop.

Alec watches on with amusement as April pulls her chair up as close as it will get to Shane's, telling him she'd love to come see him play at the concert hall sometime, and, I shit you not, twisting a strand of her brown hair around her finger.

"That's surprising," I butt in cynically, "since you've never once expressed an interest in the place in the two years that I've worked there."

She scowls vaguely in my direction, her catty blue eyes like a pair of laser beams.

"Jade's got a point," says Alec, pointing his fork at April. "All you ever listen to is Beyoncé anyway."

"Would you two just shut the hell up?" she hisses, her cheeks getting redder by the second. Alec and I look at each other and laugh. Pete sits eating quickly and quietly, clearly wanting to have dinner over and done with so he can go out with his mates.

"I'll be happy to get you a ticket for one of our upcoming shows if you'd like," says Shane graciously, and April grins widely, her previous embarrassment all but forgotten.

"I'd like that very much, Shane," she practically purrs at him.

I mouth the words *thank you*, and he smiles, waving off my gratitude. I know that he doesn't have to humour my sister, but I'm glad that he's being nice to her.

Yet again, this man has managed to warm my heart.

Ten

After dinner I tell April and Pete they're on washing-up duty, to which I receive a whole array of complaints. I fold my arms and give them both my best death stare, and finally they get on with the task. Shane follows me upstairs to help me select an outfit for tonight.

The bedrooms in my house are pretty small, so basically my double bed takes up the entire space. If I got a single I could have more room, but there's just something so depressing about sleeping in a single bed. It's like, *Yeah, I've been alone for so long that I've given up hope of ever sharing my sleeping quarters with another human being.*

Seriously, the only people who should be sleeping in single beds are children and hospital patients. And yes, sometimes having an empty side can be just as depressing, but I generally remedy that problem by sleeping in the middle all spread out like a starfish. Try it. It might fuck your spine up something fierce, but it will be the cosiest snoozing experience of your life.

Shane eyes my walls, which are decorated with pale blue wallpaper that's got golden sparrow patterns all over. I'm kind of obsessed with sparrows, hence my tattoos.

The symbolism of freedom is a big deal for me.

Old paperbacks line my window ledge and various pictures adorn my walls, mostly random art I've collected over the years. My bed is pushed right up next to the window, and on the other side is my wardrobe. Shane sits on the bed and scans the titles of my books. And yeah, he would have to select the copy of D.H. Lawrence's *Lady Chatterley's Lover* to peruse. And let me just get out there that it's not the new Penguin version with just the title on the cover, but an older version with a big sexy picture of a full-on naked woman on the front.

"What oh what is this?" Shane asks with a devious grin.

Okay, so I have been known to read some absolute filth in my time, but this one Lara brought over so that we could read it to each other over a bottle of non-alcoholic wine and have a giggle. I do a wicked Sean Bean impression.

"That," I say, pointing a finger, "is not mine."

Shane laughs long and hard.

"I swear! It's Lara's. It's also a classic."

He suppresses his smug-as-fuck smile. "Okay, I believe you. Millions wouldn't."

"Whatever." I toss my hair over my shoulder and open my closet to search for something to wear. Peeking at Shane out of the corner of my eye, I see him flicking through the pages, clearly searching for the dirty bits to embarrass me further.

I'm considering a plain black dress when, God help me, he starts to read out loud:

"He drew down the thin silk sheath, slowly, carefully, right down and over her feet. Then with a

quiver of exquisite pleasure he touched the warm soft body, and touched her navel for a moment in a kiss. And he had to come in to her at once, to enter the peace on earth of her soft, quiescent body. It was the moment of pure peace for him, the entry into the body of the woman.

She lay still, in a kind of sleep, always in a kind of sleep. The activity, the orgasm was his, all his; she could strive for herself no more. Even the tightness of his arms round her, even the intense movement of his body, and the springing of his seed in her, was a kind of sleep, from which she did not begin to rouse till he had finished and lay softly panting against her breast."

I have to close my eyes when I hear his low, sensual voice reading the passage. I'm grateful for the closet door, which is shielding my face from him as I grip the edge of it so hard my knuckles have turned white.

"You're evil," I say, shaking myself out of whatever that just was.

He chuckles softly. "I was trying to embarrass you, but now I have to admit I'm kind of turned on."

And I'm dripping fucking wet. This man's voice is just as alluring as the music he plays, if not more so.

Grabbing a pillow from the bottom of my bed, I throw it at him and tell him to put the book away. I don't fail to notice him "fix himself" as he slots it back onto the window ledge. Oh, Christ, what made me think it was a good idea to invite him up to my room? I'm so used to being around sexually nonthreatening gay men like Ben and Clark that I seem to forget Shane and I walk a very thin line between friends and lovers.

Trying to distract him, I pull out the black dress alongside a dark blue one to ask him his opinion.

When I turn back around, he has his violin out, looking ready to spin me a tune. He starts playing a riff from the start of David Bowie's "Fashion," and I roll my eyes.

"Very funny. I never would have pegged you as a Bowie fan," I say, amused.

He feigns indignation. "I love Bowie!"

"Uh-huh. I'm not quite sure that song works on the violin, though. You need a double bass, my friend."

He shrugs. "I try my best."

"So, which do you think, the black dress or the blue one?" I ask, biting my lip. I don't know why I always get so nervous for these parent teacher things. I guess I feel the need to overcompensate since I'm not Pete's actual parent.

"The black one. It's, how do you say? *Très chic*," he answers, putting on fake French accent. Somebody's playful this evening.

"I was going more for responsible and adult, but that will do," I say, putting the blue one back in the closet and digging out my very precious Hermès scarf box from the bottom.

"What's that?" Shane asks, playing a random little tune.

"It's probably the most expensive thing in my wardrobe, but I managed to snag it for only a hundred euros on eBay. I spent a fortnight bidding, and I finally got my hands on one."

When I place the box on the bed, he recognises the brand. "Oh, Hermès. Yeah, my grandmother used to wear those scarves."

"Your grandmother was a classy bird, then."

Opening the box, I pull out the red, navy, and gold silk and run my hands over its smoothness.

"Feel," I say, holding it out to Shane. "One hundred percent pure silk. It's like heaven in a fabric."

His lips curve as he reaches out casually to touch it. "If you say so."

"Oh, so unimpressed. I suppose all the kids from Dalkey grow up with silk pyjamas and Egyptian cotton sheets on their beds. Here in the liberties we're lucky not to be subjected to those old scratchy war blankets," I say sarcastically.

His amusement is clear as he watches me rant. "I grew up wearing Spiderman pyjamas, if you must know."

I can't help grinning at him. There's just something about this man that manages to lure a permanent smile out of me. "Shut up."

Going to the bathroom so that I can change in privacy, I bring my makeup bag along with me to reapply my mascara. Once I'm done, I return to my room, where Shane is still playing his violin. I guess that to get as good as he is, he needs to practice when and wherever he has the chance.

Standing in front of the full-length mirror by my wardrobe, I twist my hair up into a bun and then grab the silk scarf to tie around my neck. Next I slip on a pair of black heels, and I'm done. Shane pauses the song he's playing to let out a low whistle.

"Looking good, Bluebird."

"Why, thanks," I reply, smearing on a dab of lip gloss.

I tell Shane he can leave his violin in my room while we're gone and that I'll lock the door. He nods and we go, walking to Pete's school since it's fairly close by. When we get there, the parking lot is full to the brim with cars and the lights are on in the classrooms. This isn't the same school I went to; in fact, it's one of the better ones in the area. I haven't been back to my old school in a long time, and I never will. Too many bad memories there.

"So," Shane says jokingly as he ushers me in the entrance, "how shall we play this? Am I your boyfriend, lover, gay best friend?"

"Oh, God, I didn't even think of that. What do you want to be? I think gay best friend is out, though," I say, laughing.

His eyes light up with a plan. "How about we tell them I'm your fiancé?"

"Hmm, that does have quite the classy ring to it," I agree while a little rush goes through me at the idea. I'm a performer, a street artist, and I like to play pretend. Tonight I'll pretend to be Jade Lennon, fiancée to Shane Arthur, concert violinist extraordinaire.

"That's what we'll say, then," he replies, voice low, eyes intent on mine like he's trying to decipher my reaction or something.

I pull out the piece of paper Pete gave me with his list of teachers on it. The first is Mr. Hegarty, his science teacher. As we approach the classroom, Shane subtly slides his hand into mine. I'm about to pull away out of instinct when I remember the roles we're playing. Holding hands is a perfectly normal thing for two engaged people to do.

Mr. Hegarty is a plainly dressed man in his fifties. He greets us as we walk in and asks whose parents we are. I can tell by the look on his face that he's thinking we're both far too young to be parents to a teenager.

"Um, not parents. I'm Pete Lennon's sister, his legal guardian, actually, and this is my fiancé, Shane." I cough, the lie feeling ridiculous when I say it out loud. Still, this man doesn't seem to notice. His expression immediately turns sour when I tell him I'm here for Pete.

"Right, well, let me see," he says, flicking through a stack of folders before finding the one he's looking for. "Your brother holds a rather unimpressive D average in my class, and I'm sorry to have to be frank, but half the time he doesn't even bother to show up. If he wants to have any chance of passing his Junior Cert exam, then he's really going to have to buck up."

"He doesn't show up?" I ask in alarm. "But the school never contacted me about any absences. Aren't they supposed to do that?"

Mr Hegarty sighs and rubs at the crease in between his eyebrows. "The new attendance swipe cards they've brought in make things harder for us to tell when a student is absent. It's a ridiculous system, in my opinion. The students are supposed to swipe them through the scanner once in the morning and then again after lunch. So we get a lot of kids having their friends swipe their cards for them, or else they come in, swipe them themselves, and then leave the school. It's a big problem."

"Right," I say with a disgruntled heavy breath. "So this is clearly what Pete has been doing. He's seriously in for it when I get home."

"Miss Lennon, I've had kids like Pete coming through my doors for years. If they don't want to be here, then there's not a lot you can do beyond supervising their every move."

"Yeah, and I definitely don't have the time for that."

"I suggest you have a talk with him, try to get him to understand that neglecting his education isn't going to benefit him in the long run."

I talk with Mr. Hegarty for another few minutes while Shane sits quietly by my side. I wonder what he thinks of all this. The next couple of teachers pretty much tell me the same thing, and a few of them don't even know Pete since he's absent so often. It's all a big old slap in the face, really. I knew Pete wasn't exactly the most functional of teenagers, but I didn't think it was this bad. And I'm also wondering why he even told me about the parent teacher night at all. Was it a cry for help, or simply a big fat middle finger?

It's only when we go to visit his music teacher that I get some good news, a little trickle of hope. His teacher is a thirty-something balding guy wearing a paisley shirt, and he tells me that Pete's been doing some amazing things in class when he bothers to show up. I'm getting that this guy is more into teaching modern music than taking the classical approach. I mean, it's pretty obvious, since he didn't recognise Shane when I introduced him.

So, apparently Pete's got a whole bunch of music creator apps on his smart phone and has been creating his own tracks. Other than when he blasts all this trance and dance stuff from his bedroom, I didn't even know he was that into music. Just goes to show that teenagers tell their parents (and guardians) sweet fuck-all.

I thank the music teacher and then get up to leave. When I reach the corridor, which is full of parents going from classroom to classroom, I slump back against the wall for a minute, wracking my brain for ideas. I need to think of something to get Pete back on the straight and narrow, but it can't be all the obvious stuff like grounding him and taking away his PlayStation. That kind of aggressiveness never works for long. I need to take a softly, softly approach. Something less all guns blazing and more intelligent.

I only realise that Shane's still with me when suddenly he's folding me into his arms in a hug. I exhale against the smooth fabric of his shirt, and the tension in my body falls away. It's amazing the things a hug from another human being can do.

"You'll sort him out, don't worry," he says, his chin resting on my hair.

"Yeah, but how?" I ask, not really expecting any kind of answer.

A minute of silence passes before Shane suggests, "I could talk to him, teach him some stuff about music, if you like?"

I pull away slightly and eye him. "I'm not sure how much you could teach a kid who creates dance songs on a smart phone app, Shane. You're a world away from that."

"All music is music, Jade. I've been classically trained. I can teach him some important basics, and if he has something to focus on, then maybe everything else in his life will fall in line."

"He has been hanging out with a bad crowd. Perhaps some music lessons will keep him occupied and off the streets," I say, coming around to the idea.

Shane smiles. "Exactly."

I smile back. "Okay, we'll give it a try."

He pulls my hand up between our touching chests and squeezes, something meaningful in his expression. Letting out a long breath, he pulls away, and we walk out of the school back to my place. It's late when we get there, given that there were queues outside some of the classrooms with parents all waiting to see the same teachers. Mostly Shane and I sat and chatted while he would intermittently give me these heated stares and I'd try to ignore the way it made me feel all hot and bothered.

As I look at Shane now, he seems tired, so without thinking I reach over and run my hand affectionately over his cheek. He practically melts under my touch, and I pull away immediately, asking myself what the fuck I think I'm doing. He's such a wonderful person, and I have no right to lead him on.

"I'm just going to put the kettle on for a brew," I say, clearing my throat and handing Shane the key for my bedroom. "You can go get your things upstairs if you like."

Silently he goes, and I'm left alone with my guilty thoughts and the whistling of the kettle as it boils. The steam rises up into the air in the small kitchen, shaping itself into disappointed faces. I swipe my hand through them, annoyed at their presence. Leaning one hand against the counter, I rub the creases from my brow with the other.

"I called for a cab," says Shane, entering the room from behind me. "It should be here any minute."

"Oh, good. Well, thanks again for offering to spend some time with Pete. I'll talk to him about it tomorrow, see what he thinks."

Shane dips his head and looks around the room like he can't bring himself to keep staring at me, and I don't even have to ask myself why. My stupid body language can be a bitch, and just now she offered Shane something I can't give him and then a second later snatched it away.

"I'm sorry if…" I trail off, the fire burning in my chest preventing me from continuing.

"You're sorry?" Shane asks.

I scratch my head and practically whisper, "Yeah, I'm sorry if I've been giving you mixed signals."

His mouth flattens out as he reaches up and runs a hand through his hair. "Jade, I don't see why we can't just explore where things go between us. I understand you've had a bad experience in the past, but so have I. I think that's a good thing — it means we both know what it's like to be hurt, and we'll do whatever we can not to make another person feel that way."

He's talking a lot of sense, but still, I'm scared. "Friends" is comfortable; "lovers" is an unknown hole in the sky where anything could happen.

I can't start drinking again.

With that thought in my head, my perseverance returns. "I'm sorry, Shane, but a friendship is all I have to offer you."

His optimistic expression falls, and his hands drops to his sides. "Then I guess I'll take what you have to offer, Bluebird."

"Thank you," I whisper as I watch him pick up his violin case and walk out the door.

Eleven

At seven the next morning I get up, dress, have some breakfast, and then go to Pete's room, where he's still fast asleep. I sit on the edge of his bed and study him, his child's face that's slowly transforming into an adult. I've been a mother to him since our own one died, since he was just eleven years old.

I can't help but wonder if I've somehow fucked up the job.

He wakes up then and startles when he sees me sitting at the foot of his bed.

Rubbing at his eyes, he rasps, "Uh, what the hell, Jade?"

"Why did you even bother to tell me about the parent teacher evening?" I reply abruptly, folding my arms across my chest. So much for the softly, softly approach.

He speculates over what to say for a minute as he eyes me. Finally he says, "If you didn't go, they would have contacted you, so you would have found out about everything anyway."

"I don't get it, Pete. You're a clever kid, yet you're just barely passing by the skin of your teeth, and if you don't start attending again soon you're going to be failing."

"School is pointless," he sighs. "There are so many better ways for me to spend my time."

"School isn't pointless. If you keep at it, you'll get to go to college."

"How many people from around here do you know who went to college, Jade? Yeah, that's right, a big fat zero."

"Well, somebody always has to be the first. And what do you mean, there are much better ways for you to spend your time?"

He just shrugs.

"Does it have something to do with the fact that you have those brand-new Nikes under your bed, not to mention a new iPod? Where did you get the money for those?"

He just looks at me now. "Where do you think?"

"I swear to God, Pete, this better not be drugs."

Storming out of the bed, he answers, "So what if it is?"

"'So what'? Are you fucking joking me? Are you telling me you're dealing?"

His face transforms with anger, and it actually surprises me. I've never seen him so enraged. "Yes, I am dealing, Jade, and you'd better get used to it because it isn't going to stop any time soon."

Oh, he's so not getting away with this. "Yes, it is going to stop, even if I have to chain you up in this bedroom until you see sense. And just you wait until Alec hears about this."

"Ha! As if he wasn't doing the exact same thing at my age."

"Alec did it for a very short time before he realised how stupid he was being, and he got out before he was in too deep. And that's exactly what you need to do."

"I'm not quitting," he seethes.

"Yes, you are. Now get dressed for school. I'm walking you."

"Fuck off."

"Swear one more time, Pete. Go on, see what happens," I warn him, and I must have a scary look in my eye because he backs down.

When I leave the room, I find both April and Alec standing outside with identical looks of horror on their faces.

"Did I hear all that right?" Alec asks, working his jaw.

I sigh and slump back against the wall. "Unfortunately, yes."

"I'll talk to him," he replies in a soothing voice, and comes to rub my shoulders. "You go and have a lie-down. You're all worked up."

"Could you take him to school, too?"

"Sure, I'll even wait to make sure he doesn't try to sneak back out."

"Thank you," I whisper, and April looks at me sympathetically.

I didn't even get the chance to ask Pete if he'll take music lessons from Shane.

Mustering my strength, I pull my sister into my room and ask how she's getting along with Mia. We talk for a little while, and then she has to go and get ready for work. At least one of my siblings is doing okay. My shift doesn't start until the afternoon, so I decide to don my costume and go busking for a while.

Standing in front of my mirror, I hold my tub of white face paint in my hand, using a sponge to rub it over my skin until it erases all of my features. When I'm done I feel like a blank canvas waiting for an artist to come and paint on some lips, a nose, and a pair of green eyes.

It used to take me forever to become "The Blue Lady." Now it takes me a grand total of ten minutes. I have it down to a fine art. I step outside my house in my full costume, blue wig, wings, and all, locking up before I set off. My neighbour Linda who lives across the street is standing at her door in her pyjamas, a cigarette in one hand and a mug of coffee in the other.

She sucks in a long drag of her smoke, watching me like I'm a flying pig that just sailed into her mundane little world. Most of the people in my area are well used to my antics by now, but still, I doubt they like what I do. I'm the local freak. If it weren't for what they all know happened to my family eleven years ago, then I'm sure they wouldn't be so accepting of my eccentricities.

Normally, in a place like this you can't be different. Everyone has to be the same. I once read about an experiment where they put an albino turkey in with a bunch of regular turkeys, and because the regular turkeys couldn't understand why the albino was different, they killed it.

In this particular case, I'm the albino turkey.

But because of the tragedy that befell me, nobody is going to kill me. It's sort of the same way nobody wants to be seen to be cruel to a blind girl or a girl in a wheelchair. So I get a free pass to be as different as I like.

Ten minutes later I've reached my usual busking spot on Grafton Street. I wave hello to Marcus, who's setting up a couple of shops down. He's a flamenco guitarist who plays mostly on weekday mornings. You make more money on the weekend, but I think he's a bit frightened of the bigger crowds. They can become rowdy sometimes.

One Saturday lunchtime about a year ago, I had a guy grab my money hat and run off with it. Of course I got down from my box and chased after him, but he'd easily disappeared into the crowd, and all the cash I'd made that day was gone.

I like to imagine it made for a good visual, though, even if I did get robbed. Imagine it, a woman with wings all dressed in blue chasing a thug through the street like her life depended on it. Yeah. Perhaps I entertained a few people.

Hat on the ground. Box situated. I step up onto my little stage, which is probably about two square feet at most, and I become something else. I'm a statue in a museum full of priceless art. A mythical creature turned to stone in the White Witch's courtyard in Narnia. A marble angel wrought by the hands of Michelangelo in a church somewhere in Italy.

Or just a girl on a box who finds comfort in the anonymity of white paint and fake hair.

A group stops to look at me, and I'm as still as a feather in a world with no air. One of the women smiles and steps forward, dropping a two-euro coin into my hat. Ah, for this she gets a present.

Some living statues give lollipops to kids. Some give pretty flowers. I, on the other hand, slowly reach up and tug a blue feather from my wings. Graceful as a dancer in the Bolshoi Ballet, my arm comes down as I bow to her and present the feather. Smiling whimsically, she takes it from my hand and says thank you. I allow the faintest of smiles to touch my lips in return as I rise back to my upright position.

After another minute or two, the group moves on.

I don't give feathers to all the people who leave money in my hat. It always depends on the person. It's like I have this internal radar that tells me who will throw the feather away at the nearest dustbin, and who will bring it home, put it somewhere safe, and cherish it like it's a precious diamond they found buried deep in the earth.

When I go home, I replace the feathers by sewing in new ones. I have a big bag of them stuffed in my bottom drawer. One time when I was babysitting Mia for Lara, I left her in my room playing with her dolls, and when I returned I found her sitting on the floor surrounded by blue feathers.

I didn't stop laughing for at least half an hour.

The sneaky little thing had discovered my secret stash. For weeks afterward I was finding blue feathers in random places around the house, and every time I found one it would make me smile to think of Mia's face full of delight as she threw them up into the air and giggled.

A couple of hours of standing still pass before I call it a day. On the way home I count my money, which amounts to fifty-two euros and thirty-four cents, one brown button, a five-cent coin from Singapore, a piece of paper with the words "Art Slut" scrawled onto it, another piece of paper that says "I love you," and a Trebor Extra Strong Mint.

Nobody can say this work isn't colourful.

Also, I think "Art Slut" would be a great name for an all-female punk band.

Reaching my house, I take a shower to scrub the paint from my hands and face, have a quick bite to eat, and then head off for my shift. An American travelling orchestra are playing tonight. I don't like the disappointment of knowing I'm not going to see Shane, but I soldier on.

I hate the way we left things last night, and I haven't heard a peep from him since. Not a single call, text, voicemail, or Facebook message. And believe me, I've been checking. Perhaps he's waiting for me to make the first move?

Ugh, I hate thinking about this stuff.

Deciding to be brave, I shoot him a quick text telling him the address to meet me at on Sunday if he's still up for coming. Then I shove my phone in my pocket and go to take my place at the bar. Hopefully I'll lose myself in work, and I won't be fidgeting to check my messages every five seconds.

As it turns out, the bar is packed even though it's an hour before the event. We have a nice spacious place here, so often people like to come and socialise before the show. Also, since you're not allowed to bring any alcohol into the actual concert hall, people like to get their drink on in advance.

Now that I'm sober, even the smell of alcohol turns my stomach slightly, but I've learned to tolerate it — kind of the same way you get used to the cloying smell of petrol when you work in a gas station. And I used to work in a gas station, as it happens.

I've worked in a lot of places.

"Hey, could we get a Heineken and a white wine spritzer?" comes an unsettlingly familiar voice from behind me.

It's almost time for the concert to start, so the bar has emptied out a good deal. I pause, as I'm crouched low, slotting bottles into the fridge. I haven't yet turned around, and I'm not sure if I'm physically able to. Just as I regain the ability to move and slot the final bottle in, it slips from my fingers and crashes to the floor, liquid and broken glass going everywhere.

My hands are shaking.

The bar is loud because of the music streaming through the sound system, so I don't think he heard me drop the bottle. It's times like these that I wish they'd put two people working on this bar instead of one. That way I might be able to avoid seeing my ex-boyfriend, Jason, a man I haven't set eyes on in years.

Unfortunately, there's no one else around to serve him but me.

I don't get what he's doing here. He never listened to classical music when we were together. Turning around, I find him standing by the bar in a dark shirt, with a red-haired woman beside him. She's a little older than he is, and there's an air of class about her that enlightens me as to why Jason is here. The concert was obviously her idea.

His eyes widen when he recognises me, and within the next three seconds a whole barrage of memories hits me fast. Him going out and having sex with other women. Me drinking a bottle of vodka and spending the rest of the night in the bathroom puking my guts up. Fights. Break-ups. Make-ups. Sex. Sex. Sex. Parties. Drinking. More drinking. More fighting.

I blame him for the fighting. I can't blame him for *all* of the drinking though. That started long before he came on the scene.

My heart is going ninety as I swallow down what feels like a rough stone jammed in my throat.

"Jade, wow, it's been awhile," he says, eyes flicking between me and the woman he's with.

"Hi, Jason. Yeah, it has. I thought you moved to London," I say, trying to appear casual and busying myself making the drinks he just ordered. Better to get this over and done with quickly rather than drag it out.

A Heineken and a white wine spritzer.

Heineken. White wine spritzer.

He scratches his head and smiles. "I did. That's where I met Beth. She's my fiancée."

The redhead, Beth, smiles at me, probably thinking I'm just some old acquaintance, and flashes me her ring. Well, now, it's some rock, and it surprises me because Jason was never the type to fork out for flashy items.

"Oh, gorgeous," I say to her, putting the pint of Heineken on the counter and going to fetch the wine.

"I moved back to Dublin six months ago. My company set up new offices over here."

Perhaps he finally got his act together and scored a high-paying job. It would definitely explain the several-thousand-euro ring. It's kind of annoying to realise you were the shit part of a person's life before they moved on to the good part. And here I am, still working for just over minimum wage, still living in the same house where I grew up.

"Cool, well, here are your drinks. That'll be eleven euros, please."

Jason hands over the money and stares at me weirdly. Maybe he's annoyed I've abruptly cut off any chance of a conversation. He has no right to be if he is. My life with him is the past, a past I'd much rather forget.

Beth takes her wine and walks over to a table where a group of men and woman are sitting. They must have all come together. Jason stays at the bar, and I don't get why he isn't going with her.

"You look good, Jade. How's your family?"

Looking up, I raise an eyebrow and fold my arms. "Are we seriously doing this right now? Go and have fun with your fiancée, Jason. And please, if you could make it so that you don't come here again, that would be great. I'd rather not see you at my place of work, if it's all the same to you."

His mouth flattens as he yet again runs a hand through his dark blond hair. He always was overly fond of those locks. In this moment I feel like taking a razor blade and shaving them all off.

My anger is warranted. The last time I saw him, he was going down on some brunette in our dingy studio apartment. That was the tipping point for me. I packed up my stuff and moved back home. Two months later I gave up drinking altogether. Several months after that Mum passed away.

"I'm sorry — did I do something to offend you?" he asks abruptly.

"Yeah, you've done plenty."

"You're being rude." He pauses, and a sly gleam comes into his eyes. "I should have a word with your manager."

He definitely hasn't changed a bit. Still the petty fucker he always was. "Do it, and I'll tell your pretty fiancée all about your previous antics. I think she'll be particularly pleased to hear how you slapped me across the face because I wouldn't give you money to go out drinking with your mates."

His expression turns glacial, and my heart pounds. It hurts to even think about our history, never mind put it into words.

Go. Please, just go.

"You're a little bitch."

I just stare at him, hoping that if I stare long enough I'll realise that the last five minutes were a figment of my imagination and that Jason was never here at all.

He stands back and taps his toe on the floor, like he's waiting for me to apologise or something. Finally, he gets the message, picks up his drink, shakes his head, and walks away. I walk straight to the back of the bar and let out a long exhalation like I've been holding my breath under water.

Tears catch in my throat, but I swallow them all back. I can't start blubbering in the middle of work. A buzzing comes from my pocket as my phone rings on "silent." Pulling it out, I see Shane's name on the screen, and that in itself soothes something inside me.

"Hello," I answer, my voice a little shaky.

"Hey, just calling to let you know I'll be there Sunday," he says, somewhat hesitantly. I guess he's unsure where things stand between us after last night.

"That's great. I'm really looking forward to it."

Shane laughs, and there's a faint note of relief to the sound. "Me, too, even though I don't know what we're doing. Hey, is everything all right? You sound a bit off."

I rub my forehead. "I'm working, and I just had a run-in with my ex-boyfriend."

Shane sucks in a breath. "You mean *the* ex-boyfriend? The one who made you swear off all relationships?"

The lilting, almost teasing tone of his voice makes me feel better than I did five minutes ago.

"The one and only. He's still a prick."

"A giant gaping prick," Shane agrees. "You're too good for him. Don't be sad, Bluebird. You're too pretty to be sad."

"Aw, shucks, you know just the right things to say to a girl." I laugh. "So what have you been up to today?"

I hear some movement before he replies, "I went for a run, then practiced and watched *House of Cards* on Netflix."

"Good times. Well, I suppose I'll see you Sunday, then."

"Yeah, see you Sunday, Jade."

Stuffing my phone into my pocket and feeling a whole lot better after only a short conversation with Shane, I head back out to the bar. The bottle I dropped earlier still needs to be cleaned up, but the bar is empty since the show has started. Going to the storage closet, I grab a dustpan and brush and a mop.

All the doors to the hall are closed, muffling the sound of the music. But then one of my co-workers slips out and hurries off on some errand; the door catches and doesn't shut properly, so now I can hear the music full throttle.

Paul Dukas's "The Sorcerer's Apprentice" streams out, and my heart lifts. Leaving the cleaning for a moment, I close my eyes and listen.

Dum dee dum dee dum dee dum dee dum...
Dum dee dum dee dum dee dum dee dum...

And then comes what I like to call the big extravaganza, that part of a piece where the whole orchestra comes alive and the power of the music feels like it could knock you off your feet. The music goes quiet again, building, building...

The roll of industrial paper towels on the counter starts to twirl, unwrapping in a long train of blue. It sails to the liquid on the floor, soaking up the spillage, then balls itself up and shoots into the bin. The dustpan I've left by the bar moves the tiniest bit. And again. I smile. Both dustpan and brush rise into the air and shuffle toward the broken glass. Sweep, sweep, sweep, empty. Sweep, sweep, sweep, empty.

Now the mop comes to life from its spot resting against the bar. It shimmies to the site of the accident and twirls in a dance as it cleans away the sticky spot of beer left over. Soon the floor is shiny and clean again.

"Jade, you can go on your break now," says my floor manager Ciaran as he approaches the bar.

"Thanks, Ciaran," I say, pulling off my half apron and grinning like I know a secret. All the bad feelings from Jason's unexpected appearance are gone completely.

I love music. And I love my brain.

Twelve

My Sunday morning Tai Chi class feels like it's heaven sent. All the stress of a long working week floats out of my body on a sea of calm. I go for coffee with two of the women from the class afterward, and then I head home to throw together a family dinner.

We don't always get to eat together, but I try to at least have everyone at the table on a Sunday. I spoke to Pete last night about letting Shane teach him some music stuff, but he adamantly refused to do it. I'll keep working on him, though. I'm not going to force him, but he could agree to it eventually.

Evening arrives, and I dress up nicely in a calf-length swishy silver skirt and a cream knitted top. I leave my hair down and put on some natural-look makeup. I know that tonight with Shane isn't a date, but still, I like to make an effort.

When I reach the place I told him to meet me at, I see Shane standing by the steps that lead to the front door. He's tapping on his phone, so he hasn't noticed me approaching yet. I take the opportunity to study him dressed uncharacteristically casual in denim jeans, a dark grey T-shirt, and a black jacket. He looks good. I mean, really good, so good my breath catches a little.

Deviously, I sneak up behind him, whispering, "Boo!" into his ear. He jumps, and I break out into riotous laughter before giving him a friendly hug hello.

What sounds like the loud yet melodic bang of a cymbal echoes from the house, and you can hear the people boisterously chatting inside even though the door is shut tight. It's a brown door on a three-storey Georgian building with a red and black ladybird painted on it.

I lead Shane to the door as he murmurs something about me looking beautiful. He says it so quietly, though, that it's easy enough for me to pretend I didn't hear. Taking the knocker into my hand, I bang it once, then three times, then five times fast. A minute later it swings open, and I'm greeted by Mary, a long-haired brunette in her fifties, the resident hostess.

"Jade! We haven't seen you in a while. Come in, come in," she says, welcoming me into the packed hallway. Sitting on each step of the staircase are the members of a folk band playing a dreamy version of "Just Like Tom Thumb's Blues" by Bob Dylan. A bunch of people stand in the hall, holding drinks and swaying to the music.

"I've been busy with the family," I say to Mary. "This is my friend, Shane. It's his first time here."

Mary's eyes light up as she smiles and shakes Shane's hand. "Wonderful! Welcome to Ladybirds, Shane. I hope you enjoy yourself." And with that she saunters off to take care of other guests.

"What is this place?" Shane asks excitedly, keeping close to my side as I lead him out to the back garden.

"Hmm, do you want the straightforward answer or the urban legend?" I reply.

"Both, I guess."

We reach the garden, which is lit up with glowing white fairy lights and Chinese lanterns. There are people all around chatting and drinking, and on the grass a woman is standing on some plastic sheeting while a guy paints her entire naked body in silver and gold. Shane raises an eyebrow and suppresses what I'm thinking is an embarrassed grin. We sit down on a bench to talk.

"Well, the straight answer is that it's an artist's club. It's open to all, and you can use the rooms for practice space. On the weekends they throw big shindigs like this one. The urban legend says that the house was bought by a homeless street performer in the late eighties. A guy named Bob Farrell who used to sit on O'Connell Street with his dog and play guitar for passersby. One day after finishing up, he looked in his hat to find the usual bits of change, but there was also a crumpled piece of paper that turned out to be a lottery ticket. Can you see where I'm going with this?"

Shane's golden-brown eyes dance in the darkening light. "Sort of."

"So Bob goes to check the numbers, and lo and behold, he's won the jackpot. Keep in mind this was the late eighties and the jackpot was probably only a couple hundred thousand at the time. Still, he managed to afford to buy this house smack dab in the middle of the city and opened it up to his fellow struggling artists. When he came to view it for the first time, he found two little ladybirds on the windowsill in a room on the second floor. From there on out he christened the place 'Ladybirds,' and it's been a haven for art ever since."

"That's some story. Where's Bob now?"

"He's still here. He lives upstairs, but he's pretty old, so you don't see him around all that much. Sometimes, though, he'll make an appearance and play a few songs on his guitar."

"Is he any good?"

I nod, remembering the first time I'd heard him sing and how it gave me goose bumps all over. "He's got one of those Tom Waits character voices. Sometimes an out-of-key singing voice feels more real to me than a perfect one, especially if the emotions are raw."

"I'd love to meet him sometime. What he's done here is amazing."

"You haven't even seen half the inside yet. Come on, I'll show you."

I take his hand in mine, tingles shooting through my skin with the contact as I feel his trademark hardened fingertips. Musician's fingers. They're not callused, but they're slightly leathery from the friction of constantly pressing on strings.

I lead him upstairs to the first floor, where there's a big open room. Every year Bob hires someone to paint it entirely white, making it a new canvas, and encourages guests to paint pictures on the walls. Since it's late in the year, there's not much white left now. The room is a riot of colour; some parts of the walls look like they were done by master painters, while others are more amateurish. I glance to the spot over one of the windows where I painted a blue sparrow flapping its wings as though trying to break free of its two-dimensional concrete prison and fly out into the sky.

I know, sparrows again.

Everybody's got a theme, I guess, and those birds are mine.

Shane walks into the room, running his hand over the gigantic mural of a woman's face, tears streaming down from her sad, dark eyes. Then he glances up. A couple of months ago a group got together to paint the ceiling indigo and glue scrunched-up pieces of tin foil to the plaster to look like stars. They twinkle and shimmer against the lights, giving off a magical effect.

"This place must be the best-kept secret in Dublin," he says, coming to stand in front of me.

"Yep," I reply, tapping the side of my nose conspiratorially. "You've got to know the right people to get in. Luckily, you met me."

He breathes out slowly. "That was lucky."

We eye each other for a long minute before Ben's recognisable voice calls, "Jade, Shane, over here."

Shaking myself out of the tension, I turn and put on a smile for my friend. Ben and Clark are sitting on a red heart-shaped love seat in the corner. I hadn't known they were coming tonight, but I'll admit I'm relieved they're here.

Whenever Shane and I are alone together, there's this palpable tension, like I'm constantly aware of how much distance there is between us and how easy it would be to close it. That brief chance I got to feel his skin the first night we met wasn't nearly enough, and so even though my brain knows it's not a good idea to give in, my hormones are raging for me to fail.

"Shauna's dance group is starting in a minute," says Ben excitedly. "Come and sit."

Shauna is a friend of Ben's who teaches interpretive dance classes. Most people roll their eyes at me when I mention the words "interpretive" and "dance" in the same sentence, but this group is really good. It's not all prancing around. I mean, some of the stuff they can do with their bodies is just incredible.

The room is packed with people, so aside from the space that's been cleared for the performance area, there aren't too many places to sit. Shane tugs on my hand just as the lights are dimmed and the music starts up. Before I can react, he's pulling me to sit between his legs, my back against his chest, while he leans against the edge of the love seat Ben and Clark are perched on.

For a moment I fumble, unsure of what to do with my hands. In the end I just rest them in my lap, since that feels like the safer option rather than putting them on Shane's thighs. Unfortunately, I'm not out of the woods yet, as his arms come casually around my waist and I think I stop breathing for a second.

His mouth is close to my ear when he bends forward and asks, "Is this okay?"

I catch Ben's eye as he watches us with a pleased expression. I don't want to make a big deal of it, so I simply nod and focus my attention on the dancers. There are six of them in all, and they've formed a crouched circle in the centre of the floor. A soft, piano-based instrumental song plays as they slowly rise to stand, then begin twirling in practiced patterns. They're all dressed in white and remind me of a cloud floating gently across the sky.

Shane's hand moves along the cushioned part of my stomach ever so slightly, and if I weren't so aware of him, I probably wouldn't have noticed it. He stops for a moment, then moves again. I wonder if he's aware of how much he's turning me on. Just the barest brushing of his thumb over the fabric of my top seems to have the ability to completely unravel me.

I let my body relax deeper into his. I'd been holding myself up a little, wary of getting too close. But now I can't resist feeling his hard chest press into me. I close my eyes for a second, and I can feel every ridge of muscle. His arms around my waist tighten, and a whoosh of breath leaves me. I turn my head a fraction, and his mouth is right there, hanging slightly open.

Making the mistake of looking up into his eyes, all I see in them is want. They've grown hot and needy from just a minute or two of having me close to him. Christ, is a platonic friendship even possible for us? I feel like the only way I won't find him attractive is if I go to hypnotherapy or something.

Which, by the way, doesn't work. I tried it when I was weaning myself off alcohol. The guy told me I didn't have a suggestible enough mind, whatever that means. I think he might have been a bit of a charlatan. And there's a hundred euros I'm never going to see again.

The dance comes to a close, and the assembled audience claps. Then the group gets into formation for the next routine. This one is completely different from the first; the music is edgy, with drums and electric guitar, and the dance is fast-paced. The lights that have been set up are flashing all different colours. In other words, all of the attention is on the performers, and it feels like I'm in my own private little world with Shane.

His face moves to my hair as he sucks in a deep breath, scenting me. My hands, which had been resting idly on my lap, go to his thighs, holding on rigidly as though begging him to stop.

"Shane," I whisper, but I can't tell if he hears me over the loud music.

His hand keeps stroking my belly, bringing all sorts of sensations to life between my legs. I'm aching for him, and when I adjust my body on the hard wooden floor, I feel the stirrings of his erection nudge against my lower back.

Why is he doing this?

"I can't help it," he breathes into my ear, and I realise I asked the question out loud.

"Stop."

His hand stills, and his arm around my waist loosens. He doesn't say anything, but at least he's done as I asked him to. A couple of minutes later the lights come back on, and the performance is over. I practically leap to my feet, mumbling about needing to use the bathroom, and then I hurry from the room, leaving Shane with Ben and Clark.

There's a small bathroom just down the hall, and it's mercifully unoccupied as I step inside and close the door tight behind me. Walking to the sink, I turn on the tap and splash some water on my face, hoping to cool the redness of my cheeks. What just happened in there with Shane was too much, provoked too many sensations.

What the fuck do I think I'm doing, being friends with him?

Playing with fire, that's what I'm doing. But the pain of cutting him out of my life would be worse than the agony I go through when I'm with him, the willpower I have to expend in order to keep things in neutral. It's not my fault he has this subtle way of pushing things into high gear.

When I return from the bathroom, I find Shane still with Ben and Clark, but they're talking to a thin blond guy I've seen around before but have never met. He's wearing a long white shirt, open to display his pale, scrawny chest. His hair is long and hangs down below his shoulders. On his chest somebody has scrawled the word "Happy," which immediately informs me he's something of a character.

Perhaps he used a mirror and wrote it on himself.

"This is Keith," says Ben, introducing us. "He wants to know if we'll take part in his interactive art installation."

"Ah," I reply, folding my arms and going to stand by Shane. "And what does it entail?"

I can't hide the sceptical note in my voice. An interactive art installation usually equals embarrassment in some form or another. It could be anything from sitting on a stack of mattresses while people throw basketballs over your head to stripping naked and frolicking about like a nudist on a tropical beach while a choir sings the lyrics to "Over the Rainbow."

Not that I've done either of those things. Ahem.

Keith starts to explain excitedly. "You partner up with someone, but it has to be someone you know personally, and you use a non-permanent marker to draw the first words that come into your head when you look at different parts of their body on that particular body part. I call it 'Words and Skins.' There'll be a small audience watching. It's all about opening up and losing your inhibitions."

Christ, I knew it was going to involve nudity. Didn't I *just* say it was going to involve getting naked? Sometimes I think these "installation artists" are simply perverts who spend their time coming up with ways to see a few tits and arses.

"So we have to strip for this?" I question, my cynical eyebrow almost hitting the ceiling.

"Just down to bras and knicks," Ben puts in with a cheeky wink.

"Bras and knicks, you say? In that case, I hope you wore your good ones tonight. Otherwise your date might be unimpressed," I quip, nodding to Clark.

"Actually, I went shopping in Ann Summers this week. The word 'crotchless' was involved," Ben shoots back.

I nearly choke on my laughter when he says it, which puts me in a good enough mood to turn to Keith with a grin and reply, "Okay, I'm in. How about everyone else?" Then, turning back to Ben, "Also, Ann Summers? You classless swine. Get thee to Brown Thomas the next time, or I'll refuse to have any further associations with you!"

Ben looks to Clark, who's sputtering a laugh.

"Have you been teaching her how to speak like a dandy again?" he asks him, hands on hips.

"I might have been," Clark manages to get out past his laughter.

Ten minutes later, we're in a different room to the rear of the building. There's a large stage set up, and about twenty people are sitting on bean bags on the floor. The audience, I presume. I watch Shane as he chews on his lip, and I place a hand lightly on his arm.

"Nervous?" I ask with a touch of a smile.

"I have no idea how I managed to be talked into this," he replies, letting out a quick breath.

"It was probably the prospect of seeing Ben in his crotchless lingerie that got you going," I joke, and he gives me a little amused scowl.

"But seriously, you can back out. This night is supposed to be fun. However, I will remind you that you wanted me to teach you how to live, and this, my friend, is living," I say, gesturing around the room.

He gives me a confused look. "Stripping off in front of a bunch of strangers and baring your feelings is living?"

"It's all about throwing away your inhibitions and putting your trust in other human beings. Believe me, letting this bunch see me in my unmentionables isn't something I'm comfortable with, but I want to push my boundaries, see how fearless I can be."

"You stand on the street in the middle of the night in a fairy costume. That's fearless enough for one person, Jade," he replies, reaching out to stroke my cheek. "And now that you mention it, I'm kind of looking forward to seeing those unmentionables."

"Ah, I knew you were a scoundrel," I reply with a laugh.

"A total cad and a bounder," he says, voice low and hushed as he leans over to my ear. The way his breath caresses my neck gives me tingles and by the look on his face I'd say he knows it, too.

"You're a cruel master, Shane Arthur, to tease me the way you do," I tell him with false indignation just before Keith starts ushering us up onto the stage.

Those participating in the installation include me, Shane, Ben, Clark, and three other pairings, all male/female. Keith puts on some peaceful sort of meditation music and hands us each a marker, and then we begin to take off our clothes. I'm aware of the fact that this is going to be the first time Shane has seen me sans clothing, and me him. I caught one or two glimpses of him at the photo shoot, but nothing substantial. The night we had sex doesn't count because it was dark and we only exposed the parts we, uh, needed to expose.

Although I'm not getting into my full birthday suit on this occasion, so there will still be parts left to the imagination. I'm like a high-class French courtesan who knows that partially covered flesh can be far more enticing than stark nudity. The unknown is sexier than the revealed. All magic tricks are a disappointment once you learn how they're done.

Not that I want to be enticing here. Ah, crap, this really isn't working.

Shane is already in his boxer shorts by the time I've dragged myself from my thoughts. He's watching me, waiting. Only a minute ago I was the one telling him not to worry, and now I'm the one who's stalling. Quickly, I lift my top over my head, revealing my ivory silk bra. I undo the zipper at the back of my skirt and shimmy it down my legs until there's nothing left but the matching panties underneath.

"Do you want to go first?" Shane asks, his voice throaty, his eyes on the swell of my breasts.

I grip the marker in my fist, my palm growing sweatier by the minute. I'd been so caught up on the stripping part of this installation that I didn't get the chance to think about which words I'm going to write on his skin. What do I see when I look at him?

I nod and swallow before stepping forward. Like all Band-Aids, it's best to pull them off quickly.

Uncapping it, I raise the marker to his collarbone and begin to write.

Thirteen

A few seconds later the word "vulnerable" is scrawled across Shane's collarbone. For some reason he has his eyes closed, and I'm glad he probably isn't going to be able to see half the things I've written on him unless he gets his hands on a mirror.

I'm hoping he decides to forgo the mirror and simply wash himself clean, because this shit is going to be embarrassing in the cold light of day. I lift his hand, and on each finger I write one letter until they form "skill." His eyes are open now, and his attention is solely focused on what I've written.

I take his other hand and turn it palm up before scribbling "warmth." On his abs I simply write the word "hot," and he cranes his neck to see, looking pleased with himself when he reads it.

"Did you ever think this was what you'd be doing when I asked you here tonight?" I say, smiling up at him as I lower myself to my knees.

"In all honesty, I had no idea what to expect. You're full of surprises, Bluebird."

"Hmm, that was a good answer. By the way, those two girls sitting on the red bean bag are eyeing you up like you're a prize turkey."

His eyes crinkle. "Really? I hadn't noticed."

"Sure," I reply sarcastically before lifting my marker to the defined muscle on his outer thigh and writing "strength."

"Jade, you're on your knees, and your face is right by my crotch. That's the only thing I'm noticing right now," he replies, all husky.

I start at his words and glance up at him again. Our eyes lock, and there's a definite moment, though what we're trying to communicate I couldn't say.

"You've got a dirty mind, Mr. Arthur."

"And you've got the best cleavage, Miss Lennon. I mean, like, the best cleavage I've ever seen. I just want to put my mouth on it."

"Somebody's feeling frisky," I observe, trying to sound calm and ignore the hot blush that's spreading across my chest. In my head all I can see is Shane bending over me, his tongue flicking my nipple.

I stand again and move on to his shoulder. For some reason the word "regal" pops into my head. There's something refined about the sharp lines of his muscles there that reminds me of royalty. On his inner forearm, the one that holds the bow when he plays, I write "strings." On the left hand side of his chest, right where I imagine his heart to be, I write "pain." I don't know how he's going to react to that, but I'm being honest when I write it. When I look at him, I see a heart that was badly broken and is only just sewing itself back together.

He stares at the letters for a long time and swallows deeply, his Adam's apple moving. His eyes close then, and I wonder what he's thinking about.

"You see a lot," he whispers a moment later.

"We all see a lot when we decide to truly look," I respond as I write "sex" on the "V" of his hip. He opens his eyes to see what I've written, and his gaze heats up.

"Why sex?" he questions intensely.

I smooth my hand over the word and bite my lower lip. My voice is barely a whisper when I say, "Because when I look here, all I can think about are your hips thrusting when you fucked me."

"Jesus."

"You asked the question."

From across the room where he's sitting in the audience, Keith rings a little bell and calls, "Okay, now it's time to switch."

Looking anywhere but at Shane, I screw the cap back onto my marker and wait. I was wrong when I thought being the "writer" was the hard part, because being the "writee" is much worse. The anticipation of knowing you're going to find out what someone thinks of each part of you strips you bare. You're completely at the mercy of their judgement, and that judgement could make you either plummet or soar.

This whole thing suddenly makes sense. Who we think we are is completely dependent on what others perceive us to be.

I now realise that Keith must have had a moment of pure genius when he came up with the idea for this installation. And to think I thought he just wanted to get his rocks off.

The first place Shane decides to write is on the side of my neck. I hold completely still, barely breathing as the soft brush of the marker moves across my skin. His other hand is on the opposite side of my neck, as though to keep me in place, but the only thing it's really achieving is making me burn. Jesus, I'm practically panting here, and all he's doing is touching my neck.

"What did you write?" I ask on a deep swallow once he's finished. "That felt like a long word."

To be honest, it probably just felt long because every second he has his hands on me feels like an hour.

"Wait and see," he replies, and when I meet his gaze I find his eyes still haven't lost their heat.

His marker goes to my breasts, where he scrawls "soft," and then to my hip. I have to bend slightly to see he's written "need." Oh, God. His attention moves to my chest again, to my heart, and I swear I feel tears forming when I see him write "too big," but I swallow down the emotion. Let it sit in my belly; better there than to seep through my eyes.

He turns me around, brushes my hair aside and begins writing along the expanse of my shoulders. It doesn't feel like he's writing, though. It feels more like he's drawing something. I twist and glance over my shoulder, but it's pointless. I can't see a thing.

"That's cheating," I pout, and he reaches up quickly, rubbing his thumb over my bottom lip. I suck in air.

"You look cute when you do that."

He bends down and writes something on the lower part of my arse, and again, I can't see what it says. Damn him, it's almost like he's intentionally selecting parts he knows I'm not going to be able to read. His hand cups my cheek lightly, the touch making my heart pound. Moving along, on the top of my belly he writes "still" and on the bottom "life."

Ha. That was clever. When I'm being a living statue, I find stillness in my core. I'm alive but I'm also a statue.

He takes my hand, and on each finger spells out the word "touch." Then he turns it over and writes "me" in the centre of my palm. Wow. Does that mean he wants me to touch him?

I look at him, and it's like he can read the question in my head because he answers, "All the time."

My entire body is burning up, and right now I'm just hoping for this to be over so that I can wash his words off me and try to forget how he makes me feel. A moment later I get my wish when Keith rings his bell, signalling the end of the installation. Unfortunately, movement catches in the corner of my eye, and I realise that it's not quite over yet.

Curtains that have been hung all around the stage, and which I thought were there simply for decoration, begin to be pulled back to reveal dozens of mirrors. There are big ones and small ones, round, square, and rectangular ones. Some of them have fancy wooden or metal frames, while others have no frames at all.

Okay, that Keith is one evil genius. I really hadn't been expecting this, hadn't thought that there would be a big finish. The audience is clapping and gasping as the lights in the room reflect off the mirrors.

Suddenly I'm catching glimpses of myself from all different angles. The other couples are going to the mirrors to study themselves and see what's been written on them. For a long time I can't move at all, afraid of what I might see. Then somebody's taking my hand in theirs. Shane. He pulls me over to a large full-length mirror and positions me in front of it.

I stare at his elegant handwriting, and now I don't want to wash it away. I want to tattoo it onto my skin so that I can keep this feeling, become the beautiful thing he thinks I am.

On my neck he's written "swallow," but for some reason I imagine the bird rather than the action. He knows I have a thing for birds. I turn around and crane my neck over my shoulder to see my back. My eyes trail to my arse cheek, and I giggle when I see the word "peach." But that's not what holds my attention. What holds my attention are the musical notes he's drawn from one shoulder to the other. "What do they mean?" I ask.

He purses his lips, holding in a smile before answering, "It's the musical notation to 'Lucy in the Sky with Diamonds' by The Beatles."

I laugh. "I love that song!" Sometimes I think my brain might be a Beatles track. You know, one of the trippy ones that don't make any sense.

"Well, I would imagine so. You did write it in another life," he teases.

"Ah, yes, very true," I agree with a pleased nod.

He lets the smile free now. "It reminds me of you, the girl with kaleidoscope eyes."

"My eyes are green."

"Not to me. I see a world of things in your gaze, Jade," he replies mysteriously.

I look at him through the mirror for a second but I don't get the chance to question him because Keith hops up onto the stage.

"Ladies and gentlemen, I give you 'Words and Skins,' and I'll leave you with one question. Is your identity an organic thing or dependent on what other people perceive of you? Thank you, and I hope you enjoyed this installation. If you'd like to take part in the next one, you can contact me on Twitter, Facebook, or through my website."

The audience claps, and I go to grab my clothes. As I'm pulling on my top, Shane comes up beside me, buttoning his pants. "I think he kind of ruined the message with the social media bit at the end," he whispers jokingly.

I roll my eyes in agreement, trying not to stare at his bare chest. "I know. I was thinking he might have some real substance until he did that."

The doors are opened as the audience members start to leave, and loud music streams in from the other room. Once I'm dressed I look around for Ben and Clark, but they've already gone. They're headed home to shag each other's brains out, no doubt. Not that I'm jealous or anything.

Shane and I go in the direction of the music, back to the big room with the painted walls. Inside are an instrumental band that consists of an acoustic guitarist, a keyboard player, a drummer, a violinist, and an accordion player. Mary is going around the room with a tray of drinks as the band plays a rendition of Coldplay's "The Scientist." She hands Shane a plastic cup with some sort of orange cocktail, and I wave her off when she tries to give one to me. I can smell the rum in it from here.

We go and sit on a couple of pillows a few feet away from the band, and I notice the violinist's eyes widen when he sees Shane. He definitely recognises him. Perhaps he's even a fan. This is so exciting. I'm friends with a "sort of" famous person. I think Shane's noticed, too, because he's shifting uncomfortably as he sips on the cocktail Mary gave him.

"How's the drink?" I ask.

"Completely awful," he replies, and I burst out laughing.

"Why are you drinking it if it's awful?"

"I didn't want to be rude."

I shake my head and take the cup from him before setting it aside. The song comes to an end, and I watch as the violinist goes to whisper animatedly to the guitarist. The guy is only about nineteen or twenty, so it's very likely that Shane is someone he looks up to.

My suspicions are confirmed when both the violinist and the guitarist start waving Shane over.

"I think you're wanted," I tell him with a pleased expression.

His posture goes rigid. "No, I'm not."

I nudge him with my elbow. "Yes, you are. Now stop being antisocial and go over there and talk to them. Make some new friends."

He gives me a long-suffering look before getting to his feet and walking to the musicians. I watch as the violinist gives Shane a big excited handshake and a pat on the back. The band all clamour around him, chatting animatedly. I sit back and watch. They're obviously trying to get him to play a song with them because Shane's shaking his head and I'm lip reading a whole bunch of "no" and "I can't" responses.

I wonder how he can be so comfortable playing on stage with an orchestra, or even before with his string quartet, and yet he looks like playing here for this relatively small gathering of people is the last thing he wants to do. Perhaps it's because there isn't an actual stage here. There's no formal line between him and the general public. Here he is the general public, and not some untouchable virtuoso on a grand platform. There's no shield of distance.

Finally, it looks like the band has convinced him to play. He's nodding his head and then making his way back over to me.

"They want me to play a song with them. Just one song. You don't mind, do you?"

"No, not at all." I smile. "Go knock 'em dead."

He gives me a small smile in return and then goes back to join the band. The violinist hands over his instrument to Shane and then retreats into the audience. The band starts up, and it takes me a second to realise they're playing a modern song. Apart from his attempt at David Bowie in my bedroom, I haven't yet heard Shane play a non-classical piece. I recognise it immediately as "Just The Way You Are" by Bruno Mars. The beat of the drum fills my ears, purple sound waves drifting up to the ceiling. The violin is like the voice, the rest of the instruments the backing track.

Whoa, he looks hot up there. He catches my eye then and doesn't stop looking.

Feeling uncomfortable under his attention, I try to fix my stare on the other players, but it's no use. I can still sense his gaze on me. Some people get up and start dancing to the catchy beat, some even sing the lyrics. It's the kind of song that you can never feel sad after.

Once it's over, Shane accepts some applause from the room before returning the violin to its owner.

"That was amazing," I exclaim when he reaches me and sits back down. "I didn't know you played modern songs, too."

He shrugs, his eyes alight. I've noticed he always seems more energised after playing, more centred. "I learn them sometimes to take a break from my usual repertoire." Pausing, he looks like he's considering whether or not to tell me something. "My counsellor encouraged me to learn that one."

It's news to me that he sees a counsellor, but I don't want to pry about it. "The Bruno Mars song?"

He grimaces. "She said I should learn some happy songs. There was a period of about six months where all I could play was funerary music."

This piece of information concerns me, but I file it away for later. Deciding to make light of it instead, I whisper, "Did you go through a Goth phase, Shane?"

He laughs. "No, I was just sad."

I venture a guess. "Because of Mona?"

"She was a part of it. Anyway, once I agreed to move on, I was glad. Funerary violin is beautiful, but it's also pretty depressing."

"I can imagine. So, have you had fun tonight?"

He grins. "Yes, in the most bizarre way possible."

"Will you come again? Get to know the people." I nod over to the band. "You've already made some new friends."

"I'll come again, but only if you're here."

"I'm here every few weekends. Next time I'll bring you up onto the roof. It's great to just sit in the dark and look at the night sky, see how many stars you can count, see if you can count any at all."

Shane doesn't say anything, and when I look at him his attention is focused intently on my mouth. He looks into my eyes then, and I get caught. I hadn't realised until now just how close we are, just how cosy we must look sitting huddled together on these pillows.

He swallows hard and says, "Can I ask you something?"

"Of course."

"Promise not to get mad at me or not want to be my friend anymore?"

Wary now, I reply, "I'll try not to."

He moves even closer, taking my hand into his and smoothing his fingers over my knuckles. It feels nice.

"When we're around each other there's this...tension." He pauses for a second.

Yeah, he doesn't need to explain further, because I know exactly what he's talking about.

"It's fucking agony, Jade, not to touch you," he continues, like he's baring his soul. "And I know you're not interested in a relationship, so I was thinking we could have an arrangement."

I raise an eyebrow, not liking where I can see this heading.

"'An arrangement?'" I question. He stares at me and I can't take the atmosphere, so I have to crack a joke. "I hope you're not suggesting a *Pretty Woman* scenario here?"

The ghost of a smile touches his lips. "You know that's not what I'm suggesting." He draws closer so that he can whisper into my ear. "I want to be inside you again."

I whimper, and his tongue flicks over the shell of my ear, turning my entire body to jelly.

"You want us to be fuck buddies," I say, my voice barely audible.

"I prefer the term 'friends with benefits.' I have so much respect for you, Jade, and I promise to treat you like a queen, but I need you. I'll be your friend, but with more…"

"Shane, I…"

"Please don't say no."

"I have to think about this."

He pulls me to him, resting his forehead against mine and exhaling. "Okay."

"I'll let you know…I mean, I think we need to call it a night." I draw away, but he grips my hand.

"I'll drive you home." His eyes flick back and forth between mine as though trying to decipher my thoughts. "Jade, tell me I haven't fucked up."

"You haven't fucked up."

"Promise?"

"I promise."

And with that he pulls us both up to stand, leading me from the room and out of the building.

Fourteen

The next morning I'm chatting with my neighbour Barry a couple of houses down from mine when I see Pete leaving for school. I say my quick goodbyes to Barry before cutting down a side alley that I know will bring me directly onto Pete's path.

"Hello, stranger, fancy meeting you here," I say as I fall into step beside him.

His sleepy eyes drift to me as he shakes his head. "What do you think you're doing, Jade?"

"Taking a stroll," I answer with a shrug. "Thought I'd keep you company while I'm at it."

A sigh. "I know what you're up to."

He's not getting mad at me, which is a good sign. "Uh, *yeah*. Like I said, I'm taking a stroll."

"Herding me to school, more like."

I let out a big long chuckle and smack him lightly on the shoulder. "Oh, you teenagers are such suspicious creatures."

He doesn't say anything, and we continue walking. Once we're around the corner from his school, I wave him off. He takes a few steps before turning back around.

Scratching at his head, he asks, "Does your friend still want to give me music lessons?"

I'm surprised he's asked this, and given the open-ended way I left things with Shane last night, I'm not certain what's going to happen between us, but I'm sure he'll still work with Pete if I ask him to.

"Of course."

"And he's not just doing it because you're making him?"

"Of course not!"

"Okay, well, you can tell him I'll do it."

Wow, that was easier than I thought it'd be. I imagined I'd be in for at least another couple weeks of sulking before he came around. I salute him, then turn on my heel and head home.

Last night Shane dropped me off at my house, walking me to the door and giving me a long, question-filled hug. We parted ways, and I haven't been able to stop thinking about him since. I hardly got a wink of sleep, which is why I was up early enough to make sure Pete got himself to school this morning.

When I think about what Shane's asked of me, my entire body screams that it's the worst idea in the history of Jade Lennon. And believe me, there have been some bad ones. Every part of me wants to be with him, but at the same time every part of me says that I won't be able to keep my emotions from getting involved.

At around lunchtime I get a text from him politely asking how my morning went. Politely skirting the real question. Even seeing his words on the screen of my phone makes me feel all anxious, and I can't bring myself to reply. Later on I arrive at work and check the roster to find I'm on the front of house box office. This makes me relax a little, because Shane won't be able to come see me like he does at the bar.

Midway through my shift, Lara ventures over from her station in the merchandise shop to slide a walnut whip through my window slot.

"What's this for?" I ask with a grin.

"You look a bit down in the dumps today. I thought chocolate would be a good cure."

Really, this girl has a heart of gold.

"You had the right idea. Thanks," I say before she moves out of the way so I can deal with my next customers. There's a show about to start in fifteen minutes, so the lobby is packed with people queuing to get to their seats. I've barely even noticed what's on since I've been in such a daze all day.

"We have tickets reserved for collection," comes a vaguely familiar voice as my next customer steps up to the booth. I slide the walnut whip under my seat and glance up to find Mirin standing before me with a man I presume to be her husband beside her. He's got the same brandy-coloured eyes as Shane, but that's the only resemblance.

My heart pounds. God, why did she have to come to this booth? I feel anxious enough right now as it is, since last night her son had the good grace to proposition me with an arrangement my brain refuses to work its way around.

"Oh, hello, Mrs Arthur. Are the tickets under your name?"

"No, my husband's. Reginald Arthur."

"Right," I say as I flick through the reserve drawer. Mirin doesn't bother to introduce me to Reginald, which leads me to believe she doesn't want him to know me. Finding the tickets, I slip them through to her. All the while she's staring down at me like I'm a slice of stale bread someone's just put on her plate. She swipes the tickets up into her talons, I mean, hands, and away they both go.

Thank fuck for that being short and sweet.

Once the show starts, I join Lara in the break room to enjoy my walnut whip with a cup of tea. Lara has one, too, and we both chow down in contented silence. I always get a craving for sugar after a long day. She tells me how pleased she is with April as her child minder, and I'm pleasantly surprised that my sister's actually taken to the work. I've even seen a marked improvement in her mood, since she's now got a purpose and some regular money in her pocket. And there haven't been any older men calling to the house, which is a plus.

Now it seems I've just got Project Pete to contend with.

Towards the end of our break, my supervisor comes and asks me if I'll prepare the refreshments for the orchestra's dressing room during the interval. The girl who'd been on duty there had to go home sick. I tell him I'd be glad to, but all the while I'm cursing him out in my head. Making my way to the bar, I find a rider of requested beverages, mostly water, teas, and fruit juices.

The members of the symphony have this great big dressing room with mirrors and bright lighting, like backstage on a Broadway musical. It's basically a giant room with long lines of tables and mirrors, each one belonging to a different musician.

I know exactly which one belongs to Shane because he probably got the seat of the concertmaster who left. Checking the rider, I see all he asked for was a bottle of water. I quickly place it on his table and move on. At the rate I'm going, I won't be done by the time the interval starts, given I have almost a hundred people to cater to.

Normally there are two workers to do this task, but we must be short-staffed tonight, which means I'm all by my lonesome. I can hear the recognisable melody of the *William Tell* Overture coming to a close, and then the musicians are making their way to the dressing room. I've still got about twenty tables to do, so I hurry up.

Water.

Coffee.

Ginger tea.

Water.

As I approach the next table, I pause and glance up because somebody is standing in my way. Shane's deep eyes look into mine, and I swallow hard.

"You never answered my texts," he says as he studies me.

We're nowhere near his dressing table, so he obviously sought me out. I move by him and set another water down on a table.

"Sorry, I've been busy with work, and I left my phone in my bag in the staffroom. Was it anything important?" I say, trying my best to be casual.

Shane sighs. "So this is how you're going to be, huh?"

I flinch as I transfer more refreshments onto dressing tables. There are people moving by all around us, which makes the situation even more stressful.

"What do you mean?"

"I mean you're acting all flustered and pretending like you've forgotten what we talked about last night."

"I'm not pretending," I say.

I've just finished with the last table, and a female cellist grins at me appreciatively, taking a sip from her orange juice.

"And I haven't forgotten, Shane," I continue quietly. "I'm still considering things."

We reach the door leading out of the dressing room, but he puts his arm in my way to stop me. "Don't freeze me out. I'm dying here," he pleads, and the sound of his voice makes my stomach clench with guilt for making him wait, despite the fact it hasn't even been twenty-four hours yet.

I set the wheelie tray aside and give him my eyes, placing my hand on his arm in a gentle grip. "I'm not going to do that. I just need more time."

He stares at me seriously, and he must see something that puts his mind at ease, because his body loses some of its tension. I can feel eyes watching us through the dressing room door, but I ignore them. I never read any rules about not being allowed to have a personal relationship with a member of the orchestra. We work in the same building, but you wouldn't exactly call us co-workers, so I don't really care about people assuming things.

A long stretch of silence elapses between us before I say, "By the way, Pete's agreed to the music lessons."

A smile splits his lips, a real one, too. He genuinely wants to help my little brother. "That's great, Jade. I'll let you know when I've figured out which day will be best. We've got a lot of shows coming up, and I haven't fallen into a proper routine yet."

"That's cool. Call me when you know," I say, moving to go by him. "I need to get back to work now, okay?"

Reaching out, he tucks a strand of hair behind my ear that's fallen free of my bun. "Okay," he breathes, and then he goes back inside the dressing room. I hurry to restock my tray, and then I return to see if any of the musicians need refills. I'm busy, but I can feel Shane watching me from where he sits quietly sipping on his water.

The other violinist, Avery, has the dressing table right beside his, and she's chatting away to him. I wonder if he's even listening because his eyes haven't once left me. All of a sudden my white blouse feels too tight, my black skirt too restricting. He has this way of making me feel stripped bare even when I'm fully clothed.

It's customary for me to do the rounds of the entire room, and when I get to Shane he says yes to another bottle of water. I know for a fact he has no intention of drinking it. He's just doing this so that we'll have to interact. Avery doesn't want anything else and turns to fix her hair in a French twist.

When I hand Shane his second water, his fingers purposely graze mine, his stare hot, and I practically trip over my own feet to get moving on to my next stop. I can't be certain, but I think I see his lips curve in a smirk.

Soon the interval is over, and it's time for the performance to resume. I couldn't be happier for the reprieve.

When I'm helping with closing up later on, I see Shane with his parents and a few other people in the lobby, all chatting in a group. Everything about them screams money, from the clothes they wear to the subtle gestures they make as they talk. Lara shoots me a funny annoyed look from across the way, where she's closing up on merchandise. Clearly, she wants all the stragglers to push on so that we can close up properly and get home to our much-needed beds.

I keep feeling my eyes drifting shut due to my lack of sleep last night, so I have to continually blink to stay focused. I cash out my till and then go to assist Lara in fixing the merchandise shelves. Straining my ears, I try to hear what Shane and the people he's with are talking about, but they're too far away.

When he catches me looking, he says something to his dad before leaving the group and walking toward me. Great. I brought this on myself by staring at him like a love-hungry teenager and I know it. Still, I busy myself with the DVD shelf and try to pretend I don't know he's standing right behind me.

"Busy night?" he asks, one hand resting on the shelf above my head.

"No busier than usual. Did you play well?"

"I did. You didn't get a chance to come see?"

I shake my head and give him a little smile while continuing to stack DVDs. "I rarely do. I'm hardly ever on duty in the auditorium. They mostly put me on the bar or the ticket booths."

Shane rubs his jaw. "Yeah, I noticed it's always the old matrons who usher."

I grin now and whisper, "They've got it all sewn up. They're like the concert hall mafia. Ushering is the easiest job. Oh, and don't ever call them old matrons to their faces. Otherwise, you'll be sleeping with the fishes."

Shane moves closer, chuckling low. "I'll remember that."

His hand strokes my neck. I gasp and step away. "You might be off duty, but I'm still working," I remind him, not meeting his eyes.

"It must have slipped my mind," he mutters, his eyes boring holes into the side of my head.

His mother calls him back over, and he whispers goodbye before leaving me. I let out a long breath and look to Lara, who's standing several feet away and who obviously observed everything just now.

"Ben's right. He really does want to stick his Channing in your Tatum," she says on a giggle.

I feign throwing a DVD at her head and laugh at how catastrophically badly she just messed up that sentence.

***

"I want you out of this house right now," I demand, standing in the kitchen doorway in my nightgown.

It's nine o'clock in the morning and Patrick, the good-for-nothing father of my three younger siblings is sitting at the table. There's a half-empty bottle of whiskey in front of him and a half-smoked cigarette dangling between his dirty fingers. I hate it when all his other options have dried up, and he decides to come and burden himself on us.

His dull eyes flick to me as he takes a drag. "Greta kicked me out. I'll need to stay here for a few days."

"This isn't your house, and you're not welcome, Patrick."

His fist slams hard down into the table, and I jump in fright. "I'll stay as long as I like."

"You'll get the fuck out, or I'll tell Alec to throw you out."

"My son doesn't take orders from you. And you'd do well to behave," he replies, the threat obvious.

I can't stand him. A couple of months before Pete was born, he and my mother broke up for good. I can't get my head around why she put up with him for as long as she did in the first place. Mum was an intelligent woman, but she must have had a touch of low self-esteem to ever think this fool was what she deserved. I had to put up with him as a shoddy substitute father for way too long. The last time he came here, he stole fifty euros out of my purse and went to the bookies.

Then he showed up at three in the morning, shouting to get in because I'd locked all the windows and doors. After about an hour of banging and yelling, and after he'd woken half the neighbourhood, he finally gave up and left. This is the first I've seen of him since.

I fold my arms. "I suppose you're here to pay me back that fifty?"

"What fifty?" he answers casually, as though butter wouldn't melt.

"That's it. I'm getting Alec."

Strolling into the hallway, I call for my brother, but then my stomach sinks when I remember he's working today. Patrick must know this already because I can hear him laughing. Now all I've got is an empty house and a drunkard gambler in my kitchen. Deciding to face the music alone, I march back in and lift the landline from the receiver on the wall.

"Get out or I'll call the police."

He stubs his smoke in an empty mug and gives me a look that says, *I dare you.*

I give him a steely look in return and begin dialling those three little numbers. When the operator swiftly answers, "Nine, nine, nine. What's your emergency?" Patrick's chair squeals against the linoleum as he gets to his feet.

"Fine. I'm going," he spits, and I hang up the phone just as the front door opens and slams shut. Hmm, he must have been in a spot of bother with the police recently and doesn't want any more run-ins.

Patrick's not clever enough to be completely evil; however, he is an addict and a leech. I can't afford to have him in this house wreaking havoc with everyone's routines. He's never been a dad to Pete, April, or Alec, and the only reason he ever comes here is for money and a roof over his head.

As I go to find breakfast, I look down to see that my hands are shaking, so I make a cup of camomile tea in the hopes that it will settle my nerves. I try to steer clear of anti-anxiety medication, because like Patrick I'm an addict and I can't do drugs of any sort in half measures.

Perhaps that's why I can't stand to have him around, because in a way he's like a mirror held up to my own flaws.

After breakfast I get ready for work, and I'm late so I flag a taxi on my way. There's an afternoon as well as an evening event today, so my shift is going to be a long one. The roster tells me I'm on the ground floor bar, which is a lot busier than the one on the first floor.

And it's just my luck that when I get there both Shane and Avery are sitting on stools and sipping on coffees.

"Hello, Jade, isn't it?" Avery greets me as I step out from the back room. Shane stays quiet and lifts his cup to his mouth.

This woman is nice, I can tell, and since I've always kind of felt sorry for her after Noeleen told me of her wedding obsession, I don't like the idea of Shane using her. The fact they're both sitting here is either a coincidence, or he's trying to make me jealous. Okay, so maybe I'm just a little on edge after my encounter with Patrick this morning and feeling extra suspicious.

"Yep, that's right, and you're Avery. I hear you're wonderful on the violin." I haven't heard that, but I know she plays, and for some reason I feel the need to give her a compliment.

She smiles modestly. "Thank you. Shane was telling me about the place you took him to on Sunday. It sounds amazing."

"Oh, Ladybirds? Yeah, it's a great club. You can come with us next time if you like."

Her eyes light up, and I sense an innocence about her, a sheltered life. "Really? I'd love to."

Shane's eyes warm as he takes me in, and I suddenly realise that I was wrong. He wasn't trying to make me jealous. He's just trying to make a new friend, like I've been encouraging him to do. He sees the same innocence in Avery that I see, and he likes that I'm being nice to her.

"Great. Shane can pick you up."

"I'd be glad to," Shane puts in.

I wipe down the bar and go to serve a customer sitting at the other end.

"Jade Lennon, you're in big trouble!" I hear Alec's voice boom jokingly around the room as he walks toward the bar. I sigh, taking in his dirty work clothes and his dishevelled Mohawk. Only my brother wouldn't think twice about walking into a classy place like this in construction gear. He slides onto a stool and gives Shane a sturdy handshake before nodding hello to Avery and winking. Her cheeks redden, and I let out another sigh. Alec never met a vagina he didn't like.

"To what do I owe this unexpected pleasure?" I ask as I use a dish towel to dry some glasses.

"I heard you had a visitor this morning. I'm working on a site close by today, so I thought I'd drop over and see if you're all right."

"I can handle your dad, Alec."

"I know that. But he can be a prick at the best of times. Did he say anything to you?"

"He said a few things. He always does. Had his mind set on staying at ours, but I threatened him with calling the police and he skedaddled. We probably won't be hearing from him again for a while."

Both Shane and Avery are quiet as they listen to our exchange.

"Yeah, he rang me, giving out hell and calling you every name under the sun. I told him straight that he couldn't stay."

"I'm sorry, Al. I know he's your dad and all, but I can't have him in the house. I'm only starting to make headway with Pete, and you know if Patrick's around all that will go to shit."

"I know. I don't want him there, either."

When I glance at Shane for a second, I find concern and protectiveness etched on his face. It makes my heart stutter.

"Do you want a drink?" I ask Alec. "Or I could grab you something from the restaurant. Have you eaten yet?"

He pats his stomach. "Nope, haven't had the chance. If you could get your hands on a sandwich, I wouldn't say no."

"Okay, I'll be back in a minute."

The concert hall houses a restaurant to the front of the building and I'm friends with a couple of the kitchen staff, so I know it won't be a problem getting something for Alec. When I return with a chicken and bacon club, I find Shane gone and Alec sitting on his vacated stool next to Avery, too close really.

I put the sandwich down in front of him, and he gives me a grin in thanks.

"So, how long have you been in the orchestra?" he asks her, and I watch with interest.

I don't like the idea of my brother with this girl, mainly because I can see him chewing her up and spitting her out, but I'm still fascinated. The two of them are so different, her refined and well-bred, Alec unrefined and rough around the edges. In some ways they're like me and Shane. Although I like to think I'm not as rough and ready as my brother.

"Just over a year," Avery replies shyly, focusing intently on her coffee cup as she drains the last of its contents. She looks like she might have a heart attack from Alec's attention. "I'd better get going. It's not long before the afternoon concert starts."

Just as she slides off her stool, Alec puts down his sandwich and grabs her hand, pulling it to his mouth and kissing it. I try to hold back my laugh. He can be such a little chancer at times.

"Hopefully we'll bump into each other again sometime," he says as he looks up at her.

Avery lets out a tiny gasp and blushes yet again before quickly stealing away.

Alec turns back around in his stool and resumes eating his sandwich, a pleased gleam in his eye. I shake my head at him.

"Smooth as ever, bro."

He grins. "What can I say? I think I've just acquired a taste for posh birds."

I point a finger at him. "You leave her alone. She's not like your usual type."

"Oh, so it's all right for you to punch above your weight, but not me?" he chides me playfully.

I scowl. "What's that supposed to mean?"

"The half-Asian pretty boy. I know you've been getting yourself a slice of action there."

"We're friends, Alec. Believe it or not, some people are actually capable of maintaining friendships with the opposite sex."

"Some people, but not you two. I'm not blind."

God, he's so right. I hate that he's right. "Whatever."

He lets out a loud, boisterous laugh. "Ha! I knew it. To be honest, I'm glad for you, sis. I was beginning to get worried. You haven't had a bloke since that fuckhead Jason years ago."

"We're not together, not like that. We just had a bit of a thing…"

"Okay, stop right there. I don't want any details," Alec interrupts, wiping some crumbs off his mouth with a bar napkin.

I raise an eyebrow. "Don't worry, you won't be getting any." Sex talk with my brother is not something that's on my bucket list, thank you very much. I serve a couple of customers while he finishes his food.

"So, I suppose I'm on dinner duty tonight," he says, setting the plate aside.

"Yeah, if you don't mind. I'm working until ten."

"No problem, I'll grab some Chinese."

A few minutes later he heads back to work, and I get busy as the bar starts to fill up. When the early evening crowd have gone and it's time for my break, I find a message from Shane on my phone from a few minutes ago.

Sorry I had 2 leave w/out saying goodbye earlier. Come c me in the dressing room?

I wonder what he wants to see me for. I have to grab something to eat while I'm on my break, but I suppose I can spare a few minutes to go talk to him. The dressing room is mostly empty when I get there; Shane's sitting, scrolling through his phone when his head comes up and he spots me approaching. I slide my bum onto the table in front of him and fold my arms.

"I saw your message. What's up?" I say as he tucks his phone back in his pants pocket.

"Have you eaten?" he asks and winces suddenly, lifting his hand to rub the side of his neck.

"Not yet," I say, and frown. "Are you okay?"

"Yeah, just a bit of neck strain. It happens when you spend half your life with an instrument tucked there." He gives me a half-hearted smile.

"Ouch. Come here," I reply before I've properly thought it through.

He comes to me willingly, and I lean closer so I can gently rub his neck. Letting out a low groan, he melts into my touch, and the noise stirs a tingle between my legs. His hand rests on my thigh as I continue to massage his sore spot.

"That feels amazing. Can I hire you as my personal masseuse?"

I chuckle quietly. "I'm afraid you couldn't afford me, sir."

Another low groan. Wow, that noise is such an aphrodisiac it's not funny. "Name your price."

I just shake my head and keep rubbing until I feel him loosen up. "Any better?"

His eyes move to mine, hot and seeking. He seems to be considering something, but then simply answers, "Much better," and pulls his chair back to its original spot. "So, do you want to go grab some food?"

"Sure. I was going to get a burrito. I need the carbs when I'm on my feet all day," I reply. "Does that suit you?"

"Suits me fine," he says, grabbing his coat.

We walk to the nearby burrito bar and then decide to sit in the gardens just behind the concert hall to eat.

"My brother was chatting up Avery at the bar after you left, you know," I say before taking a big bite.

Shane looks surprised. "Really? I wouldn't have thought she'd be his, uh, type."

"Alec doesn't have a type. He likes all types. But anyway, maybe you could warn her away from him? I don't want her getting hurt when he takes her for a one-night stand and then never calls her again. She seems like a sensitive girl."

"Oh, right, that sort of behaviour must run in the family," Shane teases me.

I stare at him. "That's not that same thing."

He can barely conceal his grin. "So you're saying I'd have seen you again if it hadn't by chance turned out that I played in the orchestra?"

"Of course you'd have seen me again. Every time you walked down Grafton Street, you'd see me standing there all in blue," I tease him back.

"Ah, so I'd get to admire you from afar."

"Exactly."

"Kind of feels like that anyway," he says quietly.

"That's not true. You're always close, Shane. Too close."

"Not close enough."

A silence falls. I take a couple more bites of my burrito, but I know I can't finish it. All of a sudden I've lost my appetite. I wrap it up in the foil and put it in my bag. Perhaps I'll eat the rest later.

"I'm not sure if I can agree to what you've asked," I say softly.

He turns to face me, his brows knit together. "Why not?"

"I just don't feel up to that sort of an arrangement," I answer, my voice breaking slightly.

Understanding in his gaze, he recognises my inner struggle and nods, putting his arm around my shoulder and pulling me to his side. "Okay, Bluebird. Let's forget I ever brought it up."

I rest my head on his shoulder and stare straight ahead, whispering, "Thank you." And for the next while we sit in quiet, listening to the water crash in the garden waterfall close by.

Fifteen

People are all around me, but I'm alone in my own little world.

The rush of Friday shoppers flows by like a gushing river, so much movement, and yet I'm absolutely still. When I'm standing on my box, I like to focus on something tiny, something nobody else even notices.

On the building on the other side of the street, a piece of red ribbon has gotten caught on a shop sign. It flutters in the breeze as though dancing. I've been watching it for the last two hours, completely transfixed. I've been watching it for so long that it's no longer a single object. Now it's cheap thread and red dye; it's the shine when it catches a certain slant of light. It's the distant music I hear when it dances with the wind.

I prick my ears then, because outside my deep meditation something is breaking through. Something other than the din of the crowded street. It's real music, music I recognise.

Curiosity wins out, and with the slowness you'd expect of a statue that has suddenly sprung to life, I change my pose so I'm looking in the direction the music is coming from. Just a few yards away Shane is standing outside a shoe shop playing "Carmen Fantasy" on his violin.

What's he doing here?

When he sees that I'm watching him, he winks. Winks!

Well, now he has my attention, not to mention the attention of several people who have stopped to listen to him play. Soon a crowd has formed to watch the virtuoso on the street. Living statues never really attract crowds. We connect with one or two people at a time. Music is where the big money is at when it comes to street performance. That or circus acts. Anything that involves fire and stilts always attracts interest.

Unless of course you happen to set yourself on fire or fall off your stilts, and in my years doing this I've witnessed both. Though in all honesty, the accidents bring with them their own audience.

I like this piece he's playing. It reminds me of a tango dance. Shane does this really cool vibrato, and the crowd cheers. All of a sudden people are pairing off into couples and tangoing down the street. And don't even ask me where the women got all those frilly dresses from, or the men their fancy black tuxedos.

Soon I'm surrounded not by shoppers but a street full of ballroom dancers. The bright blue sky darkens, the outdoor air drifts away, and I'm indoors in a ballroom that extends forever. Chandeliers hang from ceilings, light glittering through the cut crystal. Antique candelabras all around are lit with long, thin candlesticks.

A couple struts around my box. The man dips the woman low and runs his hand down her thigh, which is exposed by a deep slit in her dress. He lifts her up and twirls her away from me. The piece approaches its finish, and the room begins to brighten. The enclosed ceiling turns back into the open sky, and the glittering chandeliers are replaced by dull white clouds.

Shane's music ends, and there are no dancers anymore, just ordinary shoppers like before. Sometimes I hate it when the music stops, hate the finality. Lots of people put money in the open violin case at his feet, and he thanks them gracefully. I smile when he packs up his things and walks toward me.

I haven't moved a muscle since I turned to see where the music was coming from. He looks up at me as though admiring a work of art, his eyes landing on my wings, my white face, the waistline of my dress. Standing before me, he gives a deep bow, then rises and walks away, a smile on his lips all the while.

Okay, that was possibly the sweetest thing anyone has ever done for me. Needless to say, I've never had a man come and play music while I stood on the street in my costume. All of a sudden a loud involuntary laugh bursts out of my mouth. It's so full of simple happiness that I find it difficult to breathe.

What is he doing to me?

Why is he doing this to me?

He doesn't even know it, but he's making me love him.

***

When Sunday comes I have to work, so I can't make it to Ladybirds like I promised Shane and Avery. They agree to put it off until another week, since they both have a concert to play anyway. A week and a half passes by, and somehow every time I'm busking on the street Shane manages to show up to play me a song.

Sometimes it's hours before he makes an appearance. Other times it's only minutes.

I'm beginning to think he must be psychic because I busk on different days each week, but he always knows when I'm going to be there. I guess he figures it out by checking to see if I'm working. When I'm not working I'm almost always busking, unless April or Pete need me. Mostly though, they need me less and less these days. There's something quite heart-breaking about watching the kids you've cared for transform into adults.

I'm smiling from ear to ear as I stroll home on a Wednesday afternoon. Shane came and played "Dance of the Sugar Plum Fairy" to me by finger-plucking the strings; the whole time my belly was fizzy with emotion. The grey street was transformed into a glowing forest awash with mischievous winged creatures. One night he came and played "Clair de Lune," and I paid a visit to my friend the moon, sitting on his round white head while I listened. Another time he played "Estrellita" and I was sufficiently seduced. Of course, he didn't know that.

I don't know what I'd do if I couldn't hear him play again.

Dropping into a nearby newsagents, I grab some milk, bread, and other necessities, paying for it all with a whole bunch of coins because it's the last of my money until I get paid on Friday. One downside of relying on the money people give to you on the street to buy stuff is that you end up having to pay for everything with small change. The girl at the checkout lets out a sigh when she sees me coming. I shop in here quite a bit, so she knows I'm the chick with the coins.

Sometimes I go to the bank and get it changed to notes, but I don't always have the time for that. It seems to me that banks open some of the shortest hours of all businesses. I mean, unless I want to spend my entire lunch hour queuing, I'm not going to make it there between ten and four.

When I reach my street, pulling my box along on its wheels with one hand and carrying my shopping bag in the other, I spot Barry in the tiny patch of grass that makes up his front garden. Local authority housing in the city centre doesn't exactly allow for large garden spaces.

Anyway, back to Barry.

It's an unseasonably warm day, and he's brought an armchair out from his living room and placed it in a nice sunny spot. Beside him is a plastic foldaway table on which sits a radio streaming commentary for a football game, alongside a bottle of Budweiser.

He's lounging back in his chair, his hands clasped behind his head, eyes closed as he soaks up a few rays. The picture of contentment. I have to admire him for how much he doesn't give a shit about being weird. I think that's the main reason why he's the only neighbour I actually get along with.

I suppose that once you reach fifty, have worked your arse off all your adult life to support a family and have lost half your hair, you're entitled to do as you please. The commentators get riled up as one of the teams scores a goal, and I'm guessing it was Barry's team because he jumps up from his armchair and pumps his fist into the air, letting out a bellow of triumph.

I laugh as I walk to my house.

"I see you're making the most of the sun while it lasts," I call out to him.

"Yes, yes I am," he replies, grinning and reaching for his beer bottle. "And I'm not the only one, it seems."

He nods in the direction of an apartment block that overshadows our street. It's got those metal frames on the windows that aren't quite a balcony and aren't quite a window box. One of the windows has been thrown wide open, and there are two shirtless teenage guys sitting on the ledge with their legs dangling out, sunning themselves.

"You do it better," I tell him. "And safer. I can see one of them falling from that window if they aren't careful."

"Feckin' eegits," Barry agrees, and returns his attention to the radio.

Just as I'm stepping out of the shower a half hour later, my phone starts to ring, the number of an agency I sometimes work for flashing on the screen.

"Hello," I answer, multi-tasking talking on the phone and rubbing my hair dry with a towel.

"Hey, Jade," Jonathan, the HR guy who used to get me regular temp gigs before I started working at the concert hall, greets me. "Please tell me you're free tonight."

"Free as a bird. Have you got some work for me?" I ask with interest. Last-minute agency jobs usually pay decent money, and I could do with a little cash injection. I'm expecting my electricity and gas bills any day now.

"I might. You've got silver service experience, haven't you?"

"I do indeed. I've been a server in a couple of hotels over the years."

"Yes, I thought I saw that on your resume. Right, well, we're providing the manpower for a charity event tonight. It's a dinner-auction affair, and one of our servers has had to pull out. Can you fill in for her? It pays one-fifty for the whole evening."

"I'll be there with bells on. Where's it being held?"

Jonathan fills me in on the details, and I memorise them before hanging up and throwing a sandwich together for lunch. I'm not scheduled to be at the concert hall until tomorrow evening, so I can afford to work late tonight. There's a knock at the door, and since I'm the only one home I go to answer it.

Pete's scumbag "friend" Damo and two other boys in their late teens stand on the doorstep.

"Pete's at school," I tell them, and go to close the door. Damo sticks his foot out to stop me.

"You'll tell him we've been looking for him, yeah?"

The aggression in his voice raises my hackles, so I kick his foot away from the door. "Aren't you a little old to be hanging around with Pete?" I ask, because sometimes I can't help myself but to invite trouble.

Damo narrows his eyes to slits, looking outraged that I just kicked his foot. "You ever do that again, and I'll put a brick through your window," he threatens me.

Okay, now it's on. I step forward, and all three boys back up a bit. Yeah, I can be scary when I want to be, and there's something about the mother hen in me that makes me get all protective when it comes to my younger siblings. People harming my family is a big trigger for me.

"You break my window, and I'll break your face. Now fuck off, and don't call here again."

Damo's threatening stance falters for a split second, but he quickly puts it back in place before his two friends notice. "Just tell Pete we were looking for him," he spits, and then nods to the others to follow him before stomping away.

Yep, I definitely won that round. I'll keep that drug-dealing piece of shit away from my brother if it's the last thing I do.

A couple of hours later Pete arrives home just as I'm placing a lasagne and salad on the table for his dinner. He looks exhausted and, if I'm not mistaken, a little bit haunted. It concerns me. Dropping down into a seat, he lets out a long sigh and then starts silently eating. I lean against the side of the fridge, studying him.

"Damo and two of his friends came knocking for you earlier," I say, and watch his reaction.

His eyes widen, and he seems flustered when he responds, "Did they say what they wanted?"

"Nope."

"Okay."

"Has something happened?"

He swallows a mouthful of food. "Uh, not really."

"Are you in trouble?"

"Nah." He's quiet for a long time before he says, "I might have seen something that freaked me out."

"Like…?"

He scratches the spot below his ear. "This guy Damo was dealing to wouldn't pay up, said he gave him shit coke, so Damo beat him."

"And you were freaked? This is the world you said you wanted to live in, Pete."

"I'm not talking about a few slaps, Jade. He beat him so badly he had to be hospitalised. Fucking hell, I can still see the lad's face…all bloody, all wrong." His voice starts to choke up, and then tears are running down his cheeks. Shit. I hurry to his side and throw my arms around his shoulders. Sometimes it feels like he's growing up so fast, but really, he's still just a kid.

"It's okay, it's okay," I murmur as I hold him to me. "I'll get Alec to have a word with Damo, tell him to stay away from you."

Pete's head comes up as he wipes at his tears. "You think he'll listen?"

I grin. "Have you seen your brother these days? Of course that skinny little shit will listen."

Pete nods and seems to calm down. Then he gets embarrassed when he realises he'd just been crying in front of his big sister. He pulls away, clearing his throat, and then finishes his food. I go upstairs to get ready for the agency gig, a feeling of relief washing over me. Pete is finally seeing sense that Damo is bad news.

The charity event is in the Convention Centre on the quays. I've always thought it was a strange-looking building, kind of like a gigantic glass cylinder tilted on an axis. Or a gigantic glass cock tilted on an axis. Whatever architect designed it must have been smoking some strong shit at the time.

When I arrive I'm immediately handed a uniform consisting of a white blouse, tight black trousers, and a black waistcoat. The guy who gives it to me quickly runs me through the proceedings for the night, which will consist of a three-course meal for a thousand people and a jewellery auction with pieces donated from a well-known Irish designer to raise money for breast cancer. There'll also be some high-profile bands playing on stage.

Normally when I work on these sorts of events I'm put in charge of a couple of tables, but since this is all so high-end there's a server for each one. Mine is close to the stage and seats eight people. Before any of the food is served, we have to bring out the drinks. There's a choice of red or white wine, pink Prosecco, or champagne.

Back in my drinking days pink Prosecco was my celebratory tipple for birthdays and such. Now it holds absolutely no appeal.

My heart stutters when I'm carrying the first tray to my assigned table and I clock a handsome profile and a dark head of hair. Shane. He's sitting with his mother and a few others. His dad's not there, though.

Of all the awkward coincidences.

It suddenly makes sense. The charity Mirin runs must be the one holding this event.

Shane doesn't seem happy to be here. In fact, he appears downright miserable. He looks up as I approach and is taken aback when he sees me, but then a big warm smile shapes his perfect lips. That smile is what gives me the courage to keep going.

He doesn't say anything while I place the drinks on the table, and Mirin is caught up chatting with an older man beside her so she doesn't notice me. Women like her rarely take note of the people who serve them.

Shane selects a glass of champagne and knocks back a long gulp. For whatever reason, he looks like he needs it. I stand close to him, and his voice is low when he asks in amusement, "Just how many jobs do you actually have?"

My mouth curves in a barely there smile when I reply just as low, "I work events like these occasionally."

Subtly he reaches for my hand out of sight of everyone else and gives it a quick squeeze. "You don't know how glad I am that you're here. Someone must have taken pity on me, because I really needed to see a friendly face."

I give him a curious look, not understanding what's going on with him. It's only as I'm stepping away to return to the kitchen that I recognise the couple sitting at a table one row down and everything clicks into place.

She's even prettier in real life, Mona Campbell, perched beside Justin, her new husband-to-be.

I can't believe Shane's mother invited them, knowing how they went behind Shane's back. I wonder if she even told him they were going to be here, or if she just sprang it on him when he arrived. What a thorough-going bitch.

I almost gasp when Mona rises from her seat in her floor-length evening gown, a gown that is doing nothing to disguise her small rounded baby bump. Ah, shit. That's not something Shane needed to see. Not only is his ex-fiancée moving on with his ex-best friend, but she's also very much pregnant with Justin's baby.

I feel like putting aside all my professionalism, running to him, and giving him a massive hug in front of everyone. But I don't do that. Perhaps I'll be able to catch him in private at some point. Twenty minutes later the starter is served, consisting of seared scallops and a fancy pear sauce. When I put Shane's plate in front of him I allow my body to brush off his, a small token of my moral support. Then I'm back in the kitchen, rushing around the massive, humid room helping to get everything ready for the next course.

The one thing I don't like about these kinds of events is that there isn't much camaraderie among the staff, since not everyone knows each other and we're all in such a frazzle to get things done on time.

With the starter finished, I collect the empty plates and realise just how self-absorbed Mirin is because she still hasn't recognised me. Shane's on what must be his third or fourth glass of champagne already. I put my hand to his shoulder for a second, leaning down and murmuring, "I know why you're miserable, but getting drunk isn't going to help. Don't let the bitch get to you." I pause and amend, "Either of them." Because his mother is just as much of a "see you next Tuesday" for inviting Mona as Mona is for cheating.

I'm just about to move on when Shane catches my hand to stop me. "I'm leaving once the meal is done. My dad's out of town on business so I told Mum I'd be her escort, but I can't take much more of this. Come home with me?"

Looking into his pained eyes, I'm not sure what he's asking, but his expression is so agonised that I find myself nodding and whispering, "Okay." I probably won't get paid the full amount if I leave early, but Shane needs me, and I find myself unable to refuse him right now.

A few minutes after I serve the dessert, a chocolate fondant that makes my mouth water just looking at it, I make a quick run to the bathroom. After doing my business, I return to my post just in time to see Shane standing so abruptly from his chair it falls over behind him, making a loud clatter in the process. Then with an angry look on his face he marches right out of the room. Not knowing what else to do, I follow him.

When I reach him he's pacing back and forth in a quiet corridor. He looks up at my approach and his expression is agonised. A moment later he lets out a long sigh.

"Are you okay?" I ask, stepping up to him and putting a hand on his shoulder. He stops pacing and raises his lowered head to me. His eyes are full of stark emotion.

Startled, I take his hand and lead him to the end of the corridor, where we won't be disturbed. Then I pull him into a hug and whisper, "What's wrong?"

"She's fucking pregnant," he grits out, his face nestled in the crook of my neck.

"I know," I murmur, rubbing soothing circles into his back to comfort him.

What he says next almost knocks me off my feet. "She aborted our baby, and now she's having one with him." His words are so choked that I'm not sure I heard them at first. Jesus, no wonder he's so fucked up.

I put both my hands on either side of his face so that his sad eyes meet mine. "Hey, do you want to get out of here?"

His quick, fervent nod is all the answer I need. Keeping a hold of his hand, I take him with me as I go to get my things from the temporary locker I was given when I arrived.

The locker room is empty, since all the staff are busy working the event, so I manage to slip out of my uniform and back into my own clothes quickly. I'll probably get an angry phone call from the agency tomorrow for my disappearing act, but Shane needs me.

We leave through the back exit so as to avoid his mother and then catch a cab back to his place. His house is quiet when we get there, and I sit him on the couch in the living room before going to make some tea.

When life kicks you upside the head, a hot beverage is always a much-welcome comfort.

Returning to the living room, I place two steaming mugs on the coffee table and sit down beside Shane.

"That's what messed my head up the most, you know," he says quietly. He didn't speak a word the whole journey here, almost like he was stuck in a trance since he told me about Mona having an abortion in the empty corridor. "For months I could feel her drifting away from me, so when I found her with Justin I was angry, but I wasn't exactly surprised. A few days later I found a crumpled receipt in her coat pocket for a cheque made out to an abortion clinic. I confronted her, and she admitted to being pregnant with my kid several months previously. She said she wasn't ready for a baby and knew I'd never agree to getting rid of it, so she kept it a secret." He stops and lets out a joyless laugh. "She had the gall to tell me that what I didn't know couldn't hurt me."

Bringing my hand up, I brush his hair away from his forehead in an affectionate gesture. "People are shit. The day you stop expecting decency from them is the day you'll free yourself from getting hurt."

He shakes his head and turns his body, shifting closer to me. His anger has long since dried up, but I can tell seeing Mona tonight is still affecting him. "Not all people are shit. You're not. You're the opposite of shit."

I grin at him and make a joke. "Why, thanks, Shane. That's one of the nicest things anybody's ever said to me."

A full, throaty laugh escapes him, and my heart lifts to see him smiling. "You're so fucking cool, you know that?" he says, running his hand through my ponytail.

"Ah, so many compliments tonight. Stop, or I'll get a big head."

"You're like a salve to all the crap I've been through. I sit and have a conversation with you, and poof, all the pain is gone."

"Well, I'm happy to be able to help."

We fall into a silence as I lean forward and pick up my mug, taking a long, hot gulp. My other hand has somehow found its way into Shane's, and he's tracing circles with his thumb on the inside of my wrist. I place the mug back down and turn to look at him. His hair is a little dishevelled from stressfully running his hands through it one too many times. His beautiful gaze is shining and intense, focused in on me like I'm the bull's-eye on a dart board.

"I like how you've been coming to play for me on the street," I say, breaking the quiet.

His smile grows wide. "Who says I was playing to you?"

I give him a look. "Weren't you?"

"Maybe."

"It's kind of becoming the highlight of my day," I blurt out honestly.

"Hearing me play is the highlight of your day?" he asks in genuine surprise, like he thought maybe I was just tolerating his eccentricities or something.

"I didn't mean to admit that," I reply bashfully, and focus on the movement of his thumb at my wrist. "But yeah. It's nice. Kind of makes me feel special to have a virtuoso come and perform just for me."

He sucks in a breath, his thigh moving and nudging against mine. "Explain to me why we're just friends again?"

"Shane…"

"No, seriously. I know I'm not the only one who's feeling this."

I stare up into his eyes, some kind of recklessness forming inside me. I want to feel every inch of him, want to put my lips on all his gorgeous skin.

So the next thing that comes out of my mouth is probably going to be the biggest regret of my life, but I can't seem to stop myself. My voice barely a whisper, I ask, "That arrangement you suggested, is it still on the table?"

Sixteen

The grin that spreads across Shane's face makes my pores tingle. It's almost…predatory. His thumb moves from my wrist up and along the veins on the inside of my arm.

One eyebrow raised, he murmurs deeply, "I thought you said you couldn't handle it?"

With my free hand I gesture between the two of us. "I can't, but I can't handle *this,* either. So why deprive ourselves when it's going to hurt either way?"

Shane sucks on his lower lip. "I don't want to hurt you."

"And I don't want to hurt you."

"Then we won't hurt each other," he says with a determined look in his eyes as his face hovers inches from mine.

"Okay, it's a deal, then," I say backing up a bit, thrusting my hand out to him and laughing out of nervousness. "Nobody gets hurt, and we both get to enjoy some incredible no-strings sex."

Shane doesn't breathe a word while he shakes my hand, his gaze growing dark with thoughts and need. In the back of my mind I know what I've just said is the most untrue statement of the century, but I need to fool myself into believing this is a solid plan. Kind of like when you convince yourself to eat that slice of chocolate cake, since you're going to be starting a diet in the morning; in a tiny corner of your mind you know the diet's about as likely to happen as Brad Pitt walking through the door and declaring his undying love.

With my hand in his, Shane pulls me into his body so that our chests slam together and we're both breathing quickly. He leans forward and brushes his lips over mine, just a whisper of a touch, and yet I feel it right in my core.

"I didn't say we have to start right away," I rasp as he trails those lips from my mouth over my cheek to the line of my jaw.

"Just a taste," Shane mumbles against my skin, and my entire body breaks out into goose bumps. "I want to taste you. I've been thinking about it almost every day since we first met."

A small chuckle escapes me as I watch him kiss his way down my neck. "You little pervert."

His hand glides along the outside of my thigh to the inside before skimming up to the apex of my legs. He rubs lightly through my jeans and says in a voice that's deliciously lustful, "I want to suck on your clit until you scream."

Wow. My sophisticated concert violinist has a dirty mouth, and it thrills me.

"Jesus, Shane…"

His hand comes up, and his thumb brushes over my bottom lip before dipping inside my mouth. I gasp and then touch my tongue to it, sucking hard. He groans.

"You're beautiful," he murmurs, his eyes on me the entire time.

"I'm a sure thing, you know. You don't have to butter me up with flattery," I joke, my voice strained.

He stares at me for a long time, slowly shaking his head. "You're the most gorgeous thing I've ever seen," he says firmly, each word enunciated sharp and precise, like he's sending a message. Reaching up, he unbuttons my shirt to expose my bra. He trails his hand over the lace before pinching my nipple through the fabric. I let out a little whimper, and he grins full-on, moving down to undo my jeans. I lie on his couch, transfixed, unable to bring my attention away from him as he casually undresses me. It's like he's been doing it all his life.

Soon my jeans are gone, thrown onto the floor. He licks a line across my abdomen, nipping and kissing my belly. I gasp softly when really I want to scream for him to take everything off me. I'm hardly taking part in this at all, too fascinated by how sexy he is, so focused and attentive. I think it's true what they say about the shy ones being the complete opposite in the bedroom.

Turn off the lights and turn off the shyness.

Shane's got this subtle confidence in his sexuality that can't be taught. I'm totally at his mercy. His teeth graze the edge of my knickers, teasing, hinting at the fact that he could probably rip them off me if he wanted to. Instead he slowly pulls them down, exposing me inch by agonising inch. I'm breathing like I just ran five miles, heaving, obsessed with how his golden eyes drink me in.

He kisses my mound, and for a second I'm relieved I keep everything neat and tidy down there. Then I'm not thinking at all. I'm only feeling his tongue as it flicks over my folds, soft and feather light, almost like a question. His warm hands push my legs farther apart, and he looks up at me, gaze hooded, as he goes deeper. Every time he licks me, so carefully, so skilled, a spark of pleasure rips through my system.

Groaning, he parts my lips and finds my clit, rubbing circles into it with his thumb and making my body shake. Then he moves fast, his mouth going to the tiny bundle of nerves and sucking hard. Before I can think another thought, he thrusts two fingers deep inside me, and I let out a moan so loud I actually feel like blushing. Me. Blushing. Has the world turned upside down?

How have I survived this far without knowing the pleasure of having this man worship me with his mouth?

"You're...really...fucking good at this," I gasp, letting my fingers drift into his hair.

I can see him smiling, but his mouth is far too indisposed for a response. His fingers start to pump hard and fast as he begins to swirl his tongue around my clit. Jesus Christ, but he knows what he's doing.

His other hand moves up my body to squeeze one of my breasts. I practically cry when he drags his mouth from me and pulls me up to sit.

He seems to see the question in my disappointed gaze because he replies, "We need this off, Bluebird."

I understand then as he unclips my bra and throws it onto the floor with the rest of my things. I'm suddenly aware that he hasn't removed a single item of his own clothing, so I make quick work of disposing of his shirt. Before I get the chance to take off his trousers, he's moving back down my body, his mouth doing all sorts of amazing things to my most intimate parts. He reaches up and pinches my nipple, rolling it between his thumb and forefinger. Then he begins moulding my breast with his hand.

"How are you so good at this?" I breathe as a fire starts to build in me. I'm going to come in seconds if he just keeps circling my clit with his tongue. Unfortunately, I was dumb enough to ask a question.

He comes up for air and replies low, "Maybe I spent a little too much time imagining doing it to you."

Okay, that was the best answer. The. Best. Answer.

I moan. "Don't stop."

His grin is intolerable, and then his tongue is on me, his fingers are inside me, and I feel like I'm going to explode. I hold onto his hard shoulder with one hand, my other hand gripping a cushion so tight I might rip a hole in it. It's a good job cushions don't need to breathe; otherwise, I'd be suffocating the thing.

"You feel amazing," he says as he licks me, his words vibrating through my sex.

I whimper as I feel myself reach my climax, pleasure ripping me apart. I've never come so hard with a guy. Never. It's almost like this has been building up for days. Being around each other and not touching at all is like the most torturous kind of foreplay.

He keeps on tonguing me, even after I've come, and it's so intense that I have to beg him to stop. He kisses his way up my body until he reaches my mouth and starts nipping at my lips. I pull his mouth to mine and kiss him deeply, needing to taste him. It's a heady sensation, the mix of the two of us.

He hooks one arm around my back and the other under my legs, and then unexpectedly lifts me from the couch. I slide my arms around his neck and hold on.

"Where are we going?" I whisper.

"My room. You're tired."

"I should go home…"

"You're not going anywhere. We're sleeping, Bluebird. Just sleeping."

"That's kind of crossing a boundary, isn't it?"

He shushes me, and then we've climbed the stairs and he's kicking open the door to his room. The walls are bare, and the bed is gigantic. He puts me down on the mattress and flicks on a low lamp. There's a wardrobe, a chest of drawers, and a tonne of book shelves. In the far corner there's a small couch with a bunch of sheet music spread messily across it.

I stay sitting on the bed, stark naked, not knowing what to do. He wants me to stay over, but I'm not sure that's a good idea. I mean, what are the rules here? Do I return the favour by going down on him? Do I leave early in the morning before he wakes up so there's no awkwardness? I've always felt that ideas seem much better at night than they do in the harsh light of day.

Will I regret this tomorrow? Probably.

Do I want to stay here now and let him hold me as I sleep? Most definitely.

God, this is such a shady situation with way too many grey areas. He pulls back the covers and drags me under with him, curling his body around mine, his arm tight around my middle. He traces shapes over my skin, the soothing touch causing me to close my eyes and drift to sleep.

When I wake up it's morning, bright light streaming through the window. Groaning, I stretch out my body, remembering where I am and the exact events that brought me here. Yep, hasty decisions definitely seem better at night. A feeling of dread is forming in my gut, not because I didn't enjoy what happened between me and Shane, but because I enjoyed it *too* much.

We took to each other like we'd been together forever, not like it was only the second time we'd been intimate.

I'm alone in the bed, but I can hear someone pottering around down in the kitchen. I look about the room and remember that I left all my clothes downstairs, so I grab a clean T-shirt of Shane's from one of his drawers and throw it on. It hits me mid-thigh, which is just enough coverage to be considered decent.

When I go in search of him, I find him sitting at the table, topless, a cup of coffee in front of him and a violin in his lap. His back is turned to me, so he doesn't know I'm there yet. The muscles in his shoulders move as he puts new strings on his instrument. The movement sort of holds me transfixed. I never imagined this would be a strenuous activity, but by the looks of it, it is. His muscles tense up and release as he works.

I step fully into the room and walk around the table to sit across from him. His hands pause, setting the violin aside, and his eyes come up to meet mine.

"Morning," I whisper, feeling strange about being here. Though by the way he's eating me up with his gaze, I'm thinking he's not feeling the same way.

"Is that my T-shirt?" he asks, smiling widely.

"Yeah, we left my stuff in the living room, remember?" I reply, folding my arms over my chest and shifting uncomfortably as my stomach chooses that exact moment to rumble.

Shane chuckles. "Do you want some breakfast?"

I stand up and nod, needing something to do to keep my nerves at bay. His eyes follow me as I walk to the fridge and open it. "Sure. What have you got?"

I spot a carton of eggs, some bread, milk, butter, the usual mainstays. Then I feel his breath hit the back of my neck and the warmth of his body tingle along my spine. His hand slides across my belly and then dips down under the hem of the T-shirt I'm wearing. My thighs drift apart slightly as I gasp and he cups me right between the legs. His lips brush over my neck, causing goose bumps to scurry down my spine. He caresses my sex, and I'm instantly wet for him, so full of need.

A surge of arousal rushes through me, and then all of a sudden I'm taking the lead.

I turn around swiftly and push him over to where the kitchen opens up into a sun room extension. I push him again, down onto a narrow sofa before straddling his hips. He watches me as he lies there, mouth open, chest heaving. His eyes glitter in the sunlight, and I'm so turned on I don't even care that we're in a room made of glass for all the world to see.

I reach down and try to get the fly of his jeans open. I have absolutely no underwear on, grinding my sex against him. Once I have them open I pull him free, practically shaking as I run my hand down his length. He's perfectly long and thick, just what I need.

Raising myself up, I position his cock right at my entrance and then slowly lower my body down all the way. I can feel every inch of him as he fills me, and a loud moan erupts from the back of my throat. Shane lets out a guttural groan, his hands fisting at my hips. Then I start to ride him, pushing myself up and down on his cock slowly, seeking pleasure from his body and giving him a show in the process.

He grips the hem of my T-shirt and drags it up over my head, my long hair falling through it and my breasts bobbing free. His eyes are glued to my chest as I ride him, and I feel his cock hit every sweet spot inside me. If I thought standing up was good, it had nothing on being on top. This is the deepest he can possibly get, and it's maddening. All my inhibitions fall by the wayside as my sounds fill the room.

"Incredible," he rasps. "We fit so good together, Bluebird." His hand moves up along my hip to my ribcage.

Those words momentarily break my lusty haze. They're too romantic, have too much meaning, and they make this something it's not supposed to be. Now I'm no longer lost in the sex. Unprotected sex, might I add. Completely my fault, too, since I practically jumped on him without thinking of the consequences. I'm on the pill, so pregnancy's not an issue. Diseases aren't really an issue, either. We're both mature and responsible enough to keep track of those kinds of things.

It's the intimacy that's the problem.

Being skin on skin. No barriers. It creates an emotional, almost soul-deep connection that's not supposed to happen between friends with an "arrangement." But God, it feels so good to have him inside me, to be able to feel all his hot, silky skin, that I almost don't care about the implications. Almost.

He reaches up and grips my neck, pulling my mouth down to his for a deep, earth-shattering kiss. Now I'm not the one riding him anymore; the pleasure is so much that my body has gone limp. My bones have turned to mush. Now he's moving his hips from his position below and pumping up into me.

"Babe," he murmurs as I drag my mouth from his so I can bury my face in his neck. It's warm here, and nice. This way I don't have to look into his beautiful, deep eyes and feel things I'm not supposed to be feeling. Hands clutching my hips again, he starts to pump faster, and I rise up, all of my insides tightening with impending release. Now we move together, fast and frenzied, coaxing each other to that perfect place where for seconds that feel like hours there isn't a single thought in your head, there's only the feeling of coming.

So in tune with one another's bodies, we orgasm together, my walls pulsing around his cock, milking him dry. He swears profusely under his breath, because swearing is the only way to express how amazing this feels. I swear, too, because I know this is bad, really fucking bad.

Anything that feels this perfect needs to be vocalised with a couple shits and fucks.

We stare at each other for a long time, me above and him below. Absolutely connected, having a conversation without words.

Yeah, we're both completely screwed.

Once my breathing has started to slow down, I lower my body to his and wrap my arms around his neck. His hands pet at my hair, as though trying to reassure me that everything is fine. Fine. Fine. Fine. I drift off for a while, half asleep, half not, and then finally I move off him.

"Can I use your shower?" I ask.

He nods. "Go ahead. I'll cook us some eggs while you're showering."

I grin. "I thought you couldn't cook."

"It's more of a 'not having time to cook' issue than not being able to. I get by," he says, and then pats me playfully on the bottom.

I go into the living room to collect my discarded clothes from last night. Upstairs I turn on the shower and then step under the hot spray, almost feeling sad that I have to wash Shane's smell off me.

And that right there is why this whole thing is one big old bad idea.

Can I back out of the arrangement now that it's been… consummated? Perhaps since we've fucked each other's brains out a second time, the need will have dissipated. Though even as I'm thinking this I can already feel the hunger for him re-fuelling. This is scary, and not something that's going to go away after one or two sessions.

Sometimes I wish my brain didn't always have to warn me about things. Stupid people seem to live such easy, carefree lives.

Stepping out of the shower, I dry myself off with a towel and wrap up my wet hair. Then, like any decently curious human being, I go snooping. God forbid I actually ask for a tour. No, I'd rather be nosy in private, thanks very much.

It's a four-bedroom house, but only two of the rooms have actual beds in them. The other two are sort of office slash practice rooms, full of stuff I assume he's accumulated over the years. There are lots of music books. You know, those old thick cream ones with pages upon pages of sheet music and music theory inside. There are also several violins, some shiny and perfect, hanging in cases on the walls, and others battered and bruised. Clearly these are the ones he practices with. He doesn't have to care about breaking cheaper instruments.

For some reason, I see more life and spirit in the cheap violins than I do in the pristine ones in their sealed protective cases. On a stool there's a bow with half the fibres broken off. I pick it up and run my hands along the snapped horse hair, imagining the demons Shane worked out as he sawed it into the violin so hard it broke.

Because I know he has demons. On the outside he's like his polished, perfect violins, but on the inside lies a battered and broken one. I need to know what happened to him. He told me about Mona and the abortion, but I sense more. It's probably hypocritical of me to want to know, since I've got demons I never plan on revealing to him.

In the corner of the room there's a black leather trunk; the lid is open, and inside there are a bunch of paintings in fancy frames. He must not have had the chance to hang them yet, which makes me wonder just how long he's been living here.

There's a sort of half-finished feel to the place, so I'm thinking not that long.

Pulling up a seat, I flick through the paintings, admiring them. Most of them are modern art, a bunch of shapes and colours on the canvas that mean something different to every person who looks at them.

I gasp out loud then, because the next painting I come across is eerily familiar. Before I've even pulled it out of the trunk, I recognise the brush strokes.

They belong to my mother.

Then, when I've pulled it out and laid it on my lap, something strange catches in my throat. How on earth does he have this?

The picture shows a city street, pedestrians walking hurriedly by, and in the background there's me. The Blue Lady. Mum did lots of paintings of me when she was alive and this is just one of them, but the question is, when and how did Shane acquire it?

The feeling of betrayal is an ugly emotion.
Sometimes it's so virulent that it makes you want to die.
He stood on the edge of the famous Reichsbrücke.
Sucking in what he envisaged would be his very last breath, he jumped.

***

Healing a broken body is easier than healing a broken heart.
His limbs had long since knit themselves back together, but the silly organ still ached.
His only solace was the painting on the wall, the one of the woman in blue.
She gave him hope.

Seventeen

Heading downstairs on shaky legs, I carry the painting with me under my arm. Shane is busy setting plates on the table, so he doesn't immediately notice what I've got. I prop the painting on a chair and sit down, leaning my chin on my hand and looking at him speculatively.

Shane turns from the cooker with the hot pan full of scrambled eggs. He dishes them onto the plates and then pauses when he sees me. His eyes travel from me to the painting and then back again. He swallows, turns around, and puts the pan back on the cooker. Wiping his hands off on a dish towel, he comes and take his seat on the other side of the table.

He picks up his fork, scoops up some eggs, and shoves them in his mouth. A minute later he nods to the painting. "Where did you find that?"

If I'm not mistaken, his voice sounds hesitant.

"I was looking in your practice room, saw your art collection and started browsing. You'll understand my surprise to find one of my mum's pictures there."

I start eating now, too, watching his reaction all the while. It suddenly makes sense why he took an interest in Mum's art when he visited my house.

"I've had that piece for a while," he says, voice low.

"You mean from before you knew me?" I ask in genuine surprise. For some reason I had it in my head that he got his hands on it after we'd met.

He nods. "Yeah, that's why I was watching you that first night. I felt like I'd walked into a dream. There you were, the blue woman from my painting."

A small smile tugs at my lips. "I thought you were just drunk."

"I was a little tipsy," he admits. "Otherwise I probably wouldn't have been so blatant about staring at you."

I bob my head and eat some more of the breakfast he made for me, a strange fizzing sensation in my belly. This is just kind of weird. Weird, but also a little wonderful. "So where did you get it?"

He raises a brow. "The painting?"

"Yeah."

"It's from my parents' house," he explains. "It was hanging on the wall in the spare bedroom, and I'd been staying there for a while after, well, after my entire life fell apart, thanks to Mona. I don't know why, but that painting was a huge comfort to me."

"Wow," I whisper, feeling odd to discover that a man I didn't even know had been deriving comfort from a picture of me. It makes me wonder who else might have my mum's paintings. She was pretty prolific, so there could be hundreds, if not thousands of them in circulation around the country, even around the world.

"I asked my dad where he got it from, because I loved the style and I wanted to buy another. There's this peaceful quality about your mother's work, kind of like she's trying to tell the world not to fret on things," Shane continues. "Like she's telling you everything will be all right in the end."

I get that. There's always been a warmth in Mum's art, almost like a maternal affection for the world. The way she depicted things showed her heart.

"And what did your dad say?"

"He didn't know. So I asked Mum, and she couldn't remember where they'd gotten it from, either. She thought maybe it had been given to her as present at some point. It was a little mystery, and I was kind of disappointed that I'd never be able to find another work like it. Then I was out that night and I saw you, my painting come to life. I don't normally approach strangers like that, but I just had to know you."

"That's sweet," I tell him, smiling. "And you took it from your parents' place when you left?"

"Yeah, it was like a comfort blanket. I couldn't let it go."

I frown. "How long had you been staying with them?"

His eyes shift away from mine. "A while."

"How much of a while, Shane?" I press.

There's a long pause before he finally answers. "Six months."

My jaw drops. "That's a long while." I stop talking then, considering what to say next. "At the photo shoot when you were off getting changed, your mum said something weird to me."

His face grows serious. "What did she say?"

"She said you were vulnerable. What did she mean by that?"

"I don't know."

"Shane."

"What? I said I don't know. Now just leave it."

"Fine," I reply, not liking his snappy response. I stand from the table and carry my plate over to the sink. "I'm going home now. I have a shift later on."

I don't look back at him as I turn to leave the room, but he quickly catches up to me. He grabs me by the waist, hauling me back against his chest. "Don't run off. I didn't mean to get pissed. It's just that she had no right to say that to you."

I turn in his arms so that I'm facing him. "She was warning me away from you."

"That sounds like Mum all right."

My hand trails from his chest up to his neck, resting just under the line of his jaw. "If you have issues, Shane, I need to know about them. This thing between us could go badly wrong if we're not completely transparent with one another."

I search his face, and what I see is turmoil. If he has mental health problems, which is what I got from Mirin telling me he was vulnerable, then I need to know about them. I need to know where to tread lightly.

"Right after I found out about Mona's abortion, I did something stupid. I was at my lowest, and you have to understand that this wasn't typical behaviour for me. It just felt like everything in my life was a lie." His words are hushed, quiet, like he's ashamed or something.

"I know all about stupid, Shane. Believe me, nothing you've done could hold a candle to the stupid I've committed over the years."

"I jumped off a bridge in Vienna. On purpose," he says, abruptly cutting me off.

Whatever words I was about to say next immediately die on my tongue. Suicide. Shit. There were times, particularly in my mid to late teens, when I would have happily ended my own life, but somehow things never got extreme enough for me to go there.

Perhaps I thought death would be too easy, not punishment enough.

I pull him into me and wrap my arms tight around him. "Don't you ever feel like you can't tell me stuff," I whisper to him soothingly. His body melts into mine with what feels like relief. Fucking hell. This man. All I want to do is fix him. Is it even possible for a girl this scarred to fix a broken boy?

"There's no judgement here. Okay?" I ask, pulling away slightly so I can see his face.

He stares back at me, all beautiful and sad. "Okay, Bluebird."

I smile and rub his arms, coaxing a smile from him in return. "Are you playing tonight?"

"Yeah, Beethoven and Mendelsohn," he answers, seeming happy for the change of subject.

"Cool. You want me to come see you in the dressing rooms before you go on?"

He gives me a firm nod. "I always want you to come see me, Jade."

There's some meaning in that sentence that I try not to read too much into. I press my lips softly to his and then go to grab the rest of my things. He offers to drive me home, but I say no, telling him I have to run a few errands on the way. I do have some things to do, but I also need some space from him. Some room to clear my head and figure out what exactly we're doing.

After what I just found out, I can now confirm that although his mother is a bit of a bitch, she was right about one thing. Shane is vulnerable. Never mind about my feelings getting hurt and me turning back to alcohol — I need to consider his feelings, too.

I want to be respectful of him, let him know that I'll never treat him the way Mona did. But how do I tell him that when we're not supposed to be anything more than fuck buddies? Even though it's a liminal situation, I like where we are right now. I like not having to completely define things and just go with what we feel. Touching each other when we want to be touched, and not touching when we don't want to.

When I arrive home I'm greeted by Alec's smug face as he sits in the kitchen, reading the newspaper.

"Well, look who it is. My sister, the dirty stop out. Where were you all night?"

He puts the paper down and folds his arms. I give him a long-suffering look, relieved that Pete and April aren't around. The two of them aren't exactly children anymore, but I always feel a little bit guilty when I stay out all night. Still, I did text Alec to let him know I wouldn't be back so that he'd stay in and keep an eye on them.

Not that it happens often. In fact, this is the first time it's happened in a long time.

"None of your business," I tell him. "Just like it's none of my business what you get up to in your own time, Alec."

"Okay, so you're gonna be like that, eh? Anyway, I've been meaning to ask you, you wouldn't happen to have that Avery chick's number, would you?"

I raise both eyebrows at once while shaking my head. "No, I wouldn't. And I thought I told you she was off limits."

"Come on, Jade, you know that only makes me want her more," he replies with a cheeky wink.

"She's in the orchestra, Alec. I barely know her. Why on earth would I have her number?"

"Huh," he says, chewing on his lip. "Maybe I'll look her up on Facebook."

"Yeah, you do that. But don't come crying to me when it all goes belly up and she starts to get clingy."

Alec grimaces, and I let out a laugh. I knew he wouldn't like that imagery. My brother is about as commitment phobic as you can get. A typical twenty-one-year-old male who wants to sow his wild oats without any thought to the consequences.

"I'm a man, Jade. I don't cry." He pauses and amends humorously, "I might whine to you something fierce, but you'll never see me cry. Not in public, anyway."

I point a finger at him before letting Specky in from the back garden and scooping her up into my arms. "You leave that girl alone. She's done nothing to deserve you. Stick to the mean girls. At least you know they deserve it."

He chuckles. "Okay, I'll think about it. By the way, I had a word with Damo. He'll be steering clear of Pete from now on."

A quick breath escapes me. "That's good news. What did you do to him?"

Alec intertwines his fingers and flexes his hands. "I didn't have to do anything. The prick remembers when I kicked his older brother's arse a few years ago. I think that was warning enough for him. All those fuckers only pick on little boys because they know they'll be easy targets."

Stroking Specky's soft head, I ask, "Are you sure he got the message? Pete really broke down with me yesterday. I feel like shit for not realising what a hard time of it he'd been having."

Alec eyes me. "He got the message, sis. Don't you worry."

I nod, believing him, and then go upstairs to my room. I spend a couple of hours reading and lounging in bed with Specky before I have to get to work. When I arrive I find a small white envelope in my cubbyhole. I open it up and discover two tickets to a show the orchestra is playing next week. There's a note that reads:

Tickets for April as promised. I hope you'll come, too. I spoke with Lara, and she says you're not working that night. Been thinking of you all day.

Shane.

xxx.

My heart squeezes as I hold the tickets in my hand. I'm not sure if April still remembers she was promised them, since she hasn't asked. That probably means there's some other guy on the scene for her to focus her attentions on.

My shift is a busy one, but a couple of hours in I get a break and manage to slip off to the dressing rooms. The orchestra had a rehearsal earlier, so a lot of the musicians are still hanging around for the evening concert. Shane's sitting in his spot, a book open on his lap as he sinks his teeth into an apple.

Memories from last night flood my senses. And yeah, I'm kind of jealous of the apple.

Like before, I slide my bottom up onto the table in front of him, and he brings his attention from the book to me. He looks pleased to see me as a handsome smile shapes his mouth. I take a sip from the peppermint tea I'm drinking in a paper cup I snagged from the staff room.

We don't say a word, simply staring at each other in the same silent communication that's becoming something of a habit. Close by someone's streaming music from a radio, the faint melody of "Cosmic Love" by Florence + the Machine in my ears, moons and stars and hearts seeping into my subconscious. A landscape of emotion.

Whichever people can actually pull off friends with benefits without their feelings getting involved, I lift my hat off to those heartless fuckers, because I'm failing catastrophically.

Shane pulls his chair forward and runs his hands up my legs, stopping mid-thigh.

"Thanks for the tickets," I tell him, clearing my throat.

His gaze flicks to mine. "You gonna come?"

His words give me a little jolt, and the dark look in his eyes tells me meant every ounce of that double entendre.

"I hope so," I finally respond, and shift my bottom a little so that we're a fraction closer.

He sucks in a breath and starts moving his practiced hands up and down my thighs, slow and torturous. "The PR company that handles the orchestra wants me to do a television slot tomorrow morning."

"Really?" I ask excitedly. "What for?"

"It's to promote the upcoming season of shows. I'm shitting a brick, to be perfectly honest."

"Have you done TV before?"

"Once or twice in France and Germany, but that was with the quartet, and the other guys did most of the talking."

"Do they want you to do it alone?"

"No, I'd be going on with Henry White."

The name rings a bell as I reply, "That's the conductor, isn't it?"

He nods and tells me sheepishly, "One of the agents got it into her head that I'd be a big selling factor with female ticket buyers, which is why they're pushing for this."

A grin tugs at my lips. "Oh, yeah?" I reach over and fix his collar. "She might be right. Plus, Henry would be an added bonus."

He narrows his eyes, and his hands pause on my thighs. "What does that mean?"

I shrug and tease, "He's seriously hot. There's something about conductors, you know. All those vigorous movements, kind of like they're fucking the air."

Shane purses his lips, clearly trying to suppress a smile. "You're being mean. I don't want you to find anyone else in this place attractive other than me."

I lean closer so that my mouth is above his ear when I whisper, "After last night, you have nothing to worry about. *Absolutely* nothing to worry about, Shane."

"That's good to hear, but I might need a little more convincing," he says, bringing his mouth to my chin and giving me a little nip. A man a few seats away is blatantly watching our interaction, but I'm enjoying this far too much to care right now. Turning my face quickly, I catch Shane's mouth in mine and kiss him softly. Just a whisper of a kiss, a promise of more to come later.

"Will you come with me tomorrow?" he asks then, voice low.

"Would you like me to come?"

His nostrils flare. "I'd love you to."

"Then I'll come," I say, pressing my lips to his one last time before sliding off the table. "I've got to get back. Good luck with tonight's show."

"Yeah," he replies, and I can feel his eyes glued to my behind the entire time I walk away.

Eighteen

The next morning I'm woken at six-thirty by my phone ringing. Yeah, that's right, six flipping thirty in the mother-effing a.m. Peering at the screen through squinted eyes, I see it's Shane who's calling, and I remember I agreed to go with him to the television studio. What with him playing a concert last night, we didn't get a chance to hash out the details.

I was exhausted after my shift and so was he after playing, so unfortunately we didn't have the opportunity to take further advantage of our "arrangement." Hopefully, I'll get to remedy that tonight, or maybe even today if I'm lucky. I answer the phone groggily, and Shane tells me he'll be picking me up in half an hour. There's a smile in his voice; clearly he can hear how tired I am. I don't know how the people who work on those morning shows manage getting up so early every day.

I feel like a zombie as I take a quick shower and get dressed. I don't have time to dry my hair, so I twist it up in a loose bun. For an outfit I throw on a nice peach-coloured shift dress with my biker boots, mixing prim and proper with some urban decay. There's a knock at the door soon after, and Shane greets me with a smile and a takeaway coffee cup.

We're quiet on the drive, with him giving me heated looks every once in a while. Where does he get his energy from? I'll need at least two more coffees and something carb-heavy before I'll feel like the living.

"That's a nice dress," he murmurs, turning a corner into the studio parking lot.

I rub my palms on my thighs, smoothing out the material. "Thanks."

When we go inside, a runner leads us both to the wardrobe section, but Shane says he's happy to wear what he has on already. He looks good, too, in light grey slacks and a tailored white shirt. Smart casual.

Henry White, the orchestra conductor, is already there, having his salt and pepper hair fussed over by a stylist. Shane takes the seat beside him and gives him a smirk, at the same time waving off the offer of having his own hair primped. I always wondered whether the people who go on these shows are forced to endure the wardrobe and makeup part or if they have a choice. Seemingly, from what I've seen so far, they get a choice.

Opting out is probably better, because you can always tell when the person feels uncomfortable in what they're wearing and the makeup that's been piled onto their face.

Shane introduces me to Henry briefly, and then I have to excuse myself to go to the bathroom, nature calling. I almost get lost as I search through corridors that all feel identical, people rushing this way and that, busy bees. From what I can tell, the show is live on the air right now, but Shane and Henry aren't going on until the final ten minutes.

At long last I find the ladies room, and then on my way back to the hair and makeup department I see Shane walking toward me. Before I can react, he's pulling me into an empty closet and shutting the door. Then his hands are in my hair, pulling out my bun and letting it fall over my shoulders. His mouth crashes down on mine as he inches the hem of my dress up my legs.

"I couldn't wait until after," he groans against my lips, pressing the hard length of his erection to my inner thigh.

I let out a sharp hiss of breath at the feel of him, a thrill in my belly. He was so desperate for me that he's doing this here. Here! An idea pops into my head as I kiss his neck, and then I draw away from him so that I can lower myself to my knees.

In the dimly lit closet, I see Shane swallow deeply as he watches me. The only light is streaming through the cracks in the door from those fluorescent bulbs that line the windowless halls.

I rub him through his slacks and nuzzle my nose against his cock over the fabric. Then I draw down the zipper and pull him free, luxuriating in the feel of all that silky, hot hardness.

"Jade," he whispers, his voice low with need.

"Let me," I whisper back before tipping my tongue, feather light, to the head of his penis. He shudders. I take him into my mouth, just the barest inch, then draw away and dip my head to lick him from the base of his cock all the way to the tip.

"Fucking hell," he groans, his hand going to my cheek in a caress.

Opening my mouth wide, I take as much of him in as I can. I'll never be able to fit all of him. He murmurs lots of sweet things to me as I bob my head up and down slowly. I grip his thigh for support and then go deeper. His answering strangled moan tells me he likes it. Increasing my speed, I swirl my tongue around the head of his cock, and a salty drop of pre-cum hits my mouth.

His hand moves from my cheek and slips down the front of my dress, under my bra and directly to my breast, where he squeezes. I feel myself growing wet between my legs when he pinches my nipple, continually applying pressure and then releasing.

I'm sucking him fast now, the tempo increasing as my own desire builds. I'm so turned on I feel like I might come simply from the way he's pinching my nipples. He's doing it to both of them, pinching and releasing. His cock is hard and wet in my mouth. I drag my teeth along his length, just a tiny hint of pain, and I'm rewarded with a masculine groan and more pre-cum.

I lick him from the base all the way to the head one more time before I take him back inside and suck him with vigour. I'm dying for him to come into me, dying to taste him. I've never felt such a need to pleasure a man as completely as I do with Shane. He's so gorgeous, such a beautifully pained soul, and there's this deep need in me to make him feel as good as I possibly can.

One hand releases my breast and goes to my hair, fisting it right at the nape of my neck. He tugs ever so gently, and I gasp around his cock. Looking up into his eyes, I see him almost smiling, his gaze dark with desire. Every time I suck on him he pulls, and every time I can't help my muffled gasp.

Then I feel his body tense up; his cock gets so hard and big that I can hardly fit him anymore, and he cries out as warm spurts of semen fill my mouth. I keep moving my lips on him, up and down, up and down, until every last drop has been released. I swallow, and he pulls me up to stand, pushing me harshly against the door and slamming his mouth onto mine.

His hand slips beneath the hem of my dress and right inside my drenched underwear. I moan as his fingers rub at my folds, finding my clit and giving it a little pinch.

"So wet," he breathes, his tongue licking a line from my ear to my jaw.

My hand goes to his cock and rubs; he's hardening again already. His fingers whisper over my entrance before plunging inside, and I have to hold onto his shoulder to keep upright. My legs turn to jelly as he finger fucks me hard and fast. Pleasure ripples through me, and the noise of my heavy breathing fills the tiny space. The sound of his fingers slapping against my wetness echoes in the background.

"So tight," he goes on, his fingers still fucking me, his mouth doing pretty things to my neck.

"I wish we were somewhere else," I manage to whisper, because I don't want this pleasure to end. I want him to fuck me with his cock for days. Unfortunately, we're in a storage closet in a television studio with dozens of people rushing by right outside the door. So for now his fingers will have to do. Not that they're doing a bad job. No, not at all.

"I don't," he replies, his voice a hot caress. "I like it here. It's sort of forbidden. The danger of being heard, getting caught."

Well, now, isn't he just a little kinky bastard.

At this he thrusts his fingers right up into me, and I moan far too loudly. His answering chuckle makes me want to smack him, but I'm enjoying what he's doing far too much for that. His thumb starts to flick at my clit, building a fire inside me.

I gasp and moan, pressing my face into the hollow of his neck. I nuzzle his earlobe and then lightly take it between my teeth and bite. He rewards me by rubbing a hard, torturously slow circle around my clit with his thumb, his fingers inside me slowing down. I feel him hit every pleasure spot now, the lack of speed somehow making this better.

"Come for me, baby," he urges as he nuzzles my nose, encouraging my face to move from his neck so he can see my eyes again.

"I'm going to. Soon," I tell him in response, my words all shaky as everything inside me builds to what is going to be a fucking intense orgasm. Our gazes locked now, I let out a breath, and he sucks it in. Breathing each other's air. My fingernails dig into the fabric of his shirt where I'm clutching his shoulder, and I practically yelp when all of a sudden he pumps fast again, sensation shattering from my core and outward into my whole body. His thumb presses hard into my clit and I come, moaning and sighing all at once, tremors wracking my body.

I hold onto him for long moments after they've subsided, my head all in a daze. His arms go tight around my waist, and mine go around his neck. We kiss and peck at each other, not saying a word but silently acknowledging that what just happened between us was incredible. And needs to happen again — as soon as possible.

Shane moves and brings his wrist to his line of sight to check the time on his watch. Quickly, he lets out a string of swear words and untangles our bodies.

"What's wrong?" I ask, disappointed that he's pulled away from me.

"I have to get back. We're supposed to be on the air in five minutes."

Oh, shit. I step back and take a look at him, fixing his hair while he buttons his trousers. Opening the closet door, we step out into the light and hurry to the studio. Along the way Shane's phone rings in his pocket. He stops and pulls it out, staring at the screen long and hard but not answering. I study his face, wondering why he looks so pissed all of a sudden. Then he ends the call and shoves the phone back in his jacket.

A harried runner gives Shane an annoyed look when we finally show our faces. Shane takes a peek at himself in the mirror; he's still a little dishevelled after our encounter, so he straightens his clothes and fixes his hair some more.

Henry gives him a knowing smile, and then they're both being escorted to the set. I follow behind. I've never been in a studio like this before. I take in all the equipment and lights, the behind-the-scenes team making sure everything runs smoothly.

There's a male and female duo presenting this particular show, and right now they're reading off a teleprompter, doing the intro for Shane and Henry. An overweight man in his fifties who looks like he's in charge talks swiftly to the two of them in a hushed voice, and then they're both walking onto the set and shaking hands with the presenters. They take their seats on the red sofa, and the male presenter, whose name I think is Jim, asks the first questions. I stand close by on the side lines, watching and listening.

"You're both very welcome. Now, tell us a little bit about the new season that's coming up. I hear you've got lots of exciting shows happening."

Henry nods and dives straight into a practiced spiel about the orchestra's upcoming events. I hardly pay him any attention as I focus on Shane. He looks flushed, and I guess he has reason to be, given the last half an hour.

The female presenter gives him an appraising look, her expression showing that she likes what she sees. Huh.

There's a long table nearby with tea, coffee, and various pastries. Me being me, I clocked it right away as we walked onto the set. Stepping over to it, I pour myself a cup of coffee, dumping in three sachets of sugar and some milk. I also grab an iced Danish and take a big hungry bite. Free food, you have to love it.

When I settle my attention back on the show, Shane's eyes meet mine past all the cameras, and he smiles.

Wow. I'll never get used to how his smiles make my heart go *pop*.

"I hear you'll be having some fabulous musicians from the around the world coming to play with you," says the female presenter, trying to bring Shane into the conversation.

He doesn't say anything. Oh, shit, I think his nerves might be getting the better of him...or maybe he's too busy smiling at me to hear her. There's a moment of awkward silence before Henry comes to the rescue.

"That's right," he says. "Philippa Sedgwick and Ian Hughes will be with us next week."

"And is it true that Mona Campbell might even be making an appearance?" the presenter goes on.

Now she has his full attention as his face whips to her. Suddenly, my focus is no longer on Shane's gorgeous smile. It's on the brief look of horror that quickly passes over his features before he puts a casual mask back in place. Uh, what? Mona's going to be playing at the concert hall? From the looks of it, Shane had no idea about this.

Henry replies in the affirmative, and my gut sinks. The presenter brings her focus onto Shane again by asking, "Isn't it true that you and Mona have a romantic history?"

"Yes, a long time ago," Shane answers, trying to be polite.

The presenter smiles, like this is all fun and games. "I suppose sparks will be flying at the reunion."

Shane gives her a cold look. "As I said, it was a long time ago."

"Mr. Arthur and Miss Campbell will be playing Brahms' Hungarian Dance No. 1 and 5 together," says Henry.

Now Shane cuts his eyes to the conductor. Obviously, this is the first he's heard of any planned duets. Henry goes into more detail about that particular show, but I tune him out. Shane's jaw is tight with tension, and he looks like he wants to get up from the sofa and leave. Take that, live television.

Thankfully, he doesn't leave.

I will his gaze to meet mine, and when it finally does I try to channel all my calming *chi* into one look. His tension visibly slips away as he gathers himself and settles back into the interview. I wonder why the management for the orchestra has organised these duets. I only have limited knowledge, but normally it's the job of a guest musician to do solos. Then again, Shane is something of a celebrity in this world. Perhaps they wanted to drum up a bit of gossip and intrigue, sell more tickets and the like.

Soon the interview is being wrapped up, and the presenters are thanking both Shane and Henry for coming in. The two look to be having a heated discussion as they step off the set and over to a quiet corner. I move around a guy operating a camera to get closer so I can hear.

"Why the hell is this only being sprung on me now?" Shane grits out.

Henry has a beseeching look on his face. "Honestly, I thought you knew. Maybe it's a clerical error and someone forgot to contact you."

"I can't play with her. There's too much bad blood there. It'll be a disaster."

"Surely if she's agreed to do it, then there can't be that much bad blood. Like you said before, it was a long time ago, Shane."

Hmm, it can't have been that long ago. If my estimations are correct I'd say a year at most.

"This is fucking bullshit, and you know it. Someone deliberately made it so that I wasn't told until it was too late to back out. I know how this works. They think they'll have a sold-out house because people will want to come and witness the sheer fucked-upness of it all."

Shane drags a hand through his hair, and Henry gives him a small smile. "Is fucked-upness a word now?" The teasing lilt to his voice makes Shane a little less tense, and a tiny laugh escapes him.

"Shut up."

Henry clasps him around the shoulder. "You can do this, son. Believe it or not, I've had a few romantic entanglements with musicians over the years, too. I know it can be tough."

Shane looks at him and nods, seeming to come to a conclusion that he's going to struggle on. Play the duets with Mona, and get them over and done with.

I can't say I'm pleased about it, but I'm glad he's not going to let it all get to him.

Spotting me standing by a water cooler, he comes and wrap his arms around my middle, placing a kiss to the very tip of my nose. I laugh.

"I suppose you heard all that," he says, lips in my hair.

"Yeah. You handled the interview really well, despite everything. For a second I thought you were going to say some choice words to the presenter."

"Oh, there were a few on the tip of my tongue, all right. I held them in, though, for the sake of professionalism, of course."

"Of course."

At this moment the presenter in question walks by with an assistant. I still don't know her name, but she cocks an eyebrow as she takes in the two of us wrapped around each other and then keeps walking. Shane says his goodbyes to Henry and then leads me by the hand out of the studio.

I breathe in the cold, crisp air once we get outside. There's something kind of depressing about the lack of windows inside.

"Want to go for a drive?" Shane asks as he slides into the driver's seat.

I shrug. "Sure. Where do you have in mind?"

He glances at me and then straight ahead through the windscreen, tapping his hands on the steering wheel. "Let's go see the ocean."

Nineteen

I keep staring at him as he starts the car and pulls out of the parking spot. While he drives I turn on the radio, messing around with different stations until I find something I like. Once I settle on a song, I sit back and enjoy the ride.

His phone rings again, and again he ignores it, waiting until it goes to voicemail. I'm starting to become a little too curious about who he's avoiding speaking to.

Somewhere along the way, Shane reaches over with one hand and squeezes my thigh. He leaves his hand there, only moving it when he needs to before quickly putting it back. I watch him, remembering when he'd been doped up at the hospital and blurted out that watching me drive was like foreplay. I kind of get it now. His arms strain beneath his shirt when he steers, his profile beautiful and strong at the same time. It kind of makes me hot and bothered.

I look at his hand currently grasping my thigh and realise that he hasn't had the opportunity to wash it since we were in the closet. He'd done the entire live television interview with me all over him, and I'm still on him. The idea causes a little shiver to dance down my spine.

A while later we're at Bray strand, and Shane's parking again. It's not a warm day. In fact, it's kind of chilly out. It's a good thing I brought a coat. Getting out of the car, I shrug into it and button it up all the way. There are hardly any people on the beach, just one or two folks walking their dogs. There's a good deal of wind, creating waves that bash against the shore.

Right now the tide is fully in, making the sea seem that much bigger and closer. Shane leads me down to the sand, where he finds a decent spot and sits. He pulls me between his legs, my back flush with his chest, and puts both his hands over mine to keep them warm. He's wearing an expensive black wool coat, and the collar brushes off my cheek when I turn to briefly press my lips against his.

"I didn't even remember to ask if you're working today," he says, breaking the kiss as the wind sings through the air. We're nothing but spots of rust inside a giant's thin whistle.

"Not until six. Lots of time to do lots of things," I say, and give him a wink.

By the hot look that comes over him, I'm betting he knows exactly what I'm talking about. Turning his body slightly, he looks behind us at the street beyond the beach that's lined with hotels and bed & breakfasts.

His breath makes me tremble when he brings his mouth close to my ear. "We could get a room. I don't think I have the patience for the forty-minute drive it will take to get back to my place."

My eyes flicker between his when I turn to face him, a feeling of reckless abandon coming upon me. For a girl from the Liberties, renting out a hotel room just to have sex in would be considered quite lavish, extravagant, even. I mean, we're going to pay for it and not even stay the night.

"Let's do it," I whisper before kissing his perfect lips again.

Pulling me up to stand, we walk arm in arm across the road and down the street. After a few minutes we finally settle on a hotel and go inside. It doesn't take long to get a room. I try to protest when Shane hands over his credit card, but he won't hear a word about me paying. It's a good thing too, because I'm quite low on cash. I've never been with a guy who could be considered a gentleman, so it's a whole new feeling to be paid for like this.

We touch each other in subtle ways until we reach the elevator. Shane punches in the number for our floor, and then we're ascending. Hardly a second passes before he's pushing me against the wall and devouring me with his mouth, his lips, his tongue. Everything he does makes me melt, makes my body pliant, a willing supplicant to whatever he sees fit to do with me.

Ping, the elevator doors open.

The hushed sound of our feet stepping swiftly across thick carpet.

He slides the key into the door and then pushes it open, dragging me along, hardly taking his mouth off my neck the entire time. I'm vaguely aware of the room being nice, but not overly fancy, and then my bottom's hitting the mattress. Shane pushes up the hem of my dress until it reaches my belly and then drags the entire thing over my head. Now I'm only wearing my bra and knickers, pretty matching cream ones, I note happily.

I'd been in such a rush to get ready this morning that I couldn't remember what I put on.

Shane starts to undo the buttons on his shirt and I watch, my chest heaving as he reveals inch after inch of his perfect lightly tanned skin. The hint of Asian blood in him means he doesn't have pasty pale skin like most of the men I've been with. He's so beautiful, from a whole other world, really.

I shiver as a cold breeze sweeps in through the window that's slightly ajar. The maid must have left it open to air the place. Shane sees me tremble and walks, now topless, over to the window to close it. I'm still in the exact same spot he left me in when he comes back and climbs on top of me, whispering, "Come on, Bluebird, I'll warm you up."

Oh, my *God*. I'm certainly in for something right now. His string-roughened fingers push my legs apart as he settles between them. His mouth moves to the curve of my cleavage as he buries his face there, and let's just say there's a lot to get buried in. I smile, thinking of how preoccupied he can be with that part of my body, yet he rarely refers to them directly. Almost like he's too shy to say he likes them.

I find that shyness incredibly appealing. It's so rare to find a man like that these days.

There's no shyness in him now, though. There rarely is when we're being sexual. When we're alone. It's other times that he gets bashful, like how he'd blushed when I'd talked about him fucking me outside the concert hall the second night we met. Anybody could have heard. Such scandal.

"What are you smiling about?" he asks, all raspy as he looks up from my breasts. At the same time he pulls my body up slightly so he can unclip my bra and do away with it.

"I was thinking about how you're a study in contrasts," I murmur, and squeeze my eyes shut with pleasure when his tongue flicks across my nipple.

"Oh, yeah?" he says while his mouth busies itself on the tightening peak of my nipple, one hand pinching, one mouth sucking. A strangled cry comes out of me before I speak.

"Around other people, you're all polite and reserved. But then when we're alone, you're all take charge and throw me down on the bed."

His answering chuckle radiates from my nipple in his mouth right into my breast and throughout my entire body. I'm immediately wet. Wow. My skin goes all goose pimply again, but not from the cold air this time. His hand moves between my legs, rubbing at my underwear, which is a little worse for wear after our encounter in the studio.

He grips the side and pulls them down my thighs. I whimper in frustration when his mouth leaves my nipple so he can remove my knickers completely. Then he's spreading my legs apart so wide I feel a strain, and his mouth is right over my sex, breath heavy and humid on my flesh. His hands grip either of my thighs as he brings his mouth directly to my clit and sucks.

Oh, shit. I cry out, fisting the sheets so hard they might rip. My neck arches back, my head thrashing against the pillow. He continues to suck as his fingers thrust inside me and pump, hitting my G-spot perfectly. Just as I feel I'm about to come, he withdraws. I moan unhappily this time as he brings himself to kneel between my legs. His hand slips inside his pants pocket, pulling out a condom.

Then he's shoving off his pants and freeing his gorgeously hard cock. He rolls the condom on, his eyes not leaving me the entire time. I'm almost grateful that he left me hanging when he shoves his thick length into me in one swift movement. I'm so primed that I feel it more intensely than ever. My body is on the cusp of orgasm, and as he starts to push his hips back and forth, driving his cock into me again and again, I feel the most intense release building. A release the likes of which I've never felt before.

Our gazes lock as he takes both my hands in his and lifts them above my head. He holds me captive as he continues to thrust into me exquisitely hard. It's not fast; his speed is measured and controlled. Every time he fucks me, it's so hard and deep I feel like my body is melting. Burning.

Sunlight streams into the room, and I'm suddenly aware that we're fucking in daylight. We did the other morning, too, and it's shocking because it's something I never do. Every inch of me is on display for him. Sex for me has always been at night, always in the dark. Most often with alcohol as a primer. You can hide yourself in the dark. In the light it's like an entire tapestry of your emotions is on show. Everything that's inside you is on display for your lover to see.

Before now I'd always considered daytime sex to be something that people in love do. They wake up in the morning and fall into it, still half asleep. Or maybe they feel an urge in the middle of the day. So completely inappropriate but so right at the same time.

A sheen of sweat has accumulated on Shane's forehead, on his chest, too, as he thrusts into me with a kind of determination you'd only get from a man like him. A man who practices a skill to perfection. Tremors pulse through me, the muscles of my sex tightening every time his cock drives into me.

Unable to hold back, I shift my hands out of his hold above our heads. I wrap my arms around his neck, pulling him down for a deep kiss. It's as we're kissing, our tongues sliding against each other, his chest pressed to my chest, that I completely fall apart. My muscles clench as I come on his cock, pulsing so many times I lose count.

I'm moaning and whimpering as we kiss, and he pulls back to watch me, his cock still moving inside me. I can see his movements grow more desperate as his own release builds. And then the most erotic, masculine groan I've ever heard comes out of him when he comes. He unravels and I watch him, unable to take my eyes off him.

When he's completely spent, he puts his arms around me tight and rolls us so I'm lying on top of him. Reaching down, he pulls a sheet over our bodies, pressing soft kisses to my mouth and face.

"That felt incredible," he says, voice low, as my eyes drift closed and I relish the feel of his warm, damp skin on mine.

"Mm-hmm," I mumble, sleep pulling me under. Since I got up so early this morning and only got to bed late last night, I'm exhausted.

"I love the feel of you," he continues, his voice a lazy caress. I can hear his tiredness, too. A little thrilling jolt rushes through my sleepy brain at his words. "You're so tight and wet. I want to feel you skin on skin again." His tender hand drifts over my lower back in a circling motion as he refers to the other morning. Things had gotten out of hand, and we'd neglected to use protection. It's a dangerous thought, but I want to feel that again as well.

I nuzzle my face into his neck and make a little purring sound of agreement. Seconds later, we're both fast asleep.

When I wake up, it's because I'm incredibly turned on, which, might I add, is not how I usually wake up. Shane's hand is between my legs, gently stroking. I moan and glance over at the clock on the bedside dresser. It's just after two, which isn't so bad. I still have more than enough time to get back to the city for my shift.

"Fucking hell, I want you again," he grits out as he takes my earlobe into his mouth and gives it a playful bite. Somewhere in between our nap we'd rolled over into a spooning position. With one hand on my belly, the other still between my legs, he moves me so I'm flat on my stomach. He kneels behind me and nudges my legs apart with his knee. A few seconds pass, and I get the feeling he's admiring me from this new angle. I shiver. Then he pulls me up to take me from behind. I cry out at the pleasurable invasion, feeling him from a whole new position this time. The depth is delicious as he starts to hammer into me fast.

Not knowing where to put my hands, I grip the headboard for support. I'm vaguely aware that there's no condom in the mix this time, the sneaky bastard. As I said before, I don't have concerns about him giving me something, and I know that I'm clean and on the pill, but it just feels too close like this. I practically see my heart pumping out of my chest, my vulnerable veins reaching out and attaching themselves to his.

It's hard for me to place my emotions in the hands of another person. Even if it's a sweet and caring person like Shane, there's this sense of panic. A fear of not knowing what they might do with your delicate organ. They could push you back into a destructive addiction which may cause your family to fall apart. When I was a drunk, I didn't care. I'd give my heart to the most untrustworthy, low-down men I could find. I guess that's why I'm so cautious now. I know what it's like to be burned.

Both of Shane's hands fist my hips as he swears some really lovely, sexy curse words, telling me how great I feel, how beautiful we look joined together. When we come this time, we do it in unison, my walls pulsating around him, milking his cock. I feel him fill me up, and a wave of emotion washes over me. It feels foreign and way too intense, so I push it away. I try to focus only on the sensation of him inside me. When he withdraws, he picks me up in his arms and carries me into the bathroom.

Before I know it, the shower has been turned on, and he's settling me under the spray. He comes in to join me, sliding the door closed behind him. He's brought in some tiny bottles of hotel shampoo and soap, and I laugh with pure joy as I watch him struggle to get them open. Finally he manages it and pours some shampoo into his hand before lathering it into my hair. I do the same for him, luxuriating in the simple activity, loving the feel of his wet hair beneath my fingers.

For the next half hour we wash every inch of each other, staying in the shower until the water has almost run cold. I think we both like it here. We're away from reality in a world that's only touch and water and soap. Finally we get out, rubbing each other dry with the big fluffy white towels that were resting on a shelf by the door.

Reality intervenes with the buzzing of his phone on the dresser. I pick it up and look at the screen, but there's no name, just a landline number. I recognise the area code as South Dublin. Shane follows behind and swipes the phone out of my hand, cancelling the call.

"Who's been calling you?" I ask curiously, tugging the towel tighter around my chest as I sit down on the bed. I know it's not exactly my business, but his avoidance puts me on edge. Either it's someone he just plain doesn't want to talk to, or it's someone he doesn't want to talk to in front of *me*.

Shane sighs and runs a hand through his wet hair, coming to sit beside me. He picks his phone up again and rubs his thumb along the blank screen.

"It was Mona's home number. I don't know why she's been calling," he finally answers.

I look at him in surprise for a moment, before saying, "You haven't answered at all?"

He shakes his head. "I have nothing to say to her."

"Maybe she wants to talk about the upcoming show. You two are going to have to work together then, right?"

His tortured eyes continue to stare down at the blank screen of his phone. "Yeah, probably. I'm still not sure if I'm capable of doing it." He pauses and meets my gaze now. "She brings back too many bad memories."

Reaching over, I slide the phone from his hand and put it aside, before slipping my fingers through his. "You mean your...your suicide attempt?" I whisper softly.

His nod is barely perceptible. "It's not something you're ever going to forget," I tell him, pulling him into a hug. "Unfortunately, our memories like to give us a little bitch slap from time to time. I know all about it. Use the pain as fuel, let it make you stronger. You're the best musician I've ever seen and that's because of the emotions you channel into your music. Those emotions are what make the audience love to come see you, to feel that catharsis."

He chuckles sadly. "You didn't happen to complete a psychology degree at some point?"

I give him a warm smile. "Nope. I learned all I know in the school of hard knocks. Plus, I force Clark to teach me new stuff all the time."

"Well, you can thank Clark for me. You give better advice than most of the professionals I've seen," Shane replies, rubbing his finger down my cheek.

Giving him a serious look, I say, "You're welcome, just remember it when you've got to face Mona."

"I should be able to survive the memory bitch slap," he answers warmly.

"That's the spirit," I murmur and lean in for a kiss.

We're both quiet as we dress. Shane seems thoughtful, contemplative, even. I'd give anything to know what's churning up inside that head of his. I tie my hair in a fish tail plait, a style my mum taught me when I was only little. Shane stands behind me at the mirror, fully dressed now, and runs his hand down the braid.

"Pretty," he murmurs before pressing his lips to my cheek. I smile at him, but it's half-hearted. There's a pebble of fear in my gut that I can't seem to shake. A feeling of urgency that this sweet thing we've got can't last.

On the drive home, we stop off at a restaurant for something to eat. Afterward, Shane drops me home, and I scurry about to get into my work uniform and throw dinner together for April and Pete. I'm out the door with just enough time to spare and arrive at six on the dot.

That night after the concert, Shane finds me as I'm helping with the close-up. He asks if I'd like a ride home, and I tell him yes. Although if he tries for an invite to stay over, I'm going to have to tell him no. It's not that I don't want him to stay, it's just that we tend to be pretty loud, and my entire family will be home.

We leave through the backstage exit, and I ask him how he played tonight. There was a big group of students from a nearby music college in the audience, so we had a full house. As we leave, we're stopped in our tracks by a group of girls in their late teens and early twenties who are getting some of the orchestra musicians to sign stuff.

Huh. Orchestra fan girls. I never thought I'd see the day. Unless there's a really big name playing at the venue, we don't normally get a lot of fans queuing up for autographs. Most of the time the musician or speaker will stand in the foyer to sign books or CDs.

"Oh my God, that's him!" I hear one of the girls hiss excitedly as Shane emerges through the exit.

The next thing I know they've all flocked around him, thrusting programmes and CDs in his face to sign.

I quickly get shoved out of the way, so I step back a bit, kind of annoyed at their rudeness. Looking at the CDs, I notice some of them are old ones he recorded with the Bohemia Quartet. One girl asks if he'll sign her arm, and he does so graciously. Glancing down at my watch, I realise I've been standing here waiting for at least ten minutes, and they're not showing any signs of letting Shane go soon.

I've got an early start in the morning, since the concert hall is hosting a big conference, so I need my beauty sleep tonight. I try to get by a few of the girls to tell Shane I'm going to head off, but a brunette gives me the stink-eye and elbows me out of the way, telling me to wait my turn.

"Uh, I'm not a fan. I'm his friend," I tell her, disgruntled.

She gives me a look as if to say, *so what?* and I decide I'm really not in the mood. I put both hands around my mouth and call to him over their heads.

"Yo! I'm going to walk. I'll call you tomorrow, 'kay?"

I'm surprised that he actually hears me over the excited chattering. His head whips up from a CD he'd been signing, his eyes locking with mine.

"Give me ten minutes?" he asks pleadingly, and some of the girls' gazes cut to me.

I tap my wrist. "It's late, and I've got an early start. You stay. I'm good walking."

He looks disappointed for a minute but then finally nods his acceptance, gives me a quick wave goodbye, and goes back to signing. I turn and start in the direction of home. When I reach my street, I notice somebody sitting on my front doorstep. As I get closer I see it's Patrick, looking like shit with a bottle of whiskey in his hand, intermittently taking sips. If ever there was a picture to describe the term "lowest ebb," this would be it. So much for him staying away for a couple of weeks. It's only been a few days, and he's back already. He must be having a particularly bad time of it.

I stop in front of him and tap my foot on the path. "Do you mind getting out of the way, Pat?" I ask. As it stands, he's completely blocking my entrance.

His bleary eyes move up to meet mine, and he does a little shrug. "Been knocking for ages. Alec won't let me in." His voice is all lonesome and dejected, and something stirs inside me. I know what it feels like to be Patrick. I've been at rock bottom, too, and it's the loneliest place in the world.

I go down on my haunches and study him. He glances up from his bottle and does a little huff as though to keep from crying. To be honest, his face is so messed up he could already be crying, and I wouldn't be able to tell. Somewhere in the days since I last saw him, he's gotten himself a black eye and a fat lip. Either he was in a fight, or he owes someone money that he can't afford to pay back.

"It never leads anywhere good, does it?" I ask, reaching over and tapping the glass bottle in his hand.

He stares at me full-on then, and it's hard to keep looking at eyes that bloodshot. His mouth twists, and then he finally answers, "No, it doesn't."

I don't know a lot about Patrick's life before he met my mother, but I do know a few bits and pieces. His father was a violent drunk who beat his wife and kids. The usual fucked-up family story. At times it's hard to judge Patrick when I know there's a reason for his behaviour. As I said, I've been there myself.

I take the bottle from him, and he must have completely run out of steam because he doesn't even bother to fight me. I'll probably regret this decision in the morning, but I help him up to standing, wincing at the smell of him, and say, "You can stay one night. Tomorrow I'm going to call an old friend of mine and get you booked into rehab, okay?"

At hearing the word "rehab," his entire body stills, and I can tell he's deciding whether or not to make a run for it. Is a night with somewhere warm and safe to sleep worth going into a clinic? I can practically see his mind weighing the options as he stands there frozen. A minute later he wipes a hand across his mouth, turns to me, and nods.

I open the front door and lead him into the kitchen before sitting him down on a chair and placing a pint of water in front of him.

"Drink this. You'll thank me in the morning," I say just as Alec comes down the stairs.

"Jade, I already told him he can't stay. Why did you let him in?"

"I took pity on the pathetic bastard. Come and help set up the couch for him to sleep on, would you?" I reply tiredly.

Alec scratches the back of his neck. "I'm not sure this is a good idea."

"It's just for one night. I've got a friend who works at the rehab centre I went to back in the day. She might be able to find a place for Patrick. That's where I'm sending him in the morning."

"You think it'll work? He's quit rehab at least five times already."

"I think I can get through to him if we talk. This is the last chance he's going to get, and I'm doing it for you, April, and Pete. If it's possible to get him clean, then I'll do everything I can to help. You three deserve a proper father, even if you are all grown already."

Alec keeps staring at me and then pulls me into a hug. "You're a better person than me, sis. I gave up on him a long time ago."

I smile at him tightly when we break our hug. "What can I say? I'm a sucker for a lost cause."

Because I was one, and I know it's possible to get better.

Alec goes into the kitchen, speaking a few quiet but hard words to Patrick as I go upstairs to get some pillows and a blanket from the airing cupboard. He's probably warning him not to fuck this up, because this is the last chance we're going to give him. In the living room I make the couch into as much of a bed as I can manage. It's old and threadbare, but it's the best we have to offer him at the moment.

Entering the kitchen, I find Patrick alone now, sipping quietly on the water I gave him. I put the kettle on and make myself a cup of tea. Then I go to sit down opposite him.

"How old are you, Pat?" I ask, clasping my hands around the warm mug.

He looks at me, then slurs, "Fifty-two."

I whistle. "That's old."

"Piss off," he says, but chuckles just a little.

"Apart from when you were a kid, did you ever not drink? And I don't mean just a day or two. I mean being completely sober."

He purses his lips, thinking about it. He looks a little ashamed when he replies, "No."

"And in your fifty-two years, have you ever been happy? More to the point, has drinking ever made you happy?"

Dejectedly, he shakes his head, not even bothering to form words.

I take a sip of tea. "So, every time you go drinking and gambling, you think it's going to make you feel better, but it never does, not in the long run, anyway. Maybe there's a period of about an hour in every drinking session where you feel on top of the world, but the rest of the time you feel like shit. Am I right?"

"Are you lecturing me, Jade?"

"If anyone needs a lecture, it's you, Patrick. So you go through all the money loss, the sickness, the depression, the feeling like you're twenty years older than you actually are, and you never learn your lesson. All for a pathetic hour of feeling free and many hours of feeling nothing. That's fairly fucking dumb, isn't it?"

Patrick lifts his head like it takes a great effort. "I know my life is a joke. You don't have to remind me."

"Yeah, your life is a joke, but it doesn't have to be. You get yourself sober, get a job, and a little apartment maybe. Spend some time with your kids. They're great kids, Pat, and I feel sorry for you that you've missed out on so much with them. But anyway, don't waste time regretting your mistakes — take control and make them right. Don't waste any more time."

Picking up the pint glass, he tips the last of its contents into his mouth. "I'll try."

"Don't say you'll try, say you'll succeed. Trying means you're giving yourself the option to fail. Don't give yourself that option. I didn't, and look at me. Five years sober."

"Okay," he says hesitantly. "I'll — I'll succeed."

I stare at him approvingly. I have no idea if he's actually going to clean up his act. That's all on him. All I can do is give him a little push in the right direction. After walking him into the living room, I pull back the blanket I've set on the couch and gesture for him to lie down. He slips off his boots and jacket and then drops down onto it, closing his eyes.

I'm at the door, about to leave and go to bed myself, when Patrick suddenly says, "You're a good girl, Jade. I know I've always been a prick to you, but you never deserved it."

I only nod at him, not knowing what to say. In all the years I've known him, I think this might be the first time he's said something genuinely nice to me.

"And I'm sorry about your sister," he says then, his words mumbled.

"Who, April?" I ask, my brow furrowed.

Eyes still closed, he shakes his head and whispers, "No, not April."

I suck in a sharp breath. Emotion immediately grips me, clogging my throat. I can't speak, so I simply step out of the room and close the door softly behind me. It seems I've just been dealt my own little memory bitch slap. Upstairs in my bed, I lie beneath the covers and stare at the sparrows on my wallpaper.

Those sparrows mean so much more to me than most people even realise.

For the first time in years, I think of a girl long past and cry myself to sleep.

Twenty

The next morning I almost regret having given Patrick a chance. It takes forever to wake him up, and he's hung over as fuck. The living room smells like a brewery, so I have to open all the windows as wide as they'll go to let the stink out.

Once I've wrangled him into having a shower, I go get my phone to call my old friend Cheryl. She works as an administrative assistant at the rehab clinic I booked myself into way back when. Thinking about it, it should be time for me to get a new tattoo to add to my collection soon.

When I get her on the line, I beg and plead and practically promise her my left kidney to get her to find a place in the clinic for Patrick. In the end she finally finds a way to squeeze him into a three-week stay. I really hope he stays the course. If he leaves, then I wash my hands of him.

There's only so much you can do for people before they have to take control of things themselves. It feels like I've barely had time to breathe as I rush into work after getting Alec to drive Patrick to the clinic.

I have a two-and-a-half-hour break in the middle of the day between the conference and the evening concert, so I go home to put my feet up for a while. I'm at a deli getting a chicken salad wrap made up when my phone buzzes with a text.

Shane: Hey Bluebird. You want to come over tonight? Xxx.

A little thrill goes through me at his question as I remember our time in the hotel yesterday. I do want to come over, but I don't text him back right away. There are a few misgivings rising to the surface of my thoughts, telling me I should slow things down with Shane. I mean, fuck buddies are only supposed to get together every once in a while, right? But with us it seems we're seeing each other practically every day.

At my house I'm hoping to relax and watch some mindless daytime television. It doesn't seem like I'm going to get my way as I step inside the living room to find April lounging on the couch, snogging the face off some guy. They're going at it so much that they don't even hear me come in. I have to cough extra loudly to get their attention.

Immediately they hop off each other, and I grin, eyeing the guy. I could definitely refer to him as a boy, *thankfully*, because he looks no older than eighteen or nineteen. He's got the whole skater style going on.

"Sorry to interrupt," I say, folding my arms and shooting April a raised eyebrow.

She fumbles with her T-shirt, fixing it back in place. "Uh, this is Chris. Chris, this is my older sister, Jade."

"Pleased to meet you, Chris," I say, flopping down onto an armchair and opening up my wrap. I take a big bite, chewing as I ask, "So, where did you two meet?"

"He lives in the apartment next to Lara's. We met when I was leaving her place one day," says April, a small smile on her lips. She seems nervous. She must really like this boy, and he's actually an appropriate age. I could jump for joy right now.

"Cool," I say, just as she gets up from the couch and motions for Chris to do the same. He rises, his cheeks flushed with obvious embarrassment. They're about to leave when I tell her, "Oh, by the way, Shane gave me tickets for you to see him play. Do you still want to go?"

April looks at me, and then her eyes flick to Chris. "Nah, you can have them. I'm good."

Well, no one could ever say my sister didn't have a flighty side. A new boy on the scene, and she's all but forgotten about her little crush on Shane. Although it's probably a good thing. It could get slightly weird, given I'm having sex with the man.

The front door opens and shuts, signalling their departure, and I let out a contented sigh. Peace at last. When I'm done eating, I let Specky in and she sits on my lap, keeping me company as I watch a Dr. Phil rerun. Is it just me, or is he getting bitchier in his old age?

After a while I take out my phone and read Shane's last text again. I feel bad leaving him hanging, but I really don't know how to reply. In the end, I bite on my lip and start typing.

Jade: I'm going to be working late again. Can we wait a few days? Miss you. X.

I hit "send" before realising that asking him for a few days' break from each other and then telling him I miss him is a bit of a contradiction. It's true that I miss him, though. It's just that what happens when we're around one another scares me.

My phone buzzes.

Shane: Miss you, too. Like crazy. A few days will kill me. Tomorrow?

I can't stop my heart from speeding up when I read this. I mull over how to respond for a minute.

Jade: This is only supposed to be a casual thing. I want to see you, but I think we're letting ourselves get serious too quickly. It frightens me...

Whoa. Talk about frank honesty. I feel incredibly nervous after I hit "send," not knowing what he's going to say to that, but I need to get it out there. Seconds later my phone starts to ring. Oh, no. He's calling me. This can't be good. Forcing the shakiness out of my hands, I pick up the phone and answer.

"Hey."

"Babe," says Shane, his voice low and full of affection.

"What?" I respond, unable to disguise the note of anxiety in my tone.

"You're fucking adorable, but you need to stop overthinking this."

"No, *you* need to stop being so nice to me," I blurt out, and he chuckles.

"What? You want me to be a bastard instead?"

"That's not what I meant. You're being all attentive and stuff, and I know exactly what you're up to."

There's a smile in his voice when he replies, "Okay, enlighten me, then?"

"You're making this 'arrangement' into a relationship, a serious relationship, and that's not what I agreed to."

When I dived into this thing head first without a thought for my sanity, I never considered he'd be sly like this. And the fact of the matter is, my heart loves that he's being sly. My heart is a needy thing that wants to be lavished with attention.

He lets out a long sigh, and it sounds like he's fiddling with a piece of paper or something. His voice is low and serious when he says, "That's not what I'm doing, Jade. I can't help it if I'm into you and I get carried away. Tell me where the boundaries lie, and I'll stick to them."

I bite on my lip. He sounds like he means what he's saying. "Okay," I reply warily.

There's a beat of silence before Shane says, "Are you at home or at work?"

"I'm at home."

"Should I come over so we can discuss this in person?"

"No," I answer, almost too fervently. "I have to get back to work soon. Let's just talk on the phone."

Because if I see you in person, I'll only want to kiss you, and then no talking will get done.

"Okay, stick it to me, babe. What are your rules?"

Oh, God, did I mention how much I like his telephone voice? It's so deep and masculine, like a cup of warm chocolate. And when he calls me babe like that? Fucking hell. It's not one of those contrived terms of endearment, it's like it just slips out so naturally and he can't help it.

"Well, I suppose only seeing each other every couple of days would be a good rule," I say.

"How many days is a couple?"

"Um, three?"

"Right. So I can't see you for another two days?"

I hesitate, realising I don't like the sound of that, either, but I soldier on nonetheless. "Yeah."

"That's going to be hard. What if we bump into each other when you're working?"

"That's fine. When I say 'see each other,' I mean, like, you know…"

Jesus, am I blushing?

"Fucking?" Shane finishes for me, a raspy note in his voice.

"Yes."

There's a muffled sound of him moving and then, "Okay, what else?"

"No, uh, public displays of affection when we bump into each other."

"I can't touch you?" He sounds disappointed.

"No, you can't."

"I like touching you."

"And that's something that couples do. We aren't a couple."

"Fine. Anything more?"

"I think that's it. I'll let you know if I think of more."

Specky, who had been snoozing on my lap, wakes up and hops down onto the floor before scurrying into the kitchen. I stand and follow her, opening the back door to let her out.

Shane clears his throat. "So then I suppose I won't see you until the night you and April come to see me play."

Oh, for God's sake, why does he have to sound so sad…and so appealing?

"Actually, there's a change of plans needed there. April got herself a new boyfriend and has no interest in coming to the orchestra anymore. I think I might ask Alec along. I know he'll agree to it if I tell him Avery will be there."

Shane laughs. "Sounds like a plan. Will you stay with me that night?"

My reply comes out low and shaky. "Sure."

He seems happy again when he says, "Brilliant. I can't wait."

I laugh, loving how quickly his mood can improve, especially since it's the prospect of spending time with me that improves it. Again, my needy heart is reaching out for some affection, and it'll take whatever it can get.

"Right. I'll see you then, Shane."

"See you, Bluebird," he murmurs, and then hangs up.

That night during my shift, when my break comes I decide to go outside for some fresh air. There's an emergency exit to the rear of the first floor that leads out to a metal staircase. I'm not supposed to, but it's where I normally go when I need some quiet time. I've been uncharacteristically accident prone tonight, letting a glass smash onto the floor and almost spilling wine on a woman who was ordering drinks from me.

It's all because of Shane.

The merciless man is turning my entire life upside down. Perhaps not in a way that anyone can see, but my head is a complete mess because of him. I pull a cigarette from my pocket and light it up. Lara let me steal one from her bag in the staff room. I don't normally smoke. I only do on occasions like this when my nerves are at me.

I take a long, deep drag and stare out at the tops of the trees in the gardens behind the concert hall. If I listen carefully enough, I can hear the wind rustling through the leaves like the trees are whispering secrets. The smoke flows out of my mouth, a wisp of fog snatched away by the darkness.

Hushed conversation drifts up from below, and I peer down to see two people standing just outside the backstage exit. I'm leaning against the railing, so if either of them looked up, they'd see me right away. It only takes a second for me to recognise one of them as Shane, and the other looks to be his father.

"Why won't you speak to her?" I make out his father's words. He's dressed casually, so he's clearly not here to see the show.

Shane drags his hand through his hair. He's wearing the tuxedo that all the men in the orchestra wear during performances, a black coat with tails, a white shirt with a white bowtie. I momentarily note how handsome he looks in it, how much it suits him, before he replies to his dad, "I told her I was through after the other night. How could she think it would be a good idea to invite Mona and Justin to her event?"

"Your mother didn't realise how upset you'd be. Besides, we saw you on the television the other morning. You said you'd be playing a duet with Mona for the orchestra's new season. I can't see how you can be mad at her when you've agreed to work with the woman."

Shane steps forward angrily, and his dad takes a step back. "That's got nothing to do with it. And for your information, I wasn't told about playing with Mona until it was announced to me quite inappropriately live on the air. I expect that kind of carelessness from the orchestra management. I shouldn't have to expect the same from my own mother."

"She's very sorry, Shane. She hasn't been herself since you stopped taking her calls."

"Good. She deserves a taste of her own medicine."

"She's your mother. For God's sake, have a heart."

At this Shane whips his head up to his dad, spitting out, "Is she my mother? Really? As far as I've been told, my mother is some impoverished Chinese woman who needed money so bad she agreed to sell her baby to a pair of strangers."

"Now you're twisting things. You're my son, and you're your mother's son, too. It shouldn't matter who birthed you. Your parents are who raised you."

Shane stares at his dad, his shoulders slumped sadly. "I know that. I'm sorry for snapping. You're not the one I'm mad at."

Wow. I think maybe I should head back inside. I look down at the cigarette in my hand, realising that the whole thing has burned all the way down to the butt, and I only took one drag. I'd been so rapt with the conversation going on below me that I'd forgotten to smoke it.

Looking back at the two one more time, I actually feel a little sorry for Shane's dad, stuck in the middle of a fight between his wife and son. Then I feel sorry for Shane, too. He's clearly in turmoil over what his mum did. I feel like going down there and comforting him, but that might not be my place. And anyway, I have to get back to the bar.

Leaving them to the rest of their talk, I return to my post and try not to think about how Shane is suffering right now. I know he has to go back inside and play the second half of the show, which must feel awful after fighting with his dad.

When I get home that night, I bring up Shane's number on my phone several times, agonising over whether or not to call him. Every time I chicken out, and in the end I have to toss my phone under my bed so I won't be tempted. Instead I pull out my old mp3 player and fire up the one album I have of his, *Songs for Her*. I close my eyes and listen, and once again I fall asleep to the sweet allure of his violin.

Twenty-One

I thought that two days would be lots of time to get my head around me and Shane, but seemingly I can't get past the butterflies I feel when I think of him to even consider anything else. I've thought it a very appropriate description to compare the feeling of being "in lust" with a person to having butterflies in your stomach. But at the same time it irks me, because they always fail to mention how those butterflies have wings made of steel, cutting through your insides so that all you can feel is burning.

I haven't seen Shane since the incident with his dad, which is probably a good thing, because I don't know what to say to him about how he's stonewalling his mother. Is it wrong for me to think that what he's doing is a good thing? I don't know all the ins and outs of the situation, but from what I've heard, she doesn't really deserve forgiveness.

Alec readily agrees to come with me to the concert, since I mentioned we might have drinks with Shane and Avery afterward. Of course, all I'll be having is a plain old orange juice, but the rest of them are free to get a little tipsy if they like. I put on my black shift dress and heels before twisting my hair into a fancy bun and putting on some silver stud earrings. I go light on the makeup as usual and knock on Alec's door to see if he's ready.

When he steps out, I grin from ear to ear. He's wearing a navy shirt and dark slacks. I think this is the fanciest I've ever seen him dressed.

"Are those your interview clothes?" I ask in amusement. Someone's definitely out to impress tonight.

He shrugs. "They might be. Am I driving, or are we getting a taxi?"

"You can drive. It'll give you an excuse to offer Avery a lift home, now, won't it?"

"Ah, I didn't think of that!" he says, raising his hand for a high-five. I leave him hanging, though, not wanting to participate in setting my brother up to score the shy violinist any more than I already have. I feel bad for a second before I realise that Avery will probably be delighted with the attention. My brother might be tatted up to bits, but he's definitely a looker. You'd hardly notice the tattoos with the way he's dressed tonight. All you can see is the faintest tip of a demon wing he's got inked on the side of his neck.

When he was a teenager, I always used to tell him not to tattoo any body parts he couldn't cover up: hands, face, neck, etc. I warned him he'd never get a job if he did. I'm surprised he didn't make me eat my words when he had no trouble getting work in construction.

We park outside the concert hall and go inside. It's odd, but in all the time I've worked here, this is actually the first occasion where I've come to see a show. I've sat in on one or two during my shifts, but I've never been an ordinary audience member until now.

Lara's standing in the middle of the foyer at a podium, selling programmes, when we walk in. She knew Shane gave me tickets for tonight, but she still makes a big deal as we approach her.

"Well, la di flipping da. Look at the two of you all dolled up to the nines."

Alec gives her a smooth grin, his eyes scanning her up and down. I think Lara is the only woman I know who's immune to my brother's lasciviousness. She's been around the block far too many times not to recognise a player when she sees one. Needless to say, his flirty smile doesn't work on her.

"Thanks, Lara," I say, giving her wrist a quick squeeze. She shoots me a reassuring look, knowing I must be nervous, and I feel better for it. Alec and I move on and go inside the auditorium to take our seats. There are people chattering all around us, the place only half full so far. Most people are out at the bars, finishing their drinks.

Shane got us some of the best seats, too, right in the middle. If you're too close to the front, you only have a partial view of the musicians, while if you're in the middle a good few rows back you can see everything much better.

I shoot a quick text to April, making sure everything's all right at home since she's babysitting Mia at our house tonight. She texts back a minute later telling me everything is fine and that Pete's in his room watching movies. I tuck my phone back in my bag and focus on the stage.

Alec eyes the empty seats and asks me where Avery will be sitting. I point out the second row in the violins section and then have a look at the programme I got from Lara. There are going to be three pieces played, the first of which will be Debussy's *La Mer*. I know enough French to translate that as "The Sea." Next is a piano piece called *"Une barque sur l'ocean,"* by Ravel, which means "A Boat on the Ocean." And lastly is Sibelius' "The Oceanides." Turning back to the front of the programme, I see the title of the concert is *Uisce*, which is Irish for "water." Clever.

About five minutes later the auditorium is full, and the members of the orchestra are walking out onto the stage. I see Shane right away, looking dashingly handsome as always. The audience claps, and his eyes drift across the hall until he finds me. He gives me a heart-stopping smile, and I can't help grinning in return. Fizzy excitement bubbles in my belly. I adore classical music, and it's a rare treat for me to see it live and not in small scraps like when I'm working and manage to catch a few stolen minutes of a performance.

Tonight I get to gorge myself and see an entire show from beginning to end. Once the musicians are seated and have tuned their instruments, the conductor walks out and takes his place at the front of the stage. He says a few words introducing the piece they're going to play, but my attention is all on Shane. I watch how he turns a page of sheet music on the stand in front of him and whispers something friendly to the violinist beside him.

There's a moment of quiet right before the music starts, and I relax into my seat, closing my eyes and allowing it to wash over my senses. The piece has a soft, slow start, but I can tell it's building. Suddenly, there's a loud *caw* from above, and I blink my eyes open to see two seagulls swoop low and fly right over my head.

The salty smell of the sea fills my nose and the walls begin to move, bricks turning over on themselves and transforming into wooden slats. The top of the auditorium where the organ and choir section is located begins to narrow into a point, becoming the bow of a ship. Down the centre of the hall, giant billowing sails rise up to the ceiling. The roof disappears, replaced with clear blue skies, wind fluttering through the white sails.

The boat containing all our souls moves with the music, calm waves crashing against its sturdy sides. Bright rays of sunlight shine down, caressing my skin and reflecting through the glassy waters. A dolphin jumps out of the sea in an explosion of droplets before diving back under. It emerges again, so playful, dancing alongside the moving vessel.

Then, up ahead, dark clouds form, a storm on the horizon. Rain crashes down from the sky, soaking all of us in a sheath of cold water. A clap of thunder sounds as the wind gets turbulent and waves form, rocking the boat from side to side. The ship rocks so hard to one side it almost turns over.

People clutch onto each other, but the orchestra plays on, because when everything else in life fails, there still has to be music. My heart seizes as I stare straight ahead at a dark object rising out of the water. A whale with its mouth wide open, so huge it could swallow us whole. We narrowly escape the mouth of the whale, only to crash into its tail. A crack shatters in the body of the ship, and water starts to gush through.

More and more water comes. There's no escape. We're going under. My entire body is surrounded now, only my head above, my breathing laboured, panicked. There's nothing but water and music and death.

The music stops. The audience starts to applaud, and my heart pounds like I really did just drown. One man a couple of rows in front of us rises, initiating a standing ovation. Others follow suit. Alec nudges me with his elbow and we both stand, clapping as the musicians graciously accept our applause.

There's a short intermission, and Alec goes out to grab a drink at the bar. I stay in my seat, still too moved by the music to do anything but feel the after-effects. A grand piano is wheeled out onto the stage. When the hall re-fills after the intermission, a guest pianist is introduced to play the Ravel piece.

The rest of the concert passes beautifully, and I make a promise to myself to do this more often. My phone buzzes with a text as Alec and I slowly leave the auditorium.

Shane: Come backstage.

I reply simply.

Jade: On my way.

When we reach the dressing rooms, Alec immediately goes in search of Avery. I imagine he has some big compliments about her performance all at the ready, with the intention of getting into her pants by the end of the night. I'm not sure why, but I have this feeling that the two of them could be good together, that she could be the woman to finally knock Alec on his arse.

I can't see Shane at his usual spot, but then I know why when two strong arms wrap around my middle. I smell his cologne first, something citrus and masculine.

"Three. Fucking. Days. Are you trying to kill me, woman?" he whispers huskily in my ear.

I chuckle. "That wasn't my intention, no. And I thought we spoke about PDAs?" I whisper flirtatiously in reply, turning my head to him slightly. He presses a light kiss to my cheek and pulls away.

"Sorry. I'll have to expend more willpower in the future."

I look him over, seeing he's already got his violin case with him, a backpack hanging from his shoulder. It seems he's all ready to go; he hasn't even changed out of his tux, which, by the way, I don't mind. Not at all.

He holds his hand out to me. "Shall we go?"

"Um, yeah, just give me a second," I say, turning around and trying to pinpoint Alec. I spot him a few yards away, leaning against Avery's dressing table as she brushes her hair and seemingly blushes profusely. I wonder what he's said to her to warrant such a reaction.

When I catch his eye, I mouth to him that I'm leaving and he nods, waving me off.

Turning back to Shane, I meet his gaze, and his eyes are shining. God help me, but it looks like he's got big plans for me tonight. I take his hand, and he leads me out of the building and to his car. Before I know it, I'm strapped in and we're driving in the direction of his place.

Glancing from the road to me, he asks, "Did you have a good time?"

"I loved it," I answer honestly, and bite my lip. I can't handle the intensity of his gaze, so I stare out the window at the passing scenery instead. There's something electric about him tonight, and it makes me jumpy. His hand moves to my thigh and trails up under the hem of my dress. The warmth of his skin causes a tiny moan to erupt from my mouth. I wince with embarrassment. Has three days away from him really made me this needy?

He strokes the apex of my thighs, his thumb seeking my clit over the fabric of my underwear. Shivers break out on my arms and neck. Then he moves his hands and continues driving until we get to his house. I almost protest. When he parks, he gets out first and walks around to open my door for me, helping me from my seat, his hands on my waist.

My feet hit the concrete, but we don't move. I stand there, staring up into his eyes as his grip on me tightens. He ducks his head down and presses his lips to mine, his tongue flicking out experimentally for a second.

"Better get inside, or I'll be in danger of taking you right here," he murmurs darkly into my ear and I tremble, allowing him to lead me to the house. I didn't bring an overnight bag because I don't plan on staying the entire night. I have to get back to April and Pete, but there's also the fact that sleeping with Shane, and I mean *actually* sleeping, is too intimate. Since we spoke on the phone, I realised that needs to be another rule. Just sex. No sleepovers.

"Do you want anything to drink?" he asks as we walk into his kitchen.

I shake my head, and he sets down his bag and violin case. I glance at the clock and see it's almost eleven, which means I can spend a couple of hours here before I have to leave. Seconds later he's scooping me up into his arms and kissing me so deep I ache.

Kissing and roaming our hands over each other, we fumble up the stairs, somehow finding our way to his room without tripping up on anything. He turns me so my back is to his front, and then his hand goes to my neck, gripping it possessively as he walks me over to his bed. My knees hit the mattress and he bends me over, grinding his erection against my bottom. Frenzied, he tugs my dress up over my thighs until my underwear is bared, which he quickly rids me of.

He seems to be in the mood to take the lead and I let him, revelling in it.

His mouth joins his hand at my neck, licking and sucking. "It's probably a bit late to be bringing this up, but I just wanted to let you know that I'm clean."

My brain is too fogged by desire to get what he's saying at first. Then I understand. "I'm clean, too," I reply breathlessly.

His hand on my neck tightens. "I don't want to use protection with you. Is that okay?"

Moaning as he uses his teeth to nip my neck, I nod my head. "Yeah. I want to feel you."

My response seems to please him, and he gives my bottom a little spank. I yelp and he growls, kneeling down behind me and lightly biting the curve of my arse cheek.

Emitting a low groan, he purrs, "Have I ever told you how much I love your arse?"

I laugh. "Not that I recall."

"Well, I do. It's fucking perfect."

He bites me again, a little harder this time, and then stands. Before I know it he's undoing his pants and whipping out his cock. I'm still bent over the edge of his bed, waiting, my impatient sex quivering with anticipation. When I feel him part my lips and position his cock, my muscles clench, needing him inside. He pushes in slowly, easing through my tight channel and feeling every inch of me around him.

"Every part of you is perfect," he breathes, both hands going to my hips and holding on.

He thrusts into me once hard before he starts to fuck me with quick, delicious pumps. I fist the duvet, trying to keep my arms from falling limp. When he's inside me, my entire body gets so full of pleasure that I can hardly focus on doing anything.

"Perfect," he says again, this time sounding like he's gritting his teeth. "I love doing this to you."

I can only moan in response. The sound of our skin slapping together fills the room, and I can feel my wetness running down the inside of my thighs, I'm so turned on. There was hardly any foreplay between us, and still I'm soaking wet. He reaches around the front of my body and between my legs, finding my clit and rubbing fast circles, coaxing me to a sharp orgasm. I moan loudly as I come, my channel tightening and releasing around his cock.

"Wow, babe, you feel amazing," he murmurs, kissing the back of my neck, still thrusting into me.

He keeps going after I've orgasmed, clearly not ready to end this yet, savouring me. When he finally comes, the sound he emits makes me shiver. His arms tighten around me, and he doesn't pull out. Instead he guides us onto the bed so that we're spooning. He kisses just below my ear, creating tingles at the base of my spine. I feel him softening inside me, and then he finally pulls out.

"Let's get under the blanket," he tells me, all husky and sleepy, as he pulls the duvet out from under us and then over our bodies.

"Are you tired?" I whisper.

"I could go another round if you want, but I'd rather sleep. I love sleeping with you, Bluebird."

I turn around in his hold, trying to keep from sinking into him and just letting myself sleep. Tracing my fingers over his beautiful face, I say softly, "I can't stay, Shane."

His body tenses and he frowns. "Why not?"

"It's another rule I thought of. No sleepovers. Plus, I need to get back and check on the kids."

"Shut up and sleep. That's a ridiculous rule," he says, his arms turning to steel around me, clearly getting ready not to let go. "And we both know Alec is there to keep an eye on April and Pete."

"Shane," I start, but he interrupts me.

"No, babe. I'm sorry, but I'm not accepting that rule. I can deal with only seeing you every three days and I can deal with not touching you in public, but I can't fucking deal with you not sleeping here. I need this." He pauses, face serious. "Please."

The agony in his features makes my chest pound. God, I feel like a bitch right now. My resolve withers away, and I press my lips together.

"Okay. I'll forget about that rule, then," I whisper tenderly, my words barely audible while my heart urges me to forget about all the rules.

He kisses me softly and gives me an intense look. "Thank you. Now go to sleep."

Resting my head on his shoulder, I close my eyes and let sleep take me. That night when I dream, I dream of drowning in deep, dark water, and Shane's music pulling me back to the surface.

Twenty-Two

Familiar music drifts into my consciousness, dragging me from sleep. I turn over in the bed, naked but all wrapped in blankets. I discover the music is real when I blink open my eyes and see Shane sitting in a chair by the large window, topless. The blinds have been pulled, bright light streaming in, and he's holding his violin. I love how the muscles in his arms move when he plays.

I know I've heard this song before, but I can't seem to put my finger on what it is. I smile at him sleepily and he smiles back, continuing to play. Glancing to the side, I see a big glass of orange juice on the dresser alongside a plate with grapes, cheese, and crackers.

"Is this my breakfast?" I ask softly, and he only nods, smiling again.

My heart does a somersault in my chest. I've never been brought breakfast in bed by a man before. Picking up the juice, I take a long gulp, those butterflies wreaking havoc with my insides as his beautiful playing penetrates something deep in me. I put the juice down and pop a couple of grapes in my mouth before starting in on the crackers and cheese. I feel like the most special girl on the planet right now, being entertained by a world-class musician while I do something as mundane as eat breakfast.

A couple of minutes later Shane's piece comes to an end, and he puts his violin down. I have a sheet wrapped around my chest to cover my modesty. He steps over to the bed, bow still in his hand, and uses it to lower the sheet. I'm too busy eating to stop him, and the sheet falls free. He sucks in a breath, his eyes drinking me in. I'm struck with a memory of fantasising about him stroking my body with his bow, as though playing me like an instrument.

"That was a sneaky move, Mr. Arthur," I say, attempting a scolding tone as I set down the plate and pull the sheet back up and around my body.

He gives me a hot look. "I'm not going to apologise."

"Yeah, I didn't think you would."

He perches on the edge of the bed and runs his hand from my collarbone and over to rest on my nape. "I ran you a bath," he says low, leaning forward to nip my earlobe.

"Oh, and I suppose you showered already?" I ask back teasingly.

His grin is evil. "Nope. I was hoping we could share."

"Hmm, that depends."

"On?"

"How big is your tub?"

He lets out a loud bellow of a laugh that makes my sex clench. Yeah, I definitely want to share my bath with him. He stands, shucking off the trousers he'd been wearing before holding his hand out to me. I take it and he leads me into the large bathroom, the tub filled with warm water and bubbles. I step in and sink under, sighing in pleasure at the sensation.

A moment later Shane climbs in behind me, pulling my back flush with his chest. His entire body is wrapped around mine, and I can feel his erection pressing against my lower back. He runs his hands up and down my arms for a long time and I stay still, eyes closed, enjoying being touched just for the sake of it.

His hands move to the upper part of my chest then, before sliding slowly down to my breasts. I moan softly, and he grunts. When he reaches my nipples, he pinches them lightly, and then his hands continue their descent below the water. They get to my belly and still, his thumbs rubbing small circles into my skin. Then one hand lowers between my legs, which have fallen open. He strokes my throbbing lips and then fingers the petals of my sex.

He keeps stroking me for so long that I feel like I might burst. Finally, he moves lightning fast as he plunges two fingers inside me. I let out a sigh of relief, rubbing my bottom against his cock, which is now rock hard. We continue to play this game. I swivel my hips in circles and he groans, clearly enjoying the friction. He keeps his fingers inside me, moving slowly in and out, all lazily sexual, as his other hand moves to my aching clit. He rubs as slowly as he possibly can, and I feel an intense orgasm coming on.

I want him to come, too, so I keep swivelling my hips. I move my own hands to my breasts, moulding them and pinching my nipples, letting out a long, erotic sigh of pleasure. Shane practically hisses when he sees me touching myself.

"Fuck," he mutters, breath heavy and humid against the side of my neck. "Come," he goes on. "I want to feel you come all over my hand."

"Please," I beg, needing him to rub me faster, but he continues at his slow pace, building an inferno inside me. I tug on my nipples hard, causing pleasure to ripple right down between my legs, where both his hands are hard at work.

"Oh, shit, I'm gonna come," I pant, my muscles clenching.

I feel him spurt all over my lower back as I orgasm hard, crying out wildly with the release of it. Once I've ridden out all the waves, my body melts back into his and I shut my eyes. I'm glad we're not facing each other, because if we had been, he would've seen something scary on my face just now. Something far too serious for what's supposed to be casual sex.

We stay there in that exact position for a long while. He whispers sweet things in my ear and I try not to let them get to me, but they do. I need this man far more than I care to admit. After a time Shane turns on the tap and lets in some fresh water before he washes every part of me clean. I'm too shaken by my own emotions to stay and do the same for him, so I climb out of the bath once he's rinsed my hair and wrap up in a towel. I need distance.

But I don't *want* it.

In his bedroom, I gather my clothes and start to get dressed. I've just finished when I hear my phone ringing in my bag. Pulling it out, I see it's Ben calling and hit the "answer" button.

"Hey, Ben, how are you?"

"Heya, honey, I'm as good as gold. And you?"

I cough. "As well as can be expected."

"Have you fucked that sexy beast of a man yet?" he questions blatantly. Typical Ben. I swear he doesn't get embarrassed about anything.

"That's none of your business, you nosy bitch," I respond with a laugh, and he makes a delighted sound of surprise.

"Oh, my God, you have! Spill the beans — what's he like?"

"Uh, I can't really talk right now," I hedge just as Shane walks into the room, a navy towel wrapped low around his waist. My eyes travel over his abs before I focus back on the phone call.

"Ah, you're with him as we speak, aren't you?" he says, all hushed intrigue.

"I might be. Listen, I'll call you back later."

"Yes, you fucking will, biatch. But wait, I have to ask you something. A friend of Clark's has a holiday home in Kerry, and we're driving down to stay there next weekend. It's a long weekend, so we can chillax, have a little mini break from life. You know, the usual. Lara's mum's going to take care of Mia for a few days, so she's coming, too. What do you think?"

"Well, it sounds great, but I'll have to check the rota at work. If I have shifts, I can probably get someone to cover for me."

"*Excellente!* Would you like to bring the sexy beast along as well?" Ben asks hopefully.

My eyes shift to Shane. He's put on some boxer briefs and is rubbing his hair dry with a towel. "I'll ask him. See what he thinks."

"Cool. Talk to you later, babes," says Ben, making a smacking kissy noise with his lips.

I hang up the phone and turn to find Shane watching me.

"So, what do you have to ask me?" he says with a grin.

I narrow my eyes, trying not to grin back. "How did you know I was talking about you?"

He shrugs. "Lucky guess."

I search for my hairbrush in my bag and quickly fill him in on Ben's offer. He tells me he doesn't have any shows that weekend, as there's a traditional Irish group playing a string of concerts, so he's all in. I feel slightly breathless at the idea of spending an entire weekend with Shane in the same house. If we do this, we'd definitely be breaking one of my rules.

I vaguely remember wanting to do away with all the rules last night, but the memory makes me too nervous to keep thinking about it. I start to comb my hair, preparing to style it into a braid, and Shane sits back down in the chair he'd been in when I woke up this morning. He's dressed now in a T-shirt and lounge pants. He picks up his violin and bow, and starts to play another song.

I recognise this one as well, and finally I figure out where I know them from. Both pieces are on the Bohemia Quartet record I have. The one that lulls me to sleep most nights. I can't believe it took me this long to recognise the music. It sounds a little different when it's just the violin and not the whole quartet. There's something vital about the stripped-down version, like a person singing *a capella*.

I've always thought that if there was one instrument that's most like a human voice, it would be the violin.

I want to ask him who he wrote the album for. It's called *Songs for Her*. I looked up who the composer was and discovered Shane's name. He continues to play as I take out some mascara and lip gloss, applying a little before putting both away again. Oh, hell, if you don't ask, you won't receive, so I might as well ask.

"I have that album, you know," I admit somewhat shyly.

He pauses playing and glances at me. "You do?"

"Yeah. I actually downloaded it that first night you walked me home. I was curious."

A pleased expression comes over him. "And have you listened to it?"

I give him a sheepish look and sigh. "Too many times, Shane."

"Really?"

I nod and turn back to the mirror, tucking a stray piece of hair behind my ear. Then I speak up. "I know you wrote all the songs, but who are they for?"

He gets a faraway look in his eye and turns to stare out the window. "The answer to that question is a little weird, actually. I wrote them for a girl I never met."

"Huh?"

"I was in my late teens and had just started playing with the quartet. Our manager had gotten us a couple of gigs over in the States, and I was packing up all my stuff, preparing for the long stint away. There'd been this story in the news for ages, about a girl who'd gone missing. I can't even remember her name, but I was watching the news when her body had been found buried close to the Dublin Mountains."

I'm hardly breathing as I listen to him speak. My heart is pounding. I can't function enough to form words as he continues, "People had been talking about the girl for weeks. It was a huge deal for someone to disappear back then, probably because the population was smaller. She was blonde. She actually looked a lot like you, Jade, which is why I was so struck by you when we first met and you took off your wig. You had all this pale blonde hair, just like she did."

Finally I find my voice, but it's barely a whisper, "So you wrote the album for her? The missing girl?"

Shane shakes his head. "No. When her body was found, it was all over the television stations. Reporters were trying to get an interview with her family. There was a clip of her mother talking to one of them, and her sister was there. At one point the camera focused in on the sister, and I couldn't look away. She wasn't talking, just crying silently beside her mum. She had all this crazy purple hair and a tonne of eyeliner on, so it was all running down her face like a mask of sadness. I'd never seen someone in so much pain as that girl. It made me want to cry for her, made me feel so much, like I'd lost something as big as she had."

He stops speaking, and I can't move. I just keep staring into the mirror at my own face, watching as tears slowly begin to fill my eyes.

"That night I composed so much new music I felt like my hand might fall off. It was all for her. In the morning I had to fly out, but I continued composing the songs over the next few weeks. Up until then the quartet had only ever recorded covers. *Songs for Her* was our first and only original album, and our most popular one, too. I was so busy travelling to ever find out if they caught the person who killed the girl. In a way I didn't want to know. Even if they found her murderer, there's no happy ending to a story like that."

My eyes meet his through the mirror. "No, there isn't," I reply, no tone to my voice at all.

I can't get my head around what's happening. First the painting he'd had of me, and now this. Is this like some fucked-up version of serendipity or just a complete and total coincidence? A consequence of living in a tiny city where lives can become so strangely intertwined? I stand up and straighten out my clothes, picking up my bag and throwing it over my shoulder. I might not have wanted distance before, but I do now.

"I have to go," I say, not looking directly at him.

He seems to be lost in thought, running his fingers over the body of his violin, like he's trying really hard to remember the lost girl's name. He glances up at me then, about to protest me leaving, but then he sees the look on my face and falls silent.

"Sparrow," I whisper.

"What?"

"Her name was Sparrow," I finish, just before I turn on my heel and walk out the door.

***

I catch a bus back to my house, and it's still early when I get there. I hurry up the stairs to my room and pull out my costume. After the morning I shared with Shane, I need to become someone else for a while. Putting the white paint on my face, I feel like I'm erasing it all. Erasing my confusion that we were somehow in each other's lives years before we ever actually met.

He wrote an entire album about me, an album I've been listening to on "repeat" for nights on end. As I put on my wings, I consider opening up my window and flying away, like Mary Poppins with her umbrella. I leave the house in full costume, walking down the street, receiving the usual curious glances from people who don't know me or my story.

They know nothing about Jade Lennon. The girl whose twin got killed by a sick psychopath. Let her dress up like fucking Santa Claus if it makes her happy.

I reach my regular spot and set up as usual. As I stand on my box, I feel better because I don't have to be me. I can focus only on my breathing, focus on it so hard that no thoughts enter my head. Not a single one. I can listen only to the sounds of footsteps on the path, forever passing me by, and no thoughts enter my head. Not a single one.

There's no violin music this time. No sweet melodies to transport me into a scene that exists only in my own mind. I look across the street, and he's standing there alone, outside the very same shop from the first night we met. He doesn't have his violin. He's frowning at me, studying me so intensely he looks like he might burst a blood vessel.

I never move. Not once.

After a long time of me not moving, Shane buttons up his coat because it's getting cold, and walks away. I stand there for many more hours, until the day darkens to evening. When I step off my box, I feel like I might need a chiropractor, because not moving has given me a pain that runs down my spine.

I walk home.

A few teenage boys and girls shout some obscenities at me. You tend to garner negative attention when you're wearing something as bizarre as I am. I stop in front of them, twirling in a massive circle and bowing down while raising my middle finger in a silent "fuck you." I continue on my way. Opening my front door, I hear talking coming from the living room and immediately recognise Shane's voice.

What's he doing here?

I walk into the room to find him sitting across from Pete on the couch. He has his violin and Pete's got the laptop I managed to scrape together the money to buy him last Christmas open, some sort of application running on the screen that looks like a virtual recording studio.

"Hey," I say, glancing between the two of them, my voice more air than sound. "What's going on?"

Pete raises an eyebrow. "Shane's giving me music lessons, remember?"

"Oh, right," I mutter, and then look to Shane.

His expression is indecipherable. A long moment of silence passes between us, a dozen questions hanging in the air. Finally I clear my throat and ask him softly, "Would you like to stay for dinner?"

Some sort of tension leaves his body as a breath escapes him. "Yeah, I'd love to."

"Uh, Jade you're getting that white crap all over the door," Pete interrupts.

I glance to the side to find I've got my hand pressed against the wooden frame, white makeup smeared all over it. I drop my hand and take another step into the room.

"How's everything going? Have you seen Damo around at all?" I ask my brother.

Pete lets out a snort as he types furiously on his laptop. "He's shitting himself over Alec. He came to me after school, telling me to let my brother know he doesn't want any trouble."

I sigh in relief. "That's good. Is school okay?"

"It's all right. A few of the teachers practically tore me a new one over all my absences, but I can handle it."

I smile. I want to reach over and ruffle his hair, but I can't because I'm still in my costume. The wings are so big they hardly fit inside our tiny living room. I quickly duck out and go upstairs to change, using a makeup wipe to get the face paint off. I throw on some comfy yoga pants and a baggy jumper before going back downstairs to the kitchen. I find a note on the counter from Alec telling me that he fed and walked Specky this morning, but that he's got a date with Avery tonight, so he won't be home until late.

I look over the ingredients in the fridge and decide I've got everything I need to throw together a chicken curry with rice. About twenty minutes later, as I'm standing by the cooker stirring the sauce, the door opens and somebody comes inside.

Two arms wrap around my waist, and a chin rests on my shoulder. "Smells good," Shane says, voice low. "You okay, Bluebird?"

I nod, not saying anything. He holds me there for a few seconds longer and then goes to sit down. The food is just about ready, so I start dishing it onto plates. Pete comes in and grabs his, bringing it into the living room to eat, leaving me and Shane alone. April is out with her friends, so there aren't going to be any interruptions. I'm still in turmoil over whether or not I should tell him that I'm the girl he wrote all those songs for. Will he be freaked out, or think it's romantic?

We eat quietly, and I thank him for starting those music lessons with Pete. He shrugs it off, telling me he enjoyed spending time with my brother. He says that Pete taught him almost as much as he taught Pete. Shane was pretty much in the dark about all the new technological stuff that's out there.

When we're finished eating, we wash up together, and I ask him if he wants to hang out in my room for a while. I don't have sex in mind. I plan on telling him the truth. All about the strange coincidence I suddenly became aware of this morning.

In my room, I turn some relaxing music on low and then sit down on the bed. Shane slips off his shoes and does the same.

"Why did you freak out and rush off earlier?" he asks after a long while.

I turn to him, hugging a pillow to my chest as he lounges back against the headboard. "It was the story you told me, about the missing girl and her sister."

He leans forward, curious. "That freaked you out? Why?"

I bite on my lip, clasping my hands together to keep them from shaking, and meet his gaze. "Because the missing girl was my twin. I'm the sister, the one you saw on the news."

Shane's eyes flicker back and forth between mine numerous times, a dozen emotions crossing his features. He moves closer to me then, taking my shaking hands into his still ones. "Wow," he breathes.

"Yeah," I say. "First you have that painting of me, long before you ever knew who I was, and now it seems you've actually written an album for me. It's downright spooky."

Not to mention it makes my heart to do a backflip and then try to turn itself inside out.

Shane seems to be more focused on my history than anything else. The need to know my story is practically humming from him. "What happened to her?" he whispers. "I mean, did you ever find out?"

I stare at my wallpaper, at my golden sparrows, my mind wandering to a dark place. "Yeah, we found out. I knew all along who it was, but the police never released the information to the press until after her body was found. They were afraid it would compromise the investigation." I stop for a second, then tell him, "I was there when she was taken."

Shane inhales sharply and stares at me empathetically. "You don't have to talk about this if you don't want to."

I let out a small breath. "Well, it seems I'm in a storytelling mood, so you might as well sit back and listen. I never talk about her. And I mean never. I pay tribute to her in so many ways every day — she's constantly present in my world, but I find it hard to actually speak about her. Her name was Sparrow. We weren't identical, but we had the same colouring and looked a lot alike."

"Sparrow? Is that why you got those tattoos?" he asks, eyes going to my arm.

I nod. "And my wallpaper. I'm always drawing those damn birds, too. I can't get them out of my head sometimes. They're a symbol of her. She was an artist just like my mother, the good twin. I was the moody one, always trying to change my appearance so that people would see us as two different people rather than one. That's why I had the purple hair and the makeup. Sparrow never deviated from her natural blonde roots. She was so pretty. It brought her attention from people and was probably why her abductor took an interest. They always go for the pretty, innocent types, right?"

Shane just stares at me silently, empathy streaming from his every pore.

"Anyway, we were walking home from school one day, and it started to rain. We were getting soaked and began running, holding our bags over our heads to keep from getting wet. Then a car pulled up by the side of the road. It was our geography teacher, Mr. Francis. He offered us both a ride home, but I'd always had a bad feeling about him, so I said no. Sparrow, being as trusting as she was, wanted to accept the offer, but I told her not to and began dragging her away. We got into a fight because she didn't want to walk the rest of the way home in the rain. We shouted at each other. In the end I gave up and let her get in the car. I should never have let her get in the car."

"Fuck," Shane swears under his breath. "You couldn't have known."

I take a deep breath and continue, "I walked the rest of the way home, expecting Sparrow to be there already, but she wasn't. I didn't get too worried at first because she'd often have dinner at her friend's house down the street, so I thought that was where she'd gone. Mum was out doing groceries, and she had Pete and April with her. The evening progressed and everybody started to arrive home, but still there was no sign of Sparrow.

"Mum and I sat up half the night calling her friends, calling everyone we knew and asking if they'd seen her. We didn't get a wink of sleep, and finally in the morning we called the police. It took about a day before they began searching for her properly. I told them she'd gotten into Mr. Francis' car, so they went to his house to ask him questions. He told them he'd given her a lift because it was raining but that he'd left her off at her street and driven home to his wife and kids. His wife gave him an alibi, but she must have been lying. The police could find no evidence, no CCTV footage of him taking her, no proof at all. So it was the word of some Goth teenager over that of an upstanding citizen, a local schoolteacher who'd never had any trouble with the law.

"About a week passed, and still there was no sign of her, no leads. I was so angry I felt like going to his house and threatening him until he confessed. Instead I went to school early one morning and thrashed his classroom, scrawling the word 'paedophile' across the blackboard. I got a week's suspension, but Mum was too busy worrying about Sparrow to be mad at me. She believed me about Mr. Francis, and I think she might have even been a tiny bit proud of what I'd done. Two months passed by. I rallied all the students together to boycott his classes, and in the end he resigned, stating he couldn't work under such conditions, said he was being demonised. What a joke.

"It was almost three months exactly that she'd been missing when a couple walking their dog near the mountains found a suspicious-looking patch of freshly dug-up earth in an under-populated area. They called the police. The police came, and that was the day they found Sparrow buried three feet below the ground. I knew she was dead all along. I could feel it, like a part of me had been ripped out of my chest. Two days later, Mr. Francis shot himself in the head. A week after that, the results came back from the tests they'd run on Sparrow's remains. She'd been raped and then strangled to death. Mr. Francis' DNA was all over her. I wanted to die, thinking of the suffering she must have gone through, all because I couldn't stop her from getting in that car."

I pause for breath, wiping at the tears leaking down my face. Shane wraps his arms around me, pulling me into him.

"Jesus," he whispers.

"I was so full of guilt. The only thing that could numb it was alcohol, and that's where my drinking started."

"You were so fucking young. No one should have to go through what you did," Shane says, his mouth on my hair, his nose breathing me in.

I stare at my wallpaper for a long time, then draw away from him, going to my wardrobe and pulling out the sketch pad sitting at the bottom of it. Bringing it back over to the bed, I sit down beside him again, placing it on his lap. He hesitates a moment, then opens it up.

"Sparrow wanted to be an illustrator when she grew up. She was always drawing these little sketches, creating characters," I tell him as he flicks through the pages.

"She was talented," says Shane as he stops on a page, his mouth falling open.

"That was her favourite character," I explain. "The one she drew the most. She called her Evangeline Spectrum — don't ask where she came up with the name. She thought it sounded cool, like a futuristic angel." I get up and go back to the wardrobe, pulling out a big canvas, the only large-scale picture Sparrow had ever had the chance to complete. I set it on the edge of the mattress for Shane to look at. It shows Evangeline Spectrum, her blue wings spread out wide as she sits on the moon, staring down at a world full of people.

"But this is you," he whispers, his eyes taking it all in.

I shake my head. "It's not me. I re-created Evangeline as a living statue. I'd been playing around with the idea for a long time, and after a while I gathered everything I needed for the costume. Somehow dressing up as one of her characters made me feel closer to Sparrow. That's how I cope with missing her. I put her in my life in little ways, like tattooing birds on my arm or drawing a sparrow randomly on a wall in a house full of artists. It feels better than crying into my pillow or drinking myself half to death."

Shane picks up the canvas, his gaze eating it up. "You're amazing."

I let out a surprised laugh. "That's a nice way of putting it. Most people call me crazy."

He sets the picture down and looks at me dead-on. "Those people don't know what they're talking about."

A second later he's pulling me back into his arms and stroking my hair. We stay like that for a while, and then I start talking again.

"Before Sparrow died, I didn't believe in anything. I was a complete and total nihilist, thinking the world had no meaning. It just was. I had never lost anyone, so it was easy for me to believe that when people died, that was it. They were gone. Dust on the wind. There was no good place they were headed. Then my twin was dead, and I found myself believing in everything if only it would mean that this wasn't the end. It was completely hypocritical, but I was desperate for the

~ 314 ~

light at the end of the tunnel to be true. I needed to hold onto the hope that I'd get to see her again, that she'd get to live on somewhere wonderful after the horror she endured. So now I let myself see the impossible in the mundane. I let myself believe that things can happen that defy explanation. That I can fly with my fake wings or that I can be standing listening to music on the street, and suddenly I'm in a grand ballroom full of dancers. It's the only way I know how to survive without her, the only way I can convince myself we'll meet again."

Shane looks at me for a long time. His hand on my hair pauses as he dips down to kiss me on the temple. "We all have to believe in something to keep going, Bluebird," he murmurs, and then drags me down to a lying position. Somewhere along the way he pulled the blanket over us, and the music I put on earlier isn't playing anymore. It's so quiet. His thumb brushes the edge of my forehead, pushing my hair away from my face.

"Us being here together right now could be a sign, you know," he says then.

"What do you mean?"

"You want proof of the impossible, and you have it right in front of you. I saw you crying on the news eleven years ago and wrote an album of songs for you like I was possessed by music. Then years later I find myself staying in a room where a picture of you is hanging. A couple of months after that, I'm walking down the street one night, and the woman from my painting is standing in front of me in the exact same pose from the painting. If there's magic in the world, then we've both experienced it for ourselves."

For what seems like the millionth time today, tears fill my eyes. Something stabs at my heart, and I love him for every word he just spoke, even if none of it is true, even if it's all just coincidence. I look between his beautiful eyes, barely breathing, and then finally I whisper, "Thank you."

Nothing more needs to be said. He made my entire world right just now, and I'm clutching onto his words.

I'll never let them go.

It was just an ordinary night.
He didn't think anything extraordinary would happen.
Until it did.
Turning a corner onto the bustling night time street, he saw her all in blue.
The woman from his painting was a living, breathing thing…and she was so completely still.

Twenty-Three

I wake up early the next morning wrapped around Shane. We're both in my bed, fully clothed from the night before. My face feels stingy from tears, but there's a lightness in my chest, like getting everything out lifted a weight I didn't even know was there.

My body is half on top of his and I lie still, admiring how handsome his face looks when he's sleeping, how his dark lashes create shadows over his cheekbones. He stirs a little then and wakes up, blinking his eyes a few times. When he realises where he is and who's on top of him, I feel his body spring to life. His cock hardens against my inner thigh.

Suddenly he flips us over so that I'm flat on my back on the mattress and he's hovering above me. He does it so instinctively that it sets my nerve endings alight, like it's so natural for him to want to fuck me.

"How did you sleep, Bluebird?" he asks huskily as he runs his knuckles down one side of my face.

"Good," I answer, quiet. "And you?"

"Good, too. I always sleep well when you're with me." He moves his hips a little then, rubbing his erection against the centre of my thighs. A quick breath escapes me. Then he seems to think of something and pauses, squeezing his eyes shut.

"Crap, what time is it?"

I glance to the clock on my nightstand. "Eight-thirty. Why?"

"I have a radio interview at lunch, and they want me to play live on the air. I need to go home and practice, but I really don't want to leave."

There's a sort of agony in his eyes. I understand that he wants to get busy, judging from his current state of arousal, but...and then I get it. He thinks that if he goes now he won't be able to see me again for another three days.

"You can come over tonight," I offer hesitantly. "Or I could come to yours?"

He narrows his gaze. "But what about the rules?"

"Fuck the rules," I tell him brashly and he laughs, bending down and sucking on my lower lip. Damn, I really wish he didn't have to go now, either.

Pulling back, he stares at me, his gaze roaming from one part of my face to the next, his eyes glittering. His thumb brushes back and forth over my collarbone, and I keep on staring back at him, unable to break the connection.

"I feel like I'm falling," he whispers, bringing his mouth to my lips for a soft, barely there kiss.

All my words get stuck in my throat as he draws away from me and slides off the bed. I watch as he straightens out the clothes he slept in and pulls on his shoes. Why did he say that? More to the point, what does he mean? I refuse to allow myself to draw fanciful conclusions, but it seems fairly obvious what he was trying to tell me. It feels like a lifetime has gone by when I find my voice at last.

"I'll call you later. Good luck with today," I tell him softly.

"Thanks, Bluebird," he replies, looking at me for a long moment as he stands by the door. Then he opens it and walks right out. When I hear him leave the house, I sit up in bed and try to gather myself.

I'm not going to obsess over that one little sentence. I can't. It will drive me crazy. My gaze wanders to the small calendar I've tacked to the side of my wardrobe. Scanning to today's date, I let out a little surprised gasp. There's a big blue circle around the day. It's the anniversary of my sobriety, and I'm not sure how it managed to creep up on me like this. Normally I'm so aware of each day as it passes, but since I met Shane my head has been completely preoccupied.

It's six years today since I last had a drink. More to the point, it's time for a new tattoo. I'm actually glad for the distraction as I get out of bed and get dressed. I'm not due to be at work until three o'clock, which leaves me with lots of time to add another sparrow to my arm. I take care of a bit of housework and then set off for the parlour.

Just before I leave I catch a weather report that says it could snow later on, so I make sure to wrap up well. I'm actually glad for the cold weather. Somebody told me years ago that it's better to get tattoos when it's cold, because that way you don't sweat any of the ink out. It could be an urban legend, but I've always found myself following that rule anyway.

When I reach the parlour, a short walk into the city centre, it's mostly empty. There's just one guy sitting getting a piece done on his leg. Unlike a lot of tattoo parlours, this one has an open-plan setting, so unless you're getting something done in a place you don't want anyone to see, they tattoo you right out in the open.

It's daunting but liberating at the same time.

The place is decorated in a unique fashion, with kooky lopsided mirrors hanging on the walls alongside surrealist paintings. I talk for a while with the receptionist, and then the artist I always see, a tall guy called Stew with a septum piercing and wearing a tight black muscle T, comes out.

The buzzing sound of the needle and the smell of antiseptic fills me with a sense of anticipation rather than fear. It's always strangely relieving for me to add another bird to my collection, a symbol that I've survived another year. The more years I survive, the easier it becomes.

As I sit down and Stew makes his preparations, somebody turns off the prog rock music that had been playing and switches it over to a radio station. My new sparrow is going to go just past my elbow on my upper arm. Only another couple of years before I reach the top. I vaguely remember telling Shane I'd stop once I'd gotten to year ten, but maybe I won't. Perhaps I'll just keep getting these sparrows under my skin until they start calling me the Bird Lady instead of the Blue Lady.

Stew settles himself in a comfortable position, and then the needle is burrowing into my arm. I suck in a breath at the initial sting, but it's a manageable sort of pain. My attention goes to the radio and I hear the DJ speak, introducing his special guest of the day, violinist Shane Arthur.

I call to the receptionist, who's typing into a laptop close by, and ask her if she could turn the radio up. She nods, and then Shane's gorgeously masculine voice is filling the parlour. I close my eyes and allow it to wash over me, hearing his words from this morning in my head again.

The DJ asks him a couple of the usual interview questions, nothing too personal, and then invites Shane to play something for the listeners.

"This song is for my Bluebird," Shane says before he starts to play.

It's the song from yesterday, the one he'd played for me as I was waking up in his bed. My heart starts to fizz with giddiness. By the time he's finished the song and the DJ is thanking him for coming in, I glance down to see that Stew is almost done with my sparrow. Looking around the parlour, I see that it's still empty enough, with only two teenage girls waiting to have their noses pierced.

"Do you have any appointments after me?" I ask Stew, his face a blank picture of concentration as he pauses and uses some tissue to wipe away the blood on my arm.

"No, not until late afternoon," he replies, looking up from his work with one eyebrow raised. "You got something else in mind?"

My smile is barely there, the edges of my lips ever so slightly curved up. "I might have."

"Big or small?" he asks.

"Somewhere in between. I'm guessing it'll take you about an hour. What do you think?"

He shrugs. "You're the one paying. I'll do whatever you want."

And then he goes back to finishing my sparrow. I sit back, and my smile spreads wide as I picture my first tattoo that has nothing to do with the birds on my arm.

***

As I stand at the reception and pay for the two pieces I had Stew do for me today, I glance out the window and see small flecks of white falling from the sky. The weather report was right; it is snowing. I thank Stew one more time for yet another great job and for all the work he did looking up what I needed online. Then I leave the parlour.

I button my coat right up to my chin and pull up my hood. There aren't many people on the street, because aside from excited children, nobody really likes to be outside when it's snowing. A fleck lands on my nose, and I look down to see it isn't snow at all, but a tiny clear diamond.

The ground is glittering with them as they fall from the dark, heavy sheet of clouds in the sky. When they hit the pavement, they make a little pinging sound, like broken glass. My chest fills with wonder as I turn back and stare down at the street behind me; every surface is glittering with diamonds, and I gasp at the beauty of it.

My back stings with my new tattoo, but it's a good kind of stinging. The meaning behind the piece makes me feel complete, like I'm no longer alone in this life.

And no, I didn't get a tramp stamp, thank you very much.

I walk home, trying to avoid crushing the precious stones beneath my plimsoll-clad feet. Right now the world is a diamond-encrusted tiara, shimmering and bright.

At my house I gather my things for work, and by the time I'm leaving again the snow has stopped. Some thief stole all the diamonds, because all that's left on the ground is cold, wet sludge.

When I get to the concert hall, I'm greeted by Lara in the staff room. She's in top form, telling me about how delighted Mia was when she took her for a walk in the snow. I think of how much more delighted little Mia would have been if she'd seen all those diamonds.

For tonight's show Lara and I are both working side by side in the box office at the front of the house. We have a giggle as we watch people enter the foyer, making up stories for them as they pass us by. I love these blah blah blah chats we have. It's like yoga for the brain — gives it a nice good stretch but never overtaxes it.

A group of young people in their late teens enter, and we talk about how when we were their age we wouldn't be caught dead in a place like this. They're all dressed in formal wear and probably attend some fancy college where going to see the symphony is what constitutes a night out on the tiles.

Lara mentions how they all look like little right-wing conservatives in the making, and I quote Winston Churchill, saying, *"If you're not a liberal at twenty you have no heart; if you're not a conservative at forty, you have no brain."*

"So all those kiddos out there have no hearts?" Lara asks.

I shrug. "At least they have brains."

"Damn," she chuckles, "that means I've only got a couple more years before I have to throw away my liberalism. I'd better start attending some wild left-wing protests before I run out of time."

"Yeah, get burning those bras," I quip as a couple approaches my window, having heard what I just said. I cough to clear my throat as I sell them two tickets. The very second they walk away Lara bursts out laughing, and I give her a half-hearted scowl before succumbing to her laughter.

A minute later I have more customers and my laugh dies on my lips, leaving nothing but a straight sober line in its wake. In front of me are two people I recognise well, but they don't know me at all. There's an air of tension to Mona and Justin as they request two tickets, in the stalls preferably. I note how Justin's voice is all mannerly and urbane.

For a second I don't know what to do, and I certainly don't know how to interpret the flirty wink Justin gives me when Mona isn't looking. I have a crazy thought of asking them what the hell they think they're doing here, because Shane clearly wouldn't be pleased about it. But I don't. Instead, I silently sell them their tickets.

As I'm punching the command in on my screen, Justin leans closer. Mona has taken her phone out and steps back to scroll through her messages.

"I don't remember there being such hot employees the last time I was here," he says to me in a low voice, and I have a momentary daydream of punching him in the face, my fist miraculously breaking right through the pane of glass in front of me, shards flying into the air in slow motion.

I slide his tickets through the slot and shoot back, "Yeah, well, I don't remember the last time I had such a sleazy customer, so that makes us even."

Justin's eyes narrow as he swipes up the tickets, gives me a look that's half-annoyed, half-disgusted, and then leads Mona away. As soon as they're gone, I fumble for my phone in my pocket and rapidly type out a text to Shane.

Jade: Don't freak but Mona and Justin are here.

Lara watches me, clearly having heard what I said to Justin, so I quickly explain to her who he was. She remembers Shane's story from that night at my house, so she understands why I was so rude. Then I get a text back from Shane.

Shane: I know. Mum came to the radio station today and told me she's been in contact with Mona. She wants to mend her bridges since we have to play this concert next week. Apparently, that's why she'd been calling. Not gonna happen.

Jade: You okay?

Shane: I'll survive. Come to me when your shift is done?

Jade: I will. x.

When the show starts I'm tempted to go inside the hall and make sure Shane's all right. For some reason I have this vision of him seeing Mona and Justin in the audience and having a breakdown. I know he's stronger than that, though.

When my shift ends, I go to the staff changing rooms and put on the cream blouse and navy jeans I brought, since I didn't want to wear my work uniform when I go to see Shane. I let my hair down out of its bun and run my fingers through the waves. Applying some reddish lip gloss, I study myself in the mirror and decide I'll do, slipping on my ankle boots to complete the outfit.

I'm on my way to the dressing room, walking down a corridor close to the stage entrance, when I stop in my tracks. Shane is standing there, talking to both Mona and Justin. He looks fine on the surface, but just beneath it he doesn't look fine at all.

For a second I hesitate, not knowing if I should approach or wait until Mona and Justin leave. It's a terrible thought, but I wonder if Shane would be ashamed of being associated with someone like me. After all, Justin will surely recognise me from the box office earlier.

Deciding not to let my insecurities get to me, I keep walking. Mona frowns when I step up beside Shane and slip my hand in his, squeezing it ever so slightly.

Mustering my most sultry voice, I say, "Hey, baby, who are your friends?"

I press my lips to his mouth for a moment, meaning for it to be a quick greeting, but Shane sinks into the kiss, deepening it as though it's giving him strength. Tingles scurry all down my spine. Then he pulls away. "Hey, you look great," he breathes, squeezing my hand and turning back to Justin and Mona.

Justin's got a cynical look on his face, and Mona is still frowning.

"This is Jade," says Shane. "My girlfriend."

A quick swoosh of excitement goes through me at his words, and I have no intention of correcting him. Am I his girlfriend? I'm definitely more than just a friend with a particular benefit now. At least, that's the way it feels.

Mona purses her lips, and she smiles smugly. Clearly, she just remembered where she saw me before.

"I know you. Weren't you working out the front earlier?"

"That's right," I reply, nodding. I'm not going to bother to shake her hand.

"Ah, so how long have you two been together?" she asks.

"A while," I answer before Shane has the chance. She isn't getting any details because I know that's what she's after.

Justin is giving me this knowing look, like when he flirted with me earlier I was actually receptive to it, instead of cutting him down like I did. I raise an eyebrow at him, and his face immediately sobers. I should tell Mona what he said to me. I bet he's been cheating on her all over the place in the exact same way she cheated on Shane. I also bet she doesn't like the taste of her own medicine one tiny bit.

"It's a pleasure to meet you, Jade," says Justin, stepping closer and taking my hand in his to kiss it. Shane immediately bristles, and I quickly pull my hand away like there might be venom in his saliva. "Hey, why don't we all go out for a few drinks? Catch up on old times?" he continues.

"I'm sorry, but no," says Shane sharply. "We have plans."

"And I don't drink," I add for good measure.

"Okay, no problem. Perhaps another time."

Shane gives him a look like he's got his shit in bucketfuls, and Justin's face loses some of its cocky confidence. "I don't think so," Shane tells him, voice low and defensive.

"We're trying to be civil," Mona cuts in. "Why throw away years of friendship over something so stupid? Justin has missed you, Shane. All of the guys have. Even Dad says he wishes you'd come back and play with the quartet again."

Shane's body goes ramrod straight with tension. "'Something so stupid'?" He spits her own words back at her. "Are you for real? You're fucking delusional if you think I'd ever want any of you in my life after how you lied to me. And I know the only reason you're bending over backward to gain my friendship is because ticket sales for the group's concerts have fallen dramatically since I left. This all boils down to money."

Justin's expression grows angry. "Our sales are doing just fine. We're here because we want to make up for what we did to you. It was awful, I know. I hate to think I've lost you as a friend."

"Fucking hell, those lies drip so easily off your tongue, don't they? I'll never be your friend again, Justin, because you were never a friend to me."

Shane tugs on my hand and leads me away from them, down the hall toward the dressing rooms. When he get around the corner, he stops and leans back against the wall, closing his eyes firmly and taking deep breaths as though trying to keep from going back there and punching Justin in the face. Yeah, it seems I'm not the only one who's had that fantasy tonight.

I bring my arms up around his neck and pull him close, resting my face in my favourite spot just below his jaw. I rub soothing circles into his nape with my thumb, and some of the tension falls away from him.

"I'm so glad you got there when you did," he murmurs, his lips grazing my cheek. "I was on the verge of breaking his hand so he'd never be able to play again."

"You wouldn't do that," I whisper, because I know it's true. Shane doesn't have a malicious bone in his body. A minute or so passes in silence.

"I just can't believe they both had the gall to come here. When Mum came to see me today, she let it slip that she'd been in contact with Mona's dad, my old manager. Apparently he's eager to meet up with me and discuss some things. The quartet hasn't been doing as well as it used to because a lot of my fans have heard rumours about Mona and Justin, and aren't going to the shows anymore. I imagine he wants me to rejoin so they can win those fans back."

I pull away and look at him. "You'd never go back," I say. It isn't a question. I can see it in his eyes that rejoining the group is never going to happen, no matter how much they might plead.

"No," says Shane. "I wouldn't. Mona's father has clearly given her and Justin the push to come see me. I wouldn't be surprised if he was behind this whole deal with us playing a duet together. He probably thinks I'll fall for her charms and do anything she asks of me. It's kind of insulting."

The idea of Shane falling for Mona again makes my lungs hurt. Is that a possibility? Some insecure corner of my heart wonders.

"You want to get out of here now?" I ask, kissing his jaw and allowing my hand to wander suggestively down his chest and over his abs.

He swallows visibly, and a small smile shapes his lips. "Sure. What do you have in mind?"

I bring my mouth to his ear and whisper, "Your place. Your bed."

I don't think I've ever seen him move faster as he goes to collect his things and then leads me out to his car. On the drive I text Alec to make sure he's home tonight. When we get to Shane's house, he pulls two boxes of pre-made meals from the fridge and sets them on the counter where I'm perched on a stool.

"Are these courtesy of your gourmet delivery service?" I ask teasingly as I open the box and fork up some of the chicken salad.

Shane gives me a sheepish grin. "You know I never get the chance to cook."

By the time we've finished eating and have eye-fucked each other half to death, Shane prowls around the counter to me and positions himself between my legs. I gasp as his rock-hard erection hits me right at my core. He grinds it against me, and I wrap my legs around his waist. Then his mouth is on mine, kissing me hot and deep. I have a small notion in my head that I'm going to need to keep my new tattoo hidden from him. Not the sparrow, the other one. I'm definitely not ready to show it to him yet, and I kind of want to wait until it's healed.

I put some antiseptic cream on both of them before I left for work today, but I can feel the skin tightening now, getting ready to form a scab. Yeah, tattoos aren't all smooth and sexy right away. It takes weeks for them to heal, and while they do they itch like a bastard.

"Not here," I murmur against Shane's mouth. "Upstairs."

He follows my lead as I pull him to his room, his mouth nibbling at my neck, his hand pulling my blouse over to expose my collarbone. Hmm, it's actually going to be difficult to keep those wandering hands of his away from my back.

"I want you on top," I tell him, my head foggy with desire as his deft fingers undo the fly of my jeans and pull them down my thighs.

He smiles against my lips. "I think I can manage that."

Slowly, he lowers me down to his bed, the fresh, clean smell of his sheets hitting my nose. He runs his hands along my abdomen, inching my blouse up little by little, kissing my belly playfully. When he finally removes my top, his eyes zone in on the new sparrow on my arm, his fingers brushing over it tenderly.

"When did you get this?" he breathes.

"Today. Happy anniversary to me," I answer in a singsong voice.

"So pretty," he purrs, kissing each sparrow before continuing his way over my chest to my collarbone. I let out little mewling noises of pleasure as his hand drifts between my legs and cups me. Then he does one long stroke, pressing hard over my clit and sinking past the fabric of my underwear. When three of his fingers slide inside of me all at once, filling me up, I realise how wet I am.

"You're so ready for me," Shane says huskily, arousal dripping from his words.

"Oh, God," I moan as he pumps me good and hard.

He rids himself of his clothes in short order, and then he's sliding his cock over my entrance, teasing me before thrusting all the way in. The entire time his eyes never leave mine. I bring my hands up to his face, marvelling at how his hot gaze peruses me so possessively.

Suddenly, I'm struck with the thought that I could never handle losing him.

His hips move as his desire builds.

"You're so beautiful," he whispers, one hand drifting through my hair, which is spread out over his pillow. It's strange, because I was thinking the exact same thing about him. I lose myself in a haze of sex and need, his hard body working itself into mine, and when he comes, I come with him. He doesn't pull out as his sweat-soaked chest falls against mine and his breathing slows as he falls asleep.

Twenty-Four

The following week my belly is a bundle of nerves. Not only am I going to be spending an entire weekend with Shane come Friday, but this is also the week that Mona comes to play at the concert hall. Shane and I have been with each other every chance we can get, stolen moments at work and late night visits. I haven't mentioned Shane's pseudo declaration in my room last week, and neither has he.

I've also managed to avoid having him see the tattoo on my shoulders, which was some feat, given that he has this way of ridding me of my clothes before I even realise it's happening.

Catching sight of his driver's licence one evening, I saw that his thirtieth birthday is this weekend, so I make a note to do something special for him.

Right now I'm walking down a corridor at work, returning to the bar after delivering a tray of drinks to a group of businessmen having a meeting in one of the conference rooms. My heart skips a beat when I see Shane walking toward me from the other direction. He's looking casual in jeans and a dark grey T-shirt. We stop a foot apart, not saying anything but drinking each other in with our eyes.

"Hey, what are you doing here so early?" I ask while he brings his hands to my shoulders, then lets them drift down my arms. At the same time he's manoeuvring me back against the wall and sucking in a harsh breath.

"I have a rehearsal to get to, but you, babe, are a welcome distraction," he purrs, and bends his mouth to my neck.

"Shane," I gasp, making an effort to push him off but not trying nearly hard enough. "We can't do this here. My supervisor could come by."

Both his hands move up to my neck, his thumbs rubbing circles into the exposed skin at my throat. "Oh, yeah," he murmurs, his mouth curved in a wicked smirk. "Tell me more."

"I could get the sack," I go on, my protest weak.

"No man would dare sack a face this beautiful," he disagrees, kissing both my cheeks and then moving in for my mouth. He nibbles on my lips, and I feel myself tremble against the wall.

"It's a pity my supervisor today is a woman, now, isn't it?" I finally respond, and he chuckles against my lips.

"I've missed your smell," he murmurs, one hand moulding my hip, pushing up the hem of my work shirt.

"You saw me last night."

"I know," he replies with a sullen little expression before capturing my mouth in a deep, wet kiss. My knees practically buckle out from under me when his tongue plunges inside, caressing my tongue in long, languid strokes. I come alive, growing wet between my legs as I clench my thighs together tight. His mouth is like heaven, and he's kissing me like he does when

~ 336 ~

we're having sex. There's no manners to it, just hot, fevered passion. I can feel my cheeks getting warm with a blush. Before I met this man I think I probably blushed about three times in my entire life. Now it's become a constant look for me.

He draws back an inch and stares at me, his face so close I can feel his breath on my skin. My eyelids are at half-mast, and I'm clenching his shirt with my fist.

"Fuck, you're all heated up, and now I have to go," he swears, his eyes consuming me.

My breaths come out quick and heavy. "I told you we couldn't do this here."

"Yeah, well, I have a hard time listening to logic when you're around me." He pauses and bends close to my ear to whisper, "A real fucking *hard* time."

Shivers dance along my skin, and I can't keep my eyes from quickly glancing at his crotch. Yeah, he isn't lying.

"You'd better get to your rehearsal," I tell him, my breathing slowing down a bit.

He lets out a little petulant sigh. "I bet you're soaking wet right now."

"Shane," I say, giving him a small push. "You've got to go."

"I know," he sighs again, and comes in for a kiss goodbye, this one not nearly as hot as the last, and yet it still speeds up my pulse. With one final stroke of his hand down my cheek, he turns on his heel and continues his way down the corridor.

I gather myself and get back to work, wondering if his practice today is with Mona or if the entire orchestra will be there. As I do a stock take, I try to quell the desire to slip inside the auditorium and find out. After another five minutes of stock-taking, my curiosity gets the better of me, and I go upstairs to the balcony entrance. That way nobody below will notice me come in.

As quietly as I can manage, I push open the door and walk down the aisle, taking a seat in the first row. I look down to the main part of the auditorium to find that my suspicions were right. It is just him and Mona today. The conductor, Henry White, and two other men are sitting a few rows down from the stage. They're all chatting back and forth to each other while Mona sits at a piano and Shane looks to be tuning his violin.

He seems to have it in tune when he steps forward and calls down to the three men, "What would you like to hear first?"

"Hungarian Dance No. 1," Henry replies after corresponding with his neighbours.

Shane nods and walks back to the piano, standing only a foot away. I can't help hating seeing him so close to a woman he was once in love with. It makes me ferociously jealous, and I've never had a jealous bone in my body up until now.

I wonder how he proposed to her.

It was probably beautiful, and the bitch didn't deserve a single second of it. God, these thoughts really frighten me, and I can say without a doubt that this very moment is the closest I'll come to hitting the bottle again.

Mona seems to be trying to make eye contact with Shane, but he won't look at her. At least that's something. A moment later he starts to play; it's a fast, passionate tune, full of fire and fury. So appropriate for these two. Mona accompanies him on the piano, her part like a trickling stream of water to his hot, angry inferno. It's almost like they're fighting through music. Shane is accusatory, pained, while she is supplicant, trying to win him back.

Is that what this is about?

I know I wasn't imagining things last week when I'd met her and Justin for the first time. They didn't strike me as two people in love about to tie the knot and have a baby. They struck as a couple who has come to the realisation that all they ever had was lust and secret thrills. And that lust and those thrills have long grown stale.

Shane walks across the stage as he plays before turning back to the piano. He looks at Mona now, and there's so much emotion in his eyes that I'm not sure I can continue watching. Does he still have feelings for her, or is it only hate he's trying to communicate?

The piece comes to a dramatic, swift end and I'm glad those three awful minutes are over. I stand up from my seat and am turning to leave when I stop in my tracks. Standing just inside the door is Mirin, a look on her face like the cat that got the cream. I keep walking. I have no idea what she's doing there, watching me as I watched Shane and Mona, but I have no desire to engage her in conversation.

Just as I'm passing her by, she starts to speak. "They have so much chemistry on the stage, don't you think?"

I give her my most nonchalant expression and shrug before muttering a reply, "I'm not sure that's what I'd call it."

I shouldn't have taken the bait, but I couldn't seem to help myself. What can I say, there's something about being around a woman who thinks I'm no better than the dirt on her overpriced shoes that rubs me up the wrong way. My "rubbed up the wrong way" metre is cranked right up to eleven.

"They'll get back together sooner or later," she says, glancing down at her nails.

"Uh, I hate to break it to you, but Mona's engaged to Justin and pregnant with his kid."

Mirin's eyes gleam now, like she's been keeping the secret of the century. "She's going to leave him. She's confided in me that she's unhappy and the biggest mistake she ever made was breaking up with my son. I found it in myself to forgive her and gave her my blessing in her efforts to win him back."

I give her an astounded look. "You do know what she did to him?"

Mirin purses her lips. "All water under the bridge. Mona is right for my son. She's the most talented pianist to come out of this country in years, and Shane's star is shining bright. They're ideal for one another."

Rolling my eyes, I deadpan, "Oh, well, don't I just feel so unworthy. Your work here is done, Mommie Dearest."

"Don't you dare talk to me like that, or make insinuations..."

I laugh. "That you're Joan Crawford? I hate to break it to you, Mirin, but you're not nearly that interesting."

And with that I stride right by her and out of the auditorium, feeling triumphant at the sound of outrage she makes upon my departure. That right there was probably the finest last word I've ever gotten. Unfortunately, my satisfaction doesn't last very long, as I hurry to the staff bathroom, lock myself in a cubicle, and take several long, deep breaths.

Shit, I'm not sure I can handle this anymore.

It's one thing for Mona to be trying to convince Shane to return to the Bohemia Quartet because her dad's making her do it. It's another entirely for her to be here trying to win him back. Perhaps Mirin was lying to make me feel insecure so I'd break things off with Shane before they've even begun.

God, I hope she was lying. I mean, I can understand why she doesn't like me. I'm so far from her idea of an approvable girlfriend for her son I might as well be sitting on Mars roasting my bottom. What I don't get is her continuing support of Mona, a woman who has treated her son so horribly she could be in the running for a worst fiancée of the year award.

I mean, the woman drove him to suicide for God's sake.

I guess these people will overlook many, many flaws in favour of good breeding and a sophisticated background. Mona is the lesser of two evils in Mirin's eyes.

After a few minutes, I finally gather my nerve to return to work. Thankfully, this evening's event won't be featuring the symphony, so I can avoid Shane, his ex, and his manipulative witch of a mother for the night.

When I arrive home after my shift, I'm surprised to discover Alec and Avery in the living room watching a movie together, the lights turned low. If my estimations are correct, this must be their third or fourth date, and I've never known my brother to see a woman more than twice. I smile to myself. Perhaps he's turned over a new leaf. I take in the sight of them sitting close on the couch before quickly apologising for interrupting and ducking out of the room.

In the kitchen Specky's bent over her food bowl, eating a few doggie biscuits. I pet her head and sigh. She makes a little rumbling noise and abandons her food to come and hop up on my lap. I love dogs. They never have any shame about letting you know just how much they've missed you.

"Oh, Specky, you should have seen the drama I've dealt with today."

She makes a sound that's too tame to be a bark, sort of like a questioning noise. Before I can continue being pathetic and telling my problems to my dog, my phone buzzes loudly from where I set it on the table. I pick it up to find a message from Shane.

Shane: You coming over tonight? xxx

Jade: Too tired. Tomorrow?

Shane: I could come to you.

Jade: The walls in this house are paper thin.

I'm hoping he gets what I mean by that, because no way are we having sex here within hearing distance of all three of my siblings. That would just be too weird. Plus, after what I saw transpire between him and Mona today, I need some time to myself to think. They might not have actually spoken to each other during their practice, but the multitude of emotions that were flying around the auditorium was enough to make me dizzy.

It feels like there's still so much that's unresolved between the two of them.

Shane: I can be really quiet...

Jade: Unfortunately, I can't. How'd your practice go?

I can't believe I just asked that question, but I needed to change the subject and couldn't think of anything else on the spot.

Shane: It was with Mona. More painful than getting a tooth pulled minus the anaesthetic.

I smile at his creative description. At least he didn't lie about Mona being there.

Jade: Did you two get the chance to talk?

It takes a few minutes longer than usual for him to reply.

Shane: I don't have anything to discuss with that woman.

Jade: You sure about that?

Shane: Positive. Now, if you don't mind, I'd like to talk about what underwear you have on.

Hmm, that was a crafty change of subject. I laugh out loud.

Jade: Are you trying to sext me, Mr. Arthur?

Shane: Of course. Underwear?

Jade: Black lace.

Shane: I like you in black. Are you alone?

I stand up from the table and Specky hops off my lap, returning to her bowl of doggie biscuits. Walking upstairs to my room, I shut the door and text him back.

Jade: I am now.

Shane: Where?

Jade: My room.

Shane: Lie down on your bed.

Jade: Okay...

Shane: Fuck, I'm hard just picturing you. Take off your top and pull down your bra.

Before I get the chance to take my top off completely, April shrieks loudly from her room, yelling something about hurting her hand when trying to move her bed. Shit. I shrug back into my top and type out a quick text to Shane.

Jade: Got to go. There's an April emergency.

Shane: Babe.

Jade: I know, I'm sorry. Go get some sleep. You've got a big show tomorrow.

~ 344 ~

Shane: Okay. I hope April's all right. xxx

With that I hurry to April's room to find she was trying to rearrange her furniture and got stabbed with a rusty nail when she was lifting one end of her bed. Tears are streaming down her face, and there's a nasty wound in the centre of her palm. Too nasty to be sorted with a bit of Savlon and a Band-Aid. I wrap my arm around her and give her a squeezy hug before making arrangements to head to A&E.

My neighbour Barry drives us, and we don't get home until the early hours of the morning. I drop onto my bed, exhausted, and have just enough time to set my alarm before I conk out.

The next day I arrive at work around lunchtime, yawning all the while since I didn't get as much sleep as usual. April's been complaining nonstop about having to wear an unsightly bandage on her hand, so I'm happy to be out of the house, even if it does mean dealing with the stress of Shane and Mona's concert.

Apparently, every last ticket has been sold. Never let it be said that people don't enjoy a good scandal. If it's true that Shane's fans have been boycotting his old group's concerts, then it must be common knowledge that Mona cheated on him, despite the fact that Shane himself denies it when asked.

I kind of respect him for that. He could have played up the sympathy card, but he didn't. In fact, I've been doing a bit of covert Googling on my phone during my break period, and have discovered that before Shane came to play with the symphony no one had heard anything from him for more than a year. I'm guessing a good deal of that time was spent recovering from his suicide attempt, but still, for such a well-known musician that's a long time to be out of the spotlight.

I wouldn't normally be so determined to delve into his life before we met, but Mirin's words from yesterday are still affecting me. Still making me question what would happen if Mona broke things off completely with Justin and laid herself at Shane's feet. Would he step right over her, or pick her up and take her back into his warm, strong arms?

You see, on the outside I may act like everything falls right off me like water, but on the inside I'm as insecure as they come. My brain finds these ways of twisting things, blacking out all the signs that show Shane only has eyes for me and making me question if a part of that gorgeous gaze still belongs to Mona.

The evening comes sooner than expected, and I'm back in my usual spot, tending bar. As the venue starts to fill, I turn to serve my next customer and find Justin sitting on a stool, his elbow leaning on the bar top. He's wearing a white shirt, several buttons undone, and his sandy coloured hair is all dishevelled.

"What can I get you?"

From the slightly bleary look in his eyes, I'm guessing he's already had a few. "Are you really his girlfriend?" he slurs, and I decide I'm not going to serve him any more alcohol. He must have been warming the seats at the downstairs bar for a while, judging by his current state.

"Shane's girlfriend? Yeah," I say, not really knowing whether I'm lying or telling the truth.

He sits up a little straighter. "I'll take a double vodka."

I pick up a glass, and fill it with water and ice before placing it in front of him. "That's all you're getting from me."

He narrows his eyes and scowls at me. This is one thing I like about working here. The clientele are usually of a certain class, so when you refuse them alcohol, they become moody about it. Sometimes they'll get mouthy, but very rarely do they become violent. It's a complete contrast to a dive bar I once worked in where the patrons would glass you for so much as looking at them the wrong way.

Justin's body slumps against the bar top now as he shoves the glass of water aside. "I don't want that."

"You should drink it. Your head is going to be splitting in the morning."

"Don't care."

I give him a concerned look. "Are you all right, mate?"

He fumbles in his pocket for a minute before retrieving an expensive diamond engagement ring. He sets it down on the counter and looks at it with the most miserable expression on his face. I almost feel bad for him. I actually have to remind myself what this piece of work did to Shane.

"She gave that back to me this morning," he mumbles, and air catches in my lungs.

Fuck, Mirin wasn't lying. Mona really is planning on getting her claws into Shane again.

"She said she doesn't love me anymore, but that I shouldn't worry. She won't stop me from seeing my kid once it's born." He lets out a long, joyless laugh.

"Why did she break things off?" I ask, my voice shaky.

Justin makes a sound low in his throat. "I had sex with a waitress." He pauses, and a drunken smile comes over his face, like he's cherishing the memory. "Or two."

"Well, then, can you blame her for giving you back that ring?"

"It's not like she's a bloody saint, either. She's gonna fuck his head up all over again, you know."

I stare at him hard for a long moment. "Not if I have anything to do with it."

"Yeah, you're hot and all, but she's Mona." He pauses before continuing in a sarcastic voice, "*The* Mona Campbell. Shane's been in love with her since he was twenty."

Justin's words give me a quick, violent thump right in the chest, but I soldier on.

"He *was* in love with her. Not anymore. He hates her now."

"They always say there's a fine line between love and hate."

I can't listen to much more of this, so I go to serve my next customer. By the time I look back at the spot Justin had been sitting in, he's gone. Good riddance.

The engagement ring is gone, too. I wonder if he'll sell it off or give it to the next woman who comes along.

My supervisor slides in behind the bar once the last call for the start of the concert is announced, and asks if I could go help out in the auditorium. Fuck my life. There aren't any more people waiting for drinks, so I have no excuse. I have to go and witness this concert first hand. Yay.

She guides me through the entrance for the stalls and tells me to direct people to their seats on the far left-hand side. The chatter of patrons filling the auditorium echoes all around me, but it's not loud enough to drown out the heavy beating of my heart. I'm so on edge it's unreal. I mean, what do I think I'm going to see up there on that stage, some sort of lover's reunion?

I could probably get away with leaving once the show begins, but there's this self-flagellating side of me that wants to stay. I want to watch and prove to myself that my fears are unwarranted. That no matter how hard Mona might try, Shane will be unmoved by her efforts.

When the members of the orchestra walk out from backstage, I sink to a dark corner of the hall, leaning back against a wall and waiting. I'm half relieved that the first piece is a symphony, and not Mona and Shane's duet. I won't have to suffer just yet.

A group of women to my right are excitedly discussing the two musicians in hushed voices, talking about the rumoured love triangle and poor Shane's broken heart.

"Excuse me?" comes a recognisable voice from behind.

I turn around quickly, breaking my attention from the gossiping women to find Mirin and her husband standing there waiting to be seated. I silently take the tickets from her hand and look at the seat numbers.

"Straight down the aisle, two rows before the steps," I tell her with a reserved tone.

"Thank you," Mirin replies, taking the tickets back from me. "It's going to be a wonderful show," she continues as her husband walks on ahead. "I'm so pleased you're here to see it."

I give her an emotionless look and gesture for her to take her seat. She smiles, eyes cruel, mouth hard, then turns and walks away. I let out a long, deep breath and bring my eyes to the stage, where the symphony has already begun. Trust Mirin to be fashionably late. Shane is in his usual spot, his arm moving vigorously with the music, his violin resting just under his chin.

When it's time for Mona to come out, she gets a big round of applause, and I despise every clapping hand in the place for giving it to her. Shane stands a few feet away from the piano, and they start to play the same song from their practice yesterday. I'm not sure I can take witnessing this piece all over again, but I stand firm, studying both of them, trying to pinpoint some sign that my heart is going to get broken.

And there it is.

If I can't have him, my heart would definitely be crushed. Does that mean I'm in love with him? I think I might have loved him for a while now, far earlier than would be deemed appropriate. It's hard for me to know such a talented, beautiful, good-hearted man and not fall a little bit, just enough to zing a tiny spark into my much-guarded organ.

I should never have even agreed to be his friend, but then again, how could I have helped myself? Show me a working-class girl who doesn't harbour secret desires to be swept off her feet by a handsome, sophisticated guy.

The song ends, and the audience is clapping again, a few people getting to their feet. The next piece, Hungarian Dance No. 5, isn't as difficult to endure. It's an up-tempo, almost jovial song. The only problem is, Mona's been looking at Shane the whole time, a small smile shaping her mouth. He isn't returning the smile, but at one point he looks back at her, and I feel my chest go *pop* in a bad way.

What are they sharing? Is her smile a secretive one?

Okay, I think I've endured enough. I hurry right out of the auditorium and dash to my quiet spot, the emergency exit on the first floor. I push the heavy door open, and the sharp night air cools me, sliding over my skin like a soothing balm. Tilting my head back, I look up at the night sky, silently asking the stars for answers.

Unfortunately, none are forthcoming.

A couple of minutes later I go back inside, and it's just my luck that I bump right into my supervisor. The intermission is just about to begin, and I should have been at the bar long before now.

"Where the hell have you been?"

I start to say something, but she cuts me off. "Never mind. I had to put Lara on the bar, since we couldn't find you. Right now I need to you to prepare these drinks and bring them to Mona Campbell's dressing room. She's got a reputation for being a diva, so be quick and try not to make any mistakes." She shoves a piece of paper into my hand and I nod my head, wondering if this night could possibly get any worse.

I go to the bar and prepare Mona's drinks, which seems like quite a lot for one very slim woman. Perhaps she's expecting company. There are special private dressing rooms for visiting musicians, and I try to push away my nerves as I head in their direction. When I reach her room, tray in hand, I find the door slightly ajar. I don't know why I do, but I pause, taking a quick peek inside.

It's a good thing I did, because there's someone else in there with her right now, and that person is Shane. She's sitting on a chair in front of the dressing table, and Shane is a few feet away, leaning back against a tall closet. His hands are clenched into tight fists, and I can practically see the tension in the room, it's so thick. Keeping a hold of the tray with increasingly shaky and sweaty hands, I prick my ears to listen.

"Why have you asked me here, Mona?" Shane asks as she brushes some powder onto her nose, turning her face from side to side in the mirror to examine her appearance.

Then she swings around to face him and holds out both her hands. "Do you notice anything missing?"

Shane raises an eyebrow and replies, "A soul?"

Mona pouts and turns back to the mirror. "I'm not wearing my engagement ring."

"And this is of concern to me why?"

"Justin and I are over."

"Congratulations."

"There's no need to be so sarcastic. I've been through a terrible time of it lately. You'd think you could muster a little sympathy."

"I'm crying a river for you on the inside."

Mona sighs. "And the sarcasm persists." There's a long stretch of silence before she tells him in a soft, sweet voice, "I've missed you terribly, Shane."

"Fucking hell, you've got to be kidding me." He shakes his head, running a hand through his hair and pacing the room now.

"I have. I've been in turmoil over what I put you through. I can't believe my own actions. It was truly awful, and I want to make it better. I want you to forgive me."

"Not happening. Are we done?"

"Shane!" she cries, standing from her seat and walking toward him. She grabs at his arm, but he pulls right out of her hold. "Please give me a chance. I know it will take time, but I'm willing to work at it if you are."

She keeps on following him until he's in the corner of the room and she's standing in front of him. If he wants to get by her, he'll have to physically push her out of the way. My feet are on the verge of walking right in there and pulling her away from him, but I remain still. For some reason I need to see how he handles this, and it feels like everything is riding on it.

He stares at her, eyes dark, breathing quickly as his chest rises and falls. She takes a step closer and places her hand tenderly on his arm. "Justin cheated on me, you know. Several times, in fact. It must have been God's way of punishing me. I'm a different person now. I would never be unfaithful again."

He keeps watching her, and his breathing slows. "Why are you so intent on destroying me?" he whispers. If I weren't listening so hard, I probably wouldn't have heard him. The agony on his face, the emotion passing between the two of them, is too much to take.

One of my co-workers is passing by at that exact moment, so I shove the tray into her hands. "Will you deliver those in there for me? I've something I need to take care of."

"Sure," she replies, taking the drinks from me.

As soon as the tray is out of my hands, I run.

Twenty-Five

When I locate my supervisor, I tell her I'm sick and need to go home. She doesn't seem too happy about it, but eventually she gives me permission to leave. I don't go directly home, though — I go to the big house in the heart of the city where I've spent many an hour contemplating.

There aren't too many people around when I get to Ladybirds. Mary answers the door and invites me in for a cup of tea. I follow her to the kitchen at the back of the building and sit down on a long bench painted a muted shade of green. Rubbing my cold hands together, I watch as she puts loose leaves into a pretty ceramic teapot.

Bob Farrell, the man who owns the house, walks in and holds a pan under the tap, filling it with water. Then he pulls a bag of chickpeas out of the cupboard and pours some into it. His back is slightly hunched over from age, and he's wearing a brown shirt with cream polka dots. When he sees me he smiles.

"Ah," he says, "the Blue Lady has paid us a visit. It's good to see you, Jade."

"You too, Bob."

"How's life?"

"Complicated."

His wrinkly eyes sparkle. "Stop making me jealous. I remember complicated, exhilarating stuff."

"Want to swap?"

He grins. "The old ticker wouldn't be able to handle it, I'm afraid," he says, lifting his hand to his heart.

"Oh, well. It was worth a try."

Mary comes over and puts a steaming cup in front of me. I'm not sure what kind of tea it is, but it smells faintly of wet twigs. I lift a questioning brow at her and she explains, "It's Pu-erh, supposed to be good for when you want to lose a few pounds."

I laugh. "You trying to tell me something, Mary?"

"No, no! It's me who's on the diet. My doctor says I need to lose three stone. He's the one who suggested the tea."

I lift the cup to my mouth and take a sip. It tastes like mud and dust. "Your doctor is a sadist," I say, scrunching up my nose. Both Mary and Bob have a good chuckle.

A minute of comfortable silence passes. Mary drinks her tea — she must be used to the godawful taste — and Bob goes about preparing his chickpeas. All of a sudden, Mary leans forward and takes my hand in hers.

"Something troubling you, honey?"

I blow air out through my mouth, enjoying the feel of her soft, pudgy hand on mine. "I think I might be in love."

Her answering laugh is light and tinkling. "Well, now, there's no need to sound so miserable about it."

"He's way out of my league."

"And who told you that?" Mary responds, her tone disagreeable.

"His mother."

Bob chuckles some more as he stands by the cooker, stirring his pot.

"If you ask me, his mother sounds like a bit of a B-hive," says Mary.

Now I'm the one to chuckle. "Is that a mannerly way of saying biatch?"

"The young people aren't the only ones who like to make up slang," she replies, a happy grin on her face as she takes yet another sip of that disgusting tea.

"Oh, Mary. I don't know what to do," I say, planting my face down on the table to express just how lost I feel. She leans forward and strokes soothingly at my hair.

"What else can you do other than tell him?"

"True, but that would take guts, and I'm a gutless wonder."

"You're not fooling anyone, girl. There's steel in that belly of yours. Tell him. I can't imagine any man would find it a difficulty to have a beautiful woman confess her love."

"You have such romantic, old-fashioned notions, Mary, and I thank you for the compliment, but I wish you were right," I reply, sitting back up and trying to regain some dignity after my face plant of despair.

I spend another half an hour at Ladybirds and then head home. Walking in the door, I shrug out of my coat and slip off my shoes before going straight up to my bedroom. Checking my phone, I see that the battery has died. I'm about to grab the charger when I stop and put the phone back down on my dresser. I need a night of no contact to get my head on straight, so I decide to wait until the morning to charge it.

It's going to be difficult enough sleeping, since a vision of Shane and Mona in her dressing room, her hand on his arm, has been constantly flitting through my brain. It wasn't so much the fact that she was touching him that gets to me, but the way he'd looked at her. I couldn't tell whether it was longing or anger in his eyes. It seems that Justin was right — there is a fine line between love and hate.

I've got a couple of audiobooks on my mp3, so I browse through those until I find something that piques my interest. Audiobooks are my Ambien; after a little while listening, I'm usually on a one way ticket to Snoozeville, but not tonight. Tonight my brain has other plans, and those plans involve keeping me up until the wee hours of the morning. I've listened all the way to the end of the first book and have started the opening chapters of book two before I finally nod off.

I wake up with a headache, and somebody's licking my face. Sadly, that somebody isn't a hot violinist whose name begins with an "S," but rather another "S" name. Specky lets out a little yip of excitement and then hops off the bed. Hops back on again, hops off, hops back on again. The hyper bitch.

What? It's perfectly acceptable to call a female dog a bitch.

My bedroom door is wide open, and April's standing there, laughing her head off.

"Oh, you're bloody hilarious, April," I mutter as I sit up and rub the sleep from my eyes.

"It's after twelve, you know. Shouldn't you be at work?"

"I have the next couple of days off. By the way, I'm going down the country with Ben, Clark, and Lara for the weekend, so I want no funny business from you while I'm away."

She grins like she has absolutely no intention of behaving yourself. "Can my boyfriend stay over?"

I widen my gaze, incredulous. "You've got a boyfriend?"

"Uh, *yeah*. You met him the other week, remember?" Her eyes gleam with hope that's about to be obliterated by yours truly.

"Right, yes, I remember. And no, he cannot stay over."

"Jade, please. I'm begging you." She gets down on her knees and puts her palms together like she's saying a prayer.

"All right, step inside my office and we'll have a nice long discussion about French letters, more commonly known to you and me as *condoms*." I sound out the word just to make this even more embarrassing for her.

She holds her hands up. "No effing way. I'm not talking about sex with you."

"Then there will be no boyfriends spending the night under this roof," I tell her happily and she turns on her heel, sulking all the way back to her bedroom.

Unable to keep my curiosity at bay any longer, I grab my phone and plug it into the charger. I need to know if Shane tried to call me. I'm hoping he did, because if he didn't, that could mean he caved to Mona's pleadings and decided he's going to give their relationship another college try.

If he did, then not only might I actually be finding my way to a bottle of vodka in the very near future, but I will also have lost all respect for him.

My phone lights up, and several missed calls flash across the screen. One is from Ben, and the rest are from Shane. They span over several hours, and the last time he tried to phone me was at four in the morning.

In the words of Germans in bad situations the world over: *Scheisse.*

He never left any voicemails or texts, so I have no clue what's going on with him. There's a message from Ben, asking me if I'm all set for our weekend away and telling me that we'll leave from my house tomorrow morning. I send him a quick message back saying *I'll be ready with bells on.* Then I text Shane.

Jade: We're leaving from my place tomorrow at ten. You still coming?

It's the safest option. I haven't mentioned his countless attempts at calling me, nor have I made reference to my ear-wigging adventures last night. I sit back and wait for him to reply, but when I get no messages right away, I go shower and have breakfast. Over an hour passes, and still there's no response.

I have a couple of errands to run today, one of which involves going grocery shopping and stocking the fridge with food for when I'm away. Another is giving Alec strict instructions to make sure April doesn't sneak any gentleman callers into her bedroom.

I'm determined not to dwell on Shane's radio silence, so I get busy and head to the nearest supermarket. As I'm leaving, my hands full carrying plastic bags, I spot a familiar face staring back at me from the magazine racks. I was right when I predicted they were going to put him on the front cover. It's the edition of *Hot Press* containing Shane's interview.

Standing there for far too long, I hesitate over whether or not I should give in and buy a copy. I mean, I overheard most of what was said in the interview, but not all of it. Perhaps there will be some little gem in there that will enlighten me as to who he really is. Something that will make him seem less perfect in my eyes, like expressing a racist sentiment or declaring his support for the neo-Nazi movement.

I also have a shameful desire to slobber all of the pictures that were taken at the photo shoot. Glancing from left to right, like I'm afraid of getting caught buying a porno mag, I snatch a copy off the shelf and bring it to the register to pay before stuffing it into one of my shopping bags.

When I return, I give the downstairs of the house a spring clean and make lunch for Pete. Ever since he's started going to school again, he's been coming home on his lunch hour. I'm seeing this as a good sign. If he's at home, then he isn't hanging out with Damo and company.

Coming in the door in his uniform, he drops his bag at the bottom of the stairs and walks into the kitchen. I've already set a sandwich and a glass of juice on the table, so he swipes up the sandwich and takes a big hungry bite. Then he goes upstairs to get his laptop, muttering about wanting to show me something. When he returns, he plonks his laptop down on the table and fires it up.

I sit on the other side eating my own sandwich, Specky sitting dutifully at my feet waiting for scraps, her eyes full of hope that I'll drop a nice piece of ham or maybe a pickle. Unlike some dogs, Specky will eat almost anything. I once came home and found her trying to fit her jaws around a Golden Delicious apple.

"Okay, so I want your honest opinion," says Pete. "I'm thinking of putting it up on YouTube."

He seems nervous, and I have no clue what he's talking about. "Putting what up on YouTube?" I ask, hoping to God he hasn't filmed one of those awful Harlem Shake videos.

"The song I made with Shane. I recorded a sample of him playing the violin and worked it into a dance track I created. Listen."

I do listen as a slow, heavy beat starts up and rolls into a Dubstep-style track. About thirty seconds into it the violin comes in, weaving through the electronic bits and creating a really original sound. "Wow, it's brilliant," I tell him. "I didn't even know you two recorded anything."

Pete looks pleased as punch with my reaction but tries to hide his excitement by affecting a cool demeanour. "So you think I should put it on YouTube?"

"Yeah, go for it."

He grins full-on then, and I reach over to ruffle his hair, to which he immediately scowls. I don't care. I'm so happy that he's found something to be passionate about that for a few brief minutes I forget all about my own troubles.

Soon he has to head back to school for his afternoon classes, and I clear the table. Then I pull out the magazine I bought, running my hands over the front cover showing Shane's handsome face looking off into the distance.

Flicking to midway through the mag, I stop on Shane's interview, which has the photos of him spread throughout. There's one that really catches my eye. It's from when he'd been holding his violin and I'd made a joke. He'd smiled at me. I hadn't realised it then, but his smile was so full of affection. As I stare at it, I find it difficult to breathe for a second.

Starting at the beginning of the interview, I discover the usual pat questions, which then move on to the part where the journalist brazenly asked about Mona. He puts in a little aside about how Shane clammed up and didn't seem to want to talk about his ex, which could be a sign that there's a colourful history there. Huh. You don't know the half of it, Mister.

At about the three-quarter-way point I discover questions that were asked after I'd gone, one of which stands out.

LB: Do you think you'll ever write any original pieces again like you did for the Bohemia Quartet's album, *Songs for Her*?

SA: For a long time, no, I didn't think I would. Those pieces were inspired by a particular experience, and afterward I simply didn't have anything else that inspired me in the same way. Very recently, though, I've had a new person in my life who's made me hear music in my head again. I've actually already composed one or two pieces because I just had to get them out. I guess that's how it happens — the music burrows its way into your brain, and the only way to stop it driving you crazy is to make it real.

Oh, lord. The only new person who was in his life right then was me. At least as far as I know. For a moment my head is awash with fanciful notions of being his muse, before I force myself back down to earth and continue reading.

LB: Well, that's very exciting. I hope you plan on recording this work at some stage. I'd love to hear more about the new person in your life, though. Is it a girlfriend, perhaps?

SA: *Smiles fondly* No, just a really good friend.

LB: I bet your female fans will be glad to hear that.

SA: *Chuckles* Maybe.

And then the journalist delves into a couple more questions, asking Shane who his biggest idol is and whose career he'd like to emulate, before wrapping things up. I sit back in my chair and sigh, pulling my phone out of my pocket to find the screen depressingly free of any new messages. I'm dying to know what's up with him. Is he sulking, or has something important come up that's keeping him away from his phone? Has he fallen into a depression?

Knowing that he was once in such a low place that he considered ending his own life, I worry a little. It makes me momentarily consider going to his house to check up on him, but I don't. He's probably just busy today, and if I show up all crazy and worried about him he'll think I'm being overbearing and clingy.

The rest of my day drags along at a snail's pace, and just before bedtime I pack my bag for the morning. The weather report is predicting snow again, so I don't bother to bring anything fancy, just lots of warm, comfy outfits. Ben said the house we're going to be staying in is a ten-minute drive from the nearest town, so we probably won't be going out much. That's fine by me. I'm in the mood for a weekend of relaxation and warming my toes by a nice open fire.

I just really hope Shane decides to show up.

***

It's two minutes after ten the next morning and there's still no sign of him. I caved and tried to call him late last night, but I didn't get an answer.

"Is lover boy coming with us?" Ben asks as he helps Lara and me shove our bags into the back of Clark's car.

"I'm not sure," I answer hesitantly. "Can we wait until a quarter past and see if he shows?"

Ben gives me a pat on the shoulder. "Of course, babes."

When 10:16 hits and he still hasn't turned up, I decide to swallow back my dashed hopes and expectations, and let us get on our way. Ben allows me to sit in the passenger seat beside Clark because he has this strange aversion to riding in the front unless he's the one driving. We're just about to pull away from my house when a taxi stops on the other side of the street. My heart lifts as Shane steps out of the vehicle, a bag thrown over his shoulder and his violin case in his hand.

Wow, what relief I'm feeling right now. It's a little disconcerting.

He jogs over to the car as the taxi drives off, looking out of breath as I roll down my window.

"I thought you weren't coming," I say, my eyes drinking him in.

Shane nods, his hair messy like he didn't get the chance to comb it this morning. "I didn't think I was going to make it. I'm running terribly late. I'm sorry, everyone," he calls to the others.

"Go hop in the back," says Clark. "I've popped the trunk so you can throw your bag in there."

When Shane gets in the car and Ben starts up the engine again, I glance at him in the overhead mirror. All of a sudden, I'm disappointed that I sat in the front. I want to touch him, want to ask him why he hasn't been in contact. It's going to be an awfully long drive, an awfully long five-hour drive, to be exact.

I'm already willing the minutes to go faster so that we can stop off somewhere for food midway through. He leans forward and reaches out, squeezing my shoulder and giving me a strange look. I have no idea how to interpret it.

"Pete played the track you two made together for me," I say.

"Oh, yeah? What did you think?"

"Amazing. I can't thank you enough for spending time with him. He's like a different kid to the one he was a few weeks ago."

"Well, I'm happy to help," says Shane modestly.

"Hey, why don't we all play one of those memory games?" Ben interrupts, and the next few hours are filled with mindless chatter.

Twenty-Six

When lunchtime hits, we're all starving, so we stop off in a town called Nenagh in County Tipperary, parking in front of an old roadside restaurant. I want to ask Shane a dozen questions, but he places his hand on the small of my back and ushers me inside.

"Can we talk when we get to the house?" he murmurs in my ear, and I'm relieved that he actually plans on discussing things.

"Sure," I reply before sliding into the worn leather booth, wondering if I should take Mary's advice from the other night and just tell him. Hand him my heart, and let him decide if he wants to keep it or awkwardly give it back.

I order a tuna melt wrap from the waitress, finding myself sitting in between Lara and Clark. Damn this day. Some higher power is determined to keep me from being even remotely within touching distance of Shane. Ben's sitting beside him on the other side of the booth, sucking a vanilla milkshake through a straw and eyeing Shane with an amused expression.

"Say, Clarky, honey, didn't we see Mr. Violin here on the front cover of some fancy magazine in the shop the other day?" he chirps.

"Yes." Clark smiles. "Indeed we did. They got some great pictures of you, by the way."

Shane gets this cute embarrassed look on his face and scratches his jaw. "Uh, thanks."

I shake my head at my friend. "Since when was *Hot Press* fancy?"

Ben puts on a dramatic pout. "It's fancy to me. Though I'll be honest, I was more than a little disappointed that they didn't include any topless shots."

"Ben!" I exclaim, and he laughs uproariously.

"Oh, look, she's all possessive of her man, how adorable. Doesn't want anybody else to see the goods."

"He's not..." I start, and then stop myself from completing the sentence. "Just shut up, okay?"

"These cushiony lips are sealed," he says with a wink.

"Ha!" Lara snorts. "You wish they were cushiony."

"Well, they will be," Ben argues. "Clark's agreed to get me Botox injections for my birthday next year. Haven't you, honey?"

Clark shifts uncomfortably. "We'll see."

"Oh, Jesus, please tell me you're joking," says Lara with one eyebrow raised.

I zone out of the conversation then, because Ben mentioning birthdays has reminded me that it's Shane's thirtieth tomorrow. He must not enjoy people making a fuss, because he hasn't mentioned it. The waitress drops off our food, and I slide my phone out of my pocket, doing a search for the nearest bakery to where we're going to be staying. You know me, any excuse to eat cake.

Somebody nudges my foot, and I look up to see Shane watching me.

What? I mouth.

A small smile curves his lips. "What are you up to?"

I slip the phone back in my pocket and pick up one half of my sandwich. "Nothing."

"Doesn't look like nothing."

"Be quiet and eat your lunch," I say, sticking out my tongue at him.

When we're done in the restaurant we get back on the road, and despite it only being mid-afternoon, I'm feeling sleepy. I roll my cardigan into a ball and shove it against the window as a pillow before laying my head down on it, and try to catch a few winks.

Surprising enough, I do manage to fall asleep, and when I wake up the car isn't moving anymore. I can smell Shane's cologne, and somebody's undoing my seatbelt. Opening my eyes, I find him so close to me I could lean forward just a fraction, and our lips would be touching. It feels like it's been forever since we last kissed.

But I don't kiss him, because I want to know what's been going on with him and why he didn't contact me at all yesterday. And, to be perfectly honest, I'm a little pissed about it. I mean, why hasn't he explained himself yet? If it were something simple like he lost his phone, then he would have mentioned it already.

"Sleep well, Bluebird?" he asks, his minty breath washing over me.

I sit forward, and he moves back to give me room. "Yeah," I reply, clipped, and slide out of the car.

"I already brought your bag in. Clark's put us in the double room to the rear of the house." He pauses, running his hand back and forth over his head. "Is that okay with you?"

I study him as I question him back. "Are you okay with it?"

"Why wouldn't I be?"

"Well, for a start, you ignored me all day yesterday, and then you show up for this trip late, like you weren't sure you were even going to come."

"Let's go inside and we'll talk about this," he says, stepping forward to take my hand, but I move out of his reach.

Frustration grips me as I look around. The house is gorgeous, a long bungalow with a wraparound porch, surrounded by woodland. It's getting dark and it's cold out, so I turn away from him and walk inside anyway. I'm not in the mood to have a fight out in the open.

Ben and Clark are in the kitchen, unpacking the food supplies they brought with them.

"Where's my room?" I ask, standing in the doorway, hands on hips.

Ben gives me a funny look and replies, "The last door at the end of the hall."

I nod and walk out, making my way down the hall. I don't realise Shane was hot on my heels until I open the door and he pushes me in, shutting it behind him.

"I don't get why you're pissed. You seemed fine earlier," he says as he stalks me to the other side of the room.

Letting out a sigh, I apologise, "I'm sorry. I think the car nap might have made me cranky." Going to sit down on the bed, I look up at him. "So, are you going to tell me what's been going on?"

He sits down beside me and takes my hands into his. "The other night at the concert, Mona asked if we could talk. I should have told her no, but she wouldn't stop pestering me, so I finally gave in and went to her dressing room."

"I know," I say quietly.

Shane looks confused. "You know?"

Pulling my hands from his, I begin to pick at my nails and confess, "I was sent to deliver drinks to that room. When I got there I saw you both inside, so I waited in the corridor and listened."

"Jade."

"Look, I know it sounds bad, but I couldn't help it. I wanted to know what you were doing there."

His expression is unreadable now, and it makes me nervous. "So you must have heard how she broke off her engagement to Justin and that she wants me back."

"Yeah," I whisper, swallowing hard. "I didn't stay and listen to all of it, though. I couldn't."

A period of quiet falls between us, and I wish he'd say something. After several minutes he does. "She threw herself at me."

"Threw herself at you in what way?"

"She kissed me," he answers, eyes gauging my reaction.

My heart rate starts to speed up. "And did you kiss her back?"

"Of course not! She took me by surprise. I pushed her away immediately and told her she was being absurd. If you had stayed, you would have heard what I said to her afterward. I told her…"

He falls silent, and I grip his hand in mine. "You told her what?"

Everything hangs in the balance as I wait for his reply, my entire being on a knife's edge.

His voice is barely audible as he lifts his eyes to mine and murmurs, "I told her that I was in love with someone else, in love so deep that it makes me understand what I had with her was never love at all."

I gape at him, open-mouthed, as my heart sings in my chest, thumping a mile a minute in glee.

"You're in love with…me?"

"Yes," he answers, the one word spoken with agony as his eyes fall away from mine. "You must have known. I'm so ridiculously smitten with you, Jade. I have been since the first night we met."

Running my hand down his cheek, I ask, "Why do you sound so sad?"

"Because I know it's not what you wanted. I promised you an arrangement, and love was never supposed to come into it."

"Oh, Shane."

"I can go if you want me to," he says, still staring into his lap. "I can get a bus or a train back to Dublin," he continues before I interrupt him by pulling him to me and planting my mouth on his. He groans into me, grabbing onto the kiss like it's a life raft and he's about to go under.

Our tongues do battle as his chest presses hard against mine, his hands running through my hair. I break the kiss, my breathing erratic, as I stare at him with glittering eyes. "You're not the only one who feels…" I trail off, unable to finish.

He squeezes his eyes shut before opening them again. "Babe, please finish what you were going to say," he begs.

An idea strikes me. Instead of speaking, I stand up from the bed and slowly pull off my top. His watches me heatedly, and then I turn around. A loud gasp escapes him as he takes in my tattoo for the very first time. I stand there, as still as if I were the Blue Lady performing on the street. A moment later I feel his warmth against my skin. He's behind me now, his fingers tracing the ornate musical notes that have been inked along my shoulders, musical notes to the very first track on 'Songs for Her.'

He looks awestruck. "Are these?"

I nod my head, swallowing down a lump of emotion that's gotten stuck in my throat. My eyes are watering with tears, and I don't even know why. Shane keeps tracing the notes, like if he stops they might disappear.

"You once told me there's nothing more committed than ink under your skin," he says in a silky voice laden with pure pleasure.

"I might have said something along those lines," I whisper.

"You're shaking, honey. Why are you shaking?" he asks, turning me around to face him. When he sees my tears, he brings his fingers up and wipes them away from my cheeks.

"Because this is fucking scary."

"Loving me back is scary?"

"I never said…"

His fingers move to my lips to shush me. "The ink says it all, Bluebird. Tell me, what made you get this tattoo?"

I laugh through my tears. "It was a moment of reckless insanity, I guess. I was in the parlour having a new sparrow done, and you came on the radio playing the song you wrote for me. Getting the tattoo just felt right."

He studies me for a long moment. "Do you regret getting it?"

I look back at him, not a flicker of uncertainty in my words when I say, "No, and I never will."

Even if this love isn't forever, I'll never regret meeting him. He's changed my world irrevocably, and the markings on my back symbolise us so completely.

His arm wraps around my waist, his hand going to my shoulders again like he can't get enough of the feel of the ink.

"You're my muse," he murmurs into my lips. "And I love you, Jade Lennon."

For a long time I just stare at him, before at last the right words come to me. "I love you, too, Shane Arthur."

***

Believe it or not, we don't immediately jump into bed and shag each other senseless. We do, however, lie in each other's arm, touching one another in small ways. He still hasn't told me why he was AWOL yesterday, so I ask him.

He gives me a sketchy look as he turns his head to me on the pillows and answers, "Right after I set Mona straight, Justin showed up drunk off his face."

"Oh, no," I breathe.

"Yeah. He swung for me, clearly looking for a fight. I tried to calm him down, but there was no talking to him."

"And?"

"And I punched him in the face. There was nothing else for it."

I burst out laughing. It's more the way he says it than the actual idea of him hitting Justin that sets me off, his phrasing so polite and proper. So one of us did get to punch the bastard after all.

When I finally gather myself, I quip, "I sincerely hope you broke his nose."

Shane grimaces. "I did, actually. It was pretty bad. An ambulance had to be called."

"Shit."

"Anyway, I thought I was done with him once he was taken to the hospital. I went home and tried calling you, but your phone was switched off. You were probably sleeping, since it was fairly late. I was going to come see you the next morning, but the police showed up at my house to arrest me. Justin had reported me for assault."

I sit up straight now. "Oh, my God!"

Shane grimaces and strokes my hair. "I was angry at first. They brought me to the station and everything. It was hours before I managed to contact Mona to come and tell them that I only hit Justin in self-defence. In the end she showed up and gave a statement. I was off the hook. The problem was, she'd brought Mum along with her, and after I was let out of the station, they decided to stage an intervention."

"Uh, what?"

"They said they wanted to have a talk and persuaded me to come back to my parents' house. I reluctantly agreed. Big mistake. They sat me down in my dad's study and basically talked at me, telling me what a bad decision I was making by not giving things with Mona another shot. I seriously thought I'd stepped into the Twilight Zone. I mean, Mum must have the shortest memory in history if she thought being with Mona would be good for me."

"I don't think it's about Mona being good for you, Shane. I think your mother would simply prefer you to be with someone like her rather than someone like me."

His thumb brushes over my temple as he leans down to give me a kiss. "And that right there proves that Mum has the worst taste possible. You're the best person I've ever met. Mona is quite possibly the worst."

I laugh and move to straddle him. He stares up at me and slides his fingers into mine. "Oh, you do love to flatter, Mr. Arthur," I purr at him.

"Perhaps I'm hoping it will get me somewhere," he replies, his voice pure gravel.

I move my hips a little, and he responds immediately, the bulge in his pants getting harder. "You're in with a good chance, but first, you need to finish your story."

He lets out a long sigh. "They kept me in the room for hours, arguing with me and, as Mum put it" —he pauses and makes bunny ears with his fingers— "*trying to get me to see sense*. Mona even broke out the waterworks at one point. It was pure hell. I wanted to leave, but it's difficult to get out of a room when there are two hysterical women standing in your way. Eventually Mona pulled a strop and left. Then it was Mum's turn to start crying. I didn't know what to do, so I tried comforting her and asking if she could just let me live my life in a way that would make me happy. She'd knocked back a couple of shots of gin at this point and got all soppy, bawling her eyes out and saying she only wants what's best for me. A while later she fell asleep. Dad came down then and helped me get her to bed. He'd been hiding upstairs all night, pretending to be dealing with some urgent work matters."

"As you would," I put in, laughing.

"Indeed. After that I was so exhausted from dealing with everything that I fell asleep on the couch. I woke up at nine this morning and barely made it home to pack for the trip. I'd been so stressed when the police came to take me to the station the day before that I forgot my phone. That's why I hadn't contacted you."

My lips curve. "So you weren't ignoring me?"

He brings his hands to my hips and squeezes. "I would never ignore you, babe. In fact, you're kind of impossible to ignore."

I'm about to bend down to kiss him again when there's a light knock on the door, followed by Ben exclaiming, "Come and look, it's snowing out."

I shake my head. "He's like a five-year-old sometimes."

Keeping a hold of my hips, Shane slides me off his body. "Come on, Bluebird. Let's go see the snow."

We leave the room and go to stand by the sliding doors in the kitchen to stare out at the falling sheet of whiteness. It comes down so hard that the entire ground is covered in a thick blanket within an hour. After we eat dinner, Ben suggests a snowball fight, and I think I'm the only one who's against the idea. When they all finally wrangle me into to joining in, I go and grab a thick scarf and some gloves before putting on my coat.

The cold air makes my nose go red as I bend down and scoop up some snow, moulding it into a spherical shape. As I'm doing this, I suddenly get lobbed in the shoulder, the snowball smashing to pieces as it hits me.

Looking to my right, I see Shane standing several yards away, wearing a huge grin. There's snow in his ruffled hair, but I try to ignore how adorable it makes him look and instead run after him, snowball in hand.

He dashes through the tall trees that lead into forestland and I stop running, taking aim and flinging my snowball at him. It hits him right on the cheek, and I laugh uncontrollably. My laughter dies on my lips when he makes a deep growling noise and grabs up a handful of snow. Now I'm in for it. I run in the opposite direction, back toward the house. Shane throws the snow at me, not bothering to make it into a ball.

It hits me in the leg, but I keep running. Seconds later I'm being tackled to the ground by two strong arms. He chuckles in my ear as I struggle to get free of his grasp, but he straddles me. My thighs are caught between his legs, both his hands capturing mine and raising them over my head.

"You don't play fair," I say sullenly.

He smiles with teeth and murmurs, "No, I don't," before he dips down to give me a spine-tingling kiss. Somewhere nearby I can hear Ben letting out a loud wolf whistle. I just about manage to give him the finger, even though my wrists are still captured in Shane's grip. He drags his mouth off mine lazily and then stands up, offering me his hand and helping me to my feet.

We go inside, and Clark declares that he's going to make us all a cup of his homemade hot chocolate. I go and change into some comfy PJs, and Ben fires up the DVD player. When I enter the living room, Shane's sitting on one of the couches, his stare hot as he takes in my fleece pyjamas. By the way he's looking at me, you'd think I was wearing some slinky lingerie.

I sit down on the other side of the couch, but he pulls me closer, wrapping his arms tight around me and nipping playfully at my ear. His hand settles on the lowest part of my belly, which means that when Ben starts the movie I can hardly concentrate on the story at all. Clark comes in with a tray of hot chocolates, and I take mine gratefully. The warm liquid and dollop of cream on top soothes my nerves.

This is a good feeling, I think. To have great friends. To be loved. I don't know what I did to deserve the man I'm currently wrapped up in. Then a dozen recollections flit through my mind.

Looking into the eyes of the devil who killed my sister as he pretended to be innocent.

Puking up blood and vodka as I hunched over a toilet bowl.

Going through alcohol withdrawals. God, the withdrawals were the worst.

Okay, so maybe I do deserve this moment. But I'm still slightly on edge, like I'm going to wake up from a dream. It's not like I haven't spent half my life imagining fantasies to try to escape the darkness. I remember him telling me he felt like he dreamt me the first night we met. Perhaps he feels the same way. Perhaps I'm just as much of a miracle to him as he is to me.

What he said to me is always in the back of mind, that how we met is proof that there's magic in the world. Those words are always there, making me feel a little bit better about living this life full of pain.

As the movie comes to an end, Shane's hand has started to play beneath the elastic of my pants. I clench my thighs together, thinking of all the things I want him to do to me tonight. Clark asks if we'd like some cheese toasties, but I'm too full of butterflies to eat anything else.

Shane offers to help with the toasties, and I go to our room for a breather. One of those little mundane things in life that bring me pleasure is to dive with all my weight onto a bed without a care to the possibility that you might break it. And that's what I do.

Jump up.

Dive.

Fall.

Relax.

Then I just lie there, my head turned to the window, counting the flecks of snow as they drift like beacons through the dark night. Fairies perch on their edges, hitching a ride down from their secret world in the sky. They are just as pretty and cute as you might imagine, but don't get too close, or they'll bite.

Someone coughs from the doorway, and I look to see Shane leaning against the wall. It feels like he's been there for a while.

"What were you thinking about just now?" he asks with an indulgent smile.

I shrug and turn back to the window. "About fairies that bite."

"And here was me thinking it might have been sex."

I laugh. "Well, that, too."

Shutting the door firmly behind him, he strides from his spot by the wall. With one knee levelled firmly on the mattress, he stares down at me, and this action alone makes my heart speed up. Then he crawls up my body, stopping when he gets to my stomach. He pushes up my top and presses his face to the rounded part of my lower belly, breathing in deep.

"I fucking love the smell of your skin," he purrs.

"My skin?"

"It smells like the beach, sun, and sand."

"I'm hoping this is a classy beach we're talking about," I joke.

"It's beautiful. Not a bit of sewage in sight," he replies with a devilish wink.

"Well, that's all right, then."

His fingers run along the edge of my pants, nudging them down little by little. I stare as he pulls them clean off me and then lowers his face to my mound. His lips press down hard over the silky knickers I'm wearing and I tremble beneath him, heaving, expectant.

His finger traces a circle on the innermost part of my thigh before moving to my underwear and shoving them aside, baring just part of me. I can feel how wet I am as he dips a finger in and groans with pleasure. Two fingers come together to slowly slip inside me, his hungry eyes watching my every reaction.

He works them in and out as my channel clenches around them. God, I need more. Using his teeth, he tugs my knickers down and off me at long last, and I moan loudly when his mouth dives right in. I have to stop myself from moaning a second time, aware of the other people in the house. His tongue laps at me as his fingers pump. The hand he's not using travels up my body to pinch at my nipples, and I think I might combust. He never neglects a single part of me, ensuring I feel him everywhere at all times. I have never felt more possessed, claimed.

He sucks my clit into his mouth, releasing it with a loud *pop*. I cry out and tense my legs, an orgasm approaching. When I come, it's with his mouth licking me hard, his fingers moving faster and his other hand pinching my nipple to the point of pain. Shudders wrack me, but as he moves up my body I realise he has no intention of giving me a break.

His clothes are gone within the next ten seconds, a distant memory. My sex is still sensitive from so recently coming, so when he positions himself and thrusts his cock deep inside, I become boneless.

Mouths meeting, tongues colliding, I taste myself on him, and it's the most erotic sensation. Like not only has he claimed me, but in a way I've claimed him, too. His brown eyes shimmer with gold under the dim lamp light as he breaks the kiss.

"Love you," he pants.

I stare right back at him, unable to form words, but silently communicating that I feel the same say. Fucking hell, if there's magic in the world, then this is it. He comes with a violent thrust, growling and biting gently on my collarbone. I adore this exact moment, the quiet after he's poured himself into me, the peace that comes over him as he wraps his arms around me and holds me close as though in reverence.

"Happy early thirtieth birthday," I whisper with a smile.

I can feel him grinning into my skin, when he replies, "Was that my present?"

"Wait and see. I just might have more surprises in store."

I stroke his dark hair, loving the feel of it. His face is buried in the crook of my neck, and then I notice he's humming a tune, humming it so softly that I can only barely make it out.

"What's that?" I ask, my tender voice echoing around the room and mixing with his hum.

He nuzzles me. "Just a song."

"One you wrote? It sounds like a lullaby."

He shakes his head ever so slightly. "I haven't written it yet. It came to me just now."

A flush marks my cheeks as I comprehend the fact that he thought of new music while he was inside me. Electric tingles prick at my skin, my every pore coming alive.

To be a muse is to be a wonder in someone else's eyes, flaws and all.

Twenty-Seven

Six months later…

By some strange twist of fate, I find myself in the southwest of the country again. This time I've travelled with Shane for a performance. He was asked to come play as a guest with the Symphony Orchestra at the Cork Opera House.

I love seeing him play in the symphony back home, but there's something extra special about his solos. It's like I'm getting to view all the passion and emotion that's inside him from the comfort of my seat in the audience. I get to witness how his playing affects others, how he sometimes brings a tear to their eyes and often brings them to their feet with applause by the end.

I'm really excited for tonight and have even splashed out on a new dress for the occasion.

I know, fancy dress, fancy man. I still feel a little like I'm playing a role when I go to these types of things, but then again, I do enjoy assuming a persona. Or maybe I can be me and be fancy all at the same time. I will shun perfection in order to remain a caterpillar. In fact, I've always thought that butterflies are overrated. Caterpillars may be pests, but they do have a certain quirky charm, bumbling along with all those legs and eyes.

Instead of becoming poised and sophisticated, I will continue to bumble.

Speaking of which, Mirin has been slowly coming around to the fact that this caterpillar is going to remain a permanent fixture in her son's life. I have a feeling Shane might have had a good long talk with her about it, because she came up to me in the concert hall a little after the whole Mona drama and apologised for how she'd treated me. I accepted her apology with quiet grace, while a small surge of triumph settled itself in my chest.

At the moment we're staying at a swanky hotel, but Shane left just after lunch to go to a rehearsal. In reflection of my unsophisticated ways, I changed into my dress and then decided to treat myself and order a slice of chocolate cake from room service. In fact, I ordered two slices so I could keep one for Shane for when we get back later.

Ever since our weekend break in Kerry, I've been reminiscing about cake. I got up early the morning after our first night, leaving Shane snoozing in bed, and got Clark to drive me to the bakery in the nearby town. They didn't have anything that was as grand as what I'd been envisioning, so I went wild and purchased three large cream sponge cakes. When we arrived back at the house, I stacked them one of top of the other to create a super cake, planting a three and a zero on top and lighting them with the flick of a match.

Now that's how you say happy birthday, Jade Lennon style.

Shane woke up and came sleepily into the kitchen to be greeted by me, Clark, Ben, and Lara yelling "surprise!" at him, blowing on party whistles and wearing ridiculous cone party hats on our heads. I'm surprised we didn't give him a heart attack. After all, these sorts of surprises are generally an evening affair. I got it into my head that doing it in the morning would bring an extra level of excitement.

I mean, cake in the morning? It's so wrong it's right.

Shane's eyes lit up when he saw the cake on the table, looking a little more like a monster cake than a super cake, if I'm being honest. I didn't know what his reaction was going to be, but then he laughed harder than I'd ever heard him laugh, clutching his stomach, happy tears rolling down his face.

That day we had cake for breakfast *and* lunch. Take that, Marie Antoinette. By the time dinner came around, none of us wanted to look at another slice for at least a month. Anyway, long story short, nowadays every time I want to treat him, I buy him a cake.

So, back to my current cake debacle. I'm so ravenous to shove it down my gullet that I end up dripping a load of chocolate sauce onto my lap. And yeah, I'm so busy enjoying myself that I don't even notice the error of my ways until I'm at least four bites in. Panicked, I shove the cake aside and pull the dress up over my head. It takes forever but I manage to salvage it by dabbing the sauce off with a damp towel in the bathroom. A tip for getting out stains: dab, don't rub.

By the time I get outside the hotel I'm seriously late, and it doesn't help that it takes forever to hail a cab. I mutter swear words to myself all the way to the Opera House, shoving a twenty in the driver's face and not even bothering to wait for change. The concert tonight is Vivaldi's *Four Seasons*, and as I'm being seated by an usher I note that they're already playing the Summer concerto. There are some grumblings as I pass people by, but at last I reach my seat. It's in the second row, and as I look up I see Shane standing in the middle of the stage, diving right into Summer Presto.

I remember him practicing this in our hotel room this morning while I was taking a bath. It sounded wonderful then, but now with the accompaniment of the entire orchestra it's like it's a living, breathing thing, invading every one of my senses.

A shower of colourful petals bursts out of the strings section like confetti at a wedding.

Roots explode from the stage floor, crawling swiftly up the walls, making me feel like Jack staring aloft at a gigantic beanstalk. Daisies sprout around my feet, and a bunch of lilies falls into my lap, filling my nose with their pretty scent. Pink chrysanthemums twirl down from the ceiling as though dancing through the air.

Bringing my attention back to the stage, I meet Shane's gaze, his bow sawing into the strings in quick, vigorous movements. I mouth the word *sorry* at him, apologising for my unexpected lateness. He only smiles with warm eyes in return, a smile so hot it makes me feel a burning underneath my skin. Whoa, he really is sexy when he's up there performing. There's a sheen of sweat on his brow, but that only adds to his appeal.

I relax back into my seat, unable to close my eyes and let the music wash over me because I simply can't stop staring at him. He's wearing a perfectly tailored suit with a white shirt, the first two buttons undone, no tie. The vision of his exposed neck causes all sorts of vivid images to corrupt my thoughts.

He walks across the stage, playing his part effortlessly, like it's second nature. The piece of wood resting beneath his chin is his glittering soul in tangible form, an expression of all he has felt and all he has experienced. He may be playing music composed almost three hundred years ago, but this is his interpretation, and it is an expression of this very moment. It makes me imagine things most would deem impossible, and that's why it reassures me. I glance down at the hand resting on my lap and smile. One of those diamonds that fell from the sky outside the tattoo parlour that time made friends with some eighteen-karat gold and found its way onto my ring finger.

Standing at the very edge of the stage as the piece come to its dramatic finish, Shane is watching me still.

I hope he never stops.

***

A single raindrop falls on my head, but I don't wipe it away. Statues can't wipe away the rain, after all. A light shower came down, covering my body in a delicate coat of water. No matter. The sun is peeking its face out over the clouds. If I stand here long enough, I'm sure it will dry me off.

Clink.

Somebody drops a few coins in my hat and walks away. A pity they were in such a hurry to move on, or I might have bestowed them with a precious blue feather.

I decide it's time for a change of position as I slowly raise my arms into the air. I hold them out on either side of my body, like I'm mimicking the branches of a tree. It's a difficult position to hold for very long, but the best for getting dry.

Earlier today I got a surprise to find Patrick sitting in my living room. Alec had let him in. We hadn't heard from him since I sent him off to rehab, and to be honest, I had no clue whether or not he stayed the duration or quit. I decided to avoid calling to check up on him, because the responsibility was on him to get better. In the back of my mind I never thought he would actually stick it.

As I joined him on the couch, I marvelled at his well-put-together appearance. I mean, it actually looked like he'd been showering regularly. His complexion was brighter than I'd ever seen it, and his eyes weren't as dull as they'd been before. We talked for a long time, him telling me about his journey to sobriety and how he stayed away until he knew he was on the straight and narrow. He'd been on the housing list for a while but finally got allocated a small one-bedroom apartment in Harold's Cross. I did my best not to well up when he took my hands in his and told me it was all my doing. If I hadn't told it to him straight that night, he probably never would have realised he needed to make a change.

Alec was unusually silent throughout the exchange, too shocked at his father's dramatic turnaround to speak. Avery, who's been a regular visitor to our house in recent months, stood by his side, holding his hand. Seeing my brother happy is the greatest gift in the world.

It seems it's true that leopards can change their spots. Not too long ago I'd considered Patrick a complete and total lost cause. Now look at him.

Rays of sunlight shine down, breaking through the clouds, the warmth caressing me in my damp costume, drying the sodden feathers of my wings. Somewhere on the street, music trickles its way into my consciousness. A lullaby in strings. It's the song Shane heard in his head as we made love, so sweet and soft yet full of unspoken declarations.

Out of the corner of my eye I notice a bird land on my outstretched arm. I've been so still that it must have thought I really was a tree and not a human at all. Too curious, I turn my head to the side and gasp in surprise. Sitting happily on my arm is a blue sparrow, a bird that must be rare because I've never actually seen one in the flesh.

Oh, wow. I don't think I ever want to move again.

The bird flaps its wings and takes flight, sailing off into the great big sky. I imagine it's an incarnation of my Sparrow, flying happy and free under the golden sun. Reaching around to my wings, I pull a feather out and make a wish that one day she'll get born into a happy life with a happy ending while I seek my own in this one. Somewhere, someday, Sparrow will die an old lady surrounded by the ones she loves. I release the feather and it floats away. I keep watching it until it's nothing but a speck of blue far, far, in the distance. Now I'm still again, never moving, not an inch. Come and see the Blue Lady — you'll get a feather for your trouble.

Shane's violin plays on and I savour the melody. I wonder if I have taught him something about life like he wanted me to. All I know is that I'll never let him try to silence his music again. Looking off into the sky where the blue sparrow has now disappeared, I wrap this one moment in a box and stick it with a label.

It reads, "The Most Beautiful Way to Live."

Thank you for reading. Please consider supporting an indie author and leaving a review. ☺

About the author

L.H. Cosway has a BA in English Literature and Greek and Roman Civilisation and an MA in Postcolonial Literature. She lives in Dublin city. Her inspiration to write comes from music. Her favourite things in life include writing stories, vintage clothing, dark cabaret music, food, musical comedy, and of course, books.

She thinks that imperfect people are the most interesting kind. They tell the best stories.

Find L.H. Cosway online!

Facebook.com/LHCosway
Twitter.com/LHCosway
www.lhcoswayauthor.com

CPSIA information can be obtained
at www.ICGtesting.com
Printed in the USA
BVOW03s1045070118
504648BV00002B/408/P